THE LONE WOLF #9: MIAMI MARAUDER

THE LONE WOLF #10: HARLEM SHOWDOWN

by Barry N. Malzberg

Stark House Press • Eureka California

MIAMI MARAUDER / HARLEM SHOWDOWN

THE LONE WOLF

Carrying nothing but a big sackful of heroin and a few hundred dollars, Wulff had grabbed a hitch on the outskirts of Los Angeles and was now heading toward Chicago. With plans, of course, to ascertain that his former partner Williams was alive before he took the last and biggest risk.

It was a hell of a situation but Wulff had one comfort. It was coming toward a conclusion now. He could feel it. Win or lose; all the chips were riding on Calabrese.

If he could kill this one, he thought, he could break the trade. And if he could not, then the answer was that he had never been big enough to do it, no man could do it, it could not be beaten, it was insanity to think that one man no matter how skilled, angry, lucky could make a dent—

—But, oh Jesus, had he tried.

"Hang on for a wild ride through the dangerous darkness of America in the Seventies!"
—George Kelley

Some Notes on the Lone Wolf

By Barry N. Malzberg

Don Pendleton's Executioner series started as a one-shot idea at Pinnacle Books in 1969. By 1972 George Ernsberger, my editor at Berkley, called it "the phenomenon of the age." Eventually Pendleton wrote 70 of the books himself and the series continues today ghosted by other writers. Mack Bolan's continuing *War Against the Mafia* (the working title of that first book) had sold wildly from the outset and less than three years later, when Pendleton and Scott Meredith had threatened to take the series from a grim and obdurate Pinnacle, New American Library had offered $250,000 for the next four books in the series. Pendleton stayed at Pinnacle—the publisher faced a lawsuit for misappropriated royalties and essentially had to match the NAL offer to hold on—but the level established by the properties could not fail to have inflamed every mass market paperback publisher in New York.

A few imitative series had been launched by Pinnacle itself—most notably The Butcher whose premise and protagonist were a close if even more sadomasochistic version of Pendleton's Mack Bolan. It was Bolan who had gone out alone to avenge his family incinerated in a Mafia war while Bolan was fighting Commies in Southeast Asia. Dell Books launched The Inquisitor, a series of books on the redemptive odyssey of Simon Quinn (by a then-unknown William Martin Smith, who under a somewhat different name was to become famous in the next decade), Pocket Books and Avon began series the provenance of which is at the moment unrecollected and Ernsberger at Berkley, under some pressure from his publisher, Stephen Conlan, was ready to start his own series.

What he needed in January 1973 was someone who could produce 10 books within less than a year and although my credentials as a Pendleton-imitator were certainly questionable (they were in fact nonexistent), there was no question but that Ernsberger had found one of the few writers close at hand who clearly could produce at that frenetic level. In 1972 I had written nine novels, in 1971 a dozen, in 1970 fourteen; ten books that quickly were not an overwhelming assignment. What he wanted was a series about a law enforcement guy, say maybe an ex-New York City cop, thrown off the force for one or another perceived disgrace, who would declare war upon the drug trade. The cop could be a military veteran with (like Bolan) a good command of ordnance; it wouldn't hurt if he had a black sidekick either still on or just off the force so that they could get some *Defiant Ones* byplay going in those pre-Eddie Murphy days, and the violence was to be hyped up to Executioner level as the protagonist, after an initial festive in New York, took his mission throughout the States and maybe overseas. Ten novels, $27,500 total advance with (it is this which caught my total attention) 25% of it payable upon signature of the contract. Only a brief outline would be necessary and the tenth book was due to be delivered on or before 10/1/73.

I had never read a Pendleton novel in my life.

Hey, no problem; $6750 for a five-page outline at a time when I perceived my nascent career to be in a recession-induced collapse cleaved away scruple and, for that matter, terror. I read Executioner #7, which struck me as pretty bad, mechanical, and lifeless (like most debased category fiction it depended upon the automatic responses upon the reader, did not create characters and an ambiance of its own), wrote the usual promise-them-a-partridge-in-a-pear-tree outline, signed the contracts and began the series on 1/16/73. The third of the novels was delivered on 2/14/73.

Incontestably I could have delivered the entire series by May (the early plan was for Berkley to bring out the first three novels at once, then publish one a month thereafter) but George Ernsberger asked me to stop after *Boston Avenger* and wait for further word. There was a problem, it seemed. In the first place, I had given my protagonist, Wulff Conlan, a name uncomfortably close to that of the publisher whose name at the time I had not even known, and in the second place Conlan's victims, unlike Mack Bolan's, were real people with real viewpoints who seemed to undergo real pain when they were killed which was quite frequently. Would this kind of stuff—real pain as opposed to cartoon death that is to say—go in the mass market? Berkley dithered about this while I sulked, wrote a novelization (never published) of Lindsay Anderson's *O Lucky Man!* for Warner Books, and waited around to accept an award for a science fiction novel, which award caused me much difficulty, you bet, in the years to come. (See the letter column of the 2/74 *Analog* for any further information you want on this.)

Eventually, Ernsberger called—during dinnertime, in fact, on 3/16/73—to say that I could go ahead with the series and would I please change the name of the protagonist? Grumbling, fearing that I might never get back to the center of those novels, I started again and in fact did deliver the tenth book on 10/1/73 after all. (The first three were published in that month.) As is so often the case with imitative series, sales steadily declined from volume #1 which did get close to 70,000) but held above unprofitability through all of those ten, and I was allowed two sequels in 1974 and then two more in conclusion (at a cut advance). I insisted upon killing off Wulff in #14 against the argument of Ernsberger's assistant, Dale Copps, who reminded me of Professor Moriarty.

I signed off on #14: *Philadelphia Blowup* in 1/75. That means that I am now at a greater distance from these novels than many readers of this anthology are from their birthdates ... and for that reason my opinion of the series is not necessarily any more valid than would be the opinion of Erika Cornell on her essays in ballet class in the mid-seventies.

The purpose and development of these novels would, in any case, be clear to anyone, even the author. It is evident to me now as it was then that Mack Bolan was insane and Pendleton's novels were a rationalization of vigilantism; it was my intent, then, to show what the real (as opposed to the mass market) enactment of madness and vigilantism might be if death were perceived as something beyond catharsis or an escape route for the bad guys. As the series went on and on and as I became more secure with the voicing and with my apparent ability to circumvent surface and not get fired, Wulff became crazier and crazier. By #13 he was driving crosscountry and killing anyone on suspicion of drug dealing; by #14: *Philadelphia Blowup*, he was staggering from bar to bar in the City of Brotherly Love and killing everyone because they obviously had to be drug dealers. Finally gunned down for the public safety by his one-time black sidekick, Wulff died far less bloodily than many of his victims while managing a bequest of about $50,000 to his overweight creator. The novels sold overseas intermittently—Denmark stayed around through all 14; the other Scandinavian countries bailed out earlier; the gentle Germans found it all too bloody and sadistic and after editing down the first 10 novels quit on an open-ended contract, paid off and shut it down. I haven't seen anything financially from these since 1979 but entries in various mystery reference sources and the invitation to discuss the series in this anthology suggest that it might have found a particle of an audience. (My real pride in this series, beyond its ambition and sheer, perverse looniness is that I was able to run it through the entirety of its original contract and manage four sequels as well; no Executioner imitator other than those published by Pinnacle went past four or five volumes.) The vicious Rockefeller drug laws ("drug dealers get life imprisonment") were being debated and eventually rammed through the New York State legislature at the time I was writing through the midpoint of the series. It was a propinquity of event which led to some of the more profoundly angry passages in these novels and imputed a certain timelessness as well. (The laws were horseshit and we are still living with their existence and terrible consequence.) Calling a crazy a crazy, no matter how anguished may have been the aspect of the series which was the most admired but for me the work lives in the pure rage of some of the epigraphic statements, notably Kenyatta's. Writing these brought me close to some apprehension of how Malcolm, how H. Rap Brown, how the Soledad Brothers might have felt and how right they were: The Lone Wolf was my own raised fist to a purity and a past already obliterated as they were written, rolled over by the tanks and battery of Bolan's ordnance. (Operating under Bolan's pseudonym: "U.S. Government.") Bolan killed to kill: I think Wulff killed to be free. It all works out the same, of course.

THE LONE WOLF #9: MIAMI MARAUDER

by Barry N. Malzberg

Writing as Mike Barry

The new drug law is going to make it open season on a lot of cops. Every pusher on the corner is going to be judge, jury, and—sometimes—executioner.

—Charles Kenyatta

He feels he's being a good soldier by staying in jail and saying nothing . . . he feels he's serving his country.

—Mrs. Gordon Liddy

In war, rules and histories are made by winners.

—Burt Wulff

PROLOGUE

The girl, Tamara, was alone in her parents' house when the man in the overcoat came to the door. At first she thought he was selling something but when she stared at him he merely looked back impassively, saying nothing for a little while, clutching something in his pocket. It was seventy-five degrees in Sausalito, humid for a change, the air lying dead and heavy outside the central air conditioning but the man did not seem to mind the overcoat. He wrapped it more tightly around him.

"What is it?" she said after a while. He gave an almost imperceptible nod. "You know what it is," he said, and then he showed her a gun, bringing out a concealed hand from a pocket. "You're coming with me."

"This is ridiculous," she said. She had been in the bedroom, napping, only a robe on her. She was doing a lot of napping these days. Since she had left Wulff for the second time she had been sleeping too much. This would all change soon, she had promised herself and her parents: she was twenty-five years old, she would make something of her life. Get a job or go back to school or head toward New York again. Maybe next week. "Ridiculous," she said again.

"I'm not arguing," the man said. He pulled the overcoat more tightly around him, using his free hand. "This is no time for argument." He was about five feet six inches maybe somewhere in his mid-forties. Who knew? Tamara was no good at ages. He pointed down the walk toward an idling, battered Camaro, someone sitting in there behind the wheel. "Come on," he said "It would be easier to do this by myself but there's some help if I need it. Let's go."

"Go where?"

"You'll find out."

"You don't understand," she said, suddenly understanding. "I left him, left him in Los Angeles. I told him I'd never see him again. He's not for me." She paused. "I told him I can't live that way anymore."

"That's touching," the man said. "Tell me more about it later." The gun came on her, closing ground, inches away now. "Tell me all about it later. Come on."

"Are you kidnapping me?"

"No," the man said, "I thought that we'd just go for a little drive." His control broke then; he looked back nervously toward the Camaro. A truck with a broken muffler rumbled down the street, gasping. "I mean it," he said, "I don't have time for any shit. Let's go."

Probably on speed, she thought. The sunken aspect of the eyes, the sudden shifts of mood. She had been on amphetamines herself, she knew the signs. They were not favorable. If people like this were being sent out to get her, it was very bad. Bad for Wulff, she thought, but even worse for her.

"I'm not wearing anything," she said.

He looked at her intently without sexual interest. "You're wearing something," he said. "You're wearing a robe."

"I don't have anything on under it. My parents will be back in just a little while. They'll miss me. You can't just take me out—"

The man reached forward with the hand that had grabbed the overcoat and seized her wrist. She could feel arteries trembling in his fingertips. "I said I don't want any of this shit," he said, "I don't have the time. Let's go."

She came onto the porch and then down the steps in his grasp. Heavy as the air was, a chill caught her and she found herself shaking as he took her down the walk. She looked up and down the block but this was Sausalito suburb in mid-day. No one was out. No one was looking. It would be an hour until school broke and then most of the children came home in cars.

"What is this?" she said as the door near the sidewalk opened and the man pushed her into the still shrouded form on the front seat. "What the hell is this?"

"You'll find out," the man said, slamming the door.

She sat there, looking straight ahead. The man came around the other side, opened the door and pushed the seat forward, the driver leaning forward, and then got into the back poking the gun against her neck. The driver slammed the door. For the first time she looked at him. He looked exactly like the other man. The car began to move.

"You'll find out," the man behind her said again.

She sank into the seat.

At the corner, the truck with bad mufflers was staggering through a left. The Camaro settled in behind it, the driver playing with the gas pedal. He seemed to have all the time in the world now.

She guessed he did. Definitely, the pressure seemed off.

I

Outside Reno the trucker Wulff had grabbed a hitch with in Los Angeles wanted a rest stop. "It isn't the stomach," he said, almost apologetically, "it's the kidneys." He patted himself on the waist. Maybe he thought the kidneys were located there.

"Suits me," Wulff said. He had been sitting upright in the cab since Los Angeles. After six hours of this he felt as if the shit had been kicked out of him. Then again, that was the way these drivers lived. "I could use some coffee." He made a checking glance as he had fifty times before, every seven minutes, at the sack of heroin neatly rolled up and jammed between the seat and the door. There it was. It hadn't fallen out, two million dollars' worth of dreams.

"Good," the driver said, "very good." He worked on the gears, preparatory to pulling off at the next exit. It was a complicated procedure and after a minute of this, the truck jolting and groaning along, Wulff was sweating almost as much as the driver, only half in sympathy. The thing moved all over the road.

They slid into the exit ramp, just barely. "Sons of bitches," the driver said, "these things are getting more complicated all the time."

"That's right."

"But we're still the same. The same men running different gears. The men never change."

"Sometimes they do," Wulff said, "but only for the worse."

The driver was short and fat and wore a high-peaked hat. At the pickup he had started talking to Wulff about all of the women he had stashed away on the road fucking for him, then he had gotten into a longwinded discussion about the teamsters who were marked as rotten but had certainly done right by him. Communist fucking press. Then it had been a little stereo Tijuana Brass out of the rig he had had especially installed and then more talk about fucking. But now gear shifting was the issue. The driver talked inexhaustibly. Little plumes of dust hanging above the land reeled back against the windshield. Desert. Wulff had been in this area before; a couple of months ago. That had been different. A different stage of his life. "Machinery is a bitch," he said.

"Ain't it all?" the driver said. He downshifted further wrenching it into third, then brought the truck down a small side road at thirty miles an hour. There was a sign, DINER AND EATS, blinking off to the right, half of the *A in EATS* missing. "I'll just leave it here," the driver said, rolling past the diner into a large, bare field just past it, set off by a gate. "I'm not going to wrench this son of a bitch into the lot for *nothing*."

He cut the engine then and looked at Wulff carefully as he hit the air brakes and then the emergency, taking the keys out. "You got money?" he said.

"I'm all right. This isn't a hitch anyway, I'm paying for the ride. Should have told you that."

"Oh," the driver said vaguely, but without resentment, "I see," and went through the door. Wulff got from his side more slowly, feeling a little network of pain stretching through his back. Too much; he had taken too much. Still you had to on. "Don't pay for the ride," the driver was saying, "that's against regulations."

"Isn't everything?" Wulff said.

"I don't know," the driver said, Wulff following him through the dark toward the diner. They went then into a vast, vacant room, a couple of truckers sitting hunched over coffee to the side, a waitress with amber-framed glasses reading a newspaper. The driver nodded to the waitress as he took a stool at the far end. Wulff followed him, then on instinct backed off at the last moment and went to the other side of the counter. It was not his ride. He thought about the sack of shit in the truck; the driver had not locked up the cab, it was there for the taking. That was very dangerous but what the hell was he going to do? Go back and bring his Santa Claus bag into the diner? No, that would not work and worse yet would be asking the driver to lock up. That would be a cold tip, not that anyone around here seemed to be interested in the heroin business. That was an urban trade.

The driver and the waitress were now locked into a close, intimate conversation. Good for him, Wulff thought. Good for him: he was no bullshitter anyway, he did have something going for him even though it seemed to be about forty and of generally poor quality. Still, who the hell was Wulff to make judgements of this sort? Each to his own. Wulff kept on walking toward the pay phone down the line, fumbling in his pocket. Plenty of change, anyway. It was an open phone, no enclosure, but then the lighting was dull and no one at the counter seemed to care about anyone else. He shrugged, thinking the hell with it, just plow on, and put a dime in, dialed O, placed a collect call to Chicago to a man named Calabrese.

"Who is calling, please?"

"Tell them it's the wolf."

"What's that? You'll need a name, more specific identification, sir. We can't put through collect—"

"Just put it through," he said harshly, and sent the operator away babbling. He ran his hand through the left front pocket with the change, turned, looked back at the diner as he listened to the empty sound of the transcontinental wire. "In the future, sir," the operator said, "you can place this kind of call directly, prefixing it with O. The local operator will help you."

"That's just wonderful," Wulff said without irony, "I'll want to keep that in mind."

He heard clicks, then buzzes on the wire and underneath that, like the sound of the sea, voices. Down the counter the driver stood suddenly and walked down the row of stools, heading toward the room marked MEN. The waitress watched him, then took off her glasses abruptly, laid them neatly on the counter and followed. They walked toward the end of the counter that way, then split, the driver heading into the room, the waitress into the kitchen. Ten to one there's no partition back there, Wulff thought.

He supposed he envied the driver—not that the waitress was attractive, that wasn't what he envied, just the certainty of the proposition—but he just did not have the time to think about that kind of stuff now. It was either behind or ahead of him; right now the engagement of bodies, grappling in the dark, did not interest him.

The operator was fighting with someone on the line now who did not, it seemed, want to turn the call over. This person wanted more information on who was calling and he was doubtful about accepting it. "Put him on," Wulff said, cutting through this, "he'll want to talk to me."

"I can't just put him on. I have to know—"

"I said, put him *on*," Wulff said, raising his voice a little and there was a click on the wire, then the operator said, "Sir, you are not permitted to talk to your party until the call is accepted." She put him into a dead space. He held the phone, palm sweating lightly, looking at the chipped walls of the diner, his back toward the counter. The two men were still hunched over. Did they live here?

"Yeah," a voice said. "Yeah, this is Calabrese."

"Hello," Wulff said. "I'm here."

There was a slight pause and then Calabrese said, "Where are you now? You coming? You in Chicago?"

"I'm on the way," Wulff said. "But I want Williams. I've had six hours to figure this out now and I make it that you've kept him alive because he's your insurance. You've got him, of course."

"Schmuck, I don't have anyone."

"Yes you do, but you aren't going to dig into him until you've got me in hand. So let me put it this way: I'm going to put this call in again in three, four hours and I want to talk to him. I want to hear his voice, know that he's all right. Until then it's a standoff. You don't touch him and I'll keep on coming."

"You think you're smart," Calabrese said. His voice was wearier, older than Wulff had ever heard it. He seemed to have perceptibly aged since the time of their last conversation, barely a day ago. "You're smart as shit."

"Those are my terms," he said, "you get him to a phone and the next time I call in I want to hear his voice and he better be sounding healthy.

Otherwise I might cancel my trip; kill you from behind. Your style."

"You have no style."

"I'm just trying to muddle this through as best as I can. I make it you've got him and he's still alive. Next time you'll prove it to me."

"You could be dead in three hours," Calabrese said. "An accident could happen on the road."

"You don't know where I am and you're not finding out."

"Maybe," Calabrese said, "but I know something *you're* not finding out either."

"Yeah?"

"I'll tell you next time around," Calabrese said mysteriously, "that next call you promise, all right?" and he was the one to terminate, hanging up on Wulff instead of the reverse as he had planned it, leaving Wulff to walk from the pay phone shaking his head. The old bastard still had moves; you had to respect that.

He went back to the counter. The waitress and the driver were still gone, he sat at a good distance from the two hunched-over men, shook his head, looked at the silverware in front of him. He guessed that he could go and get some coffee but it was too much of an effort. After a while, the waitress and driver came out from different directions, men's room and kitchen. The waitress's eyes looked confused, the driver hitched at his pants. Well, Wulff thought, well indeed and almost instantly came a flare of revulsion: it just was none of his fucking business what the truck driver did, what any of them did. He had one narrow corner to worry about; he was out of the world. None of this was for him any more. Barrel right on through now and end it. *End it.* Coming to the last scenes. He and Calabrese were coming to that moment when alone on center stage they would finish it.

The driver nodded and wiped a hand across his cheek. A slight sheen of sweat there. "Ready to go?" he said.

"Guess so."

"You haven't had anything to eat. You want anything?"

"Maybe some coffee."

"All right," the driver said. He seemed vaguely belligerent. "I guess I'll have some fucking coffee too." He looked down at the waitress who was slumped against the wall, her eyes turned inward. Whatever they had made back there it wasn't love. Wulff wondered if all of the truck driver's assignations went like this. Maybe. The waitress took a menu off the shelf and came toward them, biting her lips.

"Too much," the driver said, as they looked at her, "too fucking much, you know what I mean?"

"I know what you mean," Wulff said.

II

He had been a narco in the NYPD for three years and they had thought they were doing him a hell of a favor, taking him back from Vietnam, the only cop on the force to enlist active duty in the Army (they tended to treat him with the deference and caution due the truly insane) and giving him a plum like that one. Narco was definitely the place to be, unless you could have vice of course, but vice was practically a closed shop and was being phased out anyway, the amateur action in that area overwhelming the professional. Narco was really a gift. But they had made a great mistake, not the first in the history of the NYPD, of course.

Wulff had seen drugs in Vietnam. He had seen what they had done to a country, what they had done to the Army. There was a whole generation there, most of it barely twenty-one years old, zonked out on cheap horse and terror, many of them would die there, many more would come out with stoned minds, wandering through the deserts of the cities, their vision attuned to something terrible and private . . . and they would go from death there to death here because in the cities of America at that time drugs cost fifteen times as much as they did in Saigon and most of them would be unemployable anyway. Wulff had seen it. He had pretty well had the course. Vietnam had sent him home with two overwhelming convictions: the whole operation over there stunk, was unwinnable on virtually any terms . . . and drugs, which were what Vietnam was all about, were going to kill America.

This was not the kind of man you put on narco, which was a fun trip, but PD had thought they were doing Wulff a favor anyway. Narco was a pleasure in those days: hang around a little in the bars, groove on the Harlem scenery, work with the informers who were all on drugs themselves so that you could work a cheap tip, haul in some hapless junkie to build up the arrest record . . . and if things ever really got hot, which they did periodically with a change of commissioner or a newspaper stink, get an informer himself to take the rap. Bring in five or six of them at once, forty guys bringing in their five or six informers meant two hundred and fifty narcotics arrests which they could announce to the *Post* the next day . . . and if the arrests were all dropped for lack of evidence, if the informers were back on the street the day after tomorrow laughing, giggling, shooting up . . . well, it was all in the game, wasn't it? That was what it was: a rich, joyous New York game. Everyone had a ball and narco paid fourteen thousand a year at the bottom with a good expense allowance. The department could do no less for its one, authentic Vietnam combat veteran.

Could it now? The department in its wisdom apportioned to all as they deserved or so the department thought. The trouble was that Wulff wouldn't play right.

He had fallen into a soft spot but the damned fool didn't know when he was well off. He had had to start taking the job seriously, referring back to what he had come to understand in the Nam. So naturally hell was going to break loose, although in Wulff's case it took three years. Three years during which he went through the motions with increasing rage and disgust . . . until, finally, it all got to be too much for him. A sneering informant in a bar taunted him just one inch too many past the line, drove Wulff into a blind if transitory rage, and Wulff busted the informant for possession, the shit literally dangling out of his pockets, brought him down to the local precinct in the collar, stood willing to make out all the forms, labor through all the procedures just once to make something stick and had the informant taken from him by a very hostile desk sergeant who told Wulff that this was a precinct matter, not a narco, and he better park his ass in a separate room while they worked this out.

He paced that room for an hour, working out his case, all the angles of it, getting it cold and then the lieutenant came in. The minute Wulff saw the expression on the man's face he knew that he had been a fool: he should have carried the heroin down to the headquarters building himself. The lieutenant said that the informant was clean as a whistle, there wasn't a thing on him, and as far as the shit which Wulff was willing to swear to, there was no case without evidence. All that they were facing right now was a false arrest charge. The lieutenant said that he was pretty damned pissed off and so was Wulff's commander who had been hauled out of bed to hear about this one.

He should have expected nothing else, of course. In fact, he really had not: looking back on it not too much later Wulff could see that he had probably stepped into this coldly, deliberately because he could not take narco any longer. There were ways and ways all right, ways of doing anything you got your head into, ways of doing things that you could not consciously resolve to do. Busting an informant was a hell of a good way to get off narco. Informants made the thing run.

So he found himself the next night in a patrol car, riding shotgun to a twenty-four-year-old black rookie named David Williams, picking up a squeal about an od'd girl in a tenement on West 93rd Street. Shotgun had to take calls like this, the driver had certain prerogatives, and so Wulff, thirty-two years old, ten years senior to the rookie (they had credited his Vietnam time as full service for pension and seniority: wasn't that nice of them?) had been the one to labor up five flights of stairs to find a dead girl lying in the middle of a furnished room, her eyes bombed out, her body waxen. It looked like heroin overdose for sure.

The girl was named Marie Calvante and Wulff knew all about her. There was every reason why he should; he had been seeing a lot of this girl for almost a year now. They were supposed to be getting married soon. They had even put down a deposit on the apartment in Forest Hills.

So seeing his fiancée lying od'd out five flights up in a filthy, stinking hole of a tenement was calculated to get Wulff pretty mad. It was the kind of thing which could upset a man, even a combat veteran, even an ex-narco. What he went through for the next five minutes he was never quite able to remember, but when he came out of it Williams was standing next to him in the stinking room, pain and wonder on his young face, and Wulff was very calmly ripping his ID card to shreds under the plastic, taking off his badge. "Fuck it," Wulff said, "that's it; I quit." It seemed to be the best speech that he could make at that moment. He left Williams, although not for the last time, walked down the stairs, out the door, past the idling patrol car, a couple of kids playing on the hood, threw what was in his hand in the wastebasket at the corner and took the subway home. He never got around to filing the papers.

At that point his Odyssey began.

The conviction formed in Vietnam, flickering away through his years on narco, raised and welded through years of revulsion, had finally come through him like a knife-point: now with the girl named Marie Calvante dead there was nothing to hold him back. He was a dead man anyway. They had killed him; what had been a man named Burton Wulff was mostly left in that room on West 93rd Street. The heart of him was, anyway; only the functioning part was left.

So he went out to destroy the international drug trade.

Why not? It was time someone went out to do it and the ambition, as crazy and hopeless as it seemed, at least had nobility. Fail richly. He would take a few of them down with him anyway; the poison, the scum in their five-hundred dollar suits and Eldorados who sat behind the walls and laughed while the cities thrashed and died . . . he would let them know he was around, anyway. They would pay, they would pay for killing him.

It took him only three months and eight ports of call to send the message.

He blew up a townhouse in Manhattan and killed a major operator and his staff, assassinated another. In San Francisco he tracked a shipment and blew up the freighter carrying it: three hundred lost. In Boston he destroyed the fabric of the northeast network, bombing out an estate. Las Vegas, Havana, Chicago were next on the list. He was doing fine. Williams, the rookie, had connections to the informant and black revolutionary network and was turning into a hell of a supplier; a girl named Tamara whom he had met and pulled out of a speed-jag in San Francisco had proven to him that he could still function as a man when he cared to. Then, in Chicago, he finally ran into something first-rate, a major-leaguer named Calabrese who was in his early seventies and lived in a mansion on Lake Michigan. Calabrese almost killed him.

Calabrese *could* have killed him, but for some reason found it more interesting to ship Wulff to Peru instead; he said that having Wulff around excited him. It was a decision that Calabrese came to regret but Wulff regretted it too, began in the jungles of Peru and struggling out of them to wonder if you could live for any sustained period of time on the margin as he was, and not begin to actually look for a way out. Calabrese was putting the pressure on.

But he came out of Peru with a couple million dollars' worth of shit from a dead ex-Nazi, an interception of a shipment that Calabrese had worked on, and he went on to Los Angeles where he called Williams for reinforcements. By that time, Williams, a system-believer with a pregnant wife and a neat little plot out in St. Albans, Queens, was about ready to join him. Williams was not so sure about working within the system any more. He had taken a knife in the gut casing out a methadone trade on 137th Street and he had had a good amount of time to lie in a hospital bed and consider exactly where the system wanted to put a black man who was trying to get his. In a grave, he decided. Williams left his wife and ran out a stockade full of munitions to a trailer court in Los Angeles as Wulff prepared his war of vengeance against Calabrese. Meanwhile, Tamara walked in and walked out on him, saying that he was crazy: she couldn't live this way. Where did he ever get an idea like that?

But everything fell apart in Los Angeles; first he and Williams went at each other's throats and then in the middle of that Calabrese's troops, getting wind of their location, moved in, and they had had to fight desperately, blowing up the court, to get free. It was then, in the wreckage, that Wulff had understood that he and Williams could not possibly go on together; he had started his quest alone, the last act was coming with the kill of Calabrese, he would have to end it alone. "Go home," he had told Williams, "go home, you still have a chance to stay in the system, I'm out of it. Go back to your wife, get back into the PD, you were right, I was wrong. I'd get back if I could go inside but I'm a dead man," and Williams had listened, had taken the munitions in the U-haul back east while Wulff waited for the all-clear so that he could move onto Chicago—

—Except that he hadn't heard from Williams in two days saying that he had gotten through and then Wulff knew that what he had feared had happened; they had gotten the man. Somehow Calabrese had found him, traced him, nailed him to the ground and put him under wraps. Which meant that Wulff was not only alone with a war of vengeance, he had the responsibility for Williams as well. He had gotten the man into this. He had to get him out. Nothing was Williams's fault, everything was Wulff's.

So, carrying nothing but a big sackful of heroin and a few hundred dollars, Wulff had grabbed a hitch on the outskirts of Los Angeles and was now heading toward Chicago. With plans, of course, to ascertain that Williams was alive before he took the last and biggest risk.

It was a hell of a situation but Wulff had one comfort. It was coming toward a conclusion now. He could feel it. Win or lose; all the chips were riding on Calabrese.

If he could kill this one, he thought, he could break the trade. And if he could not, then the answer was that he had never been big enough to do it, no man could do it, it could not be beaten, it was insanity to think that one man no matter how skilled, angry, lucky could make a dent—

—But, oh Jesus, had he tried.

III

About an hour later, somewhere on Route 80, a small sedan, a Chevelle probably, passed them on the left moving fast and erratically, then swung into the lane in front of them so abruptly that the driver, screaming, pumping the air brakes was just barely able to back off and clear the rear bumper as the car, accelerating wildly then, went flat out ahead of them, moving at a hundred miles an hour Wulff estimated. Shaking, reaching out to grip the sack, his thought had been Calabrese, Calabrese had somehow tracked him but the surge of panic from the near-impact had wiped his mind clear, leaving him oddly empty in the aftermath and purged of that kind of fear. He knew that it could not have been Calabrese. No, it was only some lunatic, using Nevada for a playground.

"You all right?" the driver said, struggling with the gears, getting the van up to fifty again. Wulff looked down at his palm which was bloody;

he had not realized it but he had hit the dash hard, bracing himself and he must have been cut. He wiped the blood away leaving a little residue, just a scratch. "Son of a bitch," the driver said.

"I'm all right," Wulff said, looking down the windshield, down the long flat line of highway now empty again.

"That's what you put up with," the driver said. He seemed oddly abstracted now, not really in the cab at all. "The last fucking frontier, that's what this is."

"The frontier is dead."

"Not here it isn't," the driver said, "this is what it all comes down to." He had relaxed into the rhythm of the gears again, shifting the stick rhythmically, faint music purring out of the stereo as they got back to an even sixty. "Open season, shit, anything goes here." He looked sidelong at Wulff. "You're no ordinary hitch," he said.

"No, I guess I'm not."

"You didn't hitch because you're out of money. You had another reason."

"Something like that," Wulff said. He settled back into the shiny, porous surface of the seat. The driver was all right, he had nothing against him at all, but he did not want to talk. So far the ride had been fine; aimless and quiet, they had not even talked about the waitress. Now, two hundred miles out of there, if the driver could keep up the pace, he could see Chicago by dawn and he wanted to sleep his way there. "It doesn't matter though," he said, "the important thing is to get there."

"Get to Chicago?"

"Something like that," Wulff said.

"You got business in Chicago?"

"You could call it that. You could call it that," Wulff said, wondering how he was going to handle this, how he could stay out of contact with the driver without insulting what was after all a free ride. "More or less, I suppose."

"Has it got to do with that sack?"

"What's that?" Wulff said. The driver was looking at him now with an oafish smile. "What sack?"

"That thing," the driver said. "You haven't let it out of your sight thirty seconds since you got in the cab. Except at the diner. It all has to do with that sack, doesn't it?" and Wulff was turning toward him, trying to frame something which would both get the driver off his back and put the sack out of the question, wondering if he was heading into a confrontation of some sort when the driver saw something down the road. "Holy shit," he said, pointing, and Wulff followed the line of sight along the windshield. Something about half a mile ahead of them, maybe fifty yards off the straight, flat road was burning in a field. The flames were arcing upwards ten to twenty feet; even through the air conditioning, Wulff could smell it. The driver was already working on the brakes again.

"The Chevelle," the driver said, "I bet it's that fucking Chevy," and the van came to a halt in stages, first the front part of it coming to rest, then like an accordion the middle and the rear banging up, and they were on the shoulder of the road, maybe fifty yards downrange from the burning automobile, the driver already wrenching, reaching for the door. There was no one else on the road at all in the early dawn; no reflection of headlights in either direction. "Fucking Chevelle," the driver said, throwing his weight into the door, getting out. Wulff got out on his own side, feeling the hard tar of the road underneath him as he leapt from six feet and then both he and the driver were running toward the car. "It's going to explode!" the driver said, "it's going to blow up!" and yet he kept on running. Wulff ran with him. At this moment there seemed nothing else to do; he shared the unquestioning purpose of the driver. The thing that was in there had cut them off, had shaken them up, had almost killed them but that thing was human.

Closing ground on the car Wulff felt himself running weightless, a curious disconnection seeming to lift him from the ground, then both he and the driver were in the fumes themselves, little sputtering arcs of flame all around them as they closed in on the driver's side. Something was huddled behind the wheel, open-mouthed, staring through the windshield with an expression of horror and Wulff touched it first, wrenched the body free, the body tumbling and falling to the field against him, then the driver had the ankles and together they carried the thing in a groaning, gasping run back toward the truck. The fire was sputtering down now, coming into the core of the car and then, just as they labored back to the truck, holding the thing in their arms, the Chevelle blew up, in a curiously graceful series of motions parts of it, fenders and hubcaps, suddenly came free, dancing in the fire. Then there was the dull *whoomp*! as the gas tank seared in, crumpled upon itself. The impact put them to the ground hard and there was a second *whoomp*! then it was over. There was a faint crackling downrange. There was still no sign of traffic on the road.

"I think he's cooked," the driver said.

Wulff looked down at the thing they had stretched on the ground between them. The thing had been in its forties and was short and fat; a gold chain dangled across its vest. It was not respiring. There was no blood, no sign whatsoever of external damage. "Yeah," Wulff said, "yeah, he's dead."

"He's a stiff," the driver said, and then added almost wonderingly, plaintively, a man who would sprint fifty yards and risk his life to save a man who might have killed him, "what the hell did it to him? I don't see nothing."

"You wouldn't," Wulff said, "you wouldn't at all," and almost went on to tell the driver what he was looking at. Wulff knew what they were looking at; he had seen it once before, in a different way, on a girl in a tenement on West 93rd Street. The sign of the overdose, the white face, the stricken eyes. The blind fish. The sign of death. "Let's go," he said shakily, standing, feeling the sweating beginning within him but controlling it with an act of will. "He's dead. There's nothing to do. What the hell do we want? cops, a report, spend a morning doing this?"

"No," the driver said, standing with him, "no, we don't want that at all." The road was still vacant; there was little traffic on Route 80 in the dawn. "Let's get the fuck out of here."

They went into the cab, the engine still idling. "What did it to him?" the driver said, "what the hell did it to him?"

"He was driving on heroin," Wulff said, "he overdosed out," and the driver let out a long whistle, then said nothing, clanking the truck into gear again and slowly they moved out, passing the filaments of the dead car across from them.

"I never seen anything like it," the driver said after a while, "I never seen an overdose."

"You're lucky," Wulff said and pressed back into the cushions. The truck rolled, it rolled toward Chicago, it moved on the rope of his vengeance and he thought yes, Calabrese would have to be killed, all of them would have to be killed for this because the price was simply too high and all the sheltered, stinking, smiling men behind their thick walls . . . they would have to pay.

The empty eyes. The blind fish.

IV

Calabrese was ready for the call when it came. He had the black man Williams and his two guards in one room, he had the girl Tamara and a guard in another, both with extensions; he had his own phone ready. Wulff knew about Williams but he did not know of the girl; that would be a nice surprise for him. Calabrese was looking forward to that. He was looking forward to almost every aspect of the call but particularly hearing the sound of the bastard's voice when he knew that Calabrese had him and that his options were over. But first there was the waiting.

There was the waiting and nothing to be done about it. It infuriated Calabrese; here *he* held all the cards and yet it was Wulff who was deciding the time of the call; all that he had said was three or four hours until the next check-in and here it was going on five and no sound from the bastard. Of course that could mean the best kind of news; some freelancer, say, had spotted Wulff wherever he was and had killed him. That would be fine and actually Calabrese should not be so nervous, should not feel pressured. But he doubted his luck. No, the son of a bitch was toying with him again.

"Where the fuck is that call?" he said to the man in the room with him. The man said nothing, he was well trained. He shrugged impassively, showed his palms, looked at the floor. "Ah, fuck you," Calabrese said and went out of the room, went down the hall, looked in first at the room where the girl and her guard were, the two of them against the wall, drinking coffee, the girl looking at him with wide, luminous eyes. He wondered what it would be like to have fucked her. He would not touch, by force or desire, anything which Wulff had touched, would not corrode himself but it would be interesting. She was a piece of ass all right. "How are you doing?" Calabrese said.

She held the coffee cup, said nothing. "I said, how are you doing?" Calabrese said again, and the guard poked her.

"You're going to regret this," she said, "that's how I'm doing. Kidnapping is a capital crime."

"This isn't kidnapping," Calabrese said, "this is a pleasure," and then, feeling disgust overwhelm him, turned, went from the room and into the next one down the hall, the one where Williams was sitting with his two guards, the three of them, of all things, playing poker, nickels and quarters on the table. Williams looked up at Calabrese, nodded, then looked down at the table. He was cool, this one. He had established a wonderful relationship with the men guarding him. He was Wulff's buddy, that meant that he had qualities of adaptability.

"I'm waiting for your friend to call," Calabrese said.

"Me too," Williams said, not looking up from his hand. "Me too, I'm waiting for him to call."

"You know why he hasn't called?"

"Shit no," Williams said. "If I knew why he hadn't called I'd tell him to call because I'm getting pretty sick of this crap. I'll raise a dime," he said and shoved two coins onto the table. The near guard grunted, peered at his hand.

"You must think this is some fucking kind of vacation," Calabrese said and the guard looked up, the three of them looked up, Williams put down his hand, something seemed about to happen in that room and the phone to the left of the table rang.

Calabrese paused, waited for it to ring again so that he could be sure that this was really happening and it was not some kind of ploy with himself as the butt. Then when the phone went off he went out of the room quickly, leaving the door open, went back to his office and picked it up quickly, feeling the dampness circulating through his palm as he picked it up and straightened it against his ear. The operator said that the call was collect, would he accept? Calabrese said he would without even asking for the name of the party and after a moment the voice of the enemy came on.

"Put him on," he heard Wulff say, "put him on right now. I want to hear him."

"All right," Calabrese said. He put the phone down delicately, walked past the puzzled guard, went into the room with the door open, said to Williams. "Pick it up," and then turned, went back to his own room, picked up the receiver and listened. After a while he heard Williams say, "Hello."

"Hello David," Wulff said, "where are you?"

"Don't answer that," Calabrese said, cutting in, "don't answer that at all."

There was another, slightly longer pause and then Wulff said, "How are you making it?"

"I'm playing poker," Williams said, "with two very tough guards, right now. I've just been raised back two times but I think I can stand it."

"That sounds good," Wulff said, "how are you feeling?"

"I'm feeling wonderful," Williams said, "I've never felt better in my life. It's what I've been waiting for, three-hand poker with a couple of really tough mob guys."

"All right," Calabrese said, "that's enough. He's perfectly healthy, you see. We haven't messed with him."

"He doesn't sound too healthy to me, Calabrese," Wulff said and then seemed to laugh. "He's a lousy poker player."

"I'm not that bad," Williams said, "I'm better than you think. I've got control and patience, anyway."

"Hang it up," Calabrese said, "hang the phone up right now."

"All right," Williams said, "I think I'll just go back and raise him again. Why not? It's only fifty cents," and then Calabrese heard the phone clatter.

Wulff said, "Where is he?"

"I'm not going to tell you that."

"I think it's time we met," Wulff said. "I think it's time for another face to face."

"That suits me. That's what I'm waiting for."

"Good," Wulff said. He breathed in harshly once, a sharp intake of breath, and said, "I'm coming, Calabrese."

"Not here you're not." He had worked this out carefully, meditated it through, strung it through the channels of possibility for hours; now Calabrese knew that he had been right all along. "Not in Chicago," he said, "I don't want it to be here. We're going to make it in Miami."

"I don't like Miami. It's a sad, phony, hustler's town. It's not your kind of territory at all."

"But that's where it's going to be."

"Let him go," Wulff said, "let him go and I'll meet you anywhere you say. Otherwise it's no deal."

"Oh yes it is," Calabrese said, "it's definitely a deal. I didn't tell you about my surprise, remember?"

"I remember that."

"I have a surprise for you. I think you'll be pleased and interested if you'll hold on a moment." Calabrese put the phone down quietly, went out of the room for the second time and down the hall to the room where the girl was. Pushing the door open he found her in the same position, looking at him open-mouthed as he stared at her. "Pick up the phone," he said motioning to the desk, "there's someone who wants to talk to you."

"You won't get away with this," she said. "By now my parents have notified the San Francisco police and they've notified the Federal Bureau of Investigation. This is a federal crime; the FBI is in on it and they'll get you. There's still a death penalty for kidnapping."

"Oh for Christ's sake," Calabrese said, realizing that he had not been as irritated in this way since his wife had died twenty years ago. There was something about the capacity of women to complain which was infuriating; they were obsessive, single-minded creatures. Whatever you tried to do with them, whenever you tried to pursue a line of reasoning they would stick maddeningly at a single point. "Just pick up the phone and listen, will you?"

He motioned toward the guard, the guard shrugged and came from his seated position, moving toward the girl in an off-handed, rather menacing way. Carefully, so as not to give ground but at the same time reacting to this, the girl moved toward the desk and picked up the phone.

Satisfied, Calabrese walked out of the room, back to his office and picked up the phone again, listening to the humming, dead wire. "Your surprise is coming," he said.

"If it's the girl," Wulff said quickly, "you're out of luck you son of a bitch," and Tamara said "Hello," then tentatively, her voice barely carrying,

"Hello?"

"Tamara?" he heard Wulff say, "is that you?"

"It's me, Wulff. This *is* Wulff?"

"What the hell are you doing there?"

"I've been kidnapped. They took me out of my house and flew me here on a plane. Kidnapping is a Federal crime."

"Let her go, Calabrese," he heard Wulff say, "you don't mess with the girl. She's out of it. She has nothing to do with this at all."

"Come and get her," Calabrese said quietly, "why don't you come and get her?"

"You lousy scum—"

"That will get you nowhere, Wulff. Haven't we had enough invective here? If you don't like the situation, you've got the power to change it. Meet me in Miami and turn over the bag to me and we'll let the girl *and* Williams go. Otherwise, we'll torture them to death. I want the bag, Wulff."

"I'll meet you there," Wulff said, "not Miami."

"No negotiations. It's not going to be here because I say so. It's going to be Miami."

"Don't do it Wulff," he heard the girl say, "don't listen to him. He'll kill us anyway no matter what you do, you know that. Don't get stopped. Don't let him stop you. Do what you have to do, don't listen—"

"Shut up," he heard Wulff say, "shut up and don't tell me what to do."

"It's the only thing—"

"I'll do what I have to do," Wulff said, and Calabrese said nothing, held his breath, listened in, finding that he was enjoying himself for the first time in weeks. Let the bastard squirm, let him sweat. It was a pleasure just once to have the advantage over him, a nice change of pace, a good setup for that final advantage he would have over him when he blew his brains out. The moment was coming. "You're a bastard, Calabrese," Wulff said.

"Aren't you tired of cursing?"

"Aren't you tired of being a prick?"

"Give me the goods," Calabrese said, "turn them over to me and you can have your girl and your black friend too. I don't care. That's all I want."

"You're a liar. You don't want the stuff. You want a kill, Calabrese. But so do I. This is the end. You know that, don't you? You're in too deep now. I have to kill you."

"No," Calabrese said, "I have to kill you."

"Where do you want to meet in Miami?" Wulff said, and Calabrese resisted the impulse to hurl the receiver against the wall in triumph:

he had the bastard. Now he had him. "I'll be in the Fontainbleau," Calabrese said, "in about two or three days. Why don't you look me up then? We can have a nice chat."

"The Fontainbleau," Wulff said. "You *would* stay in that. You'd stay in the sleaziest, cheapest—"

"Don't be a fucking travel agent," Calabrese said. He wanted to giggle with joy. "It's a prestige hotel; it's got a great reputation. You'll like it; you'll really enjoy being in a resort area."

"I've been in plenty of resort areas."

"Don't do it, Burt," he heard the girl say again, earnestly. "Don't fall into his trap whatever it is. He's only going to bring you down there and kill us anyway, don't you see that? Stay away."

"Shut up," Calabrese said.

"She's right," said Williams, who had picked up his phone again. "Burt, she's right. Wherever you are, you're safe now."

"Where are the guns?" Wulff said, "did they get the godamned ammo too?"

"Don't answer that," Calabrese said, "don't answer that one," and then, feeling the conversation beginning to drift away from him, feeling his hard-won control of the situation beginning to slip, he said, "That's it, Wulff. I've got your girl and I've got your friend and they're both pretty safe now, but if you ever want to see them again you're going to play this my way. Miami," he said, "you come down to Miami."

"I'd rather kill you in Chicago," Wulff said.

"I'd rather kill *you* in Miami," Calabrese said and disconnected, pulling the master switch on the phone so that not only his but the other two extensions were cut off. Then he slammed the phone into the receiver, pushed it from him forcibly and stood, backing against the window. The impassive man in the room looked at him, then away, showing his palms at the same time in a gesture of compliance: don't look at me, I had nothing to do with this at all, the gesture said and Calabrese let it go, walked out of the room and down the hall where behind the two open doors everything seemed as it had just a little while ago. The girl was saying something to her guards about the illegality of being kidnapped, Williams was saying, "I'll raise you back." It was amazing how in almost any circumstances things settled into a routine, here, no less than at any other time, the people who surrounded him had worked out a system of habits. Perhaps it had something to do with his way of life itself. The mansion had a calming influence.

He walked into the room where the girl was and said to her, "You can't keep your mouth shut, can you?"

She looked up at him defiantly, the tilt of her chin, slash of mouth somehow sensual in this aspect and he found himself again thinking of what it would be like to fuck her. For one poisonous instant it occurred to him that he could; she was helpless, he could throw the guards out of the room and take her by force. What the hell could she do to him? and even at seventy-three, he could overpower a woman. But looking at her, looking beyond the attitude and the clothing, seeming to see into the rotten heart of her he felt that to screw her would be only to take unto himself the corruption of this other man who had already entered her body, by stain and implication the rottenness of Wulff would pass into him, juices from her juices, wounds from her wound and then Wulff would be inside him, his demon, possessing him. The thought chilled him and he moved away from her, backing against the wall, feeling suddenly old and ill, seventy-three years of mortality cooking in his veins like heroin, and did not even listen to her saying something about being out to kill him, he was always out to kill people. Fuck this, Calabrese thought, fuck it, feeling himself winding down to the end of the trail, something within him loosening and breaking away. Then he walked out of the room, past the open door of the other and back to his office for the last time where the man who was his bodyguard was still sitting in that position, feet tilted against the floor, his eyes closed, face toward the ceiling. He was smoking a cigarette, a thick ash protruding, his tie loosened, a thin glaze of sweat coming over his face.

"Get off your ass," Calabrese said and the man twitched, jumped, and came off the chair and into a posture of attention, ashes scattering throughout the room. Calabrese looked at him with disgust: a small, repulsive man who knew nothing but dim fantasies of violence, closed his eyes and dreamed for entertainment. Then like a gong the thought came within him: you made him this way. He's your responsibility. He's exactly what you wanted him to be.

Too much. Too fucking much. "We're going to Miami," Calabrese said harshly and feeling returned to the man's face, it opened into something both pompous and fearful, the two emotions chasing one another like dogs across the panes of the face, the features riven into those two parts as he groped uncertainly for an attitude and then the man said, "Miami. That's all right with me, we go to Miami. What's doing in Miami?" and then before Calabrese could answer the man had already turned from him shrugging in contrived disinterest, walking toward a corner of the room. "Miami," he said again.

Miami. Chicago, Athens, New York, Lisbon, Hawaii, London, Reno and Nevada. This man, the men like him, would follow him everywhere, Calabrese thought, because he was paid to do so; the others, the girl and the black man, would follow because they had no choice . . . but who, who he wondered would follow him for love? You're getting soft you old fool, Calabrese thought and then he went determinedly through the door to assemble himself for the trip. The girl had had something to do with it. The girl had reached something within him that he had thought had been dead a long time.

Pity it wasn't.

V

Wulff thought about the history of the railroads in America. Their history was complex and interesting like almost anything in this damned country, riddled with ambiguities and eventually, it seemed, possessed of failure. In the middle of the nineteenth century the railroads had spread across the country, joined the frontier, moved the technology of the country and made its industry possible as the century lurched into the turning point; in the early twentieth century the railroads had been kings of everything, everyone moved on the railroads (those that moved that was), so did the goods . . . and then Lindbergh flew across the ocean and suddenly everything was changed; airplanes became a practical means of conveyance and meanwhile Henry Ford and the General Motors' assembly lines were knocking out thousand-dollar cars a thousand a day for the common man . . . and all of a sudden the railroads were dead. Finished. Of course they took another thirty years to die.

They still moved the freight of course, but in their anxiety to get the profitable freight business and not have to be bothered with passengers, they did everything within their power to make transportation by railroad as miserable as humanly possible; they succeeded and by the beginning of the nineteen-sixties the only passengers were commuters, those who linked to the railroads and their freight for short, stifling, miserable hops into the cities which sustained them . . . but also in the nineteen-sixties the truckers had taken over. Freight movement by truck was cheaper, faster and more convenient than railroad; it could go door to door, it did not have to stand expensively at some station twenty miles from the central city until connections could be arranged . . . and at that point the railroads found themselves in very difficult straits indeed. They had long since driven off the passengers for freight but now the freight had gone away from them as well. The bankruptcies began. By the end of the decade every major railroad in the country was in bankruptcy, receivership or rapidly heading that way. It looked pretty bad. Railroad presidents were writing suicide notes with the same floridity and dash with which stockbrokers had been throwing themselves from buildings four decades before that. Considering that they represented the tradition of the country as it had ended a hundred years earlier, it was pretty depressing. It was also depressing for the commuters, most of whom had no alternative to riding on the bankruptcy specials. It was agreed that it looked pretty terrible. Some of the commuters were even in the railroad business themselves, to say nothing of the automobile or aviation-related trade. The government moved in.

The government reckoned that if the railroad was part of the great and ongoing tradition of America, the spike that joined the continent and so on, then it was a pretty piss-poor idea to let the railroads slide into oblivion, lousy public relations and so on. Also a large percentage of commuters could vote and swung the balance of power in the suburbs that were beginning to control the country. So the government in its generosity conceived of a plan to subsidize the railroads, trying to bring them back into the passenger trade—the freight business was already pretty hopeless and besides the government was deep in hock to the teamsters union—by pouring large amounts of money into them to provide for more amenities, faster trains, better intercity connections and so on. Of course none of these improvements had much to do with the commuter trade but then again that was government for you.

They called this new program *Am Track*, short for American Track, Wulff supposed, a government program which partially subsidized the railroads, and their flagship liners were the huge, bright, new passenger trains that sped at a hundred miles an hour between the major cities. These trains not only had the usual historical amenities of railroad travel . . . porters, bar cars, sleeping compartments, shoeshine men, partitions and what-not . . . they had separate cars linked onto the trains which accommodated passenger cars so that aged, fearful or lazier drivers could put their cars right up on the ramp and have all of the advantages of car travel to a distant city and possession of the car at destination that was, without the narcoleptic experience of driving on the turnpikes, an experience which would eventually lead even the nonaged, nonfearful, energetic drivers right down the trap to insanity. It was the perfect mating of government and private enterprise; private enterprise having proven itself incompetent enough to leech onto government funds for its survival, the government cheerfully and uncompromisingly throwing the money in because it was easier to do that then to take a long look at the country which the post-railroad era had become. Bring back the railroads and restore, wholly, the past. The past was always better than the present, to say nothing of the unimaginable future. Everyone benefitted here.

The Amtrak train that went from Chicago to Miami was called the *Floridian*, and Wulff was on it, sitting alone now in the bar car, traveling through the American night at a one-hundred-and-five mile an hour clip.

The car that he had loaded on the *Floridian* was a 1964 Cadillac Coupe de Ville with cruise control, air conditioning and autotronic eye. Wulff had an affinity for ruined Cadillacs, that was for sure. It was the fourth or fifth, he had lost count, that he had picked up during his Odyssey. There was something about all of this spoiled grandeur, all of this marvelous, rotting junk which excited him in a way that no new Cadillac could: here, seven to ten years later, you got right down to the rotten guts of America itself and saw it clear. America was an old Cadillac, all right; it was gilt and plastic long past its time and now, in the empty spaces, one could see the thin, luminous edge of its demolition peeking through. He loved the '64 Coupe de Ville. He did not love it quite enough to drive it down to Miami; he put it on the train this time and hoped for the best. The trans was wrecked, wouldn't downshift at all and slipped in high gear, the carburetor was plugged on at least one side and the power steering made noises even at idle . . . no, he could not drive this thing down to Miami. One trip to Los Angeles in a '64 Sedan de Ville had been as close as he wanted to get to the testing edge with an old Cadillac.

But the train was fine. Amtrak was fine. The car was behind him somewhere in the night, he was in the bar car putting a load on, the sack was locked up somewhere in a cubicle. He had stolen the Cadillac from a street on the South Side of Chicago; the moment he had seen its red glitter, the paint almost phosphorescent in the darkness, he had known that this was the one for him. But he knew the limits of his obsession; he wasn't going to drive this damned thing to Miami. Not in one piece, he wasn't.

Wulff sat in the bar car and listened to the sounds of the train and the night slowly overcoming him, an experience which two generations of Americans now had not known, the peace and isolation of a train at night. The bar car was deserted except for a heavy man toward the front who was slumped over in his chair looking meditatively at a glass of scotch. He had not moved in the thirty minutes that Wulff had been sitting in the car; drunk, probably, or contemplating that species of doom and possibility which trains in the night could bring upon one. Come to think of it, the incumbent President had once talked about listening to the trains at night when he was a young boy. Maybe that had given him the weary and contemplative frame of mind that had led him to declare the war on drugs at the Mexican border, to say nothing of his other many political innovations. Wulff sat with the gin glass in his hand, turning it absently, letting his mind drift away from modern-day politics and the disastrous war on drugs—which had merely escalated the graft changing hands at the border, that was the only difference, that and the uniforms of the men taking the payoffs—and onto his destination and what would happen then.

It was all drawing to a close. That sense of finality had begun to steal on him in the cab of the vast truck carrying him east, a feeling that this was one of the last times that he would be travelling the highways at night, clearly the last time that he would be going in this direction. It was coming to a close; he knew it during the second conversation with Calabrese when the certainty in the man's voice had matched some certainty in Wulff's; this was the clearly defined end that they were coming to. Then, saying goodbye to the trucker at the huge turnpike gateway to Chicago, all the roads merging at the airport at the great sign WELCOME TO CHICAGO: RICHARD J. DALEY, MAYOR (yes, it was Daley's city all right, the largest civilized center in the history of the world that could be said to belong to one man no matter how corrupt and aged), pressing his hand into the trucker's and passing on the two one-hundred-dollar bills that the trucker would look at in puzzlement some time later in a different light, not sure how they had gotten there or what he was riding with, seeing the trucker for the last time, then picking up an empty cab and getting into the South Side, appropriating the red coupe from a slum section . . . he had known then that he was grinding through the last series of an action. He was going to Miami; so was Calabrese.

Only one of them and possibly neither would get out of that place alive.

And Calabrese was right. When all was said and done the old fucker had taste after all, had a proper sense of destination and timing, for what better place now for all of it to end than Miami? Here was the final resting place of half of America, the other half wound up in Vegas but Miami was even more appropriate; it was a junk shop of the mind and heart where the pensioners lived in shacks and cheap rooming houses toward the north, while on the beaches themselves, rising layer upon layer, were the bright, pillared hotels of the damned, the sea eroding the beaches year after year, the beaches crawling up toward the hotels. And somewhere in those spaces, be it the landscape or in the cool, dead eaves of the hotels where the glittering people with faces like hammers looked for their fun as determinedly, with the same pulsing sense of vacancy that a junkie went from fix to fix . . . somewhere in there, if only you could get hold of it, was the answer to America itself, all of it there and no alternative, because America was dying; it was not only the Calabreses that were. Sometimes the death was just below the surface, other times it became manifest like the od that lurked beneath the habit of every junkie . . . but oh good Lord, good Lord, the death was there.

The man at the bar was looking at him now.

He was fixing Wulff with a stabbing gaze of great intensity and as Wulff returned it, looking into those eyes, he realized in the way that recovered information comes back only when tapped that this was not a brief glance, that the man, in fact, had been looking at him for a long time. Now, having caught Wulff's attention the eyes, suddenly luminous in the shifting light, seemed to glow with knowledge. Then the man was digging into his pocket, his fingers clutching at something in the right outer jacket and Wulff saw the shape of a gun faintly coming together there; then the man had turned fully, hand in pocket, and said to Wulff, "Let's get out of here."

The voice carried over the dim throbbing of the train above the rails, came at him with such casual intimacy that they might have been the only two people in the bar car, in the train itself . . . and then, sweeping the terrain, Wulff saw that this was so; the white-jacketed waiter who had been there to pick up the drink orders and deliver them, the small old bartender who had been standing behind the counter, flicking at it with a towel . . . both of them were gone, the car having narrowed to him and the heavy man. Looking at him now Wulff saw that he had misjudged this man severely, allowed fatigue and self-pity to overtake him past the point of alertness because this was no idle late-hour drunk confronting him but a hard, determined man in his late forties who looked like so many of the other men with whom he had struggled over the past months . . . except that if possible he looked even more competent than most of them.

The man came out of the pocket slowly with the gun, a Beretta, and said, "All right. Here it is. Now you start walking toward me and you do that slowly."

Wulff got up from his seat carefully, feeling the weight of his own gun flapping within his pocket, the gun suspended a crucial six inches from his right hand. He could get it in less than a second . . . but the heavy man would need far less than that to discharge from that gun the bullet that would kill him. So there was nothing to do but close ground slowly. He had had half of the second drink; more than anything now he regretted that. Sitting in the bar car had been stupid enough but he had been lulled by the rocking of the train, the conversation with Calabrese, the feeling that Chicago at last was behind him. But that was excusable, drinking was not. Every bounty hunter, amateur and professional, in the country had his name and photograph in their hip pocket. What was he doing drinking? He kept on walking slowly and when he had come to within two feet of the man with the gun the man said with a little smile, "That's enough." Wulff stopped, the train rocking him slightly. "That's good," the man said, "that's very good."

He turned behind him and said, "All right," and another man of roughly the same proportions but somewhat younger came from some hidden space of the car and stood, looking at Wulff with a little smile. Obviously he had come into the car while the others were clearing out, had been working in tandem with the first man but this did not explain, not quite, the absolute pleasure on this second man's face, the profound look of joy which seemed to be oozing from its pores. Wulff thought that he had never seen so much pleasure of that sort in his life. "Well," the second man said, seeming to rub his hands, "well, well, well." He beamed. "It's the wolf himself. As I live and breathe it's the lone wolf."

Wulff said nothing, holding his ground. The man holding the gun said, "Let's get him out of here."

"Oh, we'll get him out of here. I'm counting on that. As a matter of fact you could say that there's nothing I'm counting on more in the world than getting him out of here, but let me take a look at him if I may. Let me just take a look at him." The man stared, his face bright yellow in the shrouded illumination of the bar car, his eyes rolling. He might, Wulff thought, be on uppers of some sort. Certainly it was more than good spirits which were giving this cast to his face. "I'm glad to see you, you son of a bitch," he said. "I've been looking forward to this for a long time."

"Let's get out of here," the first man said, gesturing with his gun. "Come on."

"Oh we will, we definitely will. But there's no rush, is there? I mean," the second man said, rubbing his hands together, "there isn't exactly anywhere we can *go* is there? I wouldn't want to jump off a moving train, even the *Floridian* special at sixty miles an hour and it's a pleasure to see the great man close up." He walked toward Wulff then, coming rapidly and brushed by the man holding the gun and standing toe to toe with Wulff he reached up quickly and slapped Wulff across the face once, hard, the blow redounding through him. Wulff felt the bright slash of pain, then a slower lurch as that pain began to spread in thick rivulets into his gut but he held his ground. The man slapped him again.

"You like that?" the man said as if he were a salesman, say, demonstrating the capabilities of a high-performance car. "You like that now?" He turned toward the gun-holder. "He bleeds," he said, "the son of a bitch bleeds."

"For Christ's sake, Al—"

"Don't Christ's sakes me," the man named Al said. He placed the points of his long, elegant black shoes against Wulff's, then looked up at him. There was a considerable difference in height, five feet seven to six four, magnified because Al was in a slight crouch. "Just don't mess with me, Joe," he said to the gun-holder. "What I do I do when I want to do it, you understand?"

"This can't work," the gun-holder said. "This is all bullshit."

"Everything's bullshit, Joe," Al said almost conversationally. They might have been having a random debate somewhere in deck chairs, legs stretched across the sea. "Now you know that Joe, you know that as well as I do, everything's a bullshit deal from way back. You just do the best you can, don't you sweetheart?" Al said and hit Wulff across the face again, spotting the injured cheek, cracking the blow right down into that open web of pain and Wulff felt nausea, the nausea sifting through him in fine, light waves and this time he did give ground, swaying a little.

"See?" Al said, "he not only bleeds, he feels pain. He's going to cry in a minute, aren't you, you big bastard, you prick, you piece of filth. You know a man named Marasco?" Al said, "I knew a man named Marasco. The first one was for me and the second one was for him."

Wulff felt the humming of the train, little intimations of power coming up through the balls of his feet, throbs and pulsations which wove their way into the pain so that it began to spread through him like a blanket . . . but he was thinking, Marasco, yes, that was where it had practically all started, the guy named Albert Marasco, the kingpin who lived in a mansion in Long Island and who Wulff had killed in the fire. He had tortured the truth out of Marasco, working the truth from his dying pain in the midst of the fire and this man was named Al too, now that was interesting. That was really interesting, Al one and Al two, both of the Als coming together on the *Amtrack Floridian*, this one with a gun, wreaking vengeance. Why there was absolutely no limit, Wulff thought, no limit at all to the kind of trouble that a man could get himself into once he started this kind of campaign . . . delirium, he thought with the colder center of his mind, the pain had wrecked him, had made him delirious.

"For Christ's sake, Al," the man named Joe was saying again, waving the gun now in little circles, "this can't go on, we've got to get him out of here, someone's going to come back—"

"No one's going to come back," Al said, "no one is going to come back until I'm good and ready to have them do it, so get off my ass—" and at that moment Wulff hit him. He brought his fist up from floor level, sucker-punched Al in the jaw, lifting the smaller man almost two feet off the floor and then, the train swaying, Al's body pitched into the wall, his head hitting with a crack.

There was no conscious premeditation in this, it had all happened before; you reached a point finally where necessity and situation meshed at some level beneath consciousness, removed from calculation, and that was what had happened now because Wulff knew if he knew anything at all that things could only get worse, that whatever was happening was an ongoing situation where the odds would consistently diminish and finally he would find himself in a small, black tube of space with these men where there would be nothing for them to do, anymore, but kill him . . . and before they could enter that tube he had to take his chances, take them where they came.

Now, the man Al out of the picture, sagging almost comically into a padded chair against the wall, the other one, Joe, was bearing down upon Wulff with the gun, his eyes fixed with purpose, flicking his glance from trigger finger to Wulff trying to estimate distances and Wulff came out with a foot, knocked the man off balance, then kicking into a wall. The sound of the impact was horrifying; the partitions of the car were thin steel reinforced only by another layer behind it and it seemed as if the side of the car had caved in.

The man rebounded out of the wall, the instability of the partition then giving him impetus to spring back unhurt, the gun still in his hand, still levelling, and Wulff was almost caught flatfooted by the man's involuntary charge. He had not expected him to come off the wall in that way. A chair fell over and Wulff heard a thin screaming from the corridor; it seemed that a couple had come into the car, a young girl, now clinging to a man, her mouth in an *o* of distress, the man trying to pull her from the car but the girl paralyzed, shaking. They had wanted to come into the bar car for a quiet drink he supposed, well, more luck to them. The railroads were promoting themselves now as a different kind of trip; they could take this story home with them.

The man named Joe, still holding the gun, collapsed into Wulff's arms with the force of the rebound and for a moment they struggled with one another in a complex, horrid embrace. He could smell the high, dense odors coming from the man's body, odors both sweet and foul, excitement of course but more than excitement coming from him and for an instant they struggled that way in a parody of sexual embrace, Joe gasping and groaning, trying to get the gun up and against Wulff and Wulff, trying to free himself, establish some kind of distance, felt the man smothering him, swaddling him in that dense grip and then they stumbled over another cocktail table and into the wall of the car. Wulff felt himself beginning to slip then fall, the man tumbling over him.

Now the two of them were cleaving into a ball of activity and he could feel the gun pressing various areas of his body; nape, kidney, groin with a shy tentativeness that was the more dreadful because at any moment he expected it to go off and discharge the slug that would destroy him. But the gun did not fire, there was some mistake in the angle between finger and trigger and Joe could not get off a shot. Then Wulff had managed to wrap himself over and was lying on top of the man, panting, still reaching for the gun, noting with some corner of perception that the other man, Al, on the floor was stirring. He had not been knocked out by the blow then, only stunned, a resilient type this one and in just a few moments, unless Wulff was able somehow to get free of this one, it would be two against one, two with guns . . . and this energized him into one last burst of effort. He heaved against the man whose body now covered him like a cup and threw Joe off him. The man hit the floor with a thud, rolling, his knees drawn up, still holding onto his gun and stretching out flat. Wulff kicked him, feeling his toe dig into something soft, something that pulped underneath the pressure . . . and the man screamed.

And the screaming was a rope that yanked him to his feet, then. Wulff was leaning against the wall, momentarily in an attitude which he supposed would have struck the men on the floor, the couple standing at the door as contemplative, this man brooding against the wall over the two he had downed and Wulff imagined that there was something almost comical about this, this attitude of repose coming off the battle.

Then, in the next instant, a second scream filled the compartment, this one coming from the girl, her hand fluttering against her mouth, her chest struggling for the next intake of air that would give her a second, even more terrible scream . . . and there was nothing to do, he could not stop her, did not even know that he would if he had wanted. He was turning, stumbling, reeling from the car, holding the gun against him, the gun a welt in his side. He had to get out. He had to get out of here. All of his impulses were screwed toward flight and he gave into them wholly, feeling only now the panic that he might have felt back when the man with the gun had accosted him.

Wulff burst through the compartment shrouding the bar car from the next, hearing the sounds behind him. He almost stumbled over something lying huddled on the floor. Stopping for only an instant he saw that it was the unconscious form of the bartender and then he was moving onward through a sleeping car, the soft, even breathing of passengers around him. Let someone else clean up the mess in the bar car. Let someone else slap the bartender into consciousness, comfort the screaming girl, deal with Al and Joe. He would have no more of it. His options were running out.

He had to get off the train.

VI

The hotels fronted the bay, in back of them were the big, shiny motels glittering in color, in back of them were the older hotels, further back still were the ring of cheaper rooming houses and furnished apartments and then, two miles back of the ocean, the slums began, no transition, merely the passage of a street and the ruins in which the slum tenants, mostly blacks, dwelt. On good afternoons they might be able to pick up a breeze from the ocean, might be able to climb to the flat roof of one of the developments and see the Fontainbleau in the distance. In the same spirit they could get on the Harlem rooftops and watch the cars moving out across the Triborough Bridge, into the sun and the safer suburbs. Miami then was like all cities everywhere, the good and the rotten, the glittering and the corrupt all jammed up against one another, the line of segregation holding not through geography but terror.

Tamara guessed that they were pretty far back in the ring of furnished houses. They had come in quickly at night, the ride in the limousine from the airport done quickly, shades dangling from the windows of the limousine so that they could not see the streets, not that it would have mattered anyway; she did not know Miami nor want to know it. Williams, riding in the limousine, had fallen asleep during the ride. His two guards and hers had settled into a desultory conversation which seemed largely to have to do with Calabrese and how he was underpaying them—she tried not to hear any of it—and toward the last part of the ride she had fallen off herself, the droning of the motor carrying her back like water to San Francisco where she wished to hell she had stayed after she had walked out on Wulff back in Los Angeles. If she had done that instead of going back to her home she would not have been a sitting target for abduction and she would be out of all of this. Instead, it was just beginning.

Or perhaps it was ending. She did not know about that either; she had no idea what Calabrese had in mind except that clearly the old man intended to kill Wulff. He had said it over the phone, he had said it to her, and on the private plane to Miami he had settled beside her for a long, raving monologue in which he had tried to find out from her what Wulff was like and had told her that if he had one mission left in life it was to kill the man. She had decided then that Calabrese was a little crazy; for an old man he seemed to be as obsessed and single-minded about Wulff now as any fourteen-year-old might be about his father; in fact, that was possibly an angle, Calabrese that old man, was seeing Wulff as a father figure, an authority symbol of some sort and he was trying to kill him to remove all symbol of challenge in his old age. But that was all cheap psychologizing, Berkeley stuff and it was better perhaps not to think along those lines. She did not want to think along those lines. All that she wanted to do was to go home. She wished that her life had never intersected with Wulff's. Then she knew she was lying to herself.

She was on the second floor of a rooming house about two miles in back of the Miami shore. She guessed that it was two miles, hard to estimate, but it could not have been much less than that and if there were any more they would have been in the slum section proper which she saw rearing up behind them, a few blocks distant. She was doing a little bit better than she had since her abduction; she had a small room for herself, toilet facilities down the hall, a bed, a desk. The man who had been guarding her was not even in the same room, he was a few doors down the hall, alert, she supposed, to any sound of footfall if she headed toward the stairs. Williams, the black man, was in the room next to hers but he *did* have a guard with him, that was male supremacy for you; they felt that Williams was more dangerous, more likely to try to make an escape than she was. Well, they were quite right. She had no intention of trying to get out of here. It was quite hopeless, even she saw that, there was no way that she would get out of this alive unless Calabrese released her and he would only do that, she supposed, if Wulff were dead.

Either way the situation did not look very promising. If Wulff came to meet Calabrese in the Fontainbleau, and she had no reason to think that he wouldn't because he was as obsessed with Calabrese as the other way, he would never get out of it alive and if he didn't come, she would be killed, quite casually and expertly. She had no doubt of that whatsoever. Calabrese was as single-minded about such things as Wulff was.

Oh, she was really in a good position now. She was jammed between the two of them and it occurred to Tamara that in many ways there was no difference between them; Wulff and Calabrese functioned in exactly the same way. One was in the drug distribution business and the other one was out to destroy it, but they were both monomaniacal, they were single-minded and mostly they regarded the world as something that got between them and their purposes. If she had any interest she guessed she would go to the room down the hall and talk to the man, Williams, who had obviously been Wulff's partner through some part of this, try to find out some facts about him—even the guards would be terribly interested in this; they would hardly interfere in a discussion if it went on in front of them—but she did not care. She simply did not care anymore; she had lost interest in the whole thing. What she had told Wulff in San Francisco was quite sincere. She wanted to get as far from him, as far from the situation as possible. She owed him a great deal; he had saved her life, she was very attracted to him, the time that they had spent in bed together had done both of them a lot of good . . . but what was past was past; she did not care now if that quality of feeling within them might have somehow expanded . . . no, she did not care at all.

The magnitude of his obsession had been frightening. Back in San Francisco, having left him the second time, she had been able to think of putting her life together, getting back to school in the fall, working on a small, closed cycle of purposes the seriousness of which she had not been able to accept for many, many years. He and his war represented a different stage of her life, a closed chapter. She was finished with people who felt too largely, who acted too passionately, whose purposes were magnified by desire. If it were all the same to the world, if it really did not matter to anyone except herself, she would just as soon live with the self-deceiving people who coated over their desires with acceptance and whose lives were a series of evasions from the deep, frightful, meaningful issues which drove people like Wulff into death and sent people like that younger version of herself into a filthy drop point of a room in San Francisco where, if it had not been for Wulff who had happened upon and saved her, she would have died of an amphetamine overdose. Speeded out. Freaked out and dead at twenty-four. So much for living passionately.

She turned from the window where all of this had been revolving in her mind, she did not know how long, and Calabrese himself was at the door. The old man was leaning against the open panels, arms folded, looking at her with a strange, distorted expression which as she received his stare modified and then shifted into something close to pain. Then he had moved into the room, leaned against and closed the door and was waving a hand at her, almost awkwardly. She had not seen him in the light until now, she realized, only in the dim spaces of his office and then in the dark plane which had sped them to Miami; seeing him close-up it was as if she could look beyond the wrinkles and surfaces of the aged face into the corruption below . . . or was that merely imagination, a heightening of perception which had no basis in reality?

A clean old man, that was what he looked like; a nice, well-kept old man. He might have been a United States senator. All of them were nice, well-kept old men too, who made good appearances, talked softly and with many gestures and had sent a generation or two of younger men off to die. No point in thinking about that. Nothing political anymore, she reminded herself. You are not even Tamara, you are a girl named Susan Jenkins and this Tamara business will stop when you get home, stop for the last time, although it is just as well that these people think of you as Tamara because when Tamara goes away you will have disappeared too. Disappearance; to sink below the viscous surfaces of reality and be no more.

"Your friend isn't down, yet," Calabrese said. "He should have been in by now."

She shrugged, walked from the window and sat on the bed. "What do you want me to do about that?" she said.

"I don't want you to do anything. I just thought you'd like to know. He should have been down by now. I'm getting a little impatient waiting for him."

"He'll be down. I know he'll be down."

"I think you're right," Calabrese said squinting, wiping a little bit of dust from a black lapel with an elongated index finger. *Swipe, swipe*, it was just like the blade of a penknife working there. "In fact I'm sure you're right. When I return to the hotel I expect to have his message."

"So why aren't you there?"

"Why am I not there?" Calabrese said, and moved away from the wall, rubbed his hands together and then, in a surprisingly graceful gesture sat beside her on the bed, the springs rolling, then rebounding with a squeak. "Well, it can get very dull, merely sitting around a room, no matter how luxurious, and waiting for something to happen. Don't you think so?" He paused. "Aren't you getting bored?"

"I'm getting bored," she said. "Why don't you let me go home?"

"Oh I'd like to," Calabrese said, "I'd really like to let you do that, go home that is to say, go back to Sausalito and be a respectable little college girl again, but it's impossible you see. You're the only hold I've got on him."

He jerked his head toward the adjoining room where she could hear dim thumping as if Williams and his guard were doing calisthenics or beating one another up. Calabrese showed no concern. "He's certainly no ace in the hole," he said. "Wulff dumped him in Los Angeles. They had split up. Tell me," he said, his eyes becoming quite intense, "what is it like to fuck him?"

She said nothing. Certain questions were unanswerable. But she did not look away; she allowed that gaze to hold her and after a long, shuddering instant she felt her control dissolve. It was almost as if she had meshed into him. She began to understand the source of the man's power. It did not merely have to do with position; power came first.

"Tell me," Calabrese said, "I want to know. I know what he was doing with you; I'm not stupid. Any fool would know what was going on. Listen, he likes to fuck just as much as anyone; his fiancée got herself killed in New York and I know that *they* were fucking. Tell me," Calabrese said, "does he come fast or slow? What is it like, does he like to do it straight or does he fuck around? Does he get on top or does he like to be on the bottom, getting a ride, the way all those tough types really do? Did he suck your nipples hard? Did he hurt?" and then unbelievably he was closing in on her, his hands on her shoulders, digging in through the soft material of the sweater, the clothing insubstantial, the only reality the hard, biting contact of nails into shoulders, feeling the pain as he dug his fingers in deeper and then he was on top of her, grunting and struggling, his eyes at some weird off-angle looking at the wall as he stunned her with pressure, beginning to move on top of her.

"I'm going to fuck you," Calabrese said, "I've been thinking of it all the way for days, whether I should do it or not and I've got to do it. I don't want his poisons but I want his slut, I want to do it to something that he has," and she wrenched away from him desperately, shaking her head, screaming deep in her throat. "Don't think of it," he said, looking down at her then, "don't even think of screaming for help because the only help that you're going to get around this place, the only help at all, would want to watch me do it and make it a gang-bang. Do you understand?"

She understood. She let that understanding grow from her stomach, come into her eyes and she looked at him then, seeing beneath the angry, fervid surface of those eyes to something much deeper, something hurt and fearful within him that if it had had voice would whimper. The thing that she saw was seventy-three years old and was trembling and it was that which she spoke to now.

"All right," she said, "I won't make it hard for you. But I want you to know that it won't make any difference."

"I know that," Calabrese said, "I learned that a long time ago, that nothing makes a difference."

He was sliding from her, then he was on the floor standing, reaching for his belt, dropping his pants. "Nothing makes any difference but you've got to play the game as if it does, don't you? Don't you, don't you, don't you baby," Calabrese said . . . and then shrieking, mumbling, biting hard he was on top of her, tearing at her clothing, ripping her apart, trying to move inside . . . but she was not surprised that at the center of all this desperation she felt not pain but merely a gelatinous substance which rubbed and rubbed against her thighs.

And all around—everywhere—the sound of his weeping.

VII

Williams remembered how it had been outside the methadone center. Activity on the street, something seizing his attention, then, before he could even see the assailant, the quick, plunging feel of the knife within him, the sound of the footsteps moving, the feel of the sidewalk as it had rolled up at him, caressed him like waves. Something almost purifying about the pain in his chest and side, a pain that he must have been waiting for all his life, now hardly so bad in the actuality as it had been in dreams; more purgative than anything, getting my black ass in gear, he thought dreamily. Then the sirens, the emergency room, the long, black space in the hospital, the weeks after that when he had had plenty of time to think over his life and the relationship it bore to the unseen man who had knifed him. It was then that he had come, however reluctantly, to the decision that Wulff was right; any black man who truly thought that he could work with the system was a fool because the system was interested only in protecting itself and ripping off the outsider and that was what a black man would always be . . . an outsider. Wulff, a cop to the core who had vowed to get rid of the international drug trade, could have been an insider but he had dropped out to murder because he realized that it was impossible to clean up anything when you were part of it . . . and Williams, tacking the decision onto his own life, saw that Wulff was right, came home from the hospital and spent another few weeks thinking it out and then, when the call from Wulff came from Los Angeles it was as if he had merely been waiting for the trigger. He had left his eight-months pregnant wife, loaded up a U-haul with armaments from Father Justice of the Divinity & Faith Church and had gone out to Los Angeles to blow the system to hell with Wulff.

But that hadn't worked out either; Wulff by that time was in so deep that his options were restricted. Everybody had his name and picture; guerilla tactics were almost impossible when you were public enemy number one, open prey for every bounty hunter, amateur and professional, in the business. They had been pinned into a rotten trailer court for a week, the armaments tacked near them, saying that they were waiting to make a move but what they were really waiting for was the enemy to come in after *them* . . . which the enemy did but not before Williams and Wulff had had enough to do with one another to see that no team concept was going to work.

The trailer court had been blown up and so was the enemy, but it was a temporary respite; they were starting to roll in like cavalry now. It was obvious that they had to split up, that Williams would have to go back east and put the pieces of his life together, get back into the system again, and Williams had not fought that insight; he had said goodbye to Wulff without sentiment and taken the U-haul back on the roads toward New York . . . but in the early part of that long drive he had been abducted by two of Calabrese's men and brought into Chicago. Now he was in Miami and his life, he supposed, was in peril. That peril did not matter to him so much as the outcome of his wife's pregnancy: she would have given birth by now. He wondered if he had a son. That would have been something worth knowing; as far as the rest of it Williams felt himself simply to be beyond fear. It did not matter; once abducted he had taken to the capture with a virtual sense of relief. It solved his problems for the time being, the dilemma of whether he would go back and face his life or chuck it completely. This was easier. Being a captive took the pressure off, almost completely. For the first time in his life Williams was beginning to see the benefits of slavery. No wonder so many of the slaves, once freed, had stayed on the plantations, begged the masters to keep them. Almost anything was easier than a world in which will or free choice dominated.

Now, at the rooming house, Williams said to the man who was staying in the room with him, "It's time to play some more poker." The guards had taken him for granted. Apparently the word was out: Williams was no trouble. So they worked in shifts one off, one on, in twelve-hour cycles and the one who was on often acted less like a captor than another bored prisoner in the room.

Williams had no idea what was going on with the girl in the next room other than that Wulff knew her and they had apparently kidnapped her from San Francisco as an additional hold upon him. He had not said a word to her. He supposed that if he had wanted he could have gotten angry as hell about the fact of the kidnapping: wasn't he sufficient hold upon Wulff? Did they have to involve the girl too, were there no limits to the ugliness of the games they played? but he was too weary for anger and he knew the answer; there *were* no limits to ugliness. In or out of the world, ugliness predominated.

"Two-handed poker is shit," the guard said, "there's no fun in two-handed poker."

"What the hell," Williams said, "head to head. Challenge match."

"That's just for the movies. In the movies two-handed poker is a good game. But it doesn't work head to head." The guard spat on the planks of the wooden floor, ran a hand through his hair, then got a pack of cigarettes off a bureau. "It's all shit," he said.

"I'll go along with that."

"How the fuck long are we going to stay here? It's ridiculous; I'm going stir crazy."

"There's a way out of it," Williams said.

"What's that?"

"Why you can let me go. If I escaped on you then you wouldn't have to guard me anymore. You'd be out of it. We could work out an escape attempt."

The guard seemed to genuinely ponder this, cupping his chin in his hand. Both of them were contemplative types who seemed only marginally interested in their job. Maybe Calabrese had as much employment difficulty as any other small business. "No," the guard said, his head finally retreating, "it wouldn't work. It's ridiculous. And besides," he said, "Jack wouldn't go along with it." Jack was the other guard. "You couldn't imagine how seriously he takes this kind of shit. If he learned that we were trying to work something out he'd report you right to Calabrese."

"That's too bad," Williams said, "then we'll have to settle for poker."

"Jack will be back in a little while," the guard said, "you could *ask* him. Personally I don't give a damn; if you could think of a way to work it out I'd go along with you. I'm fed up to here with all of this crap, I really am. But I see no way at all."

"Okay," Williams said again, "I won't force it. We'll play poker, head to head." He dug into a pocket, rattled a few pieces of change. "Nickel ante," he said.

"Nah," the guard said pondering this, "it wouldn't work out, it just wouldn't work out at all," and shook his head, slumped into a chair, went into a deep, ponderous doze from which, at times, he would emerge, floundering, to blink an eye at Williams before retreating again. He was lolling, his hand resting on the point thirty-eight inside his jacket, nominally ready to blast Williams if Williams tried to move from the room but Williams knew that that was merely for show; he could, if he wanted, overpower, take the guard's gun, charge from the room. A certain relationship of trust and inattention had been set up. It really would not have been difficult at all.

The point was simple though; why bother with it? Why embark on a risky and dangerous escape attempt when Calabrese, if he had any sense at all, undoubtedly had the house ringed with guards who would blow his sensibility from his purpose the moment that he came outside of this two-story dwelling? Calabrese was not a fool; the cemeteries and seas were littered with men who had made that mistake, taking him for a fool, and Williams would be in that category if he thought that these guards were the first and only line of defense: the old man would not do this. The old man who had been clever enough to have intercepted him in the middle of the country and abducted him to ransom out Wulff's reappearance . . . he would not leave him to these two bored, indolent guards. If anything, Williams thought, there could only be direct purpose in Calabrese harnessing two guards like this to him: they might lull Williams into the feeling that he could indeed try to escape . . . giving Calabrese the perfect excuse that he needed to kill him.

No. No, he would not play the old man's game. It was better to wait now because he knew that Wulff was coming.

So Williams sat in the room, looking at the dozing guard, and waited for something to happen. Sooner or later you ran your options out and had to do it; you had to wait for something outside of yourself to create a change of circumstances, to change the balance. It had happened to him now; it had happened to the guards and in a sense it had happened to Calabrese himself.

All of them were simply waiting for Wulff to appear.

For a man that the outfit had sworn for death, he sure had a hell of a lot of options left.

You had to admire that.

Even if the man you were admiring was a dead man.

VIII

Wulff came into Miami in a stolen car, a 1968 Chrysler New Yorker which he had abducted from the surprised driver right off US 1. There was no time for frills or maneuvers anymore, the business of the *Floridian* had convinced him that if it was going to be done at all it would have to be done quickly and directly. The confrontation with Calabrese could not be accomplished through delicate maneuvering. Coming off the *Floridian* at its first stop, Louisville, there had been a moment of sheer doubt, indecision, with two corpses or near-corpses on this train and what was waiting for him ahead it all seemed hopeless, and he had hung on the platform stupefied for a few moments wondering if he could go ahead. Then the shrieks and sirens of distant cars had piled upon him and he had started to run. Running was simple, instinctive, he knew how to do that. The sirens meant that they had found the bodies on the train; they also meant, if his knowledge of local police was any guide, that the Louisville cops would be just as happy as they could be to do the job that Calabrese's men had fucked up. Everybody was a bounty hunter. Running with the sack dangling from his shoulder he had burst out at last into an open space, turned a corner, and then found himself at Main Street which was US 1 itself, the big apple before the turnpikes had wiped it out, the only direct route in the old days between Maine and Florida. He had gotten on a bus there, ignoring any glances which he might have been given, wrapped himself into a little sullen space of waiting while in little clumps all of the passengers had gotten off. He had ridden the bus to the end of the line and then gotten out past the suspicious, sweeping glance of the driver, walking south through the outskirts of Louisville, ruined houses lining the road, black people sitting on the sidewalks, mumbling at one another. It was another Harlem scene; despair and the imprint of drugs were universal. They had carried their damages to Louisville, home of the Kentucky Derby and the gateway to the New South as thoroughly as they had in the ruined northeast . . . and this insight had given him impetus.

He had kept on walking, a mile, two miles maybe, until the houses had thinned out and then he had turned toward the roadway, looking for a likely car. A Cadillac had passed him, a ruined one all right but driven by a black with three screaming children in the rear of the convertible, the top pulled down, the children standing and hitting one another and he figured that the black had enough trouble already. Then a couple of small domestics had passed him and he figured that these were no good altogether, but then the Chrysler had come by, exactly what he was looking for, driven by a man in his twenties, arm hanging out the window, hand on the roof, banging it in rhythm to radio music. When the car had slid to a stop at the light, probably the last light south in Louisville, Wulff had come from behind a post quickly and had done the necessary almost without conscious thought, functioning on instinct. You learned a few damned things if you were at it this long, probably the drug traffickers had the same feeling: that there was nothing between them and the outcome they wanted but motive. Considerations such as morals just did not enter into it anymore. If they ever had.

Out into the roadway, level the gun (there was no one in line behind the Chrysler at the light but even if there had been he would have gone ahead with it; who was going to interfere with him?), watch the rising dread pouring into the driver's face from all the pockets which sowed dread, gesture with the gun, no need to say a word, yank open the door, push him, spinning, from the car and then behind the wheel. The easy transfer accomplished, the car enveloped him like a gigantic mouth, strangely warm, smelling delicately of sweat and exhaust, the huge wheel already curving into his hands with a sense of total familiarity: there were women like that, they could go from one man to the other with such ease and accommodation that you wondered, really wondered, if they were making love to anyone but themselves. The same thing with this Chrysler New Yorker, brougham equipment, floor mats with Cadillac symbols beneath him (so the driver had perhaps had equivocal feelings about his car), the shouts of the driver diminishing behind him as he pulled the car into lane and at speed merged with traffic heading southward, always now, heading south.

It was easy. Once you broke free of restraints, once you functioned in Calabrese's world where your desires were modified only by the equipment you had to satisfy them . . . everything was very easy. Wulff could see the pleasures of criminality. All of that stuff the agencies gave you about how ill-paying a life of crime was and how your average criminal spent five years in jail for every one out and earned a net income of four thousand and fifty dollars a year before taxes . . . all of that was crap. They did not want to acknowledge the fact that the criminal's *way* of looking at things was simply superior to the more ordinary view and that the statistics were spoiled by a lot of amateurs and smalltimers getting lumped in with the overall statistics. Actually, the professional criminal took risks which were merely consonant with his job and he tended to make out rather well. Better than he would have any other way.

Wulff headed the car into Miami. From Louisville to Miami is not a long trip but it was somewhat longer than he thought; it must have been five or six hundred miles anyway and this meant two gas stops, the Chrysler guzzling it away at eight or nine miles to the gallon even on the road. The big cars just couldn't take it anymore, the country was clamping down on them, but aside from thinking of the gas mileage and the oncoming death of the big car Wulff kept his mind as completely blank as possible, watching the sack bouncing on the seat next to him, sweeping his glance between US 1 and the sack mechanically, rhythmically every thirty seconds or so, drawing this attention into a concentrated, fixed tube. Driving was satisfying and mindless, that was why it had to be the true American pasttime.

Somewhere around Jacksonville a radio car picked him up; he must have been doing seventy-five or eighty within the township limits and as the car came down on top of him, all the blinkers and headlights going, Wulff had a moment of indecision. Then without thinking about it further he put the accelerator into the floorboards and got the car quickly up to ninety, deciding to outrun the police car if he could. It would only be embarrassing and messy if he were picked up and he would probably have to shoot the cop down rather than get into any of it; he did not want to get into cop-killing if he could help it. It was just too complicated, it would mean more people to evade; ethics hardly entered into it at all.

They dragged down US 1 at ninety and ninety-five miles an hour, going through intersections and traffic lights as if locked together by a long chain, then, finally, Wulff began to open up a little distance on the roads, dropping the car back fifty yards or so. He could be running right into a roadblock of course, but somehow he did not think that he was; there were just not enough State Police around to justify a roadblock or even an interceptor car unless they were messing with something more profound than a speeding violation which at this time Wulff was. Besides that, if he knew cop's mentality at all and he guessed that he should, the radio car was not going to summon reinforcements. Getting help would be an admission of failure and no cop, given a choice, wanted to admit that he couldn't handle something himself. When you came right down to it, cops and criminals functioned on the same mentality; the only thing that was holding back most police from being lawbreakers themselves was the existence of a police force that managed to coat over their impulses, give them a rationalization.

Heavy thinking for a speeding chase but it beat worrying about what was going on behind. The Chrysler was surprisingly effective on the open roads. There was a miss in the engine toward the low rpm range and it stuttered and fumbled in the mid-passing zone of forty to sixty but above seventy-five miles an hour the big, aging car really came together, it handled more solidly and responsively at eighty-five than at twenty. It was really a shame that there were almost no roads in the country where the capabilities of these cars could be tested . . . crazy country this, whose production lines could turn out cars that could go at a hundred and twenty miles an hour, whose speedometers registered the fact that they could go at one hundred and twenty, whose every advertisement was inducement to try the cars at that speed . . . and then set up a network of cops, speeding violations, point systems, motor vehicle bureaus, traffic courts and insurance rating systems that made it as difficult as possible to use the cars up to that natural capacity. Crazy country: ambivalent country, maybe it was the same psychology in evidence that encouraged women to dress as provocatively as possible, which taught them from the age of twelve to be as conscious of the power of their bodies to incite, to inflame, as possible . . . and then made the natural response of men to these bodies as painful for them as possible. Maybe America took as much pleasure from denial as attainment but the sweetness of the pain could only be gauged by its difficulty . . . and his mind scuttled away from this, no point in thinking about it, no point in pushing his mind further and further into channels which would take him only toward revulsion.

The country was an exercise in ambivalence any way you took it; the drug culture came out of an advertising society which made escape-on-the-cheap as glamorous as possible and only made the penalties for that escape visible when it was too late to change. Blame not the pushers, the distributors, the network itself, when they were only responding to a need which had been created by television.

Yes, if you looked at things that way nothing made much sense at all. In his rearview mirror the pursuing car lurched, wiggled from one side of the road to another and then, all in one gathering simply disappeared, swerving right and out of the plane of sight. A high-speed blowout no doubt, the tires of the patrol car pushed past their capabilities by an engine which they could not control. Wulff allowed himself a small, tight smile of satisfaction, thinking of the sensations of the cop as the car went off the road, as terror and futility battled with one another in the cave of the dislocated car.

Let him think about it in the ditch, Wulff thought, let him think about the consequences of pursuit . . . and then he was free again on the roads, he was moving at sixty and sixty-five, cutting back to an inconspicuous pace. The car as if blooded for the first time by the ninety-mile-an-hour chase tugging away at the accelerator like an animal, pleading, teasing for a little speed but Wulff was firmer with the car in holding it down than he had ever been in coaxing speed out of it. He shoved the lever into D_1, holding the Chrysler into second speed where the engine labored anywhere above forty miles an hour and, spinning rpm's, he moved along on US 1.

He wished that he had a police radio, a short-wave receptor that is, that would pick up reports of the police bands. He would like to hear what the cowboy in the ditched car had to say for himself now. He doubted that it would be very much.

He was on virtually empty road now with the car shaken. Once, a long time ago, US I had been the only route from Maine to Miami, due south through New York, Philadelphia and Washington, one row of custard stands, drive-in movie theatres, gas stations all the way down but now that was finished, the turnpikes had taken away everything but local traffic and where he passed business now it was faded, burnt-out abandoned hulks which once had been roadside stands. What had happened to all these people? the people who sucked their lives off the highway, that was. Had they retreated into the fields back there in the darkness, little beaten houses just dimly visible from the highway, or had they pursued the population onto the vast surfaces of the turnpikes where they had all become Joes at the filling stations, Emilies hustling tuna salad in the Hot Shoppes? What happened to the people who worked for the country when the country ineradicably changed?

Well, it was no difference, no point in worrying about it, the country would go on and the people would take different shapes or roles to accommodate themselves to the beast. The country ran lives now, the country which once these people thought they had known and controlled was nothing but a beast now, a slavering beast that absorbed and excreted and there was little place in it for the Joes and Emilies, damned little place as well for the Wulffs too. Men who fought the beast, who threw themselves into its jaws to try and choke and sicken it on its own fetid juices, people like Wulff did not last very long. That was probably his greatest sin, the one that they would impale him for after all of the others were forgotten: he had bucked the system, he had defied it and you simply did not, in modern-day America, take on what fed you. He moved a hand over, poked open the sack and idly let his fingers play with the powder, the little, sticky grains adhering to his fingertips like sugar or salt, clinging to him in little teardrops. Here, properly adulterated, cut down, spooned and injected were a thousand dreams which he was clutching in those fingers, dreams for all of the Joes and Emilies of the land, dreams which would take them back to that easy, gentler time when US 1 had been the world, the boundaries of their world laid out as easily and precisely for them as the drug itself laid down murderous little patterns in the capillaries, pulsating then from those capillaries through the complex and ruined network of the system, squeezing the heart, coursing into the brain, moving out again then into the lungs, the vena cava, the pancreas, the vena cava . . .

It occurred to Wulff that he was not thinking very rationally. Strain, fatigue, the pursuit, the business of murder itself had changed him, perhaps in some permanent fashion. He was no longer rational, he was through some complex combination of that fatigue and the murder-lust driven into a condition which, without drugs, might have duplicated the mind of the junkie. He was what he despised, he thought lolling above the wheel, inclining his head toward the windshield, maintaining contact with reality in only the most tenuous and exhausting way, he had become what he had dedicated his life to destroying. He was a junkie himself. What he was hooked on did not go into the veins but it was the same thing, all of it was always the same.

He kept on driving. If he thought about it more he supposed this was the very thought that could push him over the edge, the realization that in some complicated way he had become the enemy. But maybe you had to do it: you had to become a killer to destroy the killers, a madman to purge out the lunatics . . . maybe then you had to become a junkie to squeeze all the junk out of the world.

He let his mind hang at that thought, the thought dangling like a fluorescent bulb off the ledge of his consciousness and then he was in Miami, poking and prodding through the slums at the outskirts, the Chrysler snaffling almost instinctively toward the rich, beating heart which was the beachfront—all of the seashore cities were laid out the same, it was exactly like Atlantic City—and from that time on there was little time at all to think. Maybe the residue of junk left on his fingers, the fingers resting against his nose had been inhaled and he was reacting to those mild, gentle vapors. You never knew. You just never knew. If this was a heroin jag, perhaps the Governor himself should try it.

IX

"Come on up," Calabrese said to him on the lobby phone, "just come on the hell up."

Wulff said, "You must think I'm crazy."

"I don't think you're crazy, I know it," Calabrese said. He sounded as much in control as ever, his voice firm and assured. "I'm in room seven-oh-one. Come on and we'll have a nice talk."

"Walk into it?" Wulff said, "you think I'm just going to walk into it?" He looked around the lobby. The standard: people in evening dress, bathing suits, all stages between drifting through, a busy newsstand at the far corner, jingling phones, bellboys . . . but at least three and possibly as many as five of these people had him under tight observation. He knew that. Still, observation was not capture. The call had been a reasonable risk.

"Why not?" Calabrese said, sounding cheerful. "You're not going to do anything to me because only I know where I've got the girl and your partner stashed and I'm not going to do anything to you because I assume that you've got the sack good and hid and only you know where it is. Am I right? So it's a standoff."

"That's not what I heard from you the last couple of times we talked. You don't want the sack, you want my ass. You want to kill me."

"Oh," Calabrese said and laughed, a healthy, unfettered laugh that had no trace of affection. "Oh, that was just to get your interest up, Wulff, and besides we all have episodes of temper, you've got to admit. Little outbursts; really, they don't mean a thing. I'm perfectly calm, this is just a business proposition to me now. Bet your life. You come up and we'll have a nice talk."

Wulff flicked a glance through the lobby again. If there was a net of surveillance it was deep and subtle, probably came from the desk clerks themselves because nothing looked untoward at all. Possibly Calabrese was so sure of his position now that he did not even think he *had* to observe Wulff, just let him walk into the lair and start firing . . . but there was always the chance too that the old man was telling the truth, that indeed the only thing he had in his mind was a casual chat. A casual chat between old antagonists . . . he had the sack stuffed into a big locker at the airport, the key to that locker checked into a smaller one as the only contents and the key to the small locker taped high in an abandoned alleyway three miles from here . . . yes, Calabrese was right, the stuff was pretty much under wraps. Still, did any protection justify the risk of confronting the old beast whole?

He guessed that it did and another jolt of the same force that had been hitting him in the car on US 1 came through. Of course he wanted to see the old bastard, of course he wanted the confrontation . . . it was what he had wanted since that last time in Chicago when Calabrese had mocked him and laughed at his impotence and even if the old man were holed up there with machine guns and men to operate them, even if room seven-oh-one was a cell of fire whose flaming walls could drop around to embrace and consume him . . . even if all of that were true he still wanted to go up there, to see the enemy whole. "All right," he said, "I'm coming."

"I'm glad. That's a wise move, Wulff."

"It's a goddamned dumb move, Calabrese."

"All right," the man said almost pleasantly, "it's a goddamned dumb one, but you haven't been smart yet and you're not going to start now, are you?" Hanging up the phone he guessed he wasn't.

Wulff walked rapidly through the lobby, streaming fountains in the background, soft music pulsing through him, little gusts of air purring from the central air conditioning hitting him as he walked underneath the vents. This was probably the closest that it was possible to come in the Fontainbleau to a sense of climate. Here indeed was where a certain kind of Americana had peaked: sheer insulation from the environment, the shutting off of any sense of strong, uncontrollable forces which were mysterious and deadly. To be an American was to seek relief from these forces, to move further and further up the socioeconomic scale was to move further away from the irreconcilable and the monstrous to some state in which death itself was merely an unfortunate aspect of the weather and could be held outside by rigorous technology.

Cadillacs operated on the same principle, Wulff thought, which might have to do with his affection for them but there was, he liked to think, some humor and at least a trace of irony in this obsession because the Cadillacs he loved were not the new but the seven or eight-year-old jobs where the bloom was off and where the environment came peeking in all the time: a bad muffler here, ruined tailpipe there, leak in the exhaust vent, the air conditioning, the leather seats themselves coming askew, all of the marvelous insulation falling apart so that you knew all the time what America consisted of. It consisted of holding onto a rotting, dismembered apparatus which could not perpetually deny what it had been conceived to abolish. The rich could have Cadillacs and the Fontainbleau, at least eight years' worth of Cadillacs and Fontainbleau to wall them off, the middle class could at least get a piece of them through two-week flight-included package tours and three- or four-year-old de Ville series coupes and sedans. The poor, however, had to settle either for the Fleetwood Eldorado series in very bad repair, seven- or eight-year-old cars which were literally spilling through the joints . . . and heroin. Heroin was the Fontainbleau of the poor man . . . except, Wulff thought, that the rich had all the bargains as usual. Heroin was far more expensive.

He rose up six flights in an empty self-service elevator whose speakers sung to him, the one hundred and twenty-one strings sweeping their hearts out for him, flowers and bowers, breezes and sneezes they were playing, a chorus of heavenly voices was singing about in front of them, the chorus and strings intertwining richly, ripely, lushly . . . Wulff could have thrown up if he had the energy, but of course he was merely a simple cop at heart, he could not appreciate the intricacies of beautiful music which the one hundred and twenty-one strings, as he remembered, definitely had a fine reputation for playing.

The doors came open on the seventh floor and he walked out into vacancy, vacancy glinting from the chandeliers, vacancy on the rugs, a couple of people in evening dress making their way along the hall, holding on to the walls almost tenderly, both of them in their mid-sixties. The man was whispering words of encouragement to his wife, or at least the man thought that he was whispering although there was some difficulty with his auditory sense. What he was doing was hoarsely mumbling in a rasping, carrying tenor. "Just a few more steps dear," the man was saying, "a few more steps and we'll be in our nice little roomsie and we'll shut the lights off, go beddy-bye," and the woman said, "I can't make it, I tell you, Gerald, I just can't make it anymore."

"Yes you can," the man said tenderly, rubbing a large, splayed hand over her bare back, leaving little red streaks across the freckles. "You can so make it Virginia, you can make it if only you think you can make it and once we're in our roomsie with the lights out and the do not disturb sign out you'll be a changed woman, you'll look back on this tomorrow morning and laugh."

"I'm not laughing," the woman said, "I'm not laughing, Gerald. I'll never laugh again. I don't think I even have the strength to cry," and lurched perilously into the wall, gripped it like a swimmer sinking beneath panels of water. "I just can't make it anymore, Gerald," the woman said, and laid herself out neatly, with a sense of finality, on the carpet.

The man made a half-hearted attempt to hold her, then as if succumbing to forces which were far beyond his comprehension, let alone control, he let her sink, let her spread out on the rug and then looked at her with a disgusted expression, his hands on his hips, shaking his head. He belched once, a deep, sour sound that reverberated from the plastic of the corridor and then for the first time noticed Wulff, who had been trying to get by them as inconspicuously as possible. "I guess you think that this kind of thing happens all the time," he said.

"Oh no," Wulff said, "not at all."

"Well it does," the man said, "that's the whole point of it and I might as well admit the truth, there's no sense living a lie anymore and now that we're on our vacation I can't hold it back, I just have to face the truth and be done with it. The woman's a total drunk. I thought that I might be able to bring her around, give her a little personal attention, try to talk her out of it in these two weeks that we had down here but it's hopeless. She just can't control herself."

The man burped again, a stab of heartburn took his face and wrinkled it; he put a hand against his mouth. "I admit that I've neglected her," he said, "but it's very difficult, you know, very difficult to have any kind of model marriage or romantic union when you're breaking your ass out there in the tunnels just trying to put a living together, trying to make some kind of a decent life for the wife and kiddies. I did it all for her," he said, his face slowly smoothing out as the bubble of heartburn passed, "everything that I did was for her I definitely want you to know but *she* never understood that. They never understand and appreciate what you're trying to do and then they're fifty-seven years old and all washed out and you're down in the fucking Fontainbleau. I tell you," the man said, a strange cunning passing over his face as if the belch had transmitted to him some expansive insight that he had never previously grasped, "I tell you, I should have fucking spent these three weeks in the shop, that's what I should have done. Sent her down by herself, maybe she could have picked something up."

The woman on the rug murmured something and then, convulsively began to sob, her fingernails gripping at the red ply of the carpeting. She was trying to get up but what it was seemed merely a parody of gymnastics as if she were trying an unusually complicated sort of pushup without success, the biceps failing to relay the messages passed from the impoverished brain. She subsided, muttering into the rug, then lay at perfect peace with herself.

"And it's not the first time," the man said, "it's not the first time this has happened, I want you to know that, or the second or the third. The disgusting scenes we've had; the only thing that I can be grateful for is that we're not with any of our friends. I wanted to come down with friends but it was she who said we had to have our private time together, just a couple of weeks to get to know one another again. You know what she's gotten to know?" the man said. "She's gotten to know about ten gallons of gin, that's all. You wouldn't give me a hand, get her down to our room, would you? It's seven-sixteen, it's just down the hall. I can't make it anymore, I just can't make it anymore. It's going to be the fourth time this week that I've carried her down the hall and I'm not as young as I used to be." He reeled into the wall, put his palms flat against it in a rather expert way and his features, seeming to contract in apprehension, smoothed out again.

"Yeah," Wulff said, "yeah, that's all right, I don't mind." Leaning forward heavily, putting his hands on the ankles of the woman, then heaving and tugging, he managed with the man to get her into a semi-erect position, her legs dangling in front of her in a set of curious motions as if she were dimly remembering pedalling a bicycle, and they got her down the hall in that way, her legs scuttling and pedalling beneath her, her mouth opening to emit little bursts of song.

"For Christ's sake," the man said as they got to seven-sixteen, "she's going to start singing again. I don't think I can stand it anymore, last night she was singing to me so I didn't get any sleep."

He dropped her, leaving Wulff with the full weight through the shoulders and he strained to hold her into position as the man looked through his pockets and came out finally with a set of keys and rammed one into the door. The woman was still singing, little obscenities beginning to curl like weeds through the lyrics of the song, the same song, as a matter of fact, that the one hundred and twenty-one strings had been playing in the elevator.

Groaning, the man got the door open, pushed it back into the wall, then, hands on hips, stood there, looking at Wulff, at the woman on the floor, at the key dangling from the hole, shaking his head. "If I had any goddamned sense," he said, "I'd get out of this right now, I wouldn't even stay here, I'd get right the hell back to Neponsit. At a hundred and fifty dollars a day, who needs this?"

"Let's get her in," Wulff said, bending, gripping the woman's shoulders. They shifted like sand under his grasp: he could feel the flesh, little grains, moving in that grip. "Come on now."

"Well of course. Of course I understand what you're saying. I mean who needs this, that's your attitude, right? She's not your responsibility, you were just a passerby who was kind enough to stick your neck out, get involved in this kind of thing. Isn't that what you're thinking?"

"Shut up, Gerald," the woman said softly. "Stop hounding the man, he's taken quite enough of you. Just cooperate and get me onto the bed. I think I'm going to throw up."

"Well we can't have you throwing up," the man said, "that would be absolutely ridiculous, I mean that would be the last complete, entire, goddamned utter straw; when you start throwing up in hotel corridors it's time to throw in the towel, don't you think?" He bent over uncomfortably, heaved the woman upright like a board, Wulff balanced the weight of her shoulders and they staggered into a huge suite, all of the blinds closed and drawn, the unmade bed in the middle of the room strewn with books, and pitched the woman onto a small, cleared space in the center. "She won't even permit them to clean it up," the man said, "really, she's a goddamned filthy slob, that's her real trouble and always has been. She can't even keep a hundred-and-fifty-dollar-a-day suite clean, that's her problem."

Wulff decided that it was time to get out. It was definitely time to get out; it had been time from the moment that he had run across this pair: how the hell had he gotten involved in the first place? Best not to think about that; maybe he could put it down as a refreshing break from his larger problems. One thing that this proved, drink was as pervasive in its effects as drugs, at least for the upper-middle-classes. The room reeked of scotch, of gin, of bourbon, of a hundred drinks consumed hurriedly from open bottles. Looking toward the dresser top as his eyes adjusted to the light he could now see the empties lined up like little soldiers on the glass.

The woman sighed, twitched on the bed like a frog and then subsided into a deep, dramatic doze, her eyes fluttering once and then ceasing to move. "You are going," Gerald said, "you don't want to go, do you? You can join me for a drink."

"I'm sorry," Wulff said, "I've got to see someone."

"Well of course you've got to see someone. I assume that you came up to this floor to keep an appointment and it was very generous of you to help us out in the first place, but now that you're here, won't you have a little drink? All that I have to do is to look at her passed out on the bed and do you know something?" Gerald said, "I don't find that very appetizing. I used to love to watch her sleep, when we were first married I could draw a chair up to the bed and just watch her for hours, you know, after sex, the way she would curl up with that little smile on her face, it was really exciting but that was a long goddamned time ago and she still has that little smile. Do you know," Gerald said, pursuing Wulff to the door, lumbering over the carpet, supporting himself now and then on the walls with hard, little slaps that reestablished his balance before he stood again, weaving, hands in pockets, "this hotel, the Fontainbleau, was the headquarters during the 1972 Republican National Convention for the Committee to Reelect the President. Isn't that interesting? It's a little piece of history. Why in this very room that we're in right now they might have been setting up the taps, making plans for the houseboat. For all we know John Mitchell was in this room, why the President himself might have been. It's hard to tell. You know, hotels are very stuffy about this kind of thing, they won't release any definite information and God knows I tried to find out but for all we know the President himself might have been right here. Isn't that something?"

"I don't follow politics," Wulff said, "I have no interest in politics at all."

"Well you ought to," Gerald said, holding the open door for Wulff as Wulff went through it, this less a gracious gesture than another of his necessary balancing gestures, "everybody ought to make himself more interested in politics, why if we had an involved citizenry the country wouldn't be in the sad shape that it is now. This is a kind of sentimental return for me, going to the Fontainbleau, you know. I was an alternate at the convention that year."

"That's fine," Wulff said, stepping into the hallway, "that's really fine."

"Yes indeed. I was an alternate with all rights, rank and privileges and if that bum who I was switching with hadn't been such a son of a bitch I would have had a chance to vote myself, get my name in the papers. I would have shown them a thing or two. I had some ideas I want to tell you, I was going to get a microphone and start a floor fight for the vice-presidency. Give the party back to the people, that was my motto. I had some real support in the Wyoming delegation too, I want you to know that; together we could have broken up the convention completely; put the party on an entirely different course—"

"Gerald," the woman on the bed said, "Gerald, will you please shut the hell up, you're disgracing yourself," and the man turned back to her to say something undeniably forceful and unanswerable; in that moment Wulff slipped through the open doorway and walked quickly down the hall. Only five or six yards out of their room he already felt that he had worked himself into another facet of existence entirely; they were entirely diminished, even the sound of their voices as he moved away was a frail peep, and then at long last he had turned a corner and shut them entirely away.

There was rich material there, no doubt about it; if he had been in another line of work he might have wanted to pursue this further because in a certain way this pair represented everything about America which had turned it into a madhouse lined by money and sustained by drugs . . . but the edge of his consciousness extruded elsewhere, he simply could not get involved, even psychically, with people like this, because there was a total kind of madness indeed. You could not clean up the entire world: all that you could do was to set yourself into one part of it and do the best that you could there.

At the end of the hall the arrow indicating rooms *1701-1709* pointed straight ahead and he walked down there, putting his hand inside his pocket, feeling the point thirty-eight. He took it out, cupped it into his hand. If Calabrese were waiting in ambush this gun would do him very little good but it nevertheless was comforting to have in his hand; at least he would be able to take a bodyguard or two with him. He did not think however that it would come to that. Calabrese was too shrewd to try anything like that and as he had said to Wulff, it was at this time a standoff. Calabrese wanted him dead very badly but Calabrese wanted the sack as well. He would never have gotten to this point if it had not been for the sack; the old man was too much of a businessman to make this kind of an investment in sheer vendetta.

The door of 1701 was ajar. Wulff saw the light glinting through it, falling in panels to the rug, the light cascading from the open windows of the room, heard the little viscous murmurs of conversation within and then, no sense of transition, no sense of preparation either, he stepped over the threshold, walking in quickly, holding the gun like a dense little ball clamped into his hand, and there was Calabrese, sitting, facing him across an enormous space, his hands folded on the polished surfaces of a long sloping desk. The man who he had been talking to, someone who Wulff had never seen before, a bodyguard, probably, was standing against the wall beside the desk. Seeing Wulff he slid out of position, backed his shoulder blades into the wall and walked that way around the corner. Wulff could see the gun in the man's hand; from this aspect it looked like a cannon, the hole open and gaping. He looked at it calmly. If death was going to come, he thought, it might as well come out of a big gun, it might as well happen now. Oddly he felt no fear at all. Looking at Calabrese he was not even sure that he had emotion of any sort. All of the hatred was gone; it had somehow been scraped free in the long, staggering cross-country drive and now he was scraped down to the raw bone of personality; he felt little more than a bleak kind of acceptance.

"All right," he said, "I'm here."

"Close the door," Calabrese said. To the guard he said, "Get out of here."

The guard looked at him wonderingly, then opened his hand to display the gun lying over his palm like a stone. "Do you—" he said.

"I want you out of here," Calabrese said, "that's what I want. Right now."

"I don't—"

"I can handle him," Calabrese said, "believe me I can handle him. Don't be so goddamned protective." He looked at Wulff, then, oddly, winked. "My staff is protective of me," he said, "overprotective I would say, but then again they're a very loyal and devoted staff. Aren't they?"

"Oh yes," the guard said, putting the gun into his pocket, rubbing it into place, smoothing folds of clothing over it, "oh yes, we're very loyal and protective," and he gave Wulff a look of hatred, walked to the door, went out of the door and closed it. Wulff heard the knob click twice, the second a thinner, higher sound and then Calabrese smiled, went into his desk drawer and emerged with a large gun and with a key. It was the key he showed to Wulff.

"It's locked from the inside now," he said. "The only way we can get out is to use this key." He put it on the desk within easy reach and then held the gun on Wulff. "I guess you might as well put yours away," he said.

Wulff looked at the gun in his hand and at Calabrese and said, "Why bother? You hold on me, I hold on you."

"Yes," Calabrese said, "but that doesn't do either of us any good." He put the gun down on the desk delicately, and spread his palms. "All right," he said, "have it your way. Go on and shoot. Do you feel any better now? I've got the girl and I've got your partner. If you shoot me, they go down. It's as simple as that."

Wulff held the gun on the old man. "Why do you think that's any hold?" he said. "He's not my partner; I've never had a partner. And she's not my girl."

"She seems to think she is."

"She's wrong."

"And what were you doing with that guy in Los Angeles if he wasn't your partner? You don't understand, Wulff, I've been watching you very, very closely." Calabrese coughed delicately, reached into a pocket, brought out his pack of cigarettes. In just a moment, Wulff knew, the old man would start to break them. A reformed or at least controlled chain-smoker, he seemed to get his satisfaction that way. All right. Let him do it. "I think it's time we talked," Calabrese said, "just talked very reasonably man to man without guns or demonstrations. This has been building up a long time."

Wulff looked at the gun in his hand, then he looked at the old man yet again and then, slowly, he put the point thirty-eight into his inner pocket, went back to the wall, pulled out a straight chair from there in front of the desk and sat down. "All right," he said, "talk."

It was remarkable how Calabrese had aged. He was simply not the man Wulff had dealt with in Chicago. It was not a failure of the will he could see so much as a simple collapse of the flesh; peering out through the thin folds of the face was the death's head that Calabrese would someday become. The death's head had a kind of ageless perception and resignation even more profound than that of the man who surrounded it; if Calabrese had himself been a man whose perception encompassed almost to the center, then the death's head had moved beyond that, it was the aspect of a creature who could no longer be misled, goaded, misdirected by anything. Looking into that face Wulff saw his own future. It was not only the death, the fact of his own death which he saw there . . . no, it was a certainty he glimpsed in that face which he had only dimly felt himself, driving on those roads, perhaps, in the American night. "Talk," he said again, his voice hoarse and strangely trapped within his throat, the gun hanging heavy within his jacket and he thought, what has happened here goes beyond guns, what is happening now goes beyond words. There is nothing to talk about. "I want the girl," he said, "and I want Williams. That's all. I want them now."

"In time," Calabrese said, "but I have certain requests of you as well. I want the drugs."

"The drugs mean nothing to you."

"On the contrary," Calabrese said, "very much to the contrary. That was my shipment. I worked on it very carefully. I made it possible for those goods to be gathered, they were prepared by my man to leave the country in his possession, I invested a great deal of time and effort to get them into my hands and I want them. I deserve to have them. That's a major shipment, it's not nickels and dimes, it has to do with keeping things afloat here for the next couple of years and a lot of people are depending on it. So you will please give it to me or tell me where it may be gotten. That is the first thing, the rest will then come into line."

Weeks ago, when Wulff had first met this man, it would have been inconceivable for Calabrese to have made any reference to the fact that he was in the drug trade, let alone be as specific as this. Calabrese had lived in a high estate on Lake Michigan and had walled himself off in those spaces not only from the world but from any direct contact with what had put him there. Calabrese would no more have admitted to handling drugs than a pimp, stopped for a license-and-registration check by a cop, would have explained exactly how he earned the money to drive an Eldorado. But now all of that had slipped from him; looking at him across the desk, Wulff saw that Calabrese had become that stranger inside, the death's head, and the death's head would not lie anymore. "I want those drugs," Calabrese said again. "I worked to develop them and I want them."

"I want the girl and Williams."

"You won't get them until I see the drugs. I'll kill them first."

"The shipment is the only hold that I have on you," Wulff said, "once I turn it over, you've got the whole ball game: you've got me too. I won't do it." He shook his head, feeling the decision settling into him, that decision which he must have known he would have to face this flatly and soon. "Them first," he said, "you get them out of where they are and into safety and I'll turn the stuff over to you. And then," Wulff said, "then it will be just you and me in a room like this one and we'll see who comes out of it. Because that's what you really want, isn't it?"

Calabrese shook his head, took out a cigarette, broke it and flung the pieces against a window. "No," he said, "I wanted to do that when we last spoke, when you were in Los Angeles. I wanted to kill you, Wulff, because you represented maybe the only thing I've ever found that I wasn't able to beat and because I'm an old man who's pretty afraid of losing control anyway, that was enough." The death's head winked at him, gave a half-bow from its dead, glowing eye sockets. "But that's all past now. I don't stay mad long, you can't let your temper get the best of you if you want to stay at the top in this business and that's where I am. At the top. No, Wulff, it's purely business. I just want the drugs."

"Then you know where I stand."

Calabrese leaned back, fingered another cigarette from the package and said, "You know, you're making things difficult for me. Very difficult."

"I was counting on that."

"You say that the shipment is the only hold you've got on me but what have I got on *you*? Just the girl and the black man and I'm not too sure about the black man at all. You split up with him in Los Angeles, that wasn't going to work at all. So it probably comes down to just the girl and that isn't enough, but it's all I've got and if I let her go, then what? Then you're a free agent again."

"I'm a man of honor."

The death's head smiled. Wulff had never seen anything so terrible in his life; the cold, resigned smile of a dead man lying under the glass of the outer face. "Man of honor?" he said, "you've sent five hundred people into their graves. You've dedicated your life for reasons I don't understand yet to driving the international drug trade out of existence. You've murdered, tortured, destroyed, burnt, stolen and you tell me that you're a man of honor?" He shook his head. "No," he said, "you are not a man of honor. Maybe by your own code you are; you feel that you're acting for higher purposes and that the international drug trade is composed of vermin anyway, are not truly human, so that you can do anything you wish without the normal sanctions we apply against humanity. We can leave that to the experts to argue if they'd care to. I can't trust you Wulff, that's all. How can I trust you?"

Wulff said, "You have to trust me. You've got no choice."

"Then you me," the death mask said, "then you me. You must accept this." It reached into the cigarette pack and broke another, flung it against the same spot in the window where the first had gone and then leaned back in the chair. "You must accommodate, Wulff," the death mask said, "you must learn to compromise, to accept your limitations."

Wulff looked at the thing across from him and said nothing for a while, letting all of the thoughts filter through, all of the complex possibilities which eventually, sooner or later, could only become a clear-cut decision which was both more and less than the sum of all those parts and then said, "All right. We'll work it out halfway. A compromise. A meeting of the minds. You give a little and I do too."

"You give nothing," Calabrese said, and flung yet another cigarette, this one unbroken. "You give nothing at all. Still, I will listen. I will listen to anything because I am getting tired of this and I would like to go home."

"Bring the girl," Wulff said "bring the girl and give her to me and I'll turn over the shit to you. You've still got Williams that way and I'll turn over the shit to you even though you've got him. I'll trust you. That's my offer," he said and settled back in the chair, the weight of the gun suddenly heavy against his armpit once again. Was his body sending him a signal that he would have to use it? but he had never believed in this kind of mysticism. Everything, inevitably, came up front. "That's fair," Wulff said, "that's the fairest offer I can give you. Otherwise, it's a standoff."

"Is it?"

"Don't you think so?"

"You want the girl," Calabrese said, "not the black man. But I suspected all along the loyalty which you had to him. The girl is the one that really matters, any fool can see that. Don't you think I know it?"

"Williams matters too. He matters a good deal."

"Everything matters to you then, doesn't it Wulff?"

"It's the best I can do," he said again. "It's the only trade-off I can offer. After I have the girl and you have the shit you can dump him. I'll trust you. After all, you're a man of honor."

"What if I do it the other way?" the death's head said, "what if I give you the black man and hold onto the girl? Would you still do it?"

"No."

"Why?"

"Because," Wulff said, and he found that he was finding the truth as he framed it, "because it's different. Williams knew what he was getting into. It was a conscious decision; he knew every step of the way what it meant."

"And she didn't?"

"No," Wulff said, "she didn't. She didn't know anything at all. She was only an accident. So she should get out of it first."

"There's nothing else to it? There's no sentiment at all?"

"What does that have to do with it?" Wulff said and felt the anger coalescing within him, the old, free, building anger that he really had not known since he had come into Miami. It was purifying, this anger; it cleansed him, enabled him to rise from the chair and then he was standing over Calabrese, six feet four over three feet and still the old man sat calmly, doing nothing. His hands did not even reach toward the gun on the desk; he had the peace of some great, interior knowledge. "What do you care about sentiment? I'm offering you a deal."

"I like it better the other way."

"No. It's this way or nothing."

Calabrese leaned back in his chair, seemingly oblivious to Wulff's hovering presence, and then took a cigarette out of the pack, put it into his mouth, opened the desk drawer for a pack of matches and then casually, expertly, lit it, drawing the smoke deep into his lungs on the first inhale, tossing the match with a *tic*! against the wall, leaning back in the chair then and taking a deep, relishing drag from the cigarette. "I don't like it," he said, "I don't like it at all." The cigarette did not move from his mouth. He let his hand fall away, drew in deeply again, held the smoke in his lungs then for a long, bursting instant and then exhaled all of it convulsively. "But it's the best I'm going to get isn't it?"

"Yes," Wulff said, "I'm afraid that it's the best you're going to get."

"You drive a very difficult deal."

"I know I do. Still," Wulff said, "consider my position."

"I have," Calabrese said. He seemed distracted, almost amiable, working again with the cigarette to take another enormous inhalation. Three of them now and the cigarette was almost gone. The old man, in his day, must have been quite a smoker, Wulff thought. Did you win admiration, did you get awards from the speed with which you could finish off a cigarette? Or did it merely count for prestige in the world which Calabrese inhabited? Either way, the old man was a ferocious smoker. "All right," he said, "see? See how easily I can capitulate, how cooperative I can be? You've built up a myth in your mind which is largely insupportable. I'm a completely reasonable man. Only you, Wulff, are unreasonable."

"No I'm not."

"You're completely unreasonable. You don't even know what's going on, you poor fool. Still, we won't get into that area now, will we? Where would you like me to deliver the girl? At the same time you understand, you'll have the drugs with you. An even exchange."

"On the beach," Wulff said without thinking, "the beach at night. Just the two of us and the girl, no bodyguards, no hoods, no snipers in the dunes. I'll be able to spot them; I was in Vietnam."

"I know all about that."

"You bring the girl, I'll bring the shit. A pure exchange."

"On the beach," Calabrese said. He paused. "The beach in front of this hotel?"

"Why not? I guess that's as convenient as any place."

"There are a lot of people on the beach," Calabrese said, "you envision a scenario but you have not considered witnesses."

"Four in the morning," Wulff said.

"There are people who go out to fuck on the beach at four in the morning. They consider it romantic. There are a lot of people who pay two hundred dollars round-trip air fare to fuck on the beaches of Miami in front of the Fontainbleau at four A.M. They consider it living."

"All right," Wulff said, "five-thirty in the morning."

The death mask smiled. "Now," it said, "you are beginning to perceive reality. At five-thirty in the morning, all of those couples have exhausted themselves, drained their impulses and have returned to the hotels. Five-thirty in the morning is a very promising time. The only living creatures on the beach in Miami at five-thirty in the morning are drowning fish, beached whales and derelicts. And us."

"Bring the girl," Wulff said. It was amazing how difficult it was to speak in a level tone of voice, to maintain control whenever Tamara verged near his consciousness. "She has nothing to do with this. It's not her fault. I want her free."

"I will bring the girl."

"Don't try to follow me when I pick up the sack. If you do that everything is off."

"I would not consider it," Calabrese said, "I will assume that you are a man of honor. By your own testimony, you are a man of honor, no? You will deliver the sack and I will deliver the girl. Presently I will release the black man as well and that will be the end of our dealings. You will go back to New York and I will return to Chicago. We will both be very happy because you will have your friends back and I will have a shipment which should have been mine from the beginning. Everything, everything for the best in this best of all possible worlds. Five-thirty this morning? Is that enough time for you to make arrangements?"

Wulff looked at his watch. It was four o'clock. "Thirteen and a half hours should be enough time for anything," he said, "enough time for anyone except a dead man."

"Good," Calabrese said, "excellent. So our interview is at an end."

"Is it?"

"I assume it is. That would be my assumption. Is there anything else you have to discuss?"

"You shouldn't have taken the girl."

"That is no subject for discussion."

"You shouldn't have gotten involved in this. You're an old man, you've got most of your life behind you, you've got all the money you'll ever want, the law can't touch you, you've got your private police force and you're sealed off from all of this. There's no one who can get you and you're probably not as stupid as Capone, you pay your taxes. You declare your income from legitimate business and you pay every cent, probably overpay. Why," Wulff said and paused, "why would you get into this in the first place?"

"Get into what? The drug trade?"

"Yes," Wulff said, "that's about the way I'd put it. Why did you touch it? Or if you got into it in the early sixties when everybody was, why the hell didn't you get out when the going was good? You didn't need this. You didn't need any part of it at all; you could have been home free."

"Ah," the death mask said, "ah," and it stood. "Ah, you understand nothing, do you Wulff, do you at all?" and then it picked the gun off the desk, was brandishing it, was convulsively motioning him from the room. "Get out," the death mask with the gun said, "get out right now," and Wulff said "Why?" once more and the death mask looked at him and then it said, "You do not understand at all, do you? For all of your foolishness, for all of your energy and violence you understand nothing, isn't that right? you do not understand, the quality of necessity," and then it had walked to the door, the door was open and Wulff went through it quickly, under the steaming breath which came from that figure and as he walked down the hallway it occurred to him that he knew nothing about Calabrese and as he walked further it occurred to him then that it was not necessary to know, all that you had to understand was power and it was this which sped him through the hallway, around a door, past the guard who had been lurking there and toward the elevators, Calabrese's uncertain shouts still behind him. *Son of a bitch*, Calabrese was saying, *taking shit from a stupid son of a bitch*. Just like the phone conversations from Chicago, he had lost control again.

Well. One thing. The door to seven-sixteen was closed and the DO NOT DISTURB sign was out. You took what you could get, when you could get it.

X

The rape had left her curiously untouched. She thought, in the first onslaught of feeling after the old man had left her, that she would never be the same again, that some intricate violation had occurred which she would not even be able to calculate let alone conquer for the rest of her life, but that had passed quickly: who was she, she found herself thinking, to be shaken by the act of rape after what she had been through? Pothead at seventeen, speedfreak at twenty-one, little intermezzos in which she had dealt with uppers, downers, inners, outers, shit, smack, LSD, left abandoned in a speedjag to die in a furnished room, rescued by an insane ex-cop who was out to destroy the international drug trade, a wild affair with this cop which had lasted all of three days the first time, one day the second, her insides plumbed by him in a way that none of the drugs had ever found . . .

No, she was no one who could find the act of rape scarring, particularly when the rapist had been a seventy-three-year-old man who was impotent. When was it rape? at the point of entrance? she thought, or did it start somewhere before that, with the intent? If it started with intent she had been raped, because Calabrese had been desperate to possess her, but if you only considered the act itself then she was untouched. He had not been able to get near her in any private way although he had squirreled and battered away at her desperately for fifteen minutes. No, it was not rape. Not in any legal sense of the word. Even the most militant feminist would find it hard to justify this one in a court of law. Perversity, possession, hatred, pain: no doubt about it. But not rape. No. Not classical rape.

He had tried to pierce her weeping, had failed, weeping, had left her room in the same way, a bedraggled, wretched old man (and perhaps the most repellent aspect of it, the thing that had hurt her the most, was the pity that he had leeched out of her, feeling pity she knew was the only terrible aspect of the act because it had been given freely whereas everything else had been wrenched from her and the pity was none the less painful because it was real) and she had been on the bed for a long time, trying to put herself together. Then it had passed from her, like some cloak dropping away from her shoulders; the true pain and indignity of what had happened had fallen away from her and she had known that whatever else happened, however it was recollected, she would never be able to feel that kind of pain again. Then she had dressed herself, put on makeup in the bathroom and when she had come out, her guard had been back there, his face bland and embarrassed, turned toward the wall. So he knew exactly what had happened.

So had Williams, probably. The walls were thin in this miserable rooming house, it was impossible that anything could pass between people in these rooms that was not instantly available to those not only in the room adjoining but probably all the way down the hall. It must have been a wonderful place for a family to live all together as it must have been in the old days before the section had become rundown and the house reconverted for the tourist trade. But if Williams knew what had happened he would say nothing, nor would his guards; she had passed that room only once when she had gone to the bathroom at the end of the long hall and he had been there, hunched over in one of his eternal games of poker. She could hear every word of them, every bet coming through the walls so they must have heard what had happened to her. But Williams merely looked up at her with a bleak, impassive smile, the guards had clumsily inclined their heads in a parody of politeness. None of them had otherwise made any acknowledgment of what had happened.

Still, what the hell were they supposed to have done? you had to see their side of it too.

You had to see everybody's side of it; that was the liberal ethic, the liberal dilemma for you and if there was one thing she had picked up in the Haight-Ashbury section during all those dear, dead, departed years it had been the liberal ethic. The guards had their side because they were in Calabrese's employ, they were an underclass who were in thrall and neither their environment nor their education had prepared them to do anything but accept their position as an underclass; Calabrese himself was an old man suffering from the old man's corruption and fear of death and he had been driven into her by forces as profound and symbolic as any radical analysis could find; double the profundity and the symbolism since he had not been able to function. He was suffering, the guards were suffering: everyone throughout the world was in pain as it had been all through history and who was she to cry injustice? Well, it sounded good, even though it did not quite work. What she wanted to do was kill the old man for the double insult; the attempted violation, and then, the failure to function. It was true; the only thing worse than being treated as a sex object was failing as a sex object. Well, the hell with it.

Her guard knew what had happened, of course, but he said nothing. What was there to say? Williams and the poker players down the hall might have known it too, hell, everybody knew it, but what difference did that make? Her guard tried in a few small ways to show compassion and concern, offered to get her foods from downstairs, asked if there was anything she particularly needed, babbled solicitously about the weather in Miami, how unfortunate it was that she had to be down here in this bright hellhole at all when the west coast was so nice at this time of year. Well, she'd be going back there soon, he was pretty sure of that, all of it an attempt of the fundamentally graceless to demonstrate grace, quite depressing but touching in its way as well because the guard was not responsible for what had happened to her. When you came right down to it, no one was, not even Calabrese: it was just massive social forces at work here which would lead inevitably to pain and disaster. It was just too bad that she had not been able to make Wulff see this, there had been some failure there; if he could only have seen as she did the sheer hopelessness of what he was fighting he might have stopped and if he had done so, abandoned the fight, resigned himself to living in the world as it must be . . . well, then, they might have had something between them: She was surprised to see how much she truly missed that. In a way he had reached her as no one else ever had; also there was the element of physical attraction not to be denied.

Too late now. Too late for any of it. Physical attraction and the relationship she had had were going to lead her straight to her death.

Tamara knew she was going to die. From the time they had abducted her from home there had never been any doubt of this; the surprise had been how easily she had been able to accept this. These men were simply not going to let her out of this alive. She was bait to catch the wolf and she did not think that the wolf would walk into the springing trap, but if he did, double the reason to dispose of her. She would know too much. Of course the thought had occurred to her that Wulff might rescue her, get her out of this, but she did not think so. Not against these men. All that he could do would be to involve himself in the coils of his own death and the black man, Williams, was in as bad a condition as she. There was literally nothing she could do about it. She knew that she was going to die.

All right, then, she would die. She had lived death for six years, come close to the rim of it in and out of dreams countless times; death did not bother her. She had never conceived of herself as living a long life anyway; like Martin Luther King she had nothing against a long life but not at the cost of other things and those things for her had been the necessity to live at a level of intensity. She had had her intensity all right, it had nearly killed her, now she was twenty-five and for a woman everything past that was straight downhill until forty or forty-two after which you definitely might as well be dead anyway. She had seen what menopause had done to her mother and most of the women her mother had known. No, she did not want this. The death of the body, the burial of the psyche, all of it moving on inevitably, making you merely an interested, terrified witness . . . no, she did not want that at all.

So she would not get out of Miami alive. She even said it to her guard, "I won't get out of Miami alive and you know that as well as I do," and he had made a dismissive gesture with his hand, sighed, told her to cut it out but some deeper sadness in his eyes rendered verification: he knew it. The sadness might well come from knowledge that *he* was not going to get out of this town alive either. Quite likely the only man who would would be Calabrese. That would be logical.

The guard came back into the room where he had left her alone for a little while, thinking all of this through and said, "We've got to go now. We've got to go down on the beach."

"Down on the beach?"

"Don't ask me anything about it. I'm supposed to escort you to the beach in front of the Fontainbleau."

"All right," she said. Once you had passed the point of violation as she had, everything slid into place easily, naturally, one impossibility was much like the next. "All right, I'll go down to the beach in front of the Fontainbleau."

"Not yet," the guard said, "I mean we're not going right now."

"But we have to leave the room right now."

"That's right. We have to leave the room right now."

"Well," she said feeling that she was teasing information out of him, "when are we supposed to be on the beach?"

"In the early morning," the guard said. He looked embarrassed, checked his watch. "About twelve hours from now. In the meantime we're just supposed to drive around."

"Supposed to drive around?"

"That's what they said," the guard said looking pained, "get out of the room and drive around and get to the beach in about twelve hours."

"That's a lot of driving around."

"I can't account for it. I guess that they want you out of the room, that's all. Listen," he said, moving toward her cautiously, "listen, I think you're a very nice girl. I want you to know that. I want you—"

"Is this a goodbye?"

The guard's face fell into little pieces, carefully, desperately, he reassembled it. "Oh no," he said, "oh no, it's not like that; it's just that I have these *instructions* you see, I'm supposed to drive you around—"

"All right," she said then, "all right," and she walked toward him, confronted him, the top of her head just at his chin level and said, "Drive me around. Let's go. What are you waiting for?"

The guards hands fluttered. "All right," he said, "those were the orders."

"I still don't understand what you're waiting for."

"I'm not waiting for anything. I'm not waiting for anything at all, I was told to get you out of here, that we were going to go driving around. I don't give a damn," the guard said, "if we're supposed to go driving around then we'll just do that," and he walked toward the door then. She followed him, he paused at the door for what seemed a long instant and then, shaking his head, walked through. She could see the revulsion in him, a profound revulsion which worked down all the levels of his body as he walked down the hallway, but it was a private thing. It could not help her. Nothing could help her and she must understand that now.

She passed Williams's room. The door was closed, inside she could hear the eternal murmur of their voices. It was a shame that there was no way in which she could get through to him but then why should she bother? Williams was as imprisoned as she. She could look for more help from the guard than she could from this man who had been Wulff's partner.

No, she had not expected to live a long life anyway.

But however you were prepared for that abstract quality, death, it always came as a great, uninvited beast, springing at the banquet table of life. The banquet with ptomaine.

XI

Wulff took a cab to the airport, not caring whether he was observed or not. Surely there was the possibility that he was on tail and that Calabrese's men would try to wrest the goods away from him when recovered but Wulff did not think so. They were not that stupid; they would not interpose between a plan of action and its execution. Nor did he think that Calabrese would permit this kind of thing; Calabrese obviously had worked out a plan of action with which he felt he could live, the old man had a tactic of sticking to his *modus operandi* once decided upon. Stubbornness, perhaps, or merely a habit of command, staying with your decisions, once they were made. They would make that encounter on the beach, anyway.

The girl. He had to get the girl back. It was no longer even a feeling of closeness to her, anything they might have had had long since perished in the diversion of their lives . . . but he was responsible for her. He had gotten her into this; he had to get her out. The settling with Calabrese would come after the fact. So the old man had judged correctly; he had known, truly, what a hold the girl was upon him. Calabrese was no fool. None of them were fools.

At the airport he told the driver to wait. The driver had been cursing Miami all the way, the stinking trade, the nick-and-dime tippers. As far as he was concerned the conventions had screwed up the town altogether, given Miami a lousy reputation. The good crowd just didn't seem to be coming down as they had in the old days and the city, mostly was full of pensioners. Wulff said that that was all right; pensioners had their strong points, they at least gave the city a rather placid nature and the driver got off on the subject of the Miami Dolphins; in the beginning they had done the city a lot of good when they developed into a good team but once you were on top all of the fun went out of it. People came looking to kick the shit out of you, make their reputations at your expense and anyway you couldn't rely wholly upon a running game as the Miami Dolphins did to set up your attack because the running game rested on two or three star backs and if any of them got hurt or lost his ability the team tended to disintegrate around them. Wulff said he guessed that that was true also.

He had never had any interest in pro football since he had worked a couple of Stadium patrols for big Giant games back in the early sixties. As far as he was concerned the best you could say for it is that it didn't hurt anyone except the players, but looking at the drunks reeling out of the stadium at five in the afternoon, their eyes far-gone, their faces with the bleak, staring, burnt-out aspect of men who had once again come to the realization that nothing about their lives would ever change and that all diversion could bring them back to that insight again and again, each time more painfully because they were consequently older . . . well, pro football was kind of a variety of smack too, everything was, some was legal and some was not, the only credible difference was that smack was death and the only way to conquer death was to kill it. Yes, that was what you had to do, kill death by controlling it. Did that make sense? Well, none less than anything else he had seen.

At the airport he let the cabbie go, grunting, cheering him up slightly, he hoped, with a large tip. Money was no trouble; money would never be a problem again. If he needed more he could always raise it. Into the large terminal building with the key to the small locker, open up that locker and get the key to the larger one, over to the large locker then in a different section, all of the terminal filled with the smell of plane exhaust, and then, opening that second locker he put it back into his hands again, five pounds of death. The sack, misshapen from hours stuffed into confinement, unfurled gradually in his grasp, feeling oddly warm, tingling to his touch, and he threw it over his shoulder. Midnight on the terminal clock, five and a half hours until the rendezvous. Was it conceivable that in five and a half hours it would all be over? No, it was not conceivable. It would never be over. He still had Williams to retrieve. He was responsible for the man being there. He had to get him out.

Two men were at his sides, two men wearing heavy jackets, dark glasses at midnight. Even in the empty spaces of the terminal they had come on him quickly, no warning, now he felt something protruding into his back that was unmistakably a gun. "All right," one of them said, neither moving his lips, he could not tell which one, "just start walking. Start walking and don't try anything at all," and then skillfully the man to his side had put a hand in Wulff's jacket pocket, emerged with the point thirty-eight, looked at it with satisfaction and then prodded him along. "Let's move," one of them said, "let's just keep on moving," and he did so, maintaining an even pace, the sack still jiggling against him. Neither made any move to take the sack. That move, he supposed, would come outside or in the place they were taking him. In the meantime they had a perfect setup; he was the bagman they were the observers . . . if *deus ex machina*, any airport security guard, should take a second look at them they could fade away . . . leaving Wulff to hold an enormous sack of uncut heroin.

Oh, it was a pretty setup all right; they had had this one figured nicely but all of a sudden Wulff felt himself lose patience with the whole issue. If they were Calabrese's scouts then the old man should play honorably for once instead of trying a juvenile double-cross like this and if they were freelancers, more goddamned bounty hunters, well the hell with them, let them deal with someone else. He was not going to be the target of every twobit mercenary around.

They were walking toward the main doors of the terminal now, the doors sliding noiselessly open and closed on their electronic gear as people walked through them, a steady flow of traffic in the airport even at this hour, about fifty to sixty people that he could see within range of sight in the main building and as they got close to the doors Wulff pivoted to his left, bringing the man on his right into an awkward position as he pivoted with him. Trying to see what he was doing and still holding position, Wulff swung back suddenly, using his free hand to strike this man viciously across the face. The man downed with a little squeal, one chicken-squawk of protest, lay on the gleaming floor kicking and Wulff came back toward the left where the other man was fumbling for his gun.

"Don't do it," Wulff said quietly, urgently, "don't do it, don't even think of it, you fire off a gun in this terminal and you'll have fifty witnesses," and he saw the man thinking about this, the thought buzzing around in his head like a mosquito, snapping here and there, drawing small bites from the intellect as he considered it, his eyes fluttering away and while he was thinking about it Wulff dropped the sack, reached forward, seized the man by the collar and holding him that way dropped him in place with a single left hook delivered with a radius of inches. The man screamed. Wulff kneed him in the groin, feeling the man's flesh shift underneath him, then used the hand that he had been steadying with to deliver an open-handed blow across the nose. The man screamed again, thinly, and fell on top of the other.

People were looking at them of course; he guessed that the first scream had galvanized almost everyone and now the terminal was in freeze, the traffic flow had been stopped and instead attention was focusing down upon them. But no one was moving, not even a security guard who he saw at the periphery of the crowd, the guard looking at them cautiously, hat in hand, hat waving at the floor, his other hand wiping sweat from his forehead. Obviously trying to evaluate.

The two men beneath him were lying quite still, the one who he had beaten was making little stirring gestures but there was no force in them. In an explosion of rage he kicked him again, catching him in the armpit. The man screamed again, unnecessarily, and lay still on the floor. That was better now. The other one, his eyes rolled up high, was looking at and through Wulff, seeing and yet not seeing, almost certainly unconscious. They were out of the picture, that was clear. And it had to be only the two of them because if it were a matter of having backup . . . why he would have been shot by now. He would have been dead. It was as simple as that.

He picked up the bag again, looking at the security guard, that one dark look passing whole subtleties of information which Wulff did not even have to sort out verbally: the guard was not an airline employee, he was leased out from some private agency, he did not like his work, his feet hurt, he was already collecting disability pension from the police force and he did not want to go on one hundred percent disability, not if he could help it . . . the guard did not want to get involved in this, not unless Wulff did something so drastic that not getting involved would have meant his job or his life. But that would have to be a mass-murder or something like that; Wulff would have to begin firing into the crowd, scattering people, shooting old women and children in the head in order to involve the guard. And the guard, having made the obvious decision that this was a private quarrel, that Wulff was not going to menace people outside of the two on the ground had already turned away then, one motion of the shoulders turning him three-quarter profile to Wulff, his palms extended in an unconscious gesture of capitulation and Wulff turned then, looked at the two on the ground for the last time, the pallid, twitching forms which would have taken him outside and killed him as casually and mercilessly as he could now kill them . . . except that he did not have the time to do it.

The crowd was starting to move, little darting on the edges as people ran toward safety and surely it would only be a little more time than this, perhaps in the minute, before city police were summoned. It would have been a pleasure to have killed them but it was not worth the risk and so he turned, putting them out of mind instantly, finished business, the two of them, and moved toward the flicking doors, the sack heavy and heavier in his hand, the string leaving an imprint of pain which he knew would be there for hours, leaving a deeper stain of implication which would never wash away. This was the price. This was the price that it had made him pay.

But it simply did not matter. Finished business was finished; the two on the floor were merely obstacles which he had had to overcome and he had no more feeling toward them now than he did about the guard. You functioned brutally, impersonally in his business, you did what was necessary and only invested enough emotion to keep you going, doling out to yourself little jolts of feeling every now and then simply to keep going, but you never confused finished business with unfinished.

Twelve thirty. Five hours to the rendezvous with Calabrese. He did not know if his presence on the beach would surprise the old man or if he had expected it all the time. He suspected that Calabrese, even if he had sent these two, was enough of a businessman not to care either way. You kept on moving, you kept on poking away, you kept your options open but you never expected anything but the worst and Calabrese, that grim old realist, would be waiting for him.

He damned well better have the girl.

Wulff looked behind him, no one coming yet. He flagged down a cab, not noticing until the last instant that it was with his gun hand, then as the vehicle slowed he put it away, got in and told the driver where to take him.

"You know what I thought?" the driver said when they were in motion. "It's the strangest damned thing, I could have sworn you were holding a gun when you were flagging me down. Boy did that give me a turn, a guy with a gun! I almost didn't stop. Light can play funny tricks, can't it?"

Wulff agreed that life was a trick of light down the line.

XII

Williams knew everything that was going on. How the hell could he not know what was going on? the walls were goddamned transparent. You could almost see, let alone hear, everything that was going on down the line and even if he were not desperately attuned to finding out exactly what the hell was going on with the girl and with Wulff he still would have known. As it was, with both of the guards bored and practically in his confidence, with an opportunity almost to listen at will he had the timetable down almost to the second. The girl was supposed to be down on the beach in front of the Fontainbleau at five-thirty in the morning. That could mean only one thing; that Wulff and Calabrese had worked out some kind of a switch with the girl as bait. Williams was not part of it; this did not disappoint him, the girl was more important to Wulff than he was, obviously, and she was also helpless. So that part was all right.

He knew about the rape too. He had been dozing, alone in the room, the guards down the hall, talking or whatever the hell they did together, when Calabrese came into the girl's room and seized her. It had been disgusting, it had been just like seeing the old fucker stripped naked, humiliating himself but beyond the pity and disgust there had been real horror because it was not fair that this kind of thing be done to the girl. Calabrese was living his private torment; he had no reason to act it out upon her. Essentially she was an innocent, she was not at all responsible for the factors which had made Calabrese do what he did; she was merely their victim. So there had been something profound about the old man's violation and the impulse had been strong within him to have done something really stupid and disastrous; charged that room, kicked the door down, killed Calabrese and yanked the corpse off the girl.

He probably could have done it too; Calabrese hardly sounded in there like a man possessed of alertness or one who was ready to fight.

Williams could have torn him away from the girl, he could have saved her from the humiliation . . . but really, what humiliation would he have saved her from? Calabrese had been impotent, unable to enter her regardless and killing or beating him unconscious in front of her would only have made things worse for them. This house was ringed; it was all Calabrese's territory. And although he might have taken some risks on his behalf, he could not be so reckless with the girl in here. Anything that happened to him if he made an escape attempt would happen to her and much worse. So in that sense, Calabrese had lucked into further cleverness. The girl was as much of a hold on Williams as Wulff. Everything had narrowed down.

But when he learned about the switch on the beach at five-thirty the picture changed. Now he had options, once the girl was out of the rooming house he had a freedom of action that he had not had before. He also had a sense of urgency because he was pretty sure that the switch was not going to go off. They would use the girl to lure Wulff there—and he would have to come; he had absolutely no choice—but once they had the man on the beach they would not allow the switch to go through. They would take the bag and they would kill the girl. Then they would kill Wulff.

Probably, Wulff knew it too. Wulff was no fool; he knew how these people operated and the little likelihood that this would go through as they had promised. But Wulff was helpless; if he had the drugs it was a very small thing indeed because they had the girl and the girl was the unshakable hold on him. For a man who claimed no attachments, no connections, no allegiances whatsoever to any cause other than his war, Wulff was one goddamned liar. They had a hold on him and it was a good one. Moth to flame, bird to snake, he was being dragged in.

So it came down to Williams. If anything could break the series of events which were going to happen on that beach they could only come from him; he was the sheer *deus ex machina* in the equation . . . and knowing this, the decision sliding through the tumblers of his mind, Williams came off the bed and went over to the guard who was sitting in the corner, reading a copy of *Playboy* magazine. The other one was down the hall somewhere. They worked in shifts now, both of them coming on only when it was time to start another poker game. What had been built up, Williams thought, was nothing less than a splendid relationship. Ever since the abduction near Chicago they had all gotten along splendidly; his abductors had been tough all right but when they had become his guards they had changed into kittens. They wanted no part of this they assured him; they had no more use for Calabrese and his schemes than Williams did, they even had objections on moral grounds: but what the hell could you do? A living was a living. But this was not to say that they had to be proud of what they were doing or that Williams wasn't a wonderful guy. Williams agreed that they were wonderful too. All three of them were wonderful and Williams was ahead about twenty dollars in the poker tournament; they had stripped him of his possessions of course, but they had been willing to let him play with markers. They even knew about the rape and they agreed that that was a damned shame too; a nice girl like that to be cuffed around by Calabrese. Life was shit, all right, no question about it. Still, what could you do?

"Yeah," the guard said, looking up from a four-color picture of enormous breasts. The breasts filled the page, the nipples little staring eyes at the center and little drops of the man's sweat had fallen across the areolae. "Look at this fucking piece of ass."

"I don't see any ass."

"Look at this pair of tits, I should say. You ever seen anything like this in your life?"

"Not in the real," Williams said, holding his arms straight down at his sides. "Pictures, yeah."

"I don't believe them," the guard said, running a forefinger across the page, "I don't think there's really stuff like that. They just blow it up with camera angles and so on. There ain't no such thing as a forty-eight inch pair of tits unless they're on some fat, old colored woman." He looked up at Williams suddenly embarrassed. "No offense," he said.

"No, that's all right."

"I didn't have to say colored woman. I just should have said fat old woman and left it at that. I'm not prejudiced, hell, you know that about me."

"You can say fat old colored woman. They do tend to be fatter than whites."

"Yeah," the guard said, "oh well, yeah, maybe, maybe not. Anyway, to me this stuff isn't real. They just make it up in the studios to drive you crazy."

"Could be."

"If it was real she couldn't get out on the streets," the guard said and Williams said, "I'm really sorry about this," and drove his fist into the man's adam's apple.

The man fell from the chair, straight down, the magazine arcing away from him, spattering against the wall, then falling in an explosion of pages and Williams followed the flight of the magazine, finding it preferable to the expression on the man's face as he fell to the floor. Then as the croaking and squealing sounds began Williams forced himself to look there again, see the man struggling on the floor, his hands working against the panels, an agony on his face so indescribable that Williams could not even approximate it, his face turning green, his mouth pursing, struggling for air and Williams felt a flare of hatred: it had been a rotten thing to do. He had nothing against this man; within the confines of the relationship forced upon them he had been treated decently. But there was nothing to be done, he made himself look at this the way that Wulff had done and the thought of Wulff, walking into the trap on the beach, was enough to galvanize him. Williams knelt, clubbed a forearm's weight into the man's jaw and the man mercifully rolled into unconsciousness, giving little gasps that might have been sighs of release from the greater pain.

Quickly Williams went inside his clothing, took a heavy point forty-five and a smaller thirty-eight out of the inner pockets, checked them for weight and loading and then put them in his own pockets. Then he rolled the man over quickly, extracted fresh clips from the right pants pocket and put them against the guns in the jacket. When he had done that he stood, breathing heavily, and faced the door.

Probably, he thought, the three of them, including the other guard, were the only people in the rooming house at this time. The girl and her own man had left an hour ago, there had been a surveillance detail in front of the house but they had gone at the same time, and it was doubtful if there was anyone presently watching the dwelling or in it. They had made the quite reasonable calculation that two men should be sufficient to handle Williams, who was not going anyplace except possibly his grave after the business on the beach was transacted; they had not calculated the excellent relationship which he had had with his guards but then how could they? communication such as the three of them had found was rare under almost any circumstances, this tenderness was particularly not to be expected in this context.

So it was just the guard on the floor, breathing more easily now through his mouth, his body slack and relaxed and Williams felt better about that, knowing that the man was not seriously hurt, and the one down the hall, and he had to decide whether it would be best to lay in wait for this one or to pursue him; either way was just as safe with the slight edge to waiting for the man to come back, unaware, to the room. But there was also the time element to be considered. He had to be on that beach considerably before five-thirty himself because he was sure that it was going to be so staked out that by four o'clock it would be next to impossible to get on there; they would have it tight. So knowing this, knowing that the time element was crucial and that it was now two in the morning and the other guard might well have fallen asleep somewhere out there, Williams pushed the door open quietly and stepped into the dazzle of the hallway fluorescence, the light bombarding him, momentarily overwhelming, he had not been outside of his room or seen the sunlight for several days now and the full intensity of the hallway lighting drove him to the wall for an instant while he quietly gasped and rubbed at his eyes. Chalk up another one for Calabrese. The man thought of everything.

But everything or nothing, sight came back to him in little stages and he prowled through the hallway strangely confident of his bearings despite the fact that he had seen it only once, when he had been escorted in here. He had been in his room otherwise; only emerged under guard to go to the bathroom at the opposite end, but the guards had locked him in during these expeditions, it had been the only time that they had pulled the plug on their relationship, probably orders from Calabrese to keep tight surveillance. Either that or the hallway was public as opposed to private territory; a kind word or joke might tip spies that they were getting on famously.

In any event the hall was easy to negotiate; he could hear from the far end of it the television set roaring away, some late-night combat movie with howitzers, cannons, the sounds of sirens over quiet weeping and taking the gun into his hand he kept on moving quietly, stalking. A door moved at the end of the hall exposing a sudden beam of light . . . and then Williams found that he was facing the other guard, the guard rubbing at his eyes with the back of his hand, yawning and mumbling, and he looked up and saw Williams.

"Oh for Christ's sake," he said, "you know you shouldn't be coming out of the room yourself, what the hell are you trying to do to us?" and then he saw the gun.

He reacted in slow trembling stages, first his mouth, then head, then all of his body was trembling as if being electrified by fine, subtle, stringing wire. He backed against the wall and slowly put his palms flat there. "What the hell is this?" he said, "now what the hell is this?"

"I'm sorry," Williams said. Pull the trigger, something professional within advised him. But he could not: he simply could not do it.

"Sorry? What do you mean sorry? Put that fucking gun away now, will you for Christ's sake?"

"I can't," Williams said. Now was the time to pull the trigger, fire the stunning shot and yet still he could not do it. Something held him back, something choking and burning casting loops downward to his hand, freezing it on the trigger. "You know I can't do that."

"Where is Howie?"

"Howie? Who's Howie?"

"Howie's the other guy. You mean to say you don't know his name?"

"No," Williams said, "I don't know anyone's name."

"Where the hell is he?"

"He's in the room stretched out."

"You killed him," the guard said, "you killed Howie." On the television, drifting from the room was the sound of an explosion, then heightened shrills from the air-raid sirens. The noise was grinding, insufferable. "You killed him."

"No, I didn't kill him," Williams said. "he's all right. He's just unconscious."

"He's just unconscious," the guard said, with a stupid, bemused nod. "You just knocked him unconscious."

"I'm sorry," Williams said again. "It's not the way I wanted it. I've got no choice."

"You're a real prick son of a bitch, you know that? We try to make things easy for you, make it pleasant—"

"No," Williams said, "it had to be this way. I don't want to shoot you. Is there any place that I can lock you in?"

"Lock me in?" the guard said, "you turn on me like this, you take advantage of our trust and then you ask me how you can lock me up? You stupid prick, I'm going to kill you," and it was only this that must have saved Williams, the guard's announcement of intention that was, otherwise he would have been caught flat, dumb. Suspended between the necessity and the impossibility of shooting, he might have let the guard kill him there if it had not been for that warning but as it was Williams had the necessary two seconds in which to prepare himself.

The first shot tore the guard's hand off, literally sent the dismembered limb fluttering into the wall, the second, somewhat lower, hit him in the thigh in the vicinity of the pocket holding the gun and turned him around and the third, going in at the base of the neck, pulped the guard's brain. He exploded in a fountain of blood and death and then fell to the floor in front of Williams, climbing doglike to hands and knees in a parody of activity for an instant, belching torrents of blood which spattered against the wall and Williams's fourth, fifth and sixth shots went in, hitting a shot-target within half an inch of one another in the space between the shoulder blades, firing uncontrollably, spasmodically, ripping them in because he had lost control utterly and now only wanted the man dead. The obverse signature of guilt was punishment, he thought, shit, should have known that all the time, how about that man? and finally the guard lay before him bleeding from a hundred small and large holes which crossed his body in network from neck to groin and everything between. The small thirty-eight fired at such close range had even blown out the guard's intestines; he could see them hanging in frail, greenish little loops from the violated belly. Not five minutes ago these intestines had been twitching along in their accustomed tasks, accepting, sorting, depositing, voiding, nothing in them was prepared for the embrace of open air and yet here they were, already in decomposition, their dark interior also cut and spilling open.

From too much flesh Williams turned away. He remembered Wulff telling him about his kill in Chicago, the rough one, the kill which had been too strong even for Wulff's stomach and which had made him realize that he was not fighting a war against objects or forces but against human beings who were as stricken as he, could bleed as freely, decompose as fast. Flesh, he was choking in oceans of flesh, some of it lying to pulp on the floor in front of him, more in the room behind and Williams felt his stomach heave. Death, even in the police training films, had not been such an unsanitary business. He could not take it anymore. Death in the abstract was one thing; to see it demonstrated before you in this way was quite another and these men, by their own lights at least, had been his friends. That made things a little worse.

Putting the gun inside his jacket, pedalling his feet desperately to initiate motion where the impulse for motion seemed to come from some higher, denser, more desperate part of himself, Williams urged himself down the hall, onto the steps, down the steps and clattering out the glass doors of the rooming house, then running freely in the empty air outside, running, he hoped in the direction of the beach.

It was fully five minutes of gasping, stumbling running against poles and walls, crazy, dazzling running that made him realize he was making a fool of himself and that he had to approach this systematically.

And that if he had handled it differently, he might not have had to kill the guard at all.

XIII

On the beach Wulff could see only vague forms, the impression of distances, no specifics. He had run the first cordon of Calabrese's men through sheer stealth; as he had anticipated the old man had the beach within a certain perimeter ringed with troops, forty or fifty men staking out, but he knew things about combat terrain learned in Vietnam which Calabrese could not have sensed and he was able to get into this ring by entering the water far downrange, moving in hip-deep waves and surges past the point where he could see the line and then wading ashore, his pants damp to the skin but the sack held high above his head throughout still safe, still dry. Now, having low-crawled up the beach working himself behind a lifeguard's chair as improvised cover he was able to command a good view of the beach, that central point where he was fairly sure Calabrese would bring the girl. But from where? That was the only question he had to evaluate. He had to know where they were before they could locate him.

It was quite clear that Calabrese had planned to cross him on the exchange. He had never doubted it for a minute, nor had he ever intended to go through with the switch. It was impossible for the old man to use the girl as anything more than bait, there was no way that either of them could walk out of here with what they wanted before killing the other one. So any thoughts of an honest swap had been dismissed at once.

The only thing was: could he get down here and get the girl away anyway? Could he use his presence and the bag as bait in order, somehow, to get her free? The girl was all that mattered now; if Calabrese had been willing to deal honestly, the old fool might have gotten what he wanted anyway because he was more interested in seeing Tamara free than in holding onto the sack of heroin. But Calabrese could not understand that. Nor would the old man have it that way. Looking for the corrupt, meanest, neatest way through every loophole always, he would, of course, project his motives onto others. He could not understand that Wulff might have been agreeable to an honest swap. He could not understand that in at least this one case the shortest distance between two points was indeed a straight line.

Well. It was too late for all of that now. He had the beach ringed with *soldat*; clearly he intended to encircle Wulff as soon as he uncovered his position and bring upon him enough firepower to utterly destroy him. Those forty men standing in an impassive line, ringing the beachfront were not there as witnesses or to protect Calabrese: no, each of them had to be multiply armed and each of them would be ready to fire upon signal. Execution squad.

But he was safe in the darkness. It was going to be a cloudy day; that was in his favor, the heavy cloud cover over the sun which, in October, would not be rising weakly for another hour and a half at the earliest; he had, in the meantime, an almost perfect dark with which to work and to use. The troops were murmuring to one another, their heads inclining down the line and then Wulff saw what they were reacting to. A man was coming onto the beach from far back. Under his arm was a bulky object which could only be a Browning Automatic Rifle.

A BAR! Calabrese was leaving nothing whatsoever to chance. Wulff permitted himself a grim smile; if Calabrese was moving in a BAR man to cover this he must really feel under pressure. Forty armed men and a hostage and he wanted a Browning Automatic; that was a kind of tribute, Wulff thought. It was a badge of honor; if he lived to see this one through he could always say that he was the man that Calabrese in these circumstances had put a Browning on. If the word got around it would destroy the old man's reputation, not that the old man was going to get out of this alive.

He was quite determined. It was going to be nothing equivocal; this was the last showdown. If he didn't walk out of this with what he wanted he wasn't going to walk out at all.

It did not look, however, as if he would have that choice.

The BAR man put his weapon down with a groan, then began to work in a clip. The BAR was a heavy son of a bitch, the heaviest piece of mobile combat machinery going. They weighed forty pounds and could only be fired from a stationary position; still the beauty of them, at least for platoon combat commanders, was that they could have this kind of firepower brought along with the unit. Of course your BAR man had to be strong as hell with a back made out of planks of wood and he could not be a complainer because complaining BAR men in Vietnam had a way of getting themselves shot by their own troops. In highly justifiable circumstances, of course.

The BAR man was finished now and then Wulff heard another sound; high above them all a shaking roar, growing in force, and as he looked up he could see the copter lumbering over the sea, the blades almost static in this perspective, the bird suspended in the air and at the same time, from far back, a huge spotlight came on, catching the copter in a blaze. Wulff huddled in his position, hoping that the spotlight would not sweep; it did not. It wavered, holding the copter in the center of the light, then as the bird hung motionless it locked in.

Helicopter, spotlight, Wulff thought, all of this on the beachfront not more than a couple of hundred yards downrange from the hotel and the sweep of the city itself. Certainly the man did not care, certainly he understood that he had no more than a few minutes before, no matter how deeply the guests were sleeping, the first calls came to headquarters, the police were summoned . . . and then he realized that the man did not care. This was Calabrese's play, all of the chips were on the line and he was quitting Miami. It was exactly as he had figured; all of it was going to end here.

A ladder unfurled suddenly from the copter, the rope dangling below, waving like a pennant and then a hatch opened. As that latch fell there was a high whine and then Wulff heard the sound of an amplifier seeking modulation, a high, shrieking scream piercing the beach, and then Calabrese's voice came out of that amplifier, magnified ten times but characteristically his, the slight lisp, the rolling consonants. "All right, Wulff," the voice said, "we're going to let the girl down now. Leave the stuff under the spot in clear view and she'll be coming down."

He made no move, rigidly held his position. The spot slowly backed off the helicopter, settled onto the beach, illuminating a circle perhaps six feet in diameter about twenty yards east of his position, near the waterline. "Let's go, Wulff," the voice in the amplifier said, "let's do it now. I promise you safe passage forward and back." It paused "I know you're there. I know you're on the beach with the rest of them. Now let's go."

Still he did not move. Instead he found his attention fixated on the BAR man. The man, exhausted by his trudging journey with the ordnance, had settled into the stand next to it and was smoking a cigarette, shaking his head. He looked utterly weary and not at all alert.

There was at least a chance that he could rush that position and take it. All of the troops were facing the copter, the spot had carried their attention far away from that line. Surely, he could get off a killing shot into the BAR man at just this moment. The point was taking over the gun. The point was also what Calabrese, overhead, planned.

"I'm not going to wait," Calabrese said, "I'm not going to wait this out much longer. I want the stuff, Wulff. Otherwise, we're going to kill the girl. Look now. Look at this."

Tamara's figure appeared at the hatch and then suddenly, convulsively, she was on the rope itself, struggling like a fly, impaled in that position, slowly moving downward. She struggled on the rope awkwardly, her body constricted at the joints, obviously no rope-climber, obviously a girl who had never been on a rope in her life and Calabrese said, the amplifier holding a strange, mocking note which infuriated him, "We're going to drop the girl on the beach, Wulff, and if you don't make the plant we're going to shoot her. Do you want her to die in front of your eyes? She's going to do it."

She hung on the rope desperately. Then, sinking, staggering, Tamara began to descend. The troops looked at her without pity but with fascination. The man at the BAR, revealed now in the light of the spot, was leaning forward intensely, holding the cigarette, drawn into a line of attention which locked with the girl.

Wulff watched her climb down with the motions of someone sinking to their death, he watched the frozen line of troops, he looked at the man with the BAR and he did then what he knew he would have to do very quickly and without any kind of mental set whatsoever. It was impossible to prepare for this kind of thing. You had to do what you did before thought; thought in itself could be transferred to the enemy.

He levelled the point thirty-eight, which he had been holding throughout all of this. He pointed it yards downrange and in one savage motion on the trigger as the girl tumbled the last few strands of rope he blew the BAR man's head off. The man fell into the sand kicking.

And then he charged the unguarded Browning.

XIV

Williams had been running since he had left the rooming house, he had hit the street, running, had headed in what he hoped was east, running, had paused at an intersection and then, running, had commandeered a car, not even thinking, just running, desperate to get to the beach. He was obsessed with a feeling of lost time; by his watch it was still only three A.M., hours until the rendezvous, but undoubtedly they would have the beach sealed off long before that time and there would be no way for him to get on. He had to get there; what he would do once there he did not know but around that simple essential purpose everything was focused.

The car he had commandeered, simply by going over to it idling at a traffic light, showing his gun and climbing in, was driven by a nineteen-year-old college student and his date who wanted no part of Williams at all. "Listen," the boy said, the girl huddling against him, hiding her face in his shoulder, shifting and clashing gears, "I don't want the car. You can have the car. Why don't you just let me pull over and let us out and you can take it?"

"Not necessary," Williams said, "I don't want the car either, I just want a ride. Take me down to the beachfront in front of the Fontainbleau and get out of here. I've got no quarrel with you."

"But I don't know Miami!" the boy said, "I don't know where the Fontainbleau is, I've got nothing to do with this, I'm just down here on a vacation."

"It's hopeless, Lenny," the girl said, "we're going to be killed. I come from New York, I know all about these mass murderers. First they make you do whatever they say and then they kill you. You can't change their evil desires."

"Take the car," the boy said, but he was sensible enough to keep on driving, "really you can take it, I don't want it. It's never been any good anyway. It's—"

"Don't argue with him, Lenny," the girl said into his jacket, "the more you try to reason with them the more they get to turning around and killing you. The only thing to do is to agree with everything they say. Take him to the Fontainbleau."

"I don't know where it is."

"Well don't look at me," the girl said, rearing up, wiping a hand across her forehead, then adjusting a strand of hair back over her ear in that casually heartbreaking feminine way which even now Williams found could move him, "I don't know where the Fontainbleau is, Lenny. Do you know where the Fontainbleau is?" she said to Williams.

"Just keep on driving east," he said, "I'm sure we'll hit it."

"He's sure we'll hit it, Lenny. He's sure we'll hit it, so just keep on driving east. You know, there's no need to kill us," the girl said, "you can just take the car—"

"He doesn't want the car, Jill," Lenny said, "remember? We already discussed that. I offered him the car and he said he didn't want the car and you said to stop fighting with him."

"Listen," Williams said, "listen folks, I'm not a murderer or a lunatic. Just do yourselves a favor and relax. I just have to get to the beach, fast."

"Oh I'm sure you're not a mass murderer or a crazy man," Jill said, "*I* never said that, did I? Of course I didn't. You just want a ride to the beach. So you'll get a ride to the beach—"

"Shut up, Jill," Lenny said, "please shut up." There was no traffic; they accelerated through the dead streets at forty, fifty miles an hour, Williams holding the gun on them loosely from the back seat. It was his first engagement in criminal activity unless you counted dealing with Father Justice in Harlem or running munitions to the coast or gunning down a group of troops in the trailer park in Los Angeles. He did not. All of those were legitimate acts, the kind that an ex-cop could engage in without rationalization, but this was different. Kidnapping, assault, the threat to murder. It didn't look good. It just didn't look very good at all. Still, the remarkable thing was how you were able to accommodate yourself to this. There was nothing difficult about crossing the line; it even gave you a high, dense kind of freedom. It could be fun. He hoped that he would never reach the point where he would see it in just that way.

"You don't know the way to the Fontainbleau, Lenny," Jill said, "you don't know what you're doing. You're just driving around, you're hoping that you'll come across it."

"Shut up, Jill, please shut up," Lenny said, hunched over the wheel, "do me a favor and don't say anything more."

"He's doing a good job," Williams said, "if you just keep on driving to the beach you'll hit that beachfront drive and you'll be able to see it. He's doing fine."

"Lenny, I told you I didn't want to go out tonight," Jill said, "I told you that we should have stayed in the motel. Why did you want to go out for a drive? Wasn't the motel enough for you. You spent six months trying to get me to a motel and after two nights you want to go driving around Miami. That wasn't very smart, Lenny."

"Jill," the boy said, "I can't listen to this anymore. I don't want to hear it, you've got to cut it out, Jill, this is stupid."

"Well I have a right to say it, don't I? I just don't know how you're thinking, Lenny, you beg me to come away with you, shack up in a motel and I do it finally and then on the second night you want to go out for a drive—"

"Why don't we just cool it?" Williams said, "I'm sure that everybody here has a good, reasonable point of view but this isn't doing anybody any good. Now you'll be out of this in just a little while and you don't want to do anything or say anything you'll be regretting; you want to have a good relationship, you want to keep on going with one another, don't you?"

"Don't ask me," Jill said, "ask him."

"Shut up, Jill," Lenny said. "Just shut up." He dropped down a little hill, went up a gentle rise and then Williams could see the beach in the distance, to the right, the huge sign of the Fontainbleau spilling light on it. They might have been three blocks away from the beachfront now.

"You did good," Williams said, "see that? You did fine."

"Yeah," Lenny said, "I always do fine."

"Now you can stop right here. Right here is fine, I'll hike it from here."

"He's going to get out now Lenny. Get down in the seat, for God's sake, this is when they put a bullet in your head because they don't want any witnesses."

"For God's sake," Lenny said, "I can't stand this anymore," and the girl thrust her head like an axe into Lenny's shoulder. "I'm waiting," she said, lifting a palm to cover the back of her head, "I'm ready, I'm ready."

"Oh Jesus," Williams said. The car rolled to a stop, Lenny pumping the brakes spasmodically, and Williams lifted himself against the seat, then was held by the weight of the girl. "Excuse me," he said, "you'll have to get out."

"I knew it. I knew it."

"You'll have to move, I'm sorry."

"I won't," she said. "You'll have to shoot me down right here. I won't get out. If I'm going to be gunned down it's going to be in a car with my friends."

"For God's sake," Williams said as gently as he could, "you'll have to get out because it's a coupe and I can't push by you, don't you understand?"

"Jill," Lenny said, "please get out."

"Oh all right," she said. She seemed vaguely disappointed as if something for which she had long prepared herself was not coming to pass after all; she tossed her head in a very feminine and to Williams quite infuriating way, poked more hair out of her eyes, lifted the door and got out of the car. Williams pushed through, she looked at him. "I just want you to know," she said, "that I remember your every feature and that you'll pay for this."

"Oh," Williams said, "in that case I guess I do have to kill you, right? Because we desperate psychopaths can't have any witnesses to our acts, remember?"

"Oh my God," Jill said, "oh my God," and rammed herself into the car, buttocks heaving, trembling as Lenny leaned across her dense weight to pull the door closed and then the Volkswagen yanked itself out of there, the clutch chattering. Williams watched the little taillights bob their way out of his line of sight and then he set out toward the beach, moving as quickly as he had on the street from the rooming house, pacing himself to a level, even run which could hold for distance—

—And although it was ridiculous under the highly dangerous and menacing circumstances, although he hated himself in a way for it because there was so little justification . . . despite all of that, as he ran he found himself smiling, seeing the girl's face again and then the bleaker image of the downed guard superimposed itself upon this and he was suddenly out of breath, suddenly staggering to maintain his pace, suddenly very chastened and frightened as he raced toward the beachfront.

But he kept on.

Wulff would need him.

XV

In the copter all of her fright had gone away and she had felt a level, resigned kind of acceptance unlike anything she had known before, unless you counted in the speed jags which would give her that kind of feeling but only in a flushed, overexcited way. Now she was perfectly at rest. She saw her own death, saw it plain, and having seen this she had accepted and with that came strength because she had passed a point which very few of them, the death-dealers, ever had. So, sitting in the copter, cramped up, arms around her knees, she had rocked and plunged with the motion of the craft, saying nothing, only savoring this peace which was not courage because it had nothing to do with the will to resist until the old man sat beside her and shockingly she felt the contact of his palm on her knee.

She pushed it away. "No," he said, "don't do that. I just wanted to say I'm sorry."

The engine noise was terrific; the walls themselves were shaking, the thin canvas of the bulkheads, but she could hear him distinctly. "Don't talk to me," she said, "don't say anything."

"It doesn't make any difference to you, does it?"

"Get away from me, you filthy, dirty, stinking old man!" she shouted at him and the others in the copter heard this: there were only two, the pilot, working over the controls and Calabrese's ever-present bodyguard who was apparently being airsick in a corner, his face a luminous yellow, staring down, his hands cupped to his cheeks. The pilot smiled thinly.

"All right," Calabrese said, "have it your own way, then. This isn't going to do you any good you know. You're going to go down on that beach."

"I know I'm going to go down on the beach!"

"If your friend had not been so stupid and stubborn this would never have happened. If we had worked this out in a fashion that gentlemen could, you would never have been taken from your home let alone put up here. I didn't want to do this, you know. He just gave me no choice."

She put her hands over her ears. "I don't have to listen to this. I won't listen to it."

"He can't save you, you know. If you're counting on miracles of some sort there are none. The only hope is that he does exactly as I have asked him to do. But he has never done that."

"Please go away," she said.

Calabrese shrugged. "Where can we go? We're in very tight quarters here. I thought that we might be able to make peace before the end."

"Make peace?" she said The pilot was staring at her frankly now, his hands manipulating the controls in an absent, backhanded way, his eyes flicking to them only with the most casual attention, most of him focused on her, and there was something in his eyes which was inexpressibly dirty. "There's no peace," she said, "you filthy, dirty, ugly old man, there's no peace to be made because you have none. You can't even function."

Calabrese drew away from her. "What was that?" he said.

"I said you've got nothing to apologize for. You didn't do a damned thing to require any apology. You just want everyone to think that you did something. You old bastard," she said, "you can't even fuck," screaming this over the whirring of the blades and the pilot sitting in place began to laugh, loud, obscene barks of laughter pouring like liquid from his mouth and Calabrese hit her hard then across the face, bringing flesh into her cheekbones, sending dark pain radiating through her.

Her head smacked into the wall and rebounded but she held her expression, she did not reach up a hand to rub her skull. Undoubtedly she was bleeding. All right, so be it then, she had been bleeding in many small places inside for a long time now; this pain meant nothing. "You can't even fuck," she said again, holding Calabrese's gaze, not blinking, "and you can hit me ten times but you know it and now everybody knows it," and the old man doubled over then in the limited confines of his position, put a hand to his mouth, began to make loud, retching noises, gagging and choking against his hand, the pilot suddenly very involved in the controls once again, the technique of flying the craft all-absorbing, Calabrese's guard behind them still looking at the walls from behind yellow eyes, all of this having passed through him, and then she braked her buttocks against the wall, slid away from the bulkhead and tried, clumsily to stand. She was not sure why this was necessary this time; it had something to do, she guessed, with establishing distance from him, with asserting dignity. Who was to say?

The craft rocked in the air and then took a sudden, sickening little jolt and she collapsed to her rear again, her legs coming out straight ahead, the pain of falling and the indignity of it suddenly bringing tears out of her that nothing else would have: not death, not terror, not simple fear but only humiliation could do this to her. She put her head on her knees and sobbed. Something, Calabrese's hand, yanked her chin up and then he was staring at her, his eyes full and luminous, his face filled with little pockets out of which insects seemed to be crawling, picking away at the scabs and small encrustations of the old man's ruined face. "Dirty bitch," he said, "dirty, filthy whore's cunt, that's what you are."

She shook her head, tried to crawl out of there but he held her firm. "Whore," he said, "stinking slut, was it good for you with him? Did you like it, did you take it deep? You lousy cunt, nobody says to me what you said, I don't have to take that from anyone, I'm not going to take it from any whore."

He wrenched a long, surprisingly powerful arm around her neck and began to strangle her.

She could feel the pressure on the windpipe cutting off her breath almost immediately, then when the sights of the copter began to fade away, when she began to see colors behind her eyes, she knew that she was in trouble. Struggling for breath was not so bad, it was almost pleasant to be taken out of the world in this way after suffering so much ... but the colors were vivid, too bright, too muddled to have any of the aspects of light and as they began to devour her she saw that she was going to die, trapped in his grasp. Desperately, instinctively, she brought her hands up, tried to break the grasp but it was like the flutterings of a goldfish caught in a palm. She struck the stone of him and fell away and then she felt herself surging into a long, deep pit, trying to scream but unable of course. No breath meant no screams and so she fell silently, moving away from the world until suddenly, spasmodically, the grip broke and she fell away, not into a pit but into the familiar canvas. She rolled feebly on her stomach. Someone was shouting behind her.

"You can't do it," a voice said, and she opened her eyes, peered around, saw that it was Calabrese's bodyguard who was bellowing at him. "I don't give a shit what happens down on the beach but you can't kill her in the copter, you can't kill her in front of me." And Calabrese was yielding to the shaking, his body loose, empty, flapping in the guard's grasp and some sense of the situation must have come to the guard only at that moment, the realization of what he had done, some understanding of his audacity and he released Calabrese and fell back himself against the canvas, retching. "You can't do it, that's all, you just can't do it," he said in a weak voice and then moved away, fell into the spot where he had been, put his hands across his face and said, "Oh for Christ's sakes, I'm sorry, I'm sorry, I shouldn't have," until Calabrese himself turned toward him and said, "It's all right. It's all right; I shouldn't have done it, you're right," and the guard, stunned by his own actions said nothing, looked at the bulkhead, his eyes flickering, apparently regarding the man who had just done what he had as someone else, some stranger in the cockpit.

The pilot attended to his controls, the helicopter sliding off-angles to the sea, coming in and Calabrese said again, "It's all right, it's all right, stop it now," and she felt herself moving away from all of this, like the guard. What was happening must be happening to other people here, surely she could not be living through this herself, she was eighteen years old in San Francisco and had dreamed these seven years of her life as a nightmare of warning, that was all, and then the pilot turned to Calabrese and said, "On target."

"Already?"

"Had favoring winds. It wasn't going to be that long anyway."

"All right," Calabrese said, "all right, then. You have the equipment?" His voice was level, controlled, once again he appeared to have himself under hold. That was the most remarkable thing about all of these men, even Wulff, they could do the most unspeakable acts and minutes later not refer to them at all. It was a remarkable quality. "You got it all set?"

"Yeah."

"Then help me," Calabrese said, "let's get it set up," and the guard lumbered to a standing positon, unfolded burlap behind, came out with some kind of electronic equipment and began to struggle with it and Calabrese turning toward her said, "We're going to send you down a hatch. You understand that?"

"I don't know what you're talking about. I—"

"We're going to send you out of here. You're going to cooperate with us."

"Send me down a hatch? On what?"

"On rope. On a rope ladder."

"I can't climb."

"You're going to go down," Calabrese said. "You're going to cooperate. If you don't cooperate you're going to make it that much worse for your boyfriend."

"He's not my boyfriend."

"I have no time," Calabrese said, "I have no time to argue with you." The hatch fell away and she was looking into darkness, below that darkness were sudden prickles and blemishes of light, spinning below. Rope unfurled, plunging into the darkness. "Now," Calabrese said, "get down there."

"I'm afraid," she said, "I'm afraid of that. I don't want to go—"

"Go," the pilot said, struggling with something by the hatch, "don't argue with him. Don't ever argue with him. Just get out of here."

"Please," she said. For some reason the rope terrified her; the abstract acceptance of death had gone down easily, like gelatin or a wad of phlegm, but the actual quality of this climb through the night was unbearable. "I don't want to go out there."

"But you've got to," Calabrese said, "you've got to get out there." He flicked a switch, she heard a high, amplified shriek. "You've got to get out right now."

"Please," she said, "please—"

"Believe me," the pilot said, "believe me, it's going to be much easier if you'll just go. Go." He touched her, the sliding, clamping feel of his flesh against hers somehow revolting but breaking through her as well, moving past terror into activity, perhaps exactly as the pilot had calculated . . . and then she was out in the air, she felt the dampness on her face, felt wind like breath gasping at her and then, hand to rope, rough strands to palm she was sliding through the darkness as overhead, filling all of the world, she heard the rasp and boom of Calabrese's voice.

She knew, she must have always known, if only in dreams, that it would end this way.

XVI

The Browning came into his hands roughly, even grasping it was to recover through memory a hundred fields in Vietnam where he had heard its boom, and then he was lying in prone position behind the cannon, doing nothing for the moment, merely trying to locate his position, to see what was going on. It would make no sense to begin firing wildly until he had established his position and the situation; for one thing it would uncover him . . . and as yet he had not been placed.

The shot, the single squawk of the downed BAR man, had turned the attention of the troops in that direction and they had seen him fall, but even as that had happened the girl was tumbling the last few yards in the air, impacting upon the sand and that had brought the focus of attention back to her. Several of the troops had run toward her, others were pivoting in confusion between the fallen girl and the place where the BAR man had been but in the dark none of them could see anything . . . and Wulff had been able to make his sprinting, staggering run toward the BAR without any of them seeing him; their confusion had been accentuated by the rasping and scream of the speaker above which had, perhaps, been there with the intention of distracting Wulff but had instead only upset the troops. No, Calabrese was not thinking all right.

The old man could not be functioning anymore, not the way that he used to. What had happened to him?

But, then, nobody was functioning. In the confused leakage of the spot, the big beam twitching now as its point of origin, obviously something near the beachfront, moved, Wulff could see the forms beginning to scatter freely, the line of troops broken, the enemy scattering through sections of the beach, and then his attention was riveted, the girl was up on her feet, gesticulating, screaming. She was waving at him, an insect figure hundreds of yards downrange, desperately trying to semaphore and he could not understand her gestures, sharp and intense. Moving within a small frame, she was trying to communicate but even as he watched the megaphone noise separated into distinct syllables. "There she is, Wulff," Calabrese's voice said, "there she is, *now deliver the stuff*," and he clamped down on the BAR, pointed it toward the copter thinking this is insane, he had no business to do this, his primary responsibility was to rescue Tamara . . . but how could he do it? no way to get to her . . . and then, even as his finger was coming into the trigger someone shot her.

He could see her leap in the characteristic gesture of the stricken, her form twitching. Then she was at full height spinning, trying desperately to move away . . . and the second shot hit her in the chest, a web of blood sprang from that space visible even at this distance . . . and she fell into the sand.

He went a little bit crazy then.

Well, the craziness had been there, had been lurking behind all the time: there had always been that madness, the lust for massacre, peeking out behind the curtains of personality, sometimes coming through: the townhouse on the east side, that freighter in San Francisco, the refuge in Boston, the casino in Las Vegas . . . oh yes, he knew what it was to feel that urge to murder extruding, poking densely from the torn-open scars of hatred, but what hit him now was stronger than all of those put together. As the girl went down something in Wulff went down as well, something which he did not even think was there, which had perished on West 93rd Street . . . and then, scrambling, his fingers hit the trigger and he began to fire.

He must have taken ten of them down in the first burst.

It was just a matter of guiding the BAR, the monster put down its own fire, its own profound weight guiding it through an arc of destruction, all that he had to do was to ride it out with a supporting palm, like steering a big, fast car on a straight road he merely had to pulse in little reminders now and then to keep it on course. Calabrese's men were jumping, shrieking, hopping on the beach like rabbits, and then he saw no more because he guided the BAR toward the spotlight and hit it dead center; there was an explosion of glass and then the beach slid into total darkness. All that he could hear were the cries of pain.

Men were shrieking, praying, gasping, running and he enjoyed those sounds, not only for their own sake, but because they guided his fire; they led the tracers from the BAR deliberately into their center and although in the darkness he could no longer tell how many were dead he knew that it was quite a lot. There was no thought of going to the girl, he knew that there was no point to it. She was indisputably dead; to approach her would be only to join her. He only had one mission now and that with a grim and central ferocity:

He wanted to kill everybody, everywhere, who had made her die.

So he fired off the BAR until it was exhausted. He got a fresh clip out of the shirt of the man who was lying beside him, jammed it in and fired off the Browning again and now his fire was no longer being returned. There had been at first a few feeble gunshots, experiments really, half-hearted attempts to find him in the darkness, but now the enemy had been routed past the point of returning fire. Men were jostling, screaming, the survivors were trying desperately to get up the beachfront and over the line, up on the boardwalk but the Browning tracked the screamers and knocked them down too.

He heard the explosion of copter exhaust above him and then the megaphone was screaming once more, "You bastard," Calabrese said, "you dirty bastard," and he let the Browning track the voice; bullets hit something, the amplifier went dead with a hiss, and a smell of burning drifted over the sea. Then the engine of the copter was revving desperately, five thousand cycles a minute, hitting unevenly, a bad miss in at least one of the cylinders but nevertheless fighting, fighting for altitude and then the copter was moving out of there, he could tell by the receding sound that Calabrese had somehow made good his escape. He was leaving thirty dead men on the beach but he had killed a girl, he had failed utterly in his objective but he was going to get out of this alive while the others stayed and died. Well, that was leadership for you. Wulff, screaming, weeping in frustration, fired off the Browning in the direction of the copter, hoping that a lucky shot or two would puncture the fuselage, would miraculously make the bird dead but the steadier throbbing of the engine as it pulled away was testimony that it would not, and so he could only return his fire to the beachfront, pump off shots into the last remaining troops, the few staggering forms which remained but it was no good, no good, no satisfaction to it at all, he was really shooting at Calabrese and hitting stone and he knew when the sun came up it would show the litter on the beach, the blood sunken into the sand and the police would come from five counties and they would rope off the beach up and down around ten miles but not a one of the officials, not one of the photographers, not one of the reporters or the news analysts or television cameramen or commentators or crime experts . . . there was not a one of them who would understand that everything here, this great massacre which would be remembered for fifty or a hundred years, was merely a substitution for what he really had been wanting to kill all of the time . . . and most of him lying dead, dead, dead, near the water on the ruined sands.

XVII

In the copter Calabrese passed out and did not regain consciousness until the helicopter was hovering above the Dade County airport, the pilot indecisive. What the hell was he supposed to do? nothing in his orders so far had ever anticipated anything like this. The guard was no help at all, he was hunched against a bulkhead, gibbering to himself. The pilot just hung there in the air. This would not work, he knew, they

had to transfer to another plane, they had to get out of here . . . he had
no idea of exactly what had happened down on that beach but of one
thing he was quite sure: it had been very bad. At length, Calabrese's eyes
opened and he stared at the pilot. "What is it?" he said.

"I'm waiting to descend."

"Where are we?"

"Above the airport."

"Above the airport," Calabrese said, "above the airport," and then
something convulsed within him, some flare of intelligence, and he said,
"We didn't get the stuff, did we? He didn't throw it out on the sands, did
he now?"

"No," the pilot said, "he did not."

"The girl is gone?"

"The girl is out of the plane," the pilot said, his hand tapping the
controls, "you arranged that, remember? I think that she's dead. She was
shot down there. There was a great deal of shooting going on down there.
I think, I think that he got hold of a machine gun or a Browning
Automatic."

"Shit," Calabrese said.

"There was nothing to do but to get out of there. Our men were being
massacred."

"Shit," Calabrese said again, "there were thirty-five men down there.
How could he? I mean how could he do it?"

"I don't know."

"I prepared for everything. I prepared for every single goddamned
thing. How could he have gotten out of it?"

"I don't know," the pilot said. "We've got to get out of here ourselves.
We've got to land."

"The girl is dead," Calabrese said. "She is definitely dead?"

"I think so."

"Fucking fuckheads," the guard said in the corner, "miserable fucking
sons of bitches. Fuck you too." He took out his gun, pointed it at
Calabrese. "I've had enough of this shit," he said, "I've really had enough
of it. How much can I take? It's not right, is it? I mean, a man shouldn't
have to take shit all his life. Sooner or later a man has got to stand on
his own."

The pilot sat rigid, his hands imprisoned between his thighs, looking
from the guard to Calabrese. "It's an old problem," Calabrese said, "it
means nothing."

"Sure it means nothing, you son of a bitch," the guard said, "nothing
means anything to you. Just death. Death means a lot."

"You're in a great deal of trouble," Calabrese said calmly. The calm was unshakable, the events back at the beach had purged him or at least, he thought, had put him at a level removed from feeling. He simply did not care anymore. Some capacity to be moved had vanished. The guard accordingly was simply another obstacle, more difficult than most. "You could be in worse trouble if you don't stop this. Put the gun away."

"Why should I put it away, you bastard? You killed that girl. You sent her out to die."

"I did not do that," Calabrese said. His own gun, he found himself thinking with acute clarity, his own gun was in his hip pocket, he knew he had put it there when he had left to board the copter. That solid, unresisting weight against his buttock must be it, for he had not changed its position. It would be a simple matter to get to it, to shoot the guard . . . but somehow he had to first distract the man. The guard looked distractible, his eyes blank and yet glowing, focused through Calabrese, on the wall behind him, his attention diffused over a wider area . . . but it was still too risky. He could not do it. He could not do it yet. "I did not kill the girl," he said, "she did it to herself."

"You kill everything. You make everything you touch rotten. You didn't have to kill her."

"Drop the copter," Calabrese said to the pilot. "We're going to land."

"You're not landing. You're not landing anywhere," the guard said. "You're going to die here."

"I don't think so," Calabrese said. This guard was named Nicholas and had been with him for four or five years. Before that he had worked in the household staff, getting into that position of trust through honorable work in the collections division. He had never exhibited, in all of this time, a hint of rebellion. So that core of loyalty must remain; it was merely a temporary episode, if he could pierce through and reach that vulnerable, dedicated core which had served him so well he would be in no danger. "No," he said, "I'm not going to die here. No one is going to die here. Put that gun away."

"You kill everything, you fucker. You think I don't know what's going on? I tell you," the guard said, "I can't take it anymore. I can't take this filth."

"Drop the copter," Calabrese said to the pilot again. The pilot nodded once bleakly, put his hands on the controls. "Are we over the airport?"

"We're over the airport."

"Then drop it."

"Don't drop it," the guard said. He came off position, held the gun half-crouched on Calabrese. Sweat came off him freely, little drops of it lodging in the collar of his shirt, with the free hand he pulled the shirt away from his neck. "You're not listening to me," he said, "you think that this is bluff. You killed that girl. You had no reason to do that. I can't put up with it anymore."

"But you have to," Calabrese said. It was amazing how calm he was under the circumstances; how that calm held. Having seen everything, nothing could touch him. "That's the way the world is, Nicholas. Now stop making a fool of yourself and forget this. Forget this nonsense."

"Why did you kill her? Because you raped her?"

Calabrese said nothing. The helicopter began to sink; it fell through the air as if it was water, heavily, jouncing. "We're about half a mile to go," the pilot said, "we're going to go on the far side of the field. It's going to be fast and hard so hold on." His voice shook.

"Fast and hard, Nicholas," Calabrese said, "did you hear that? A fast and hard landing. Better hold on or you'll get shaken."

"No," Nicholas said, "no, I'm not going to go through any more landings with you. I'm not going to have anything fast and hard, I'm not going to see any more death, I've reached the end of the line with this now," and his finger tightened on the gun began to bear forward. Concentration flowed in waves across Nicholas's face and Calabrese took the gun which he had managed to get out of his pocket during the last lines of exchange, wedging himself against the bulkhead and shot the guard in the throat.

Blood leaped in small jets from the adam's apple but Nicholas seemed strangely alert, completely conscious. "You son of a bitch," he said, "I shouldn't have let you get away with that," and Calabrese took another shot, this one getting Nicholas in the wrist, spinning the gun out of his hand, the gun crashing to his side, above his head. Nicholas screamed, grasping his wrist, and then spouting blood from the two sites, fell at Calabrese's feet.

Calabrese shot him in the back of the head.

"All right," he said to the pilot then, not even looking at the corpse, "proceed on landing. Put this goddamned thing down."

"All right," the pilot said, "all right."

"We're going to get out of here. We're going to get back to Chicago."

"That suits me," the pilot said. The copter was in a swift descent now. Calabrese lurched, swayed, pitched across the dead body of the guard and lay there, feeling the dead man's flesh palpating his and as he felt that death, that moistness against him, it occurred to him with an utter sense of finality that someday soon he was going to be that way too. He was going to be dead. The only thing that separated Nicholas from him was time and not very much of it. The dead flesh had a familiarity against his.

"We're going to get out of here!" Calabrese shrieked and the pilot said *yes* again and the helicopter fell gracefully toward the concrete of the Dade County airport where the private plane that would take him back to Chicago was waiting . . . but comparing the way he would board it as against how he imagined this triumphal return flight would be, he did not know if he could go through.

The girl dead, the drugs lost, Wulff free and now surely, the line of defenses ruptured, bound to attack him. And how could the victims of the massacre not be tied to him? nothing could shield him from that. He had no lines of defense. Miami was to have been the final arena of victory. Instead, it was he who fled and behind him now the avenger with multiple cause, multiple righteousness.

He had nothing with which to fight now, he thought, but fear itself.

XVIII

But the avenger did not feel like one now or anything close to it, leaning over the body of the dead girl on the beach. The beach was littered with corpses, sirens were in the air, the few survivors of the massacre had staggered to the boardwalk and were doubtless now moving along the facing streets, clear tracers to the police to lead them to the beach and yet he could not leave until he had seen the girl. She lay on her back, one bright little drop of blood in the center of her forehead, another delicate stain underneath her sweater in the place between her breasts. Head shot, chest shot, clean wounds both of them, the bullets buried so deep as to be invisible. Oh yes, beautiful work had been done upon her. But even in death she would have style. Wulff would have known that from the beginning if he had thought of it. Style in her every gesture, style in substance and act, even dead Tamara was an object molded carefully, turned out priceless. He knelt beside her and had it not been for the bloodstains and what he knew had happened, he might have taken her for sleeping. Even her face seemed poised for respiration, her nostrils about to take in another breath on the instant. But they did not.

They did not. She was dead.

He looked at her, lying that way on the beach, and he knew that he should go. The thick, prodding sounds of the sirens dense in the air now, only a matter of moments until the police flooded the beach. They would find him, they would incarcerate him and from then the end would come very quickly; there was no way that he would ever see the light again. And Calabrese would be free. He would have gone through all of this, not yet to kill the man who had caused it. It was unspeakable.

He knew that he should move.

But he could not. He could not leave her. It was as if, to him in any event, she held life and until the light of that spirit had gone from her he would hold fast. If anything, his months of massacre had given him a reverence for life, its delicacy, its difficult tenancy in the body, how quickly, absently it could be blown free. This had been a life too, perhaps the only one that had touched him and he could not leave her.

The sirens were closer yet.

He leaned over, his discarded gun falling unnoticed to the sands and touched her wrist, felt the bony patina of it as he traced up the surfaces of her forearm, tracing out delicately then the network of her body as he ran his hand under her neck, across her cheek, up the fine nose and against her forehead, brushing a finger into the delicate, already dried spot of blood between her eyes, just risen a couple of inches. As she had used to lie in bed while he did this to her, so she lay on the sands, her mouth twisted into an unspeakable expression of acceptance and knowledge. She had smiled that way in bed when he had been touching her. Touching her.

He felt the pain begin to prod within him, not the pain of fear or of rage, not even the simple fear of death which he had already known many times in his mission, but something far more complex, something that went back to another part of his life and then moved forward until he was looking not only at this girl on the beach but at another face, a face he had seen months ago, the two of them blending together and the fusion was almost unbearable, It was not fair, not fair: he was responsible for this girl's death in a way that he had not been for the first, going out to avenge the one he had somehow managed to kill her spirit in another form and thinking this Wulff collapsed, sprawled weeping across the girl, feeling all of it rush out of him, the pain that had been bottled up for so long coming out in huge, gasping convulsed sobs, sobs like a giant sea animal might make trapped in this sand.

"It's not fair," he said, "it's not fair," but her body was cold, cold, his hands ran across that body, cupped and touched her dead breasts and then fell away. "Not fair," he said, "I didn't mean it to turn out this way, I didn't want it, I would have done anything if it hadn't ended up this way but what could I have done? What the hell could I have done?" She had walked out on him in Los Angeles. God almighty, she had walked out on him in Los Angeles, said that he was crazy, said that this would lead if he continued only to madness and destruction . . . but did that destruction have to include her? Then she had been caught up in the web and now she was dead. Simple. Simple equation. "It's not fair!" he shouted again, rubbing his head across her stomach, "I didn't want it to be this way!" The sirens were almost on top of him now. How much longer did he have? A few minutes? The beach was vacant; he the only man on it, he and the dead men and this one dead girl. It could not be long now.

"You cut that out now, man," a voice said behind him.

Wulff leaped and, then, losing his balance, staggered backward, lay on his elbows in the sand, completely vulnerable, looking at the face above his. Light was starting to filter out and he could make out the features. "Enough of this, Wulff," the face said, "you and me, we've got to get our asses out of here."

Williams.

"Where did you come from?" Wulff said and then, the question unnecessary, the answer pointless, motioned toward the girl again. "She's dead," he said, "they killed her. *I* killed her. I killed her and now she's dead."

"There's no time for that," Williams said. He reached out, grasped Wulff's shoulder, pulled him upward, unresisting. "You got to get your ass out of here. We both do." He pointed at the beach, the light was coming up more fully now, Wulff could see the signs of the massacre. "They're going to see that it's going to be very bad," Williams said. "You done a job here, you've done a real job. But we have to get out of here."

"She's dead."

"I know that. I see very well that she's dead but that's not going to change anything. You did the best you could."

"No I didn't."

"I tried to get here sooner but I couldn't. I might have helped you. But you did all right on your own."

"Oh I did fine," Wulff said underneath the sirens, "I did fine, I always do. No one does better. I think I'm going to let them take me."

"No you're not."

"It's too much, can't you see? I can't take it anymore. She got killed."

"That wasn't you, it was the old bastard. The old bastard did that." Williams looked at the sack lying crumpled a few yards down. "You won," he said. "I see you still got what he wants."

"I have nothing."

"If you have what he wants then he got out of this with nothing. The last step is to kill him."

"He killed Tamara."

"Tamara was dead already, don't you understand that?" Williams said ferociously. He yanked Wulff toward him holding a tight grip, fingers biting into his wrists, then literally shook him. "She was gone, you met her in a speed factory. If it hadn't been for you she would have blinked out right there; as it is you pulled her out of it. How much longer do you think she had anyway?"

"I don't know. Longer than this."

"She was *dead*," Williams said, "once you're hooked into that shit you never get free of it, it's in the system and she was going right back there. How much longer do you think she had, a few months? You goddamned fool," Williams said, "you're not going to blow up everything you've done so far for this, are you, you're not going to let it go by because of this bitch—" and Wulff broke inside, he clawed at Williams' face, he hit him, and Williams took the slap straightway, standing there, hands dangling flatly at his sides, his eyes resigned. Wulff, after the impact, turned around, staggered away from Tamara, down the sands toward the sack.

"Okay," Williams said, "okay, now you have done it and that suits me but it's time to go. It's time to go, it's time to get out of here, Wulff, now let's go," and he came beside him, helped him raise the sack, helped him carry it along the length of the beach. "You know that," Williams said, "maybe it could have been different but it's too late now to worry about difference and we've got to kill that son of a bitch."

"It's too late," Wulff said, "it's too late to kill him."

"It's never too late," Williams said, "it's never too late for killing a monster and the man is a monster. Think of the satisfaction, Wulff. Think of the pleasure. Think of what it's going to mean to rid the earth of this vermin." They were almost off the beach now, staggering toward the slats of higher ground. "That's all, Wulff," Williams said, "you've got to do it."

"He went back to Chicago. I know that he's gone back to Chicago."

"Probably," Williams said, "he'd probably do that."

"Then I've got to go back there and burn him out. I've got to go back to Chicago and blow up the lakefront to get him but I'll do it."

"That's good, Wulff. That's real good."

"I'll get him," Wulff said, "I'll get him and then I'm turning myself in."

"You better move your ass," Williams said flatly, "unless you want to be turned in right *now*," and he pushed Wulff along, impelling him with a blow in the small of the back, the blow not at all unkind but rough, *rough*, harder than the slap which Wulff had given but not nearly as mean and Wulff thought, no, he's not a bad guy after all, he's trying to pull me out of this and he's right, he's got to be right because if I give up now, her death will indeed have been in vain and nothing will have been accomplished. You've got to go on. Whatever you do, you've simply got to go on. There were sirens all around them now.

"We've got to get a car," he said.

"You don't worry about that," Williams said, "you just leave that to me, I'm getting goddamned experienced in this business, not in your class Wulff, but I could fill in in the dark," and leaving him at streetside, he ran toward a parked Mustang, illegally sprawled on the curb, probably left by a drunk who had given up the ghost but then again it might simply be out of gas.

Williams kicked the window on the driver's side in skillfully, the safety glass spattering, and sprung open the door, vanished inside it. Standing there, Wulff watched, the sirens coming closer and closer all the time and a dull roar came out of the dual exhausts of the muffler. Then Williams had wrenched the wheel all the way around, spun up on the sidewalk, made a huge U-turn and came screaming to a halt beside Wulff, the left rear door falling open. Wulff crept into the smelly, furred cave and the door closed, Williams rammed the accelerator all the way down and they were moving along the beachfront drive at thirty-five miles an hour. Another screaming U-turn at the next corner and they were moving away from the sirens at fifty. Wulff settled back into the seat, breathing unevenly, feeling the sweat come down and around into all the empty spaces of his body.

"Nothing to it," Williams said, "nothing to it at all. Police academy technique for motorists locked out of their cars. Remember?"

Wulff remembered.

<h1 style="text-align:center">XIX</h1>

At the airport they found that a flight to Chicago had left just fifteen minutes before. That had to be it. There was an abandoned copter at the far end of a runway in the private plane section which Wulff pretty well identified but there seemed little point in checking it out. The important thing was to get onto another Chicago flight as quickly as possible, but it would be a forty-five minute wait and in the meantime staying in the terminal itself seemed an ominous proposition.

Williams bought tickets and did some hurried surveillance while Wulff went into the men's room, locked himself into a cubicle and for long, gasping instants sat looking at the floor, fully clothed, sitting on the toilet seat. Shame filled him. Miami was to be the final arena, the last confrontation and it had not been. They were both going to get out of it alive. Behind Wulff were a lot of bodies but multiple murder was not accomplishment and the girl was dead. The girl was dead.

He looked at the sack curled beneath him on the floor of the men's room and found himself saying *no more, no more*, looking at this clamped mass of death that had only brought death and then in one sudden impulsive gesture he stood, grasped it, opened the cord and dumped all of it into the open toilet, filling it with grain that became glutinous as it meshed with the water. Then he began to flush, flushing spasmodically, again and again, shaking out the sack with one hand, dumping the stuff with the other, pouring the heroin into the sewage of Miami, flushing and flushing repeatedly, coughing, tears in his eyes from the fumes that came up from the scented waters, flushing all of the death away, shaking the bag, pounding it, slapping it desperately to remove the last grains.

Finally, five or ten minutes later, he had no sensation of the passage of time, all of it was gone and he jammed the sack into the toilet, stoppering it, and walked out of the cubicle. That was stupid, he thought, not only flushing it away, but leaving the sack as evidence. At least he could have disposed of the sack somewhere else; he didn't have to tie it so directly. But he did not care. Let them worry about it. Let the porters come in and see this sack jamming up the toilet, the toilet by then with an OUT OF ORDER sign across it and wonder what had happened.

He had ditched one enormous load of heroin into the Charles River between Boston and Cambridge; enough heroin to have supplied the entire northeast sector for months. Now in Miami he was putting the Midwest out of business. So be it. Let the heroin go into the sewage system.

He wondered vaguely if like LSD was rumored to be able to, traces of heroin could drift from sewage into the water supply and freak out portions of the city of Miami. He doubted this very much. Heroin was an inert material, LSD an active, virulent chemical. Pity that he had never tried to bust the LSD business but then you couldn't have everything, could you? Besides, LSD was dead. Dead. The kids were turning away from it in droves. Damaged genes.

At the door of the empty men's room Williams met him. "No surveillance," he said, "not yet anyway. They're not watching the airports it seems; they're not into that yet. Everything's focusing down on the beach. We should be able to get out before they come into the airport unless someone down there gets bright."

"Remarkable," Wulff said. "How did you find out all that?"

"I scout around," Williams said. He looked at Wulff curiously. "What did you do with the sack?"

"I dumped it."

"In here?"

"In here," Wulff said, "where else?"

"After everything you went through—"

"Oh come on," Wulff said, "enough of this, will you? Just don't tell me what to do."

"I'm not telling you anything," Williams said. He put a hand on Wulff's elbow, guided him out of the room, into the empty, ringing spaces of the terminal. "What are you going to do now?"

"I'm going to go back to Chicago and kill him, that's what I'm going to do."

"You'll never make it."

"Try me."

"You ought to lay low for a while."

"I'm not lying low again. I'm going to go in there and kill him," Wulff said. "After that I don't give a damn."

"The girl is dead," Williams said. They walked over to a small service bar, the Chinese bartender looked at them idly. "You'd better have a scotch or something. The girl isn't going to be brought back."

"Bullshit," Wulff said. "The girl has nothing to do with it."

"The girl has everything to do with it, but she won't come back." Williams motioned to the bartender, asked for two double scotches. "You ought to go back to New York," he said. "If we're lucky we can get back there and then you can go underground."

"And you?" Wulff said, "what are you going to do?"

"I'm going back," Williams said. He took the scotch in one gulp. "I've given it a lot of thought and I'm going to try and get back into it. I don't think they want me as bad as they want you and they're pretty well smashed regardless. If I go back into the NYPD I'm too big a target to bother. You've set them back ten years, you know."

"That's a great feeling."

"Well," Williams said, "you have. I don't think I have as much to fear from them going back now. I think you ought to go back too; lie low. They're scattered, they're in a panic. It's going to be a long time now until they come looking for you again."

"I don't care," Wulff said. He looked at the scotch without interest, then drained it. "That doesn't mean anything to me anymore, can't you understand that?"

"You have more to worry about from our side. Lot of people are going to ask you questions if they can get hold of you. Also, I don't think a lot of people are too happy with the fact that you were able to do more on your own, one man, in three months, than all of these agencies, bureaucrats, narco squads and investigators were able to manage in ten years. That kind of has a tendency to show people up. People don't like to be shown up, Wulff, have you noticed?"

"It's bullshit," Wulff said again. He looked numbly at the empty glass, then pushed it across the bar, let the bartender refill it. Williams put more money out on the bar. He held the glass, looked at it for a while and then took it straight again. Williams smiled and pushed over his own glass.

"That's the ticket," he said, "that's the best way to handle it, it's going to do you more good that way. Listen, don't go to Chicago. Come back to New York with me."

"No," Wulff said, "I won't go back to New York. Not yet."

"You can get him anytime," Williams said, "that old man is dead. He's run out his options now and he's got nowhere to go."

"No," Wulff said, "I'm going to kill him. My options have run out too."

A megaphone blared and Williams said, "That's my New York flight boarding right now."

"Well good luck to you. The best of luck to you in your new career."

Williams looked at him intently. "You all right?" he said.

"Yeah, I'm all right. I'm fine. I'm great."

"I'm not going to Chicago with you. It wouldn't do anybody any good, you see."

"You're quite right about that," Wulff said, "quite right. This has to be me. Get on your plane."

Williams put down his glass. "I don't know if I'll ever see you again," he said.

"Well, it's a possibility. Everything's a possibility."

"I can't stay with you!" Williams said with sudden, desperate urgency. "I can't live like this. I've got to go back; I've got to get out of this."

"Go, good luck."

"You make me feel fucking *guilty*, man," Williams said with a forced smile and the megaphone blared again. Williams put down some money on the bar and said, "I've got to go. That's all. I wish you luck."

"Sure," Wulff said.

"I think you're the best there is, you know? I think that you're out of everyone's class. But I just can't cut it anymore." He extended a hand, Wulff looked at it for a long time and then he touched it delicately. It was as far as he could go, it was the most contact he could make. Williams drew his hand away, shook his head, muttered something which Wulff did not hear and then went away from the bar quickly, walking in an uneven, stumbling gait, heading toward the New York flight.

Well, Wulff thought as he let the bartender pour him one more scotch, well, it had been a long journey from the first time he had seen Williams until now. The rookie Williams had approached him somewhat as this renegade Williams had left, the strange, proud tilt of his shoulders, the poise of his bearing, a hint of something yielding in the center which caused him to walk subtly off-balance.

A long way from there to here but maybe not so long at all and now it was over. The girl dead, Williams gone. Wulff raised the scotch, looked around the terminal for signs of local police or leftover scouts from the Calabrese party . . . and waited for his Chicago flight.

XX

In the airplane, a routine passenger flight, Calabrese was dreaming. His head tilted back, his hands folded before him, he was dreaming of the rape again, the way that the girl had opened underneath him and in the dream he was whole and had parted her savagely, had torn inside her, feeling the smooth convolution of her cunt as it had gripped him, the smooth rising within him as he had, gliding, pumped himself toward orgasm, each stroke one of superb felicity, each stroke driving the girl into deeper and more profound paroxysms of her own.

"Oh my God yes," she was saying to him in the dream, the plane rolling slightly in diminished turbulence over Knoxville, "Please keep seat belts fastened," the stewardess had said just before Calabrese had fallen off. "Oh my God yes, this is the way I always dreamed it would be, this is the way it should be. Do it, fuck the hell out of me, lover," and her breasts slid into his mouth, the conjoinment easier than it had any right to be considering their posture; in the dream he sucked and sucked at her breasts, each suck giving him renewed invigoration to pump below and he knew that he could keep it up forever.

It was just like the old days; he could come on the spot or hold it back for hours, either way, anything he wanted, he was in utter control of the situation. Rolling and rolling in the dream he turned over all the angles of the bed on which they were copulating and finally when the girl had reached some peak of excitation her mouth fell open, her tongue moistened her lips and she said, "Now, now, give it to me now," and he had done so, unloading into her in a single rush, all of it: the pain, the loss, the fear, the desperation and above all the power. It had been power to unload into her and she had taken everything he had given gratefully, moaning, winking back at him through spasmed eyelids and holding him more tightly as he poured into her.

"Oh yes," she said then, "oh yes, that was good, that was everything I ever wanted, it was wonderful, you're the best there is, do you know that?" "Better than Wulff?" he said in the dream, the first thing he had said to her since the coupling had begun, "better than him?" "Oh yes," she said, "oh yes, you're much, *much* better than him, of course you are, he can't do *half* the things to me that you can, you were just wonderful."

He had begun to laugh then, a sheer, unstrangulated laugh of delight because at last he had beaten the bastard, beaten him cold, gotten at him through the interposition of the girl and proven himself finally in every essential sense a better man, twisting with laughter on the bed, the sheets wrapped around him, drawing little cords into his neck and shoulders, tightening on him, the girl a weight too, the girl lying across him as he laughed, her weight added to the binding of the sheets suddenly constricting, his soft prick dangling and he could not breath, he could not somehow get air into his lungs, either the girl or the sheets had cut something off, he was struggling, falling, gasping, sinking beneath the weight and the constriction and suddenly he flailed with panic trying to free himself, his arms flying to his head, the weight increasing all around.

"Stop it," he said, "stop it, I'm dying, I'm drowning, I'm choking," fighting to get free of all of this, "I tell you I'm drowning," and still the weight coming in. He was going to die, he was going to die right here—

—He woke up.

And found himself leaning back on the red corduroy of the plane seat, the fabric biting into him, the back of his neck running with sweat, all of him twisted over into a terrifying position, limbs bunched underneath one another like an insect's so he could not, for the moment, move, and the stewardess, apparently having seen him move in his sleep, was by his side, an expression of fear and concern in her eyes which Calabrese would have given almost anything not to see. It was close to the worst thing that had happened to him yet, seeing the way that this young girl was looking at him.

"Are you all right?" she said, and then remembered her training. "Are you all right, sir?"

"I'm all right."

"Can I get you something? Something to drink?"

"Yes," Calabrese said, "you can get me a double scotch, no water, no ice."

Her eyes flickered. "Are you sure—"

"Yes," he said, so loudly that the couple across the aisle looked at him strangely, "yes, I'm sure it's all right. That's exactly what I want."

"You've already had one—"

"Get me another!" Calabrese said, "you get me another right now!" and the stewardess turned, went down the aisle, the set of her buttocks showing a fury which would never reach her face. Fuck her. He was feeling a little better now.

Just a muscle spasm, that was all it had been. Sleeping in

uncomfortable posture and then the matter of the turbulence. Nothing to worry about.

Nothing. Nothing to worry about; he was not going to die. He was not having a heart attack; he was in excellent condition for a man of his age. He looked out the windows, then, seeing clouds, that child's vision of heaven, and felt sick again. Never look down. Never. He leaned back into the seat and looked back at the aisle.

Strange: strange to be travelling alone like this but probably clever, too, the cleverest thing that he could have done under the circumstances. All of his troops were back on that beach; he had no idea how many of them had survived, maybe five or six, he could assess his losses later, but there was not time to surround himself with any of them before leaving. His bodyguard dead, the pilot in the ditched helicopter could worry about that. He was going back to Chicago alone, commercial flight. For the first time in years he did not feel insulated from surroundings by a coterie of protection. He was on his own. He would have to make it on his own.

But it was a good feeling; it was the first release and peace he had known since he had left Chicago for this damned, rotten Miami adventure and with every mile that he was able to put himself away from Miami he felt a little more assured, like the old Calabrese. At least he had gotten out. Everything had been fucked up; the expedition was a total disaster, the complications and reverberations which came off what had happened here would reach through the country . . . but he was safe. He was out of it. And once he knew the province of his estate again no one could touch him. He would wall himself away. And if Wulff came for him, as surely Wulff would . . . he would meet that when it came. The man had not killed him yet. He had not killed Wulff. A standoff.

The stewardess came back with his drink on a tray, held the tray stiffly while he reached out and took it. She was really quite a pretty girl in the cold, effective way which stewardesses were trained to project, but underneath it there was something tender, he was sure, if only he could find it. Didn't they all screw like bunnies? That was the folklore on stewardesses; hell, if they screwed like bunnies there was some real tenderness there if only you could find it. "Thank you," he said to her.

"You're welcome," she said, starting to move away, but a little gust of turbulence caught her and sent her back the other way. She dug a thigh expertly into the ridge of his seat to hold on. Nice thighs, nice buttocks. It would be nice to go to bed with her. It would be nice to go to bed with all of them if only—

"Sorry I shouted at you," he said, trying to smile. "I didn't mean—"

"That's all right, sir."

"I didn't mean anything by it is all I wanted to say."

"It's already forgotten sir. Is there anything else I can get you?"

"Nothing. Nothing at all."

"Then you're quite welcome, sir," the stewardess said and moved away from him, her buttocks waggling. For a moment Calabrese thought of pursuing her, at least calling out something which would make her come back and extend the conversation until he could break through that wall, touch her as a human being . . . but no, it was not worth it. What did you get when you broke through all the way to the depths of a stewardess? A stewardess, that was what you got.

He settled back in the seat, looked at his watch. Forty-five minutes, maybe a little less, until O'Hare. The thing was that you spent forty years of your life fighting, fighting to reach a point where you had finally gotten to the top or if not the top at least a place where you had moved beyond the struggles, moved to a place where they could not touch you. You worked on an organization, nursed it along, tried as best as you could to make that organization a living, viable thing. There were rivals every step of the way, people who had already reached that position who saw you as a threat and would do anything within their power to stop you from reaching that objective—

—So you had to be shrewd, had to be cunning, had to take risks which most of those with whom you were competing would not be willing to take, simply to reach that position. At the end of it, at the end of this forty years you were most likely dead, long since knocked off in your pursuit. If you were not dead you were likely to be the next thing to it, ruined, racked up, but if you were one of the very few who had been able to follow it all the way through, who had had that correct combination of luck and ruthlessness and flexibility, the flexibility terribly important because it meant that you were willing to get out of what was dying, into what was growing without an instant of doubt and hesitation, move into prostitution in the forties, into drugs in the fifties, into harder drugs and gambling in the sixties—

—Well, at the end of all of that you were seventy-three years old and fit prey for the gravediggers anyway. Half of the people you had started off with were long dead, most of the rest of them were dying or just barely hanging on. But even though you could say that you beat them you knew that the one thing you could never beat was mortality itself, the slow corruption of the flesh, the dark, singing torment of chronology which drove you further and further away from any sense of what you yourself might have been, might have gained—

—And then there you were, seventy-three years old. Seventy-three years old and just barely hanging on. Calabrese closed his eyes against the pain of that insight, drinking the rest of his drink with his eyes closed, the liquor piling down into the gut in the familiar way, clamping, wringing him, feeling the motions of the craft moving through him and thought, I will not deal with this anymore. Everybody gets old, everybody ages, it's a condition of life. It has nothing to do with me personally, I will not take it personally. It is better to be seventy-three years and alive than to be seventy-three and celebrating the seventy-third anniversary of your birth, remember that, remember that always … and the plane lurched sickeningly, began to plunge in a long, uneven dive that brought gasps and screams from the passengers. He gripped onto the chair blanking his mind, blanking response of any sort and a thousand feet or so down the plane levelled off, began to hobble in the air like a canoe shooting the rapids with a single oar.

The pilot got onto the public address system and said that there was nothing to worry about, this kind of mid-air turbulence was common in cases like this, nothing to be concerned about, have a drink on the house, try to enjoy the rest of your flight … and then Calabrese knew it was bad, it was unmistakably bad if they were taking that approach, but as the plane rocked and shuddered in the air he could even smile at that, the drink on the house that was because the idea of a seventy-three-year-old man dying in a plane crash, why there was a redundancy if he had ever heard one.

Opening his eyes he saw that the stewardesses looked terrified.

The plane plunged again.

XXI

Coming off at Kennedy Williams found that he could not wait. He could not wait even until he had gotten out of the terminal. He went to a telephone in the Eastern terminal and called his sister-in-law. The phone rang only once; she picked it up as if she had been waiting for a long time.

"It's me," he said.

"I knew it was you."

"Is she all right? Is everything okay?"

"You took long enough to call," she said, "you didn't really give a damn, did you?"

"I'm home," Williams said, "I'm home now. Tell me. Is she all right?"

"I take pity on you. Everyone's all right. You have a son, eight pounds two ounces, born three days ago. They should be coming out tomorrow."

"A son," Williams said. He leaned against the glass, it seemed porous. "A son! How about that? What's his name?"

"No name yet."

"No name yet? How can that be? Aren't you supposed to put the names on the certificates within twenty-four hours?"

"Male child," his sister-in-law said, "they give you a seven-day extension for that. We were waiting, maybe waiting on the chance that you'd be back. That you'd like to help name your son. But we had just about given up hope. You're a real son of a bitch, do you know that?"

"That's all over now," Williams said, "that all happened a long time ago."

"Did it?"

"I'm home," he said, "I'm home. I came home to *be* home and I'm staying. What hospital?"

"Lying-in."

"Lying-*In?* That's in Manhattan. What is she doing way over in Manhattan; we had it all arranged—"

"There was kind of a speedup," his sister-in-law said dryly, "we were out for a drive and the baby decided that he wasn't having none of it. You're a real bastard, do you know that? Walking out on an eight-months pregnant—"

"I said that's all over," Williams said. He held the receiver tightly, feeling the dampness come from his palms and said, "I'm going now. I'm going to see her right now."

"You're going to have a very tough time. I don't envy your position at all."

"I'll make it right," he said, "I'll make it right. I don't envy my position either but there are reasons."

"There are always reasons," that bitterly philosophical woman, his sister-in-law said, and Williams hung up, threw the receiver on top of the phone and came out of the booth roaring inside, wanting to grip everyone who he could see in the Eastern terminal, babble out to them the news that he had a son, but of course something leaner, colder within him told him that he was acting like a fool if he did that, not that it wasn't sympathetic, and that he was in no position to call attention to himself. Right. Right on the second anyway, the first he did not know about. What was a fool anyway?

He came out of the building, got onto the cab-line, got a taxi and went off to Lying-In Hospital down the ramps, over the expressway at seventy miles an hour and so complete was his absorption, so total was his delight, that it was hours later, hours after he had left the hospital, hours after the reunion with his wife at a depth of connection that he would not have known could have existed . . . hours after all of this that he thought of Wulff even in the slightest way and then in the most detached fashion: he hoped that the son of a bitch had made it through. He really did. He wished him the best. He certainly wished him the best.

But it was no longer his battle.

XXII

He did not even read about the Chicago liner that had gone down for three days and then only idly, did not connect it to Calabrese. By that time his wife and son were home, he was applying for reinstatement to PD. He had enough on his hands.

30 September 1973: New Jersey

THE END

THE LONE WOLF #10: HARLEM SHOWDOWN

by Barry N. Malzberg

Writing as Mike Barry

For George Ernsberger and Bill Pronzini

To drive the pushers from the streets . . .
to make our cities safe again . . .

—Nelson A. Rockefeller

What is this? This is garbage.

—John A. Marchi on the *New York Times*

This is garbage.

—Burton Wulff

TO: COMMANDER, SPECIAL UNIT.
RE: BURTON WULFF; FOLLOW-UP.

Present whereabouts, plans, deeds unknown. It is possible that Wulff is dead, although this is merely an unverified hunch. Reason for speculation: there has been no evidence of activities for two months. This represents, by far, the longest period of inactivity since his war began, seven months ago. Results then were so widely publicized that we concluded that this level of activity would continue.

Brief summary incorporating materials of previous report and updating: Burton Wulff, thirty-two years old, Vietnam combat veteran (more than a few years counting toward civil service pension "good time"), ten-year veteran of New York Police Department. Various duties before three years on narcotics squad, 1970-73. Suspended from narcotics squad for allegedly making an arrest without proper evidence. (It is known that the arrestee was an informant who did indeed have hard drugs on person, and that the release was arranged by lieutenant of the booking precinct. See file #43712. Collaboration between dealers and precinct personnel not uncommon in that precinct during period of arrest. New command instituted.)

Returned, temporarily, to patrol car duty with new partner, David Williams. On first night of patrol car duty, Wulff was sent on anonymous tip to rooming house on West Ninety-third Street in New York where a twenty-three-year-old white female, subsequently identified as Marie Calvante, was found dead of heroin overdose. Apparently Calvante, decedent, was the fiancée of Burton Wulff. *This is carried as an open case, and no leads have been uncovered.* It is possible that girl did die of overdose. Based on autopsy, however, murder was not completely dismissed. There were signs of forced induction in the pulmonary vein, and decedent bore no external signs of drug addiction.

Wulff never returned to the patrol car, the precinct, or the police department. Much of what follows has been developed from public data and the hearsay of certain unidentifiable informants.

Wulff declared a "total war" on the international drug dealers, apparently believing himself and the decedent to have been "targeted" because of the previous day's drug arrest. *There is no evidence of such targeting.*

The "war" began in New York and Long Island where Wulff, apparently relying upon combat experience and knowledge of ordnance, incendiaries, and guerilla tactics, killed at least six men, three of them identified as being prominent in the higher circles of East Coast drug distribution. After blowing up a townhouse on the East Side and assassinating a major distributor (taking with him, apparently, the plans and directives for a major shipment due to arrive on the West Coast), Wulff went to San Francisco where his "war" continued, escalating into a massacre when a freighter containing the shipment, along with a large crew and many operatives on board to receive it, was blown up in San Francisco harbor. Escaping with the shipment itself, at least a million dollars' worth of uncut heroin, Wulff proceeded east to Boston, using shipment as "bait." In Boston, through continuously escalating guerilla tactics, he destroyed the fabric of extant distribution in the New England states before apparently disposing of the drugs.

Wulff then proceeded to Las Vegas where a large quantity of drugs stolen from the evidence division by a now deceased police sergeant (see file #43926) was rumored to be. Terror tactics continued, a major casino was destroyed, and several more important figures were assassinated. Returning East with stolen goods, Wulff's flight was hijacked to Havana.

Here the trail is lost, not to be picked up until weeks later when, emerging somehow from Havana, Wulff was known to be in Chicago. There he confronted Nicholas Calabrese, seventy-three, long suspected to be the kingpin not only of Midwest distribution but also of the national council of families. Apparently Wulff was entrapped by Calabrese, but mysteriously was not killed but instead exiled to Lima, Peru, from which country he again emerged in unknown ways, next being seen in Los Angeles weeks later where more violence was committed.

(There are unsubstantiated reports that throughout some of these incidents Wulff had been receiving help, both overt and covert, from David Williams, his former partner. Williams, critically injured by knife attack near a methadone center in west Harlem, was hospitalized for several weeks, left home shortly after his return, and *might* have been with Wulff in Los Angeles. Many aspects of the Williams situation are interesting, and a separate report is being prepared. Williams, as you know, has now applied for reinstatement, refusing to give details of his involvement with the subject.)

Details of Los Angeles events will be found in supplementary reports being prepared, as will details, when available, on previous episodes. Wulff left Los Angeles for Miami at the same time that Calabrese was heading there, apparently for a final "confrontation" of some sort. (It also appears that a second and even larger lot of drugs was taken by the subject out of Peru, a multimillion-dollar load of uncut heroin diverted from Calabrese, who had arranged the shipment.) In a massive guerilla action on the beach in Miami, some forty or fifty men, apparently Calabrese's employees and security personnel, were slain. Also found on the beach was the corpse of a female in her mid-twenties who highly suspect sources indicate might have been Wulff's paramour. By the time authorities had arrived, Wulff was gone. His body was not found, leading to the conclusion that he had somehow escaped. However, the failure of subject to surface during the subsequent months indicates that he might indeed have been killed in the massacre, his body somehow disposed of.

A commercial airline flight carrying Nicholas Calabrese and seventy-three other passengers crashed five miles west of Chicago's O'Hare airport on the morning after the massacre. Only the pilot, copilot, and one stewardess survived the crash, but all died within thirty-six hours of the incident.

It is conceivable that Wulff did survive the massacre with the intent to follow Nicholas Calabrese back to Chicago and kill him there, that the crash made this plan of action unnecessary, gave him the feeling that his "war" had come to a successful conclusion, and enabled him to go underground. However, this is doubtful, considering the previous record of Burton Wulff—the scope of his activities, the anger with which they were carried out, and his unswerving dedication to destruction of the international drug trade, of which Calabrese was merely one important symbol.

Supplementary reports, as noted, are in preparation and will be forwarded.

Although Wulff is a former police officer, and although he has made efforts throughout not to involve/injure/kill enforcement personnel, he must nevertheless be considered extremely dangerous. Since his capture would undoubtedly result in life imprisonment—he is guilty of several hundred murders and, regardless of the motive and the nature of the victims, many murders are still first-degree—and since he knows this and would undoubtedly not allow himself to be approached, it is reluctantly recommended that he be shot on sight, end report.

I

Calabrese dead, Tamara dead, Williams gone, the drugs destroyed, the cities burnt behind: lost, lost.

Calabrese dead, Tamara dead, Williams gone, the drugs destroyed, but here he still was, he was here, he was back in Harlem. A few months, a different life ago, his quest had started there when he had pulled a dealer from a car and choked out of him information about the next higher link in the chain. On and on he had moved then: snapping links in the chain, leaving it a slithering, broken serpent behind him as he had moved on and on, through the great cities of America into Havana, Lima, building toward that confrontation with old Nicholas Calabrese, toward that time when he would accomplish the purpose of his quest; he would kill him and be done. Behind him then was wreckage, ahead of him the darkness, but he would have Calabrese. He would find him in his lair in Chicago and kill the old man; hell, he would torture him to death.

But Calabrese dead, Tamara dead, Williams gone, the drugs destroyed, everything had come to an end and an end away from him. Getting off the plane in Chicago, the Miami-Chicago flight one hour behind the one that Calabrese had taken, seeing the panic at the airport, the reporters, the photographers, the grim men in black suits from the aereonautics agencies, the security personnel holding off the crowds that wanted to surge down the runway under the blank spotlight to see the wreckage in the distance, the fires and hoses playing upon it—seeing this he could not believe it, it was not possible that Calabrese could have gone down, denying his own vengeance. And yet, on the heels of this was a second level of feeling: an acceptance. He knew that it would have to have been this way. The old man was too cunning, clever, corrupt. He had managed all the details of his life; now at the end of his purposes, his troops destroyed, Wulff hard behind him, could not the old man strangely have willed his death and in that one megalomaniacal gesture of the heart and will brought down seventy innocents with him?

Well, Wulff was no mystic. The world was still a rational place; it was only the corrupters and the thugs who made it irrational. He would not get into that issue at all; what he had to do now was to adapt to the fact that Calabrese was dead, that he would not return, and that he, Wulff, had to get out of Chicago as quickly as possible. He had obtained the casualty information quickly and easily. The reporters were talking to anyone. Only three survivors had been pulled from the craft, the pilot, copilot and one of the stewardesses, and they were en route to the hospital now with 85 percent of body surfaces burned. No one was expected to live.

Get out of Chicago, then. First was the rage that Calabrese had used death, that trap door, to evade him; second was a feeling of emptiness, deserted purposes; but the third conviction, spilling all through him like heat and light, was that he had to save himself and he would. The shipment of drugs had been shredded and destroyed in Miami. Williams had left him for the last time to try to pick up the pieces in New York.

Tamara, who might have at another period of his life wrenched him into feeling—well, Tamara was dead, but that was all over. He was still alive. He had to survive. If he did not, everything that he had done so far was meaningless. He had to get out and back to New York because at least he knew New York, he felt safe there.

So he went to a counter and bought a shuttle service coach ticket and, accident and all, was on board on his way within twenty minutes. If he had had some vision of hundreds of Calabrese's soldiers ringing the airport, waiting for his entrance, if he had thought of hundreds of equally dedicated police carrying his photograph, alert to his return from Miami—the soldiers, if any were left after what Calabrese had invested in Miami, had undoubtedly taken for the hills as soon as they had gotten word of the crash, and the cops had other things to do. Mostly trying to hold the gapers and the press in check. He slipped through all of them like a soldier low-crawling barbed-wire and headed back toward New York, a three-hour flight against headwinds during which he had time to evaluate his position.

His position, of course, was impossible and had only been magnified by the crash that had downed Calabrese. He guessed that his plan had been to kill the old man, thus rounding off as best he could his six-month struggle in the jungles of the international drug trade, and then to turn himself in to the federal authorities as proof that the trade could be broken if a small group of trained and dedicated men were allowed to operate vigilante style outside the scope of conventional enforcement procedures. Or he might simply have slipped away, breaking through the border to Mexico. He was tired, the price had escalated, the risks now outweighed the potential for further damage, and Calabrese had seemed to be the proper murder with which to round off at least this phase of his career. But then the son of a bitch had gone and died on him.

Well, it just went to prove that you never knew. You could never be sure of anything. Calabrese himself must have had that feeling as the plane fell.

Calabrese dead, Tamara dead, the drugs shredded, Williams gone. He came off the plane at Kennedy, this beginning to throb like a litany through his consciousness: Cal-a-brese *dead*/Ta-ma-ra *dead*/drugs *destroyed*/Will-yums *gone*. He had ducked underground at once, striking out not toward the hack stand or the highways but toward the odorous, rolling swamps beyond Kennedy. There, climbing fences, moving through water, he had gotten himself to a side road in Jamaica, and only then had he hailed a cab, a cruising gypsy.

And he had had the cab take him to Manhattan, to the West Side.

Only in the saying of it, in the destination coming out of him, had Wulff understood the perfect sense that this made, the feeling of perfect circularity, closing the cycle: bless the subconscious again. Or curse it, hold no odes for the subconscious, because it knew better than he did that what had happened had begun on the West Side and here, then, it would end. On the West Side, in a stinking rooming house on West Ninety-third Street, he had seen Marie Calvante overdosed out, twenty-three years old and gutted, her body aged fifty years in the impact of the drug, her lovely body, which he had known so well . . . but it was better not to think of this, to remove thoughts of this sort from the conscious mind, because they would get him nowhere. He was beyond rage. All that he knew was that there was a compelling *rightness* in returning to the West Side.

And who would suspect his being there? Here, with the remnants of the shattered organization still staggering around, still seeking him, they would never expect him to come back to New York where it had all started. And the enforcement authorities who wanted him at least as badly as the organization, if only because he had shown them for the cheated, cheating fools they were—they too would not expect him to be here. Anywhere but in New York, with which he was most identified, and where he was most identifiable. So it was perfectly safe, it had been safer than any port in or out of the world, and when the cab had pulled onto the Triborough Bridge, it had been with absolute certainty that he had said, "Let's go over to the West Side. Drop me off in the west nineties, anywhere at all."

And they had gone into the west nineties. Going there, being there for the first time since he had seen the girl dead there had been a single moment of disconnection, lurching panic when he did not know whether he could take the sights or sounds of it anymore. But this had all gone away, he had felt the clamping certainty as the car came off at Ninety-seventh Street to make it through the transverse. He would not lose control of himself. He was back on home turf now. He could handle himself.

Into West Ninety-seventh, off the transverse road, across to Broadway, and this was where he had the cabbie stop, paid him off, got out. He was carrying only a small overnight bag. Losing the sack of drugs had lightened him down to bare essentials. In his pockets he had a .38, a .45, and four thousand in cash. Money was no problem; when he needed some he would pick it up. Take what you need, don't be greedy. Criminal mentality, he guessed. He walked south, through the midnight freaks and geeks of Broadway, turned after four blocks and found exactly what he had been looking for, what he had probably been looking for from the moment he had left Chicago.

West ninety-third Street. A rooming house.

No one recognized. Who was to recognize? A cop in uniform, as everyone in the business knew, was as close to the invisible man as the postman, the milkman, the parking lot attendant. In their roles, they had no features. He told the small, bitter man at the front desk that he would be in for an indefinite period, paid fifty dollars, two weeks rent in advance; and got a room on the second floor overlooking an airshaft. The second floor was all right.

He did not think that even he would have been able to take the fifth.

He spent two or three days lying low, getting his bearings, coming back to the New York sense of things. Everything began here; so it would end. The city was dying, but magnificently: there was more energy in one decayed strip of paper blowing on its streets amidst dog shit than in all of the vast spaces of Los Angeles or San Francisco. He blended into it perfectly. Everyone on the West Side was invisible, most of them invisible even to themselves. No one came looking for him; he had no sense of pressure or menace. He fitted right in.

The newspapers gave him a little more information. Massacre on the beach at Miami, forty-three dead, mob violence, mob vengeance, assailant's identity known to the police, intensive manhunt, no information to be released to the press at this time. Nicholas Calabrese dead in an air crash outside O'Hare, connections to the Miami massacre suspected, no definite information. Probable kingpin of the Midwest drug trade, a federal indictment was being sought for tax evasion at the time of his death. Wulff laughed at that, but not very hard. Otherwise, everything seemed fairly normal: a press service story about a possible drug panic in New England; supplies seemed to have almost vanished, to everyone's consternation. Authorities had no explanation. He laughed at that, too, again not heartily. In New York the drug trade was bubbling right along, new state laws or not, although an inordinate number of police seemed to be getting themselves shot and wounded, even a couple killed, in the process of making drug arrests. However, most of the trafficking had simply slipped across the river; the majority of deals seemed now to be taking place in Fort Lee or Hoboken. New Jersey's attorney general was going to ask the legislature for similarly harsh laws in his state so that New Jersey would no longer be a refuge for traffic. Wulff shrugged. Enforcement had nothing to do with the problem. Couldn't they see that? Enforcers were merely employees of the drug traffickers, ripping off their share in civil service salaries, defense legal fees, press publicity, and so on. Nothing would ever change inside the system. The system was dead-set for drugs; they kept it going. If any change was going to come, it would have to come from guerilla technicians, working outside the system, who had absolutely nothing to gain from their efforts but the satisfaction of knowing they were solving a problem. Couldn't they see that? Yes, he guessed they could. They knew it so damned well that they kept on passing tougher and tougher drug laws, pleading for more judges, more district attorneys, more jail wardens, more social services, more funding for their agencies . . .

After four or five days, he got sick of reading the papers and found himself ready to forage on the streets again. Nothing would ever change, that was for sure. Williams, the Williams of the beginning, before he had been knifed outside the methadone clinic, had been telling him the truth after all. The system was not about to change, it was going to go on the way that it always had; all that you could try to do was to hang loose and get your own. Give up any idea that you could make a difference. Go for the split-level or the two-family house in St. Albans, build your walls around yourself, go for the good twenty and pension at half-pay, and get the hell out, Williams had said. Well, maybe he was right.

Still, he wasn't quite ready to give up yet. Close to it but not just yet. Wulff had a few last ideas of his own; you couldn't start at the beginning, no way, but maybe you could get back to the roots just to see if you had done a thorough job, to do a little extra trimming and weeding around before standing back and admiring the finished construction. That was about what he was after now. There was no way to repeat his odyssey. But he could check back, take a craftsman's view of his work.

He went back to Harlem. First cruising the streets casually in a cab, saying nothing to the puzzled, nervous cabbie, just looking over the blocks as he had remembered them: Lenox, St. Nicholas, 125th Street, Lexington, Park. And then when he had decided that the terrain looked pretty much the same, he decided to dig in a little bit deeper.

Just to see how close he could get to the heart of the flame and still feel his own breath.

II

Animal said, "Get that white motherfucker."

The Dude followed Animal's point, looked down the street to see the guy coming toward them slowly, looking from right to left, shrugging his way toward them in a curiously graceful series of leaps, really good moves for a white man, and said, "The hell with it. You want him? *You* get him." He tapped his devil-head ring on the steering wheel.

"Fuck that shit, man," Animal said, almost pleading already. "I can't do it myself, you know that. Anyway, it's your turn. You get him."

They were sitting in the front seat of the Dude's 1971 Electra 225, custom kit, snow-white tires, rising fist for a hood ornament, trading a pint bottle of Thunderbird, just sipping a little, sliding with the wine, not so much trying to get drunk as just cement the good high that they had gotten from the Animal's very good stash about three-quarters of an hour ago in the building right across from them, which from the front appeared to be abandoned. The Dude got a laugh out of that, the patrol cars coming through five, six times a day, looking at that boarded-up storefront and checking it off as just another ruined piece of Harlem. Actually the joint was jumping. There was more action behind those fake boards than there was in the Apollo Theater at midnight; in back of those fake boards was a hidden entrance and another entrance over to the side that most of those in the know used. On the ground floor they were selling it outright; there was a nice, clean, dark basement for shooting, and on the upper levels there were even supposed to be women if you had the ambition after a veinful of that good stuff to go up and get yourself laid. The Dude had heard that that was about the best there was, fucking a woman on a horse-high, but it sure as hell wasn't for him. He could barely get up the energy after a horse high to sit behind the wheel of the Electra, tap the wheel and dream. Animal, on the other hand, became manic, wanted to get started right away on all those plans that he was dreaming up by the minute, giggling away. The stupid fuck. Still, what the hell, live and let live. It took all kinds to get along, took all ways to enjoy a horse-high, too, and if Animal wanted to react this way, the hell with him. He, the Dude, would just tap the wheel and dream, sing to the teddy bears dangling from chains in the custom kit, and get along. The trouble was that Animal was hustling him. He didn't have that old give-and-get-dead philosophy; he crawled up and down your ass. Insect-like. Someday, the Dude thought, someday soon, like maybe right after the down, he would have to straighten out Animal. Dragging. Dragass.

"*Get* the motherfucker," Animal said again and shifted position in the car, holding himself easily, nudging the Dude in the ribs with an elbow, and all of a sudden Dude felt himself build into a real sweat and rage, sitting right there in the car with Animal, listening to the guy rapping on him, some game of the soul that Animal was playing with him. "Shit, man," the Dude said, "*you* get him," looking at the tall white guy poking his way down the street easy as you please, quick glance at the trash cans, peek into an alley, finger rubbing behind his ear, free hand jammed in his pocket. Looked like he was just rambling through the territory, that was how he looked. "Son of a bitch," the Dude said, trying to get his point across, "what's this wasting him? The guy might be a narc, for one thing." Or one of the special attack force on drugs, the governor's shit, he thought. Hell, they were in enough trouble anyway.

"Waste him?" the Dude said, coming to a point of decision right then, feeling everything clicking into place like little wheels and tumblers getting together in his mind, "I'm not going to waste him, I'm going to get the fuck out of here." He jiggled the keys in the ignition lock of the Electra, trying to get them through the ignition point. Everything moved much more slowly when you were high, seemed to be taking place under water. He could not, somehow, get the keys out of the lock position. He wrenched at the wheel, bringing his right knee up to brace against the shock, trying to tear the thing into gear.

Animal's hand was suddenly on his, the fingers almost caressing the back of his own hand, a curious intimacy in the gesture that made the Dude realize something: he had never *liked* Animal. They had taken highs together, they had swung a little bit, but that didn't mean that he had to like the man. And to tell the truth of it, he did not; the Animal was crazy in a dark way, some fascination with death in the man, here he was looking at this white fucker dragging ass down the street and thinking about wasting him and that was not just sensible, no sense to it at all, hard high or not you just did not go around thinking about wasting people on sight. "Let's *go*," the Dude said, talking less to the Animal than to his fingers, "let's go, let's go," shouting, the keys finally driving through, and the starter of the Electra ground alive, but stupidly the weight of Animal's elbow pressing on his right knee drove his foot all the way down into the accelerator, mashing it into the floorboards, and the car started with an enormous, surprised bellow, like a lion caught sleeping by gunfire, and then promptly stalled, the cylinders screaming as raw gas flooded them. Still, Animal would not release his elbow from the Dude's knee, the Dude could not pull his leg off the damned gas pedal, and this position somehow struck the Animal as funny. He was very high, spitting, coughing, wrenching into laughter, and the Dude felt himself turning toward panic.

Horse-high always did it; you were supersensitive to lights, sounds, noise, heat, one minute floating easily, painlessly, above the whole motherfucking, gangbusting world, the next minute you were ditched, brought low, something in the air, some sound for which you had not accounted driving a nail through the pane of consciousness, and you were brought down again, plunged into the stinking, sinuous bowels of the earth itself where the real fucking was going on. This was where the Dude now found himself, some collaboration between the white man still walking, walking toward them and Animal's crazed laughter bucked him all the way down. The car was an intestine; red, white, and black it writhed around him. Animal was some crazed devil of the bowels trapped within. And even as the Dude was telling himself to keep it down, keep quiet, lay low, it will pass, he was scrambling out of the car, wrenching himself away from the wheel and out into the street, standing, weaving dangerously, struck by some aspect of the sunlight. He had the feeling that he was being observed, that they were pouring out of the shooting gallery to watch him, that Animal himself was pulling himself along the seat hand-over-hand to get behind the wheel of the Electra, but his attention had narrowed to the white man himself, still walking, coming toward them, and insight broke upon the Dude: the man was coming to get them. He had tracked them from 125th to the lot where the Electra was tucked, uptown to the shooting gallery, and now that they were happy and high with a few grains for extras still on them, he was going to bust them for possession. He was a narc. He had watched them for days, probably years, waiting, just waiting for the new drug laws to go into effect so that he could hook them in, and now he had them. Real shitfit, the Dude thought, I'm having a real shitfit . . . *but there was no place to hide.*

No place at all to go: he was naked, exposed upon the street, under observation from a hundred, two hundred people, and then, as if this were happening on some other street, a street with which he had no connection whatsoever, there was a roar, *gunfire*, the Dude thought, son of a bitch, that's gunfire, and looking in that direction, leaning toward the right, he saw Animal holding out a low-caliber pistol, already into the second shot: where the hell had he gotten the pistol *from*? Well this did not matter, nothing mattered, the Dude urged his legs to run, get out of there, work it all out later, but his legs were gelatinous, nothing was happening there at all, and so he could only stay rooted in posture, then, locked in position. The gun Animal was holding went off for the third time, but the big white motherfucker, untouched by any of the shots, seemingly invulnerable, possibly immortal, suddenly went inside of himself for a gun of his own, and then as the Dude watched, unable to move, unable to locate that heart of desire that would enable him to confront the situation at all, the white motherfucker fired off his own pistol, and the Dude did not have to verify, did not have to look, did not have to swing his attention to the right to know the truth that had burst within his brain, the final inescapable truth of it, that the shot had hit Animal dead on, and that the Animal was croaking, choking, smoking, singing out his life on this damned street, his body suspended against the cushions of the Electra, and there was nothing whatsoever for him to do then but to watch this as the white man lifted his gun yet again and pumped the second, unnecessary shot into the corpse, staining and ribboning with blood the interior of the car.

They were everywhere. There was nothing you could do to stop them. They would follow you and follow you and then they would kill you off. Overcome by a spasm of weeping, the Dude fell into the sidewalk, then, screaming into the stones while everything went on outside him, and for all the impression that it made on him, he might have been on another world, and all these creatures were aliens.

Horse-high.

Teach him to fuck around with it.

III

"No," Gianelli said, "don't tell me I can't do it. I want to get him."

"Too risky," Miller said. He was trying to be reasonable about this, trying to maintain his sense of balance, but fifteen minutes with Gianelli was half an hour in the ring with the heavyweight champion. He did not know if he could take the constant battering any more. "No, you can't do it."

"I'm going to do it," Gianelli said. He squeezed his hands into, then against one another. "I want to and I know I can do it. I'm going to." He showed Miller the .45 again. "With this," he said, "I can handle anything: the heavy stuff, the light stuff, but this is right. I'm going to do it."

Miller shook his head, stood, walked to the window. Hilton Hotel, seventeen stories up. There was a good view of Central Park from certain rooms here, he understood, but he wasn't in that class. Transient trade; no credentials. "I don't want you to do it," he said. "In the first place, no one's sure of where he is, and in the second—"

"He's in New York," Gianelli said. He was a pale, squat man in his sixties who claimed to have known the late Nicholas Calabrese from way back and to have once sworn a blood oath with him: if either was murdered, the other one would avenge that death. Of course, that had been a long time ago; Calabrese had gone one way, Miller another, Gianelli still a third. And Gianelli was in the worst position of all because Miller, who figured he knew everyone, did not know Gianelli. Hired muscle, he supposed, or on the fringes acting as a runner, but at sixty how much muscle, how much running, could a man do? Still, there was Gianelli back from the dead or from Kansas City, which was practically the same thing, swearing he could locate Burton Wulff and avenge the death of his old, great friend, Nicholas Calabrese. What was

Miller supposed to do? It isn't worth it, he thought: Calabrese's death, what he left behind him, was sloppy enough; there was no reason why he should have to deal with loose ends like Gianelli as well. Still, the man was here: what was he supposed to do with him?

"How do you know he's in New York," he said.

"He's got to be in New York," Gianelli said, "I've figured this out, there's nowhere else he could be. This is what he knows best, this is where his contacts all are, this is where he figures is the absolutely last place that anyone would be looking for him. He wouldn't be anywhere else. And I know I can find him."

"No one's found him yet," Miller said. "There are a thousand men looking for him."

"That's all right," said Gianelli. He cocked and uncocked the .45, giving Miller the uneasy feeling that he was going to discharge it at any moment, then in a spasmodic gesture put it back in his pocket. "Listen," Gianelli said, "I'm not asking for very much. Am I asking for a hell of a lot? Let me go out on my own, that's all."

"With a couple of men," Miller said. "Don't forget that; you're asking for a couple of men. Otherwise you're not asking for anything." Except the impossible, he thought. He looked down the airshaft, seventeen stinking levels down into the polluted hole that New York had become. Sixth Avenue, Broadway, it was all garbage. They had torn the great city apart. "And what's to say he's in New York at all?"

"He's in New York. I know he's here. I know how that man thinks; I spent weeks just thinking about him, reading up, familiarizing myself. He's uptown, probably around Harlem, and I can get him," Gianelli said. "I want to get him very badly."

"We all want to get him very badly."

"I'll do it. I'll put him out of business."

"It's too late," Miller said. "It's too late to worry about that. I'm not in New York to deal with him, I know that. I'm trying to put this thing together again."

"That's right," Gianelli said standing, going over to the window, standing shoulder-to-shoulder then with Miller, "you're trying to put the whole thing together because he's hurt all of you bad, he's changed the whole setup, you've got to get reorganized straight from the top, find new routes, get hold of new supplies. You think I'm a fool? I know all that."

"So don't say it. Say nothing."

"You're afraid to send me out," Miller said, "because you know that I can get him and I'll show the rest of you up. I'll show up your fifty-million-dollar organization for the fools and shits they are. One man, just one man with a gun and a couple behind him is going to deliver him in ribbons to your door. You wouldn't like that, would you? It would make all of you look like shit. So you'll send me back to the provinces, won't you? That's what I figure."

Miller could not take that. There were certain things that you could take, were bound to, others that you could not if you were trying to run or as in this case, desperately hold together, an organization. He slapped Gianelli flatly across the mouth, a dull, hollow, single impact.

Gianelli took it, his face broadening under the impact, his eyes springing involuntary tears. Otherwise, he remained impassive.

"Don't say that," Miller said, "don't you ever say that again."

"I'm not here to talk," Gianelli said, cautiously rubbing his cheek as if it were someone else's; this is not happening to *me*, his eyes said, someone else, some phantom Gianelli stands in this room being slapped around, the real Gianelli is merely observing this from a far distance. He wouldn't be any part of it. The real Gianelli would not undergo such humiliation. "I'm not here to talk," he said again, "I don't want to talk. Are you going to let me go after him?"

"I don't know," Miller said, "it depends. Why don't you give me your information and let *us* go after him?"

"No. It's not information anyway, it's just a feeling. I've got a feeling for this guy, I've studied him, I know his moves, where he probably is. But it's nothing I can tell you."

"We won't give you any men," Miller said. "We've lost enough men going after him. This time we're not going to take any risks at all."

"All right," Gianelli said, the knowledge sinking into him that he was going to get almost nothing. "So I don't get any men. I don't get any help. Then all I want is permission."

"Permission for what?"

"Permission to work in your territory. Permission to kill him. That is all I want."

"It's a free country," Miller said, "I can't stop you."

"No, but you can make things very unpleasant for a man operating without your permission. I know about such things," Gianelli said. "I am, after all, not any kind of a fool and I know how these things are done. If you will not give me help, you must at least give me permission so that I can avenge my old friend."

"Listen," Miller said, turning to face the window, back from the window and to Gianelli, who was now rubbing his palms together, his eyes bright and somehow limitless in their apprehension. Miller saw small, doomed images of himself pinned in those eyes, blinking, blinking, blinking away. "Now listen, Calabrese wasn't killed. Calabrese, I mean, he was *killed* all right but not by Wulff. There was no sabotage on that plane, the indications were that it just went down—"

"No difference," Gianelli said loudly, waving a hand, and Miller began to feel the focus of the conversation shift, now he was no longer in control: how had he lost control of this? It had been he who had slapped Gianelli the petitioner. Now it was Gianelli who controlled the room. "No difference, he sent my old friend to his death as surely as if he had pulled a gun on him; he was responsible for his going to Miami, he was responsible for bringing my old friend to this position, he put him on that plane, and he made him die. You know nothing of honor or vengeance," he said, little white streaks appearing on his face, "you know nothing of these qualities; you come from a generation that laughs at these qualities, mocks them, makes the words stand for something that is only cause for laughter," Gianelli said, and he was suddenly quite powerful, the dominance in the room was no longer something that Miller merely imagined. It was a physical fact. Gianelli looked years younger, his body seemed distended to great proportions, his face alive with youth—or merely energy, it was difficult to tell, they could have been the same thing. "This is for my old friend, Nicholas, and it is not for you to stand between the two of us. I do not do it for profit," he said, "I do it for honor."

Miller had nothing to say. What could he say? There was no way to respond to the old man. In fact the old man was right, he was now being put into a context that had nothing to do with the way he regarded life, tried to run it. Life for Miller was a numbers proposition, input here, output there, balance the books, try to make every loss a gain in the long run, try to stuff the gains to cover up the losses. That was management, that was what the organization was all about now in the seventies—just holding on, declaring your position, and trying to maintain it. Passion did not enter into Miller's calculations, nor did vendetta.

Calabrese's death was a disaster, of course, but a disaster that could be calculated down to the last decimal and had mainly to do with the convulsions that would be taking the Midwest in the wake of his death, the need to put the Midwest slowly, painfully together again. That was all that Calabrese's death meant; considered objectively you had to recognize the fact that the old man was seventy-three, that good health or not he was reaching toward the end of his years and that within the next five or ten the convulsions would have started anyway, possibly worse because like all the old-line men Calabrese would be trying to pass on a line of succession, and that simply did not work these days. The outfit would not sit still for it. So there would have been a power struggle, the Midwest would split into factions, the factions would crawl and slash, and in due time peace would be declared, but six or ten months might have passed by and much business would have been interrupted. It was better, perhaps, to do it this way: a quick death, a shocking removal, the troops caught completely by surprise, and in that quiet aftermath the organization had a chance to get hold of the Midwest by itself and put its own procedures in with less difficulty than it might have had otherwise.

In truth Miller cared very little about Calabrese's death. The fact of it was important and if his death looked like an attack upon the outfit it would have to be avenged, cruelly, quickly, brutally, if only to make sure that an appearance of weakness was not given. But beyond that it mattered very little. He was not here. It was not Miller's intention to shed tears because a powerful old man had gone down in a plane outside Chicago. The feelings would have to be left to the Gianellis.

"All right," he said, with surprising mildness, considering what he could have done to Gianelli for defying him like this on his own ground. "All right then. If you want to conduct your own search-and-destroy mission, that's all right with us."

Gianelli's face fell in upon itself, lines seeking lines, toward satisfaction. "Good," he said, "that is very good."

"We cannot protect you."

"I understand that."

"We cannot give you any assistance of any sort, and this is your own vendetta; if you are killed by him or others, you will not be avenged."

"I am sixty-three years old," Gianelli said. "My own life is a matter of indifference."

"All that I can promise you is that you will have safe conduct on our territory as far as we are concerned. You may conduct yourself as you see fit."

"That is what I wanted."

"But we don't control Manhattan," Miller said. "We don't control Harlem, we have only certain officials, certain procedures, certain pockets of business . . . what I am trying to tell you is that this is a violent and dangerous city, and we are as much subject to the violence and danger as anyone. We cannot pledge your protection. This is not any Sicilian village."

"I take no offense at that," Gianelli said. "I appreciate your bluntness."

"We are businessmen," Miller said. "This is a business organization. The time of the blood feuds, of the great wars are over. I am not here to perpetuate them. We are trying to hold together a business operation, that is all."

"I am a man of the times," Gianelli said and granted himself a little smile; here was a man, Miller suspected, who rationed out smiles to himself the way other men rationed out cigarettes or drinks. It was a luxury. "I am a completely realistic man and I know what you are speaking of. You can guarantee nothing. This is a dangerous city."

"So it is," Miller said, "so it is," and found himself losing interest in the conversation now. What did it matter? What did any of this matter? Calabrese was dead, the old fool gone in a downed plane, behind him all the problems of organization and control, bureaucratic charts, levels of approval. All of this was administrative, none of it personal. No time to mourn. From what he had understood, there had been no more than twenty people at the funeral, none of them from the organization. It was not like the old days; funeral attending was not something you wanted to get involved in unless it was something unavoidable, like your own. "So it is," he said, the disinterest lashing at him like the sea, "and now I'd like you to go."

"Very well," Gianelli said, "I think that our business is concluded," and with a little bow, half a salute at the end of it, he let the smile fall away from him like a woman dropping a towel to nakedness and then grimly backed out of the room, retreating step by step, out the door then and into the whispering air-conditioned hallway of the hotel. "Thank you," he said in the doorway, and pulled the door toward him. "I am sorry that you do not have feeling," he said almost apologetically and was gone.

Didn't have any feeling? Did not have any feeling? For a moment Miller felt himself tumbling into a rage so extreme that he could have leapt from the chair and pursued the old bastard down the hall shouting: What do you mean I don't have any feeling? I have plenty of feeling, but business is business! But as quickly as it had hit him, the impulse was gone and he was in his chair thinking: Feeling? What is this about feeling? Didn't the old bastard know that this was a world with which they were dealing, not a dream, and that were it not for Miller and a very, very few like him, that world would rush in, throw tentacles around him and carry all of them from their rooms and corridors to be deposited in the sewage of history? Feeling had nothing to do with it, feeling was entirely beside the point. The question was one of utter control, and toward its maintenance he would let anything, anyone, even Wulff do what they must. If only the situation would remain, for him, cold and focused.

IV

Williams had been passed up the line through a series of interviews, and now one of the deputy commissioners wanted to see him. Williams's case was unusual, exceptional, and no one knew exactly what to do with him. On the one hand he had been a competent patrolman during his time there, and what with the constant racial issue the department did not want to get into anything with those overtones by holding a black man back from reinstatement. But on the other hand, the circumstances under which Williams had summarily left the department, amounting to a defiance of normal procedures, were quite mysterious. On top of that, Williams simply would not talk about them at all. Why he had left, what he had done during those two months was his business and none of the department's. He had told this to the personnel sergeant, he had told it up the line to the lieutenants, and now he had been bucked up to the deputy commissioner. And on top of all that, there was the news item today about that murder in Harlem and the grenade thrown through a storefront that turned out to be a shooting gallery. Williams needed no prodding to know who had done *that* work.

Nor did the department. The department people weren't fools. They read the papers and they had their contacts in the underworld. Even the new, fancy, modern, computerized NYPD made out in the same old ways, scruffing around with informants and informants on the informants, and they were pretty well briefed on what Wulff's activities had been over the past six months, right up to this latest one, which was clearly his modus operandi and meant that the man was back in the city. The NYPD wanted him very badly. And for a number of reasons, they had gotten it into their heads that Williams had had some contact with him, that as a matter of fact, his mysterious AWOL might have been directly tied to Wulff, that he might have spent that period of time in his presence. The department was very anxious to find out everything they could about Wulff. Getting him was not only a matter of pride. For one thing they didn't even know if they had that much to stick him with. No, it went much deeper than that. Wulff was conducting a vigilante campaign, which in essence was pointing out every step of the way that the authorities had lost control of the situation, but that a single, grim, determined man with a multiplicity of techniques might be able to do the job that they had failed to do for decades, to make real inroads against the drug traffic. This was not the kind of news with which the authorities were completely pleased, and the fact that Wulff had started off in the NYPD made him in a sense their responsibility, gave them an unusual interest in the case, just as a group of alumni might have a morbid interest in the activities of a fraternity brother.

So they wanted Wulff very badly, and they pretty much had the idea that Williams was a lead into him. Even so, Williams might have gotten away with it, not felt the really heavy pressure. Except that the incident in Harlem was the clear giveaway that Wulff was somehow back in town and operating in the old fashion. That, with the colliding circumstance that Williams was also in town, just trying desperately to be reinstated and to get back to where he had been six months ago before what he liked to think of as the madness hit him. That was all the department needed.

The deputy commissioner, a short man with surprisingly long and graceful hands, hands that he rubbed incessantly as if he were kneading clay, looked at him with a bright and rising glare of interest as Williams sat before him, and then he looked down at the papers on his desk. They were in his office, which despite all the rumored improvements in the PD over recent years was as scruffy as anything Williams remembered from movies taking place in the old precincts—paint coming off the walls in small, dismal chips, a cluttered desk, a window with bars that looked out on a courtyard where trainees were going through some kind of a crash emergency evacuation and riot control course, complete with clubs and screams. This deputy commissioner, Williams remembered vaguely, had been a member of the opposition party; appointed as some kind of political payoff. It stood to reason that his facilities would not be of the best. Administrations had a way of changing, so did deputy commissioners, but this office would go on and on. Nothing changed. The cities were run by civil servants functioning out of offices like this, and the politicians could have all the rhetoric they wanted; the civil servants would just grunt in their shabby little offices, shrug, and go on with their paperwork. The paint chips would continue to fall off the walls, the roaches would scuttle, the battered fluorescent lights would hum, and New York City would slide off into the sea. But those who were sinking would do it on full career and salary plan.

"I don't know anything about him," Williams said for about the fiftieth time since he had started shuffling through the reinstatement route, the third time in this office this morning. It averaged eight to ten denials an interview. "All I know is what I read."

"We don't seem to think so," the deputy commissioner said. He looked at a sheet of paper lying on the top of the stack, took it off, smoothed it, then passed it across to Williams. "I've gotten a memo on this man," he said. "It's going all through the department."

Williams looked at the memo about Wulff with some interest. Apparently compiled by the police intelligence division, or what passed for an intelligence division, it dealt with a reconstruction of Wulff's activities since he had left the patrol car and the force. The work, all things considered was surprisingly accurate, although there were gaps in it, and they had missed a lot of the details as well as the relationship with the girl. He thought of the girl, Tamara, and a vision of Miami came back, the corpses littered on the sands, the girl's body among them, blood draining from her body, Wulff standing over her, Williams trying to pull him away. He pushed the image away, squeezing his eyes shut, handed the memo back to the deputy. "I don't see what that has to do with me," he said carefully.

"According to this you were with him, at least in Los Angeles."

"No," Williams said. "I don't know anything about that. I wasn't with him. I haven't seen him since that night on patrol."

"People don't accept that," the deputy said, his voice showing some irritation. He was obviously one of those men who prided themselves on their absolute control of situations. But the voice was breaking; it seemed that the deputy commissioner had made something close to a calculated decision to go *out* of control. "And I don't accept that either. I think that you've had contact with this guy."

"Not for a long time."

"He's back in the city," the deputy said. "Everybody knows that. Now that blowup in Harlem, that's clearly his kind of operation. The question I want to have answered is what is he going to do next?"

"I don't know what he's going to do next," Williams said. The thing to do was to cultivate a kind of flat calm, a patience, the same technique they taught you for interrogation: hit the same points over and over again, and after a while they might be so convinced you were stupid that they would cave in and let something enormous slip. "I don't know anything about his plans at all. I was with this guy for one night of patrol car duty, you know that. We took a call about a girl on a drug o.d. in the west nineties, and he went up and investigated it; after awhile, when he didn't come down, I thought I'd better get up there too and have a look. I go up there and I find him—"

"Yes," the deputy said, "yes, yes, we've heard all that; that's the same story we've been through time and again. I don't find that acceptable. There are some pretty reliable reports that you were seen with him out in Los Angeles, that you joined him out there, that this explains your absence. I don't have to tell you that this is a serious thing you're involved in; you were aiding the commission of a felony. Now—"

Williams looked at a large picture on the wall. The picture, the only adornment in the room, aside from the cracked and falling paint and the bars on the windows, showed the deputy commissioner shaking hands with the present mayor of New York City, the background indicating that it was a political banquet of some sort; tables, a middle-aged woman in a strapless evening gown who might have been the deputy's wife staring bleakly through huge-framed glasses through the small space opened between the mayor and the deputy. Both mayor and deputy looked uncomfortable, but for different reasons: the mayor appeared to be trying to break the handshake, wondering if the picture had already been taken, while the deputy was desperately holding on as if for dear life, wedging his hand into the mayor's, an expression of strain and pain in his eyes that might have been from trying to hold the contact or from the middle-aged woman in the evening gown. It was hard to tell. Williams supposed that if he kept on looking at the picture it would, bit by bit, yield up all kinds of insights about the deputy commissioner that in the long run he could do without. It was in full color, badly framed, and seemed to be swaying on the wall, although this was hardly possible, the air in the room being dense and absolutely static. "Listen here," he said, the photograph giving him a kind of frame for conviction. The deputy's position was as tenuous as his own; this photograph was so painful that beads of sweat seemed to be coming off it; it was impossible to conceive of the deputy as being anything other than what Williams was, a man in severe trouble. "Listen here now, I'm twenty-six years old and I've got a wife and a mortgage and I've just had a baby son—"

"I know all about that. Congratulations."

"And I've got to put my life together," Williams said. "I'm in a whole lot of trouble and I admit it; I shouldn't have taken the walk that I did, but I was very confused and I had my reasons."

"We know you had your reasons."

"Let me finish!" Williams said, his voice shaking to a kind of passion, and the deputy retreated, put both hands on his desk, pushed himself away imperceptibly but in a way that for Williams was a signal that he had temporarily gained some kind of control. "I admit that I made a mistake, and I'm the first one to say it, but does a man have to live all his life in shame because he's made one mistake? Does a whole life have to rest on one decision? I want to get back; I admit I was wrong but it didn't seem wrong at the time, and I'm willing to apologize and come back. I'm not asking for any favors, but there's a hell of a lot of training and experience that I've got tied up in me and you can't send it down the drain." Crawl you bastard, he thought. Go on and crawl. Still, what alternative did he have? He even more than the deputy knew how limited his options had become. If it wasn't the police department, what was his alternative? Send his wife back to work in a department store, take care of the baby during the days and tend night bar? That was promising. That was really promising for a guy who two years ago thought he had the game beat: you would join the system and make it work for you, laugh at all of them from behind the career and salary plan. Oh, he had learned a few things all right. He had learned a few goddamned things; the trouble was that everything that he had learned he would have been better off not knowing. "I'm asking for a chance," he said, loathing himself. "I'm entitled to a chance."

"You're entitled to nothing," the deputy said mildly, "nothing at all. But we're not out to punish people. We're not out to humiliate here; we're trying to save people."

Sure you are, Williams thought furiously, that's exactly what the PD is in, the people-salvation business. But he said nothing, merely looked at the man impassively. Nothing, nothing to say. Sooner or later you had to learn to keep your mouth shut.

"I'll offer you a deal," the deputy said, "but I don't know whether you'll be interested or not. If you're telling the truth you'll probably be interested, but if you're not you won't be."

"What deal?" Williams said and almost added, swab out latrines in the sixty-second precinct for a couple of months just to prove my loyalty to the department? Or maybe I should go out in a black T-shirt and jeans, prowl Forty-Second Street, go out on the fag patrol to get broken in. But again he said nothing. Shutting up was easy once you made a discipline of it. He should have tried it months ago.

"We're putting together a special squad," the deputy said and ran his fingers over the memo he had shown Williams, "trying to put together a special squad to find this man."

"Wulff?"

"Wulff," the deputy said flatly. "You know who I mean. He's an embarrassment to the department, and in many senses he's a departmental responsibility. He comes from New York and if certain things had been handled differently by us he never would have been in business in the first place." He looked at the ceiling, gave a half shrug. "That's neither here nor there," he said. "I'm not discussing whether we were right or wrong in handling him that way. As you know I wasn't here when all of this happened. I was appointed only three months ago. We're putting together an elite squad, some of the best men we can find, heavy weapons men, intelligence operators, men experienced in intelligence work, keeping it small and compact, trying to keep it to ten men. And I think that you could be useful on it. You have first-hand knowledge of the man, his habits, his modus operandi. For one thing you were out in Los Angeles with him."

"No," Williams said, "I was not."

The deputy stared at him, and Williams held the gaze until he could no longer, looked away, past the photograph, swinging his gaze toward the gates covering the window. No, the man was no fool. He had to face that; the photograph, the particulars of his appointment might show that the deputy was as human and fallible as any of them except Wulff himself, but this did not mean that the man was a fool. On a certain level he had his own control, own self-awareness, enough insight. Williams could not look this man in the eye and tell him that he had not been with Wulff in Los Angeles. For all its weaknesses the PD had compiled a pretty good dossier on Wulff, better than it would have been credited with achieving. Keep quiet. Keep your mouth shut. At a certain point forbearance was the only tool left in the arsenal. "I just don't know," Williams said, "I just don't know what to say about that."

"You don't want to be on the squad? You don't want to be responsible for finding your friend?"

"That's not it," Williams said.

"I think that is it. I think that's exactly what you have in mind. Do I have to spell it out for you, patrolman? This is a man who has murdered some five hundred people in six months, all of them for what he considers to be good purposes, but that does not mean that he is anything but a dangerous killer. The end does not justify the means, and as long as a man of this sort is on the loose it means that no one is safe, not only criminals, but all of us, because escalating violence involves many innocent people and also creates a state of consciousness where there is increasingly more violence."

"I know that."

"Do you really know it? Secretly in your heart of hearts, your sympathies are with Wulff. You think that he's doing a wonderful job, that he's doing a job about the only way that it could be done, because bureaucracy can't deal with criminal control and in many respects is part of the criminal system. Don't you believe that, patrolman?"

"I try not to think about that," Williams said. "I don't want to think about the ethics of the thing any more."

"Oh, you do," the deputy said, his voice rising, leaning across the desk, "you do so believe. In your heart of hearts, you have a secret admiration for this man. You may feel that his methods are a little too violent, but you and a good many police officers like to feel deep down that this is the right way to approach the situation: vigilantism, murder, that Wulff is making fools of the authorities because they can't do the job and he can by going outside the normal processes of law and order that hold our society together. That's what law and order is, Williams, not an excuse for beating heads, like certain politicians like to say in code; law and order is that fabric of rules and manners and understandings and codes that hold together a large, unhappy, polarized society such as we have today and make it possible for people to live their lives. And your man is attacking all of this; he is turning life back into a jungle, and every cop, *any* cop who believes in his heart that he's right, who is secretly rooting him on, that cop is killing himself because he's cheering on a situation in which that cop will stand for nothing, in which any man with the price of a gun and what he thinks is a set of reasons can kill that cop, make life hell for all cops."

"Listen," Williams said, mildly enough, "he's not my man. You've got this thing wrong—"

"Your man, my man, what does it matter?" the deputy said. "Listen, we're not fools, there's a great deal of Wulff-sympathy in this PD and in departments all through the country. Don't you think we know that? We've learned from informants that cops in certain cities have had information from sources that he was coming in their direction, plenty of time to mobilize for his coming, anticipate his moves, stop him if they could. But they did nothing because a lot of cops—I mean highly placed cops, men at the top levels—think he's fighting their battles, and as far as they're concerned he's taking the heat off them, taking off the pressure, maybe doing a job too dirty and risky for them. But they're crazy! This isn't enforcement, this is vigilantism, and this isn't a vigilante country any more." The deputy tapped the desk three times earnestly, more conviction in his face and voice than Williams had seen, more than he would have suspected. He could understand, at least was beginning to understand, why this man might have political connections and talent. Furthermore, he had a point. Definitely he had a point. As between Wulff attacking the system and Williams once believing in it, neither of them was completely right, but it was possible that Williams had been more right than Wulff. Because once you went outside the system you had nothing. Not righteousness, not an end to corruption, but simply *nothing*: death. The system was man's way of imposing some order, no matter how perilous, upon the essential void of reality. And this thought was too difficult for him, Williams did not want to face it, there was no end to the trouble you inherited if you started charging down channels like this because you might end up believing that anything was better than that void, any corruption, any pain, any madness, simply so that you would not have to face the darkness of no choices at all. Enough. Enough.

"Do you see what I'm saying?" the deputy was going on, apparently having continued even more passionately while Williams had been charging into his own subterranean channels. "You can't have it both ways. You can't hate the system and cheer on a man who's in effect destroying it and yet working for it at the same time. It's one or the other. Your problem is that you wanted it both ways; you wanted to be a cop because you thought it was a good living, a safe job, decent pay, good pension, but at the same time underneath you hated the system you were supporting. You thought you could be a double agent, Williams, you thought that you could have it one way on the outside and another on the inside. But it doesn't work that way. You found that out, didn't you? You found out a few things."

"I found out a few things," Williams said, "I am not denying that."

"The question is," the deputy said, "will the inoculation take or was it just a booster shot, a temporary injection with no staying power?"

Williams looked at him and at that moment felt all evasion and deception drop from him as if they had been a cloak he had been carrying around for twenty-six years. Free of it now, feeling the breezes of these new thoughts closing around him, it was as if he had not been conscious of the weight of that cloak until it had fallen. "I don't know," he said, "I can't answer that. But I do see what you're saying. I really do."

"He's up to it again," the deputy said. "He's back in town, and it's going to be the same thing all over again. This business in Harlem is just the beginning if we don't stop him, and I mean stop him now. You see, there's just not going to be any end to it. There's never a cutoff point. And no man, not even Burton Wulff, is in a position to make judgments as to how much is enough."

"All right," Williams said, nodding slowly, "all right, I understand. I understand what you're saying. You want me on your squad? I'll be on your squad."

"But do you want to? Or do you just want to get back on that career and salary plan so desperately that you'll agree to anything just so you can get hold of the tit. Because that isn't going to work. This time, Williams, it isn't going to work."

"I understand," he said, "I understand that. I'll get on the squad. I'll do the best you think I can. I'll give what help I can. I see your point," Williams said, looking up at the photograph, thinking again: this man is no fool; he looks like a fool, in a way sometimes he may act like a fool, he may be in a fool's position, but there is just no saying what the real measure of a man is and, middle-aged woman, stupid handshake and all, he is on the ball. He sees things I have not seen; he has told me things I did not know.

Maybe, he thought, and this was a strange new thought, maybe this deputy commissioner was like everyone else; he had to do things he did not like to do, become something he did not want to be, simply to be in a position where he could get these ideas across to someone and have a small chance of feeling that they were being put into practice. There was no saying what ass a man had to kiss to become a man—or what the ass kissing might in the long run mean; it might mean something entirely different from what it seemed.

Puzzling and confusing; he would have to work it all out, he would have to give it a great deal of thought. "I'll do what I can," he said again and extended his hand across the desk to the deputy. "I'll do what I can," and they shook hands then, the grip in his hand as light and sweaty as he would have thought. But you could not judge a man by his handshake either, or by the number of corpses he was willing to pile high for what he believed to be the justification of his purposes.

He saw the point.

He hated the seeing . . . but it was there.

Wulff had to get back to his quarters to think, had to reconnoiter with himself to see what was going on. But after the attack in Harlem there was almost no time; there was just no way that he could. Once again it was a feeling of events lurching out of control, mindless, insane. From the moment that the one in the Electra had pulled a gun on him, he had seen it all laid out before him, the violence, the necessity to kill, and he had met that with reluctance because he was tired, he had seen enough. And because going back to killing on the streets of Harlem was going back six months to a stage that he thought he had left behind him. If he had accomplished anything in Peru, in Havana, in Miami he had hoped that he had escaped from the shooting galleries of the inner city.

But they would not leave him alone. It had been madness to think that they would; furthermore, he should have realized that reconnoitering Harlem was in a sense asking for it. What was he doing in that blasted land if not seeking, perhaps consciously, more likely unconsciously, exactly this kind of attack? His first reaction had been rage, and he had used that to kill simply, quickly, destroying the man in the car who had shot at him, the other one reeling out crazily, gesticulating, fleeing across the street and into the shooting gallery, and at that moment Wulff had felt all his purposes coalescing: he *knew* why he had come to Harlem and what he had to do next.

Pitching the body of the dead man out of the Electra, he had taken the wheel. It was there, wrenching the car away from the curb, that he had seen that the floor of the car was littered with incendiaries, literally covered with them; these men were not only addicts but pocket revolutionaries of some sort. Amidst the bloodstains tracing out their delicate network on the floor panels of the Buick were small, rolling objects that seemed to be hand grenades, sheathed knives, unsheathed knifes, the disassembled pieces of what seemed to be a small-bore rifle. They had everything covered, these men, no doubt about it. Shoot it in, shoot it up, shoot it out.

They were coming out of the shooting gallery to see what had happened, cautious ones and pairs of them standing there, gesticulating, and at that moment the clear certainty of inspiration had hit Wulff: those were grenades on the floor of the car, and if they were grenades they were meant to be used. It would be pointless not to do so; it would not be a fit memorial to the man he had killed—he wanted to look at it that way—not to put his weapons to some use in his memory. So quickly, impulsively, not even bothering to think it over, he had picked up one from the floor—it was standard army issue—curled it within his palm, a strange, even, even heat radiating from the grenade, and then in one quick, brisk gesture had thrown it twinkling through the air toward the shooting gallery, the grenade twisting in a high arc, and it had hit dead in the storefront in the middle of a bleached and ruined *O* and then in a single *whoomp*! it had gone up.

No time for retreat, no time even to scream; there had been in the faces of those watching him only that one astonished instant of comprehension when they understood what he was going to do, but caught between the grenade and that realization they had not been able to move for the critical two seconds that might have saved them. The fragmentation from the grenade and the concussion had blown the building *within* itself, an implosion rather than explosion. It brought back memories of bodies Wulff had seen in the fields of Vietnam where it had been this way; the incendiaries driving the bodies into themselves so that they had been small, terrible ruined balls of blackened flesh. What a death that must be! driven in upon oneself, the moment of death not even a release but instead burning and blasting within, a seeking of the flesh for its ruined and rotted core!

Wulff had already been driving the Electra frantically, beating out the heart of the machine through that lever on the floor, moving the huge, rotting car through the back streets of Harlem, possessed with the necessity merely to get out of there. He could think of the explosion later. No, he would never think of it again.

There had been no pursuit, but he had not really expected that there would be. What was pursuit? What was the nature of entrapment now that he had bombed out the shooting gallery? These people were not interested in pursuit, they were not geared for it at all, all that they were interested in doing was in shooting the poison through their veins by the quart, and any interruption of that purpose was merely that, an interruption. They would not deal in retaliation No, he was safe, he was dealing with a population so bombed out, so fatigued, self-involved and desperate that there was literally nothing that could not be perpetrated upon them. Harlem was in itself witness to five decades of exploitation by generations of looters, and the map of that precinct was a map of shame; only in movies would Harlem enforcers come speeding out of the ghetto in fast, black cars to locate the thrower of the grenade and bring him to justice, extract small pieces of vengeance out of his flesh. Only in movies would this happen because only in movies was Harlem a community at all, a community that could be expected to gather around and protect its own.

No, no, Harlem was nothing like this at all. Harlem was a concentration camp or a prisoner-of-war compound in which groups of the brutalized milled around in small and smaller packs, each of them seeking only his own preservation. What a million dollars might have been for one of the distributors, what the Presidency of the United States would have been for the governor, so one more fix, one more day was to your run-of-the-mill Harlem junkie. Let the governor have his presidency, let the Calabreses have their million. The junkie would take tomorrow in the same spirit, one more step into the imponderable and unspeakable future. No one was going to pursue him. There was no will to even try.

He would read all about it in the papers.

So Wulff went back in the Electra to his furnished room in the nineties. Parking the Electra in the neighborhood would have been too complicated, and he did not even want to think of what it would have involved to seek garage space for it. The hell with it; he left it as a junker on West Ninety-fifth Street off the river, tearing off the hubcaps and throwing them down the palisades into the stinking, odorous Hudson, ripping off the antenna and laying it on the front seat, smashing in a window with a rock. It would lie there for weeks and weeks; passersby would take it for a car that had been wrecked on the highway and towed off by precinct tow trucks, left there to rot until city pickup and junking could be arranged. The cops would take it for a vandalized car and with their customary dedication would open it up and take anything serviceable out of the engine compartment. The car would sit there until some night when, for the hell of it, a neighborhood pack might throw a match into the gas compartment just to see what would happen, and then the black parody of the car would sit there for a while longer and eventually, after a long time, one of the junkers would get it. In the meantime he had nothing to worry about.

He went back to his room with the gun he had pulled from the man he had killed and with a couple of the grenades he had seen still rolling on the floor of the Electra and had picked up for possible further use. Two flights off the street, behind his police-locked door, Wulff knew that he was on the verge of a decision now, right on the perilous lip of some kind of commitment that would one way or another take him past a point of no return: he could give up, give up utterly, stop it right now when he was ahead, and turn himself in to the police who would not know what the hell to do with him but were bound to give him a sympathetic hearing, probably get him off on a few minor manslaughter charges arranged through the DA. And he would get himself jailed for two to three years, come out and make a new life for himself. Or he could go on, go on the course he had set with this latest attack wherever it would send him.

Two months or even two weeks ago there would have been no choice. He had been committed to his lonely and terrible quest no matter where it would take him. But now, since he had returned to New York, the two-to-three for manslaughter had almost looked tempting at times and for that he cursed himself. It was a hell of a thing that he would actually consider throwing himself upon the mercy of a system that he despised, that he had left exactly because of his hatred for it. But how far could he go? Certainly Miami had been the pivot. *Tamara dead, the drugs gone, Calabrese dead, Williams fled.* It had all seemed pretty pointless if it came down to that death on the beach and he might be better off out of it. Certainly it could be said that he had tried. He had done more to cripple the vermin than anyone since drugs had become the outfit's new toy in the 1960s.

But he had found out in Harlem that this was merely rhetoric, a fancy, something he had conjured up from his fatigue and pain, nothing more, no conviction. Harlem had shown him that now as always that pure, fine, high, dead lust for combat and destruction sang within him; he had listened to its voice calling him as he had attacked the vermin in the car and then the shooting gallery, and the voice had sung high and sweet, had sung out its dreadful purities in language that he could not ignore and that he knew reached him as no voice of reason or caution would. Back in his barren furnished room, pacing between stinking chest, stinking bed, stinking walls, Wulff said, "All right then, I'll do it, I'll *do* it," and saying that had not known what he had said until the import of it struck him, redounding back from those walls, and then he knew; he knew that he had said it and the impact coming back on him slowly, a fist beating upon him like a heart, the rhythm of that fist pounding slow knowledge, and he said, "I'll do it again," awed with himself, at the singleness of that conviction, at the return of the rage and the sense of mission after all he had been through. At this stage he should have known better. Certainly at this stage he should have lost that sense of commitment. But it had been there all the time, all of the time indeed, merely waiting to reclaim him.

But if it had been waiting to reclaim him so be it: he knew what to do next. From Williams, during their week in Los Angeles when they had talked about everything, he had obtained the whereabouts and nature of Father Justice's Brotherhood of Divinity and Truth Church, the storefront in Harlem behind which was a weapons shop of such awesome selection and range as to make even an infantry commanding officer turn envious. To Father Justice he went to load up on new armaments. He knew that there would be a great deal of trouble with this. In the first place, going back to Harlem after the attack on the shooting gallery was risky altogether, highly risky; and in the second place, Father Justice had leased out a large amount of ordnance to Williams on an 80 percent refund basis. This Williams had had swiped from him when Calabrese's troops had waylaid him and his U-haul on the desert on his return trip from Los Angeles. Father Justice could not be too happy about having lost so much ordnance. Williams had paid for it all, of course, and the good reverend had no claim whatsoever upon it. But if Wulff thought he knew this business as well as he did, Father Justice was not really in sales; he was in the rental business, and he could not look too kindly upon the loss of all this rare, valuable, and powerful material whether it had been paid for in full or not.

Still, no doubt about it. If he was going to go on, he was going to have to load up, and as far as loading up was concerned, Father Justice was the only place in the vicinity that he knew about. The good reverend had the goods, that was for sure. Perhaps Wulff could best risk it by not letting on that he had any connection with Williams at all. That made it a question of a single white man going up to Harlem and asking for ordnance in quantities. That, too, Wulff suspected was not Father Justice's kind of thing. Father Justice, a black revolutionary, dedicated and megalomaniacal, according to Williams anyway, was not in the business of leasing out guns to white men. This would get him nowhere; at best it would give him a sermon on conversion to the ways of righteousness and peace.

Better to lay it on the line, then.

He went up there very cautiously, checking out the terrain as if it were a foreign combat zone before he came out of the subway at 137th Street, reconnoitering carefully from that vantage point, moving uptown then exactly as one would infiltrate an enemy zone, high alertness, careful positioning, the willingness to use any part of the terrain for camouflage or cover, no matter how painful or awkward. He was ducking into storefronts, hopping buses, watching carefully in all directions as he made a sidelong, careful, circuitous passage uptown to the place where Williams had told him the storefront was. When he got there, looking at the dusty, shabby, decaying boards, the street almost deserted, the street in fact absolutely deserted as a young, terrorized female welfare worker, carrying her casebook under her arm tap-tapped her way up a wrecked brownstone and trembling into the lobby, Wulff had a moment of doubt, doubt piled upon indecision, the idea of going into this storefront, seeking arms from a lunatic seemed somehow appalling. But he drove through the point of indecision, shaking it off desperately and rammed his hand into the smashed boards of the Brotherhood Church.

The storefront was decorated with religious symbols, little aphorisms, scrawled posters announcing the date of the next prayer meeting, the social club, the breakfast club, the revival society. Religiosity and crime stalked together in the inner city, Wulff thought, both of them heightened and irrational, both of them somehow as bizarre to the nestled inhabitants of the suburbs as might be the nature of an alien star (except that the inhabitants of the suburbs knew enough to be scared to death). And it would take a greater writer or politician, certainly a greater thinker than he to point out that the two of them were the same: crime and religiosity, both of them somehow mystical over-reactions to an unbearable present. Any cop knew that, any cop's knowledge could inhabit and encompass the despair of these streets; but insight was not enough, there would have to be a way to frame it and to frame too the realization that drugs and religiosity were also the same thing, at least in their intended effects, a trip, a trip out, an effective journey out of self and into some area where connection and control reappeared, the same connection and control that were lacking in the lives that brought the penitent to this position.

But there were differences, of course. In the drug culture there were very few doubters, disbelievers, or reluctant attendees.

Drugs made fanatics of them all.

The door was opened by a black man in his mid-forties, black, black, black as the darkness, that darkness of his skin so intense that it might have been light. He was wearing a turban and religious garb of some sort, mottled pastels, and in his eyes danced a strange and merry light. He looked at Wulff appraisingly for a while and said, "The church is closed for the festival season."

"I would like to come in and discuss something with you," Wulff said.

"That may be very true," the black man said, "that you wish to have a discussion, but as I say, the church is closed until the conclusion of the festivals and also it is a specifically African, that is to say a pan-African institution. I do not believe that you would be interested in the teachings of the church or that it would speak to your condition."

Wulff moved forward against the black man, stood there feeling the heat radiating from his body, and it occurred to him that there was no way to physically overpower the man. He had run up against a resilience and determination that simply could not be overcome. You might be able to kill Father Justice but you could not overpower him. "I pass onto you the blessings of peace and of this great festival of the moon," Justice said. "I share with you our thoughts for universal connection and brotherhood at the end of this holiday, and now if you will pardon me I must return to meditations."

"My name is Wulff. I know David Williams," Wulff said and added quickly when the black man's eyes remained dead, "the man who was here weeks ago to buy a lot of ordnance. He's my partner. He was bringing that stuff out to me."

"I do not believe I know what you are talking of," Father Justice said. "We do not sell or deal in ordnance in this church, this church is a church of God. Also," he said after a judicious little pause, "not only do we not deal in ordnance, but this man who you say you know who I am not conceding for a moment that I have ever heard of, in the hypothetical instance that he existed, he has failed the mission. He has failed his brotherly and spiritual duties by a failure to return any of this ordnance."

"I wanted to talk to you about that."

"I believe there is very little to talk about."

"You're Father Justice," Wulff said. "Listen, I know you quite well through Williams. I know that you—"

"I think," Father Justice said, "that you had better come in. The street is not the proper place for concourse or devotions of any sort," and stepped aside. Wulff saw looming blackness. He walked into it, a light flicked, and he found himself in a surprisingly large room, benches front to back, seating capacity of fifty penitents at least, religious ornaments dangling from the walls. One of them, a huge, golden crucifix seemingly suspended by invisible threads from the ceiling, particularly fascinated Wulff. As he looked at it, it seemed to glint, glow, change colors. He began to feel very much out of his own area of specialization, which was a peculiar way indeed to feel.

Father Justice noted Wulff staring at the crucifix and said, "His mercy and his love is everlasting and evermore and this, as you see, is a concrete symbol of that everlasting mercy and love. Some of our congregation need concrete symbols to reinforce their feelings, but those of us truly in the church know that he is within, rather than without us." He brought his hands together, looked at Wulff in a peculiar and intense way and said, "There have been difficulties with this Williams you claim to know. He has betrayed the Church of the Brotherhood."

"Everything was hijacked out West. He was kidnapped."

"I am afraid that kidnapping is a personal problem. I am concerned with the, ah, materials that you say have been lost."

"As I understood it, he paid for those materials in full."

"The Church of Brotherhood is never paid in full," the reverend said. "Any recompense that we may take for our materials is far, far less than their actual value. In truth, we lend our materials, we do not sell them, much as the trinity lends or leases out the soul to us, to reclaim it at the moment of death. You understand that it is impossible to pay in kind for the receipt of materials." His hands came apart. "I was expecting, in short, their return."

"I'm sorry," Wulff said, "I'm sure that Williams is sorry too. But we can't be accountable—"

"Everybody is accountable!" Father Justice said loudly. He seemed to expand, rise six inches or more, his robes, falling to the floor gave a further illusion of ascension as if he were floating, suspended, within his ecclesiastic garb, moving, drifting now at off-angles to the crucifix. He looked at it with reverence. "In this world or out of it, all of us are truly accountable for our deeds and our acts. Nothing is lost, nothing is forgotten, nothing is misplaced in the giant eye of the Creator who gave breath to us all. I do not think that there is any comfort or mission I can offer you."

"I'm quite willing to—"

Father Justice made a dismissive gesture. "We do not deal in earthly goods here; we do not accept the symbols or tokens of mammon but seek a higher, a finer, a truer and if I may say a somewhat denser truth. One load of ordnance has already been lost. I cannot risk the loss of another. Also," he said, giving Wulff a look of loathing, "we are a ministry of the community and for the African, that is to say, pan-African peoples. I would not care to deal with a member of your race, a member of that sect of devils who through time immemorial, through all of known and unknown history have turned their hands against my brothers."

"I need a machine gun," Wulff said, "I need a good machine gun with full clip, an extra set of clips, and an M-15 rifle with silencer. I'm willing to pay two thousand."

Father Justice stepped back, looked at Wulff in an even way again, that cool, contained gaze flickering between crucifix and Wulff. Then he brought his hands together in that gesture again, touching the fingertips delicately against one another as if preparing to incline for prayer. "I am afraid you do not understand," he said. "We are not dealing with earthly considerations here; we are dealing with a finer, higher, darker creed, one which unites all of my brothers—"

"Twenty-five hundred dollars," Wulff said, "and not a penny more. And for that I want it to be good, dependable stuff. You'll probably never see it again but I'm taking that into account and paying you at least fifteen hundred dollars more than it's worth."

Father Justice shook his head. "You do not understand," he said, "the risks of prayer, the risks of dedication to the unearthly spirit, to the spreading and the gathering and the annealing and the dispensation of the word—"

"Twenty-six hundred dollars," Wulff said. "No more. That's all."

"I see," Father Justice said. "I see." He bent, looked at the floor as if seeking some kind of meditative answer, some equation that would wrench him past a moment of crisis, and then he said very gently, "It will be necessary for us to seek the answer to this prayer in the back room. We will have to retire into the holy of holies for further meditation and consideration and hope that therein we will find the answer."

He turned, walked back toward the wall, touched it with a delicate gesture and suddenly there was a panel that splayed open, another panel buckling with it, and there was a man-sized entrance into a huge, dark cavity behind. Quickly, gracefully, the reverend walked through it, Wulff following, and Wulff found himself in an odorous, enormous room, rich smells of wood and metal around him. As his eyes adjusted to the light, Wulff saw that he was in the largest arms cache he had ever seen in his life. From shelves piled to the ceiling fifty yards from him downrange in any direction, were the glinting aspects of ordnance: ordnance of all forms, of all apparent stages of modern history: here were hand grenades from the world wars piled neatly atop one another: here were M-1 rifles, the old dependables from World War II and Korea; shading off in the rear were the modern, repeating M-15s; there were incendiaries of the most sophisticated type used in Vietnam; a little bit closer were clumsier bayonets of the type that had inhabited every barracks since the First World War.

Remarkable. It was absolutely remarkable. Williams had not been kidding, all right; Father Justice had a cache here like nothing he had ever before seen. Conceivably army supply centers in the ordnance depots were stocked like this, but in civilian life, of which Father Justice could be considered to be a part, you would have to go long and hard to see a stockpile like this.

It would have made a religious man of the most avid skeptic, just to see what prayer and devotion had accomplished for Father Justice in this warehouse.

"Twenty-six hundred dollars is insufficient," Father Justice said, coldly. His manner once he had entered the room had changed entirely. The mask of the divine had fallen from the good reverend's face and had been replaced with seamless lines of perception and purpose. "You must think that we are fools here to sell to a white man in the first place," Justice said, "and in the second, that is ridiculous compensation for the risk involved. How do I know who you are? How can I know for what purposes you're going to use this stuff? Five thousand."

"Forget it," Wulff said. "I can't come near that."

"Where are you going to better the price? Can you go down the block, find another supplier?"

"Five thousand is ridiculous. Four thousand would be. I just made you top offer. Twenty-six hundred."

"No."

"Then why invite me back here at all?" Wulff said. "You wouldn't have asked me to step into this room unless you saw something in my offer, some territory to be explored." He paused, put down an urge to light a cigarette, looked instead at the glinting, terrible contents of the room and said, "Three thousand. But that's the last. I won't go any higher than that."

"Three thousand is a small contribution to the temple of the holy spirit."

"Three thousand is the top," Wulff said, "that's the limit for what I'm asking. I'm not asking for an army's worth of stuff, you know." Rage was overtaking him. This was the way it had been now for a long time, drift along, go through the motions, try to do the best you could reasonably, taking it step by step and a sudden stab of revulsion, some aspect in the enemy's eyes, some quirk in the situation would trigger off an eruption from the layers of grief and rage buried within, his perilous control over himself would lapse, and perhaps that would throw the adversary more than any calculation could; perhaps the adversary, looking at what this did to Wulff would suddenly realize that he had moved past the point of manipulation and could no longer dissemble. Hard to say. Hard to know. Looking at Father Justice, seeing the quickening and confusion in those eyes, Wulff began to see the phenomenon work again, that phenomenon of reversal when the adversary felt the situation beginning to slide away at cross-angles, something in his eyes like the very light of religion himself. Why, the man might indeed be a reverend, that might be the secret of his power, his conviction, guns for the eyes of the Lord. Justice said, "That is a ridiculous sum. And from a white man, to accept this kind of money from a white man is suicidal. Nevertheless I am going to do it."

"Good," Wulff said.

"I will do it on condition that the materials are returned."

"I can't promise you that. There's no way that I can make you that promise at all. I don't know where I'll be."

Justice shook his head with a kind of weary, stubborn insistence. "Then we can't do business," he said. "There are limits to this, but you must understand that I am not autonomous, I am no more a free agent than you are."

"I'm a free agent."

"Well you may be a free agent," Justice said, "although in the eyes of the Creator, as you must surely know, there is no such thing as a free agent, all of us must merely commit God's will—"

"Save that for outside. Outside this room you go into that."

"That is neither here nor there," Justice said with a hint of irony. "You may be a free agent, Mr. Wulff, although only a fool believes that he exists on his own with full options, without connection to outside forces, but I am not. I have interests to whom I answer and for whom I must be accountable. Selling to a white man is difficult enough. Giving you these weapons outright would be irreparably dangerous. You must say that you will return them."

"How do I know if I can return them? How do I know where I'll be—"

"I didn't say," Justice said cunningly, "that you *had* to return them. I said that you must *state* you will return them. Give me your firm, pledged word that you will yield these armaments back to me in the condition in which you are given them and that you will be responsible for them during the time that you have them in your hands. That is all."

"For an 80 percent refund."

"That is the way the brotherhood of the divine works," Justice said coldly. "That is the principle upon which our great church was founded. An 80 percent return for merchandise returned in good condition. You may have these ordnances on a two-week lease."

"For three thousand dollars down."

"For three thousand dollars down," Justice said, and Wulff went into his pocket, went into his pocket where the money taken from the suit of the man he had killed lay; it was a hell of a price, he thought, a hell of a price to pay for some armaments taken on a risky and speculative basis. But Williams was right: Williams had always been right about things like this, he had street knowledge and he knew how this business worked. Cash on the line, 100 percent deposit for lend-lease. There was no way around it. He had pushed the matter as far as he could.

"All right," Wulff said, "I'll go along with that. You're not giving me any choice, you know."

"Free will is absolute," said Father Justice as he smiled and worked his way toward one of the far shelves on which an array of machine guns perched. "We live in a system of choices; we can choose what we will, we are condemned to nothing, we can be whatever we wish to be."

"And those are the choices," Wulff said, following him, "those are the choices upon which the church of the divine is founded."

"Why, of course," Father Justice said, "of course. Your grasp of our theology is improving. Did you ever think that it was anything else?"

VI

Gianelli had him scented out. Gianelli had the prick scented out; he knew where he had to be, he knew that he was closing ground. He had been closing ground all the time on him in the three days that he had been on the trail; now it was narrowed down to just a couple of streets, no more than fifty houses. In one of them the vermin lurked. He would get him. He would get him and kill him.

But first things first. First things were always first; now it was time for a shot of the needle. Gianelli had been a heroin addict for forty years, piss on all of the newspaper articles and popular scientists that made it look as if you dropped dead after a few years of it. Bullshit, all of it was bullshit; it was a habit like cigarettes or alcohol or sex; keep it within bounds and you could live with it, let it get the upper hand and you were in trouble. But a strong man could keep it in perspective. For forty years he had been on and off horse; he was not dependent, he simply used it when he needed, didn't when the need was lacking. He liked to think that he took the habit the way they did in the old country; there were a lot of people in Europe who could use heroin or get along without it. But Americans, Americans, they had no sense of control.

Carefully, stirring, blending, Gianelli prepared the mix. He was in his own furnished room, a tight construct four flights up in the west seventies of Manhattan, a good base of operations, exactly the kind of place you wanted when you were on a vendetta, as he was, because you were traveling so light, had so little sense of connection to these rooms that held you that they could be barely said to exist; on the other hand—always, always, Gianelli tried to think on the other hand, see the other side to a question—you had a place to sleep when you needed it, you had an abode of some sort. You had a place to shoot some dope.

The stuff was bubbling now and he took it off the stove looking at the fluid as it lay there in the spoon, the little insolent bubbles prodding and poking themselves to the surface like little messages from under the earth. He swilled it around in the spoon to get the consistency just right and then carefully, unhurriedly, carried it over to the side of the room where the syringe and needle were, put the plunger delicately into his hand, inserted the plunger into the spoon and drew the clear, dead-white fluid all the way up behind the needle.

Nothing to do then but to slide it in, but Gianelli allowed himself that one, necessary moment of hesitation before he did so. In many ways this was the best part of all, the anticipation, waiting for the stuff to go in, extending the moments until the needle would bite in a sacred way into a vein and begin to pulse through its bright messages of salvation. No need to rush it, he had all the time in the world. Looking at the spoon, he thought that he could see not only bubbles but also little, astonished animals swimming around in it, animals that were part of the compound, small, vital, living things that would be injected into his bloodstream and were in themselves the heart of the connection. Wasn't that the folklore of horse after all? That there were little men in the fluid, little creatures swimming in the substance that added their life, their thoughts and vitality to yours so that it was not one brain but many occupying the surfaces of one's skull? Of course it was. It was very important folklore. Unhesitatingly, thinking about the rich and ancient traditions of his background that had brought him to just this moment, Gianelli put the needle into his arm, pressed the plunger all the way through, and took the rush.

It was like thunder in the head, blood in the gut, a feeling of warmth below, alertness above that had not been duplicated in anything else that he had found in his sixty-three years. Women were all right, but with women the pleasure was too quick, a few brief spasms at the end of the manic jerking and you were spent, exhausted, lying across them gasping out the heartbeats. But horse carried you on and on; liquor was all right, but the induction was too slow and sometimes in the getting there one would lose all sense of what had sent him that way. Other earthly pleasures not excluding sleep were not even worth considering. But horse, ah! horse went on forever. He felt it beating like a bird within him now, felt it rising, his heart itself enlarging like a butterfly with gigantic wings to embrace the horse as it hit his system. Then, just barely getting the needle out, just barely maintaining enough sense of the situation to get the damned needle *out* and put it somewhere on a high shelf where it would be safe for the next time, for the next sacred rush, Gianelli staggered to the bed, sat on it heavily listening to the springs whoosh and then lay straight out, feet up, arms extended, looking upward, looking at the ceiling, watching the pretty pictures that began to float across the slate of his mind.

Beautiful, it was beautiful. He writhed with joy watching those pictures: there were women being chalked upon that slate, flaring hips and gigantic breasts; there were forest images that he had not seen except under the horse for thirty years. Oh, there were a multiplicity of things, and Gianelli enjoyed every one of them, writhing, thrashing, screaming on the bed as the images blasted through. Behind all this the vague thought that he should not be doing this, that he was wasting valuable time doping when he should be hard on the trail of the Wulff was so frail, so transparent as to be negligible; he did not have to think of it at all. Later. There would be time for all of this later. Wouldn't there be? The man was at his mercy, Gianelli had the upper hand, everything was a mere matter of time and he could take the man any time he felt like it. In the meantime he was entitled to his own relaxation. Wasn't he? Of course he was. No less than anyone, his old, dear friend, Calabrese would have approved.

Calabrese would have understood why his loyal and devoted friend Gianelli would be entitled to pause during his vendetta for a little bit of the horse that he so loved and would not begrudge him this great and simple pleasure. Had not Calabrese himself, after all, shown his own sympathy and understanding for heroin by being critical to its distribution?

Of course he had.

Gianelli lay on the bed dreaming, and all sense of time or urgency perished from him as it always, always did when inside the great gong of self began to ring.

VII

Lincoln was just about to score, huddling intensely over the gleaming frame of the bar, dealing hard and fast, the deck in his hand twinkling like a magician's pack of cards in the lights, edging in, closer and closer to the score all the time, the buyer just sitting there, astounded, paralyzed by Lincoln's self-sufficiency and spiel, the vision of pure, white wonder and release that Lincoln showed in his hand . . . when everything blew up.

One moment Lincoln was working away, going into particulars, holding the deck like a wand, while the buyer, a thin cat who Lincoln had never seen in the lounge before just watched everything, fascinated, his eyes rolling like pebbles. The next moment there was a dull, pounding rush, a *whoomp!* as if the stars in the sky had suddenly punched out holes of heaven, and he was rolling, rolling, all around him the bar, maybe fifty people along its length, another couple of hundred in the front and back room, the jukebox screaming, the bells banging. Then there was a second roar, this one with light in it, and Lincoln found himself pitched into the street, pushed backward through the glass, the glass breaking all around him as he was on concrete, rolling and rolling, trying to protect himself. And then the third *whoomp!*, something final about it, he had a sensation that the bar rather than moving further outward was now collapsing within itself, layers and layers clinging to surface, and he was pressed into the sidewalk sinking like a stone through levels of concrete that rushed by him like water: no thought, no dreams, nothing but pain, and at the end of it he was on his back, looking at the sky while someone or something was going through his pockets, twitching away in those violated places as if a frog's leg had somehow penetrated him, and Lincoln was cold, cold.

Cold: he did not think that he would die this way; cold: he did not think that the lounge in which he had dealt for so many months would turn out to be a place of fire; cold: it was the shock of it more than anything else that had destroyed him. To die was one thing; to be blown off a stool and into the street, lying on your back, looking at the rotten sky with the sound of sirens all around, that was bad enough, that was not the way you dreamed your life would end when you were twenty-five years old. But you could come, you could just barely come to terms with something like this if you had had any warning, if you had known that it was going to happen to you. If you had been able to anticipate.

But lying there on his back, seeing the fires, hearing the sounds, Lincoln knew that he had been wrong; it was precisely this state of unpreparedness that was the key to death itself; you were *never* prepared for it; you were never prepared when the Man came walking down the pike and that was something that everyone, each one alone and in his own time would have to find out. Find out that it came in the night as a stranger, seized you in an embrace that felt at first like sleep and carried you off. He shook his head from side to side, feeling blood running within all the secret, broken places of his body, and someone was leaning over him, looking at him, a tall man with grey hair at the temples, infinite sadness to his eyes, infinite perception and knowledge clambering out of small, difficult holes on his face. "Give it to me," he said, and Lincoln understood that it had been the hands of this stranger probing his pockets, that touch inside. "Where is it? Give it to me right now."

Lincoln shook his head, gritted his teeth, unable to speak. He did not know how many bodies were around; he did not know the shape of the land; everything had narrowed to him and the stranger. His sight was periscopic, a small, dense tube of vision connecting only to this man, even the sounds faded away. "I don't know," he said, "I don't know."

"I want the shit," the man said almost calmly. "I know you've got it on you; I know that that's what you were dealing with in there. Be a good boy. Give me the shit, please."

"No," Lincoln said again, trying to move a hand toward his pocket, trying to see if the stuff was in there for himself, but he was paralyzed; something in his spinal cord was not relaying messages and he lay there, looking up at the stranger, thinking, Not only my body but my mind has been paralyzed; what am I going for the stuff in front of him like this? If I find it then he will find it too and that will be the end of anything. "No," he said again and lay there quietly. He licked his lips.

"Don't call me boy," he said then.

The tall man held that infinitely weary, infinitely thoughtful gaze. "Don't you hear the sirens?" he said, "don't you hear the sound of the horn? They're coming, you know. They're coming right now. Wouldn't you prefer to die fast?"

"I don't want to die," Lincoln said.

"No you don't, but you sold death."

"Leave me alone," Lincoln said, "leave me alone," and the man's fingers fluttered and probed within, Lincoln felt a sudden jab in his armpit, sensation of pressure like a knifepoint, and then the sensation went away, *there it was,* he thought, and the stranger came away with the deck of heroin. It had not been seared or scorched by the impact; it looked exactly as it had when he had flashed it for the last time and put it into his pocket. Then the explosion.

"You see?" the tall man said quietly, "there it is. It was there all the time."

"Leave me alone. Please leave me alone."

"You shouldn't have done it, son," the man said. "Dealing is very bad. Dealing fucks up people's minds and bodies and hearts and souls because you're distributing poison. Don't you know that? Don't you, son?"

The sirens were indeed louder. Lincoln was able to turn his head weakly from side to side; to his left he could see the smoke, feel the scorching heat of the flames on his cheek radiating into the bone; on his right everything was dark and wet as if something had spattered the street; the contents of the bar perhaps becoming liquid, liquefied matter pouring onto the concrete of Harlem. As hearing returned he could hear around him the faint moans, the gurgles, the sighs of what seemed to be a hundred people scurrying, sound of footsteps, stone against stone, the sounds of combat and evacuation, density, impaction; and filling his line of vision, overtaking him, swelling before him as if there were nothing else in the world was the face of the man looming over him: it was like a woman, like sex then, those final moments of intercourse when the woman became not only a part of the world but the world itself, the essential source from which the world came, life, death . . . and tumbling over the cliff of copulation then into a dead space of fading. But the man would not fade away. Lincoln knew he was going to die. Death was all right; dealing and drugs, shit, you faced that all the time. The fact of his own death had been real to him since he was five years old and began to see, looking at the landscape of Harlem, what a pretty destiny the world had figured out for him. But not like this. No, not like this. "Leave me alone," he said weakly. Speech had returned. He licked his lips, feeling the flame growing on them. "Leave me alone."

"I'm going to leave you alone," the man said. "I'm going to leave you alone for eternity." He was a white man; funny that Lincoln had not even noticed that until this moment, so overwhelmed had he been by other terrors, the man had simply been a force, not a color. But of course: of course, he could have known, should have known that when death came to take him it would be wearing a white mask. He licked his lips again. "So kill me you son of a bitch," he said, "kill me and be done with it, don't talk about it, just do it."

"I will do it," the man said, almost sorrowfully, "I have to, you see. I have no choice. You always have to go back to the beginning and do it over again, that's what I've learned, there are no ends, only beginnings." What the fuck was he talking about? Then the gun was unslung in the man's hand like a heavy prick being pulled from the pants of a urinating stranger in an adjoining pew, the fat edge of death coming over his face, and the man said again, "There's got to be an end to it. But where? Tell me where. I don't see any end, all that I see is a beginning." And the sirens were all around him, the sound of the sirens rising and falling, falling and rising, the cops were coming in and the gun came down and the man put the pistol against Lincoln's ear, tight, and pulled the trigger.

An image of a head exploding like a grapefruit came into Lincoln's mind at that moment but that head could not possibly have been his, that imploded and devastated brain must have been someone else's, had to be someone else's because this was not him, was it? He was already committed to the blackness.

Lincoln fell out of Harlem.

VIII

The formal/informal name the department gave it was the Wulff Squad, the detail of six whose full-time assignment was to run Wulff to ground and bring him alive—or, if necessary, dead—into headquarters for delivery. But in his own mind, Williams had a better name for the squad: just call them the fuckups. He was dealing with a disaster area; he was dealing with a squad that in the good old days would have been working the urinal circuits in Times Square or trying to pick up queers in Greenwich Village. Now, with the new liberalized policies and the tolerance of minorities, the department's worst were no longer able to work colorful details like this, but on the other hand there was nothing that you could do with them in normal channels. Put the fuckups into patrol cars or even behind the desks at precincts and they'd be screwing around with the public; bring them up on departmental charges and you were risking a nasty stink. Besides, what the hell could the charges be? Incompetence? Psychopathology? It was not like the army; there was no clean article system in which every condition had a label, just stick it on the discharge and pitch them out.

No. No, these men were staying. The commander of the squad, a lieutenant, had gone through a colorful adultery-and-divorce case that had gotten his picture on the front page of one of the tabloids, piling out of a motel room in his underwear, grappling desperately for his gun, which was the one article that a policeman was never supposed to be without, a hint of bare shoulders in the background. He had been shacked up with a prostitute on Route 9 near Peekskill, and his wife through a private detective had traced him. The lieutenant was very bitter about it, claiming that all he was trying to do was to satisfy some sexual urges and practices that his wife, a cold bitch, would not let him. There were a couple of fat patrolmen who had been partners in a car once until they had driven the car, in hot pursuit, clear off the docks and into the Hudson River in search of a fleeing junkie; they had not found the junkie or the stash, but they had succeeded in sinking the car, and that too had been the subject of a humorous story in one of the tabloids with a picture of the patrol car sunk to its roof line, floating on the surfaces of the oily Hudson like an inner tube. There was nothing you could do with them, either. And there was nothing to be done with the slender, unspeaking Puerto Rican patrolman, very delicate in his features and movements, who had been working in drag as a prostitute for the purposes of entrapment, but had apparently become so enthusiastic with one of his prospective customers that he had tried to take him into a hotel, had had to be literally pulled off the John's body by the pair of surveying cops who somehow got the idea that the Puerto Rican was not only on patrol; he might be an actual transvestite. It was that kind of squad.

There was no order or procedure. Williams came in the first day and heard a long, rambling talk from the lieutenant in the filthy back room of an abandoned precinct house on the West Side. The lieutenant said that he didn't know exactly why they were there or what the hell they were supposed to do, but this was the job anyway and he had passed around copies of the departmental memorandum on Wulff, the memorandum that Williams had found so surprisingly accurate, considering how little they had had actually to work with, but sloppy in small details and missing out on a lot of the stuff Wulff had pulled along the way. In the memo, Williams was not tied to Wulff specifically, which was very much a benefit. "He's a dangerous man," the lieutenant said, "a very dangerous man, he's out to kill all the junkies and dealers, it seems, but anyone gets in his way he'll kill them too, he's a killer, probably psycho," which was complete bullshit as far as Williams was concerned. But it impressed the Puerto Rican no end, he began to mumble to himself in a louder and louder voice, saying at last that he didn't want to deal with any goddamned psycho, life was too short to get involved with psychos, and then said nothing else while the ex-partners of the sunken patrol car laughed and belted him around a little bit. "We have to go pretty much on our own on this one," the lieutenant said. "You see, we're a squad, we're the Wulff squad, but we've got to split up and act as individuals, we can't move with one another, we can just spread out all over the city and create a network of intelligence, right? You refer all your findings to me and I'll coordinate." The patrolmen turned very sullen at that and asked the lieutenant exactly who the hell he thought he was. You mean to say that they were going to do all the work while the lieutenant sat on his goddamned ass and made *reports*? That sounded pretty lousy to them (they always spoke in the plural; it was *us*, not *me*), why didn't the lieutenant get off his ass and chase this killer if the department was so interested in getting him, instead of making them setups. The lieutenant said something about policies and procedures, words filtered down from headquarters, the most efficient and viable use of human resources, and so on.

Williams stood with his arms folded and let all of it pass over him. Obviously this was no time to start protesting, and he was at least half-involved in the squad *not* finding Wulff. He was on the fence about it, but he was not by any means committed to his capture. Actually, he did not know how he felt about it at all except to know that he needed his job back to fit together the pieces of his life. If he ever came up against Wulff, man to man, he would probably have a very difficult decision to make. But one look at this squad was a pretty good indication that he would not have to face that problem; these men could not have caught a hooker in a whorehouse. So much for the department's efficiency and commitment to capture Wulff.

But then again, maybe the deputy commissioner had not been such a fool after all; perhaps he had an insight, that the only kind of squad to put on a problem like Wulff was one that was in itself composed of brigands, fools, fuckups, vigilantes, the dregs of the department whose methodology in its peculiar convolutions would approach that of Wulff himself: set a thief to catch a thief, a dog to catch a dog. Wasn't Wulff the biggest fuckup of all? That had been the deputy's point, of course, that Wulff the maverick, the vigilante, the brigand, could be considered as the ultimate rogue cop, and under those circumstances the squad made a good deal of sense. Of course this was looking at things in an abstract, metaphysical fashion, as deputy commissioners far removed from the field were often inclined to do. For Williams the difference between the deputy's view of things and the squad that he had mustered was that irony that made the universe itself, hundreds of millions of years ago, reluctantly inflate and begin to go about its business.

They split up districts among the city; each taking a section of Manhattan. They had decided to focus on Manhattan on orders from above because this was where Wulff had come from and where all the internal signs indicated he was still operating. If it was the Bronx, Staten Island, or Brooklyn, it would have been impossible anyway, and Queens was unto itself at least ten cities, maybe twenty. You had to start with a modus operandi that contained possibility, and that meant focusing on Manhattan. If he wasn't in Manhattan, the hell with it. The Puerto Rican got the West Side from the Battery to Ninety-sixth Street, the two patrolmen got the east side the same way, and Williams, of course, got Harlem. All of Harlem to cover. Well, he was black, wasn't he? so it made a good deal of sense. The lieutenant seemed to be pleased at his intelligent decision, sending the Hispanic to the lower West Side, the whites to the East, the Negro to Harlem. It appeared to compose in his mind one of the few great original techniques evolved in modern police work; suiting the man to the territory. He, the lieutenant, would of course have a special phone number and a code name through which he could be reached at this precinct house during the days and at home at night. He lived with his mother in Staten Island.

All right, Williams had Harlem; he took Harlem. Burrowing through his mind was a crazy, fervid idea anyway; if anyone was going to catch Wulff, he would. These others did not have a chance; any possibility resided solely within Williams. If Wulff was catchable at all, it would be by Williams, and in that sense it didn't matter where they sent him, because wherever he was sent, there Wulff would be, in a strange, metaphysical connection of some sort, driving them toward one another. He was sent to Harlem, he would go to Harlem. The two patrolmen, mumbling about pension rights, went out of the room turning at the door to curse the lieutenant; the Hispanic signaled for Williams to join him in conversation at the improvised desk that the lieutenant had thrown up out of a set of packing crates. "Listen," he said in unaccented English, "is this man a killer?"

"Of course he's a killer," the lieutenant said with some satisfaction, "haven't you read the reports?"

"I don't want to be killed," the Hispanic said. "I don't want to deal with any killers. Do you?"

Williams shrugged. Keep it cool, play it down. He had no idea how much any of them here knew about him but it was best to concede nothing, to proceed as if he had no knowledge. The less known the better. "I don't think we'll find him," he said.

"Of course we won't, with that attitude," the lieutenant said. He hit the crate hard, causing the slats to tremble. "I don't want any goddamned defeatism on this squad," he said.

"I have defeatism," the Hispanic said, "I have a great defeatism. I do not want to be killed."

"Forget it," Williams said. He put a hand delicately on the Puerto Rican's elbow, trying to draw him out of the room. The man shuddered, little waves of motion cresting throughout his body, and shoved off Williams's hand violently.

"Don't touch me," he said. "I do not like to be touched in this way. Don't touch me!" he said, his voice breaking up an octave, "I will not tolerate this."

"All right," Williams said, "I won't touch you." He moved away from the lieutenant. "All of Harlem," he said, "I'm supposed to go through all of Harlem and find him."

"You will. Unless you give up on it now."

"I'm not giving up," Williams said, "I'm just thinking that's a lot of territory to cover."

"Ambition!" the lieutenant screamed. "It's ambition that made this goddamned department *work*, that made law enforcement possible. What if they said they couldn't get Dillinger?"

"I can't cover the West Side," the Hispanic said. "Two million people are on the West Side. What am I supposed to do?"

"Enough!" the lieutenant said. "That's enough of that!" and rose from his seat. Standing, he was six feet eight inches tall, his paunch trembling like a bombsight in front of them, leveling in, aiming at Williams.

Williams, already at the door of the room, said, "Enough, enough, I'll take Harlem, I'll *take* it," suspended somewhere between insane laughter and rage. But there was no reason for rage: what was the point? why get excited over something like this? It meant nothing at all.

The Hispanic seemed from this aspect to be about to leap on the lieutenant, impale himself upon him in some ecstasy of feeling, but backed away, some shade of disconnection had dropped between them, and the Puerto Rican felt obviously that he could push it no further. "All right," he said, "all right then, we'll show you, this will show you! I'll go out there in Times Square and get knifed to death, that's what's going to happen, and it'll all be on your head!"

Wear a dress and high heels, Williams thought he heard the lieutenant murmur, but could not be sure of this. In any event the lieutenant had subsided behind his desk, all six feet eight of him folded up neatly like a ruler, and Williams got out of there quickly, not even waiting to see what the Hispanic would do next. Outside he found the two patrolmen engaged deep in conversation; they were arguing as to where they were going to go for lunch and who had the better credit with a decent neighborhood place, but they decided that neither of them had any connections at all in this precinct, no one knew them, and this made the discussion become quite heated. Passing them without acknowledgement, Williams was afraid that they might come to blows, and what good would that do? Anyway, he had no time to get involved in a fight between these two. He had ideas.

If you were going to do the job, you might as well do it right. And Williams had an idea, a pretty goddamned good idea of where Wulff had been picking up all of those armaments that he had been using so spectacularly.

There was only one place in New York where a man traveling light could pick up stuff of this caliber quickly. And hadn't it been Williams himself who had made the referral? That made him responsible in a way that was a grim way to look at it, but he supposed that he had more at issue than he was willing to admit when he had come into the Wulff, the fuckup, Squad.

Williams went uptown to see Father Justice at the Church of the Brotherhood.

IX

Now the war had started again, but the war was working only in little bits and pieces, it did not have the grand sweep, the devastating overview that the earlier campaigns had had. Then Wulff had been working at the top, blowing up estates, smashing dealers and top distributors. He'd had the feeling that he was moving tentacles from top to bottom, squeezing the lifeblood out of the trade, and it had been good, it had been effective; no one could ever talk away what the campaign had meant to the organization. But this was different, now he had come down to the bottom again, was mucking around in the sewers, catching one by one the vermin that ripped out of that excrescence, and it was not the same; it was piecework instead of a grand overview, a sense of overriding control and majesty that he had had at times during the beginning of the campaign, even toward the middle. Now it was just wearying, plodding work.

Still, he had the shooting gallery in Harlem burned out and he had the Royal Lounge. The Royal Lounge: three hundred injuries, the whole, huge drop joint and trafficking center burned out in that one, lunging explosion; then, waiting across the street for the first bodies to come hurtling out, the flames, the explosion, the pain, the sound of sirens, and then getting across the street in the middle of that havoc to confront the dealer on the street, extending the confrontation too long, perhaps, in the middle of that chaos, letting the flames and enforcers get too near him. But he could not resist that opportunity, the opportunity to see the enemy whole, to have him at his mercy. And at the end the killing had been less one of vengeance, vengeance being long past him, but one of simple release, the man's eyes impacting into his skull, the groaning skull imploding within itself and then quickly, quickly, the flight downtown, on foot for several blocks and then by taxi. No one was going to touch him. The explosion had drawn attention from two square miles of houses and police, even a fleeing white man would not attract much attention in Harlem on a night like this. At last, at 110th Street, he had slowed, taken a cab, gone back to his room.

It occurred to him that up until this last New York siege he had not specifically been acting against the law; he had been acting outside of it, dealing with criminals, many of whom laughed at the law, administering to them his own justice, not lashing out against authority or against the uninvolved, but delivering his message of justice to those who had needed that message for a long time but could not be touched by normal processes because the framework of social retaliation had broken down. It had been that way in San Francisco, Boston, Chicago, Miami, New York the first time, Havana, Lima, and Los Angeles. None of those who had felt his vengeance would have been entitled to the protection of the law in a state where the law worked. But New York was different; on this second go-around he had to admit that for the first time he was going up against the authorities themselves; bombing the lounge and gathering ordnance for further attacks put him at poles with the enforcers, and the enforcers if they found him would be merciless now. They would have to be. He had jeopardized their own position.

So he was acting against the law, he was a lawbreaker who would be dealt with now as mercilessly as any junkie under the new drug program. And yet, back in his room, the door secured, the ordnance neatly packed in a suitcase near him, Wulff found it impossible to feel any sense of guilt or regret at this. It had been building for a long time, this last, great confrontation. He had known every step of the way that there would be a time, finally, when he would be placed in open opposition to the enforcers, and in a way he welcomed it. The lines were clearly drawn now; there would be no equivocation. He would be in contest against all of them: not only the dealers and distributors, but also the enforcers; not only against the inhabitants of the sewer, but also against those who were supposed to keep the lid on tight. All of them. He would be taking on the world.

Well, he had been a long time getting to this position; first as a rookie patrolman he had been taking on criminals, then in Vietnam something vaguely defined that was merely called "the enemy," and then back to the department again where on narco he was supposed to do something vague to people called "drug merchants" or "users," and finally in his odyssey he had taken them on in a far more forceful fashion, more forceful indeed. But he had been building toward this last and most critical step for a long time, that point at which he would be taking on all of the world. Not in pieces, not splinters of possibility here and there, but the whole damned swinging door of the world would now be coming upon him.

All right. High time.

He turned and there was someone standing in the doorway.

The door had opened so quickly, so quietly, that there had been no sound whatsoever; the construction of these old tenements had something to do with it, too. Impermeable walls, well-oiled bolts with doors that hung far above the floor in their arc of opening. That was solid construction for you, you had to admire the integrity of the buildings of old New York, although all they were good for now was for junkies and the welfare population. The man standing in the door must have taken advantage of that, and of the fact that Wulff had not locked the door when he came in. That was stupid, of course, but it simply had not occurred to him that anyone would be interested.

The man was in his early sixties. He was small, well-dressed, had one of those ruined-but-still-alert faces you see so often at the whiskey bars in the old neighborhoods. He was holding a gun in his hand, the gun absolutely level, no shake in the hand at all, bearing down on Wulff. His eyes glistened with something that might have been satisfaction and a feeling of good fellowship; he seemed, as a matter of fact, prepared to emit little cries of pleasure. "Ah," he said. "Aha!" and Wulff could see the finger begin to tighten on the trigger.

But something had happened to the old man, perhaps the strain of climbing the stairs, perhaps some element of unexpectedness in his own situation that undercut his alertness no matter how refreshed and satisfied his face appeared. The gun wavered subtly in his hand as he was trying to get off the shot. Then, in slow-motion, he was able to bring the gun to fire, and Wulff, hitting the floor, rolling already on the floor in a spasm of reflex that might have saved him even if the shot had been accurate, heard the bullet hit the wall just above him, little showers of plaster coming down, spanging off his forehead.

"Son of a bitch!" the man said, "son of a bitch!" and Wulff could hear his breath, his little aimless kicks at the floor as he concentrated on the gun, trying to get off the second shot, but the second shot, when it came, did so only very slowly, this one hitting all the way above him, splattering the ceiling. Wulff, rolling, a fine sense of aimlessness as he spun on the floor, the revolutions a disconnection, reached into his pocket, got out his own gun and fired almost blindly, pumped a single shot into the place where he thought the man was standing. "Son of a bitch!" the man screamed again, "dirty bastard!" and got off yet one more shot, completely wild. Wulff now had him placed exactly and in one careful motion bore in on the man and shot him in the gun hand.

The man screamed, the gun fell from his hand like ash, and suddenly he was hurled in upon himself, covering his wrist, yanking it against his chest like a shopping bag, an expression of fine and discrete agony coming all through his face, opening that face to an almost youthful expression. He did not look sixty in his pain, but fifteen, a young man astonished at the violation of his body. Wulff was already on his feet, drawing up his knees underneath him, scrambling to a weaving, standing position, the gun dangling from his hand like a leaf. Then, instead of closing ground on the man who had caved into a corner, holding his wrist and squealing like a rabbit, he went to the door, kicked it shut, threw the bolt and chain on it, then came back to the center of the room and looked at the man once again, an inconsequential object huddled down against the wall, shrunken and, in some reversal, aged once again, his eyes spinning him through decades of chronology so that within seconds what looked at Wulff out of those eyes was again a very old man. "No," he said, as he saw Wulff raise the gun, "no, don't do it."

"Don't do it!" Wulff said. "How can I not do it?" He concentrated on the series of actions—death was very easy to bring if you looked on it only as a matter of mechanics; let the rest of it be a religious problem, he would concentrate on the technology of the administration of death—he pointed the gun at the old man, leveling it slowly, holding it locked in place by that knot of concentration, then tensing the body to deliver the torrent of death.

Everything locked into place, froze, drifted in a moment devoid of time, the old man's mouth opening like a fish, his hands twisting, eyes fluttering; his attention seemed to shift from Wulff to something inside him then, as if death had announced itself from some secret place and was now stalking him, greeting him with upraised fist. The old man doubled into that knowledge. Holding the gun Wulff felt a sudden moment of indecision: the old man was dead now, he was dead as of this moment. If he were to pull the gun away and order him out of the room, the old man would go and never bother him again because in some intricate way he had been broken. But on the back of that was the insight that only death's apprehension had broken the old man, only the sure, swift knowledge of his own death, and that came out of certainty; remove the certainty and it would be as if nothing had happened.

No. He could not tolerate that. Wulff thought no more, did not think at all, it could be said that he had not thought during any of this but had only done what he had to do, which was to pull the trigger. The gun exploded in and out of his hand.

Gianelli's head cracked open like a cantaloupe, and in the middle of that impact Wulff could see the grayish, oozing mass of the old man's brains, slowly expanding toward the air, embraced by the air, and in sudden frieze the brains danced like a waterfall, little greyish ropes springing in the air. Then the old man had croaked, had croaked again, and with a sigh fell before Wulff limp on the carpet, his blood flowing into it gently, gracefully, gray of brains, red of blood, gray and red together puddling into the thin, green fabric of the cheap furnished goods. Looking at all of it, Wulff thought he had an insight and then, looking at it again, he knew that it was no insight at all: it was merely the same thing, the same over and over again; here some brains, there some blood, and in the whole long line of murder and vengeance that he had committed, all of them were the same in death as never before in life. Nothing changed. Nothing ever would, ever could change: all differences were resolved in blood. All that he was looking at now was a rack of dead meat.

Outside, in the dank hallway, he thought he could hear the rise of voices, but it was only his imagination. Anything could happen in New York. No one cared. No one listened.

He took the gun that had belonged to the corpse, holstered it away, and looked at the thing on the floor, deciding what he was going to do next. Any way he turned, it was death.

X

When Father Justice opened the slats of the storefront to peek out, it was with a truly reverential expression, and Williams felt like a petitioner. But then as he stared within, the eyes narrowed, the slats fell and what came to the door was not the benign, nodding Father Justice who had given him both blessings and ordnance a few weeks ago, but instead a grim, compact black man in his middle forties whose robes hung from him like a saddle might from a horse so much did he seem to resent their touch. "You," he said at the doorway, "*you.*"

"May I come in?"

Father Justice blinked and said, "Yes, you may come in," and the door opened just enough for Williams to squeeze his way through; in the trap of dankness within, he felt Justice's hands, surprisingly strong, gripping the wrist, squeezing, applying pressure. Painful as it was, Williams submitted, allowing himself to be led through the pews into the massive back room where the ordnance lurked. Funny, he thought absently, looking at the improvised altar, the crucifix, the large, sentimental portrait of the black Saviour that hung on canvas behind the podium, the little strips of fine wire pasted down on the stage with Scotch tape, probably so that Father Justice's tones could be inconspicuously amplified. Strange, strange: I've never seen a service here at the Brotherhood Church. I wonder if they *have* services. Well, that's none of my business, and in any event one thing is sure, one thing is sure as hell, I wouldn't want to see the kind of service that they have here.

He had spent half the day in plain clothes in a bar near the Apollo, drinking beer and plotting his approach to Justice. He knew he was going to go, there was nowhere else to go, it was the only possibility from the first. But in the bar he'd had to balance off a number of things, the most important being, if he could find Wulff, did he really want to confront him? Did he want to have that choice thrust upon him if he could run Wulff to ground? Granted that the deputy commissioner's point of view made a great deal of sense, granted that the Wulff Squad, as pitiful as it was, might be the proper rogue's squad to catch him, granted that he desperately wanted to get back inside the department and start building on what he had almost thrown away. Granted all of that, was he prepared to make the choice that he would have to make if he ever found Wulff? He had drunk the beers to no conclusion, no real conclusion at all, listening to the thud of the jukebox, looking at the walls, listening idly to the conversation at the bar, which had a good deal to say about the lounge just a few blocks down that had been bombed out the previous night. Some thought that it was some kind of drug dealers' war, the old organization retaliating against the black distributors who were not cutting them in and who were using the lounge as an important point of distribution; others were convinced that it was an inside job, an insurance job of some sort. But on one point everyone was quite clear: at least five people had died in that explosion, including one gunned down on the street. Thirty or forty more had been checked into hospitals overnight, and there was no reckoning the damage that had been done even beyond this in terms of the sheer assault on the neighborhood. Now even Harlem was not safe; it was going to be the same battleground that had been made of other sections of other cities. There was plenty of crime in Harlem, but it had been of the small arms, face-to-face, individual ripoff type. This was a newer and meaner construct, and people in the bar were damned scared, so scared that Williams, simply because he was an outsider, had attracted a good deal of unpleasant attention up and down the bar, people staring at him, whispering about him. Finally the bartender, flickering a towel, had come down the line to tell Williams that he thought it would be a good idea for him to get out of there, and Williams had left. There was no sense in fighting that decision. He had no ground to defend.

And that, oddly enough, had been what had tipped the balance, had sent him after all to Father Justice. If Wulff was carrying on his war in distant ports or cities; if Wulff was carrying his war to the exclusive districts where the vermin lived and walled themselves behind their guards and possessions, that was one thing. But if he was going to take it into the streets where the poisons themselves flowed, then he had to be stopped. It was simply too dangerous; Wulff might be thinking that he was attacking at the source now for his last and greatest campaign, but what he was actually doing, Williams thought, was springing his trap on the victims. The war could not reside in Harlem. Harlem was a combat zone itself, a devastated area, like Dresden in 1945 or Hiroshima. It was merely feeling the effects of the corruption, it was not causative. It was only a receptacle. So Wulff had made a very serious mistake, a misjudgment, really, his first misjudgment, perhaps, but one serious enough to swing Williams all the way over to a decision: he had to go after him. It had to be stopped. Perhaps if he could see Wulff and merely explain to him the folly of what he was doing, the fact that he was not striking back but merely *in*, Wulff would see it and desist. He would have to proceed on this basis anyway. There was another possibility altogether that Williams did not even want to consider at this time: the chance that Wulff had seen all this and simply did not care, that Wulff too had evaluated this in his mind and had decided that he *had* to bring the war home to the victims. But Williams did not have to consider that now. Maybe he never *would* have to consider it; Wulff would listen to him when they met and decide to be reasonable.

The alternative was not worth thinking about.

In the bowels of the ordnance room, Father Justice reached inside his robes and suddenly there was a gun on Williams, a .38, which is a light, inaccurate, and short-range piece, but a .38 at this range could do as much damage as a .45. When you were lying in a coffin, the quality of the weapon that killed you hardly mattered. "I've been wanting to talk to you," Father Justice said softly.

"I'm here," Williams said. "You can put that thing away." He paused, then said, "I don't think that that's in accord with the principles of brotherhood and divinity, is it?"

"You leave brotherhood and divinity out of it," Father Justice said hoarsely. He coughed, cleared his throat, hawked out a clear drop of phlegm which he leaned over to deposit on the gleaming floor. "You let me worry about brotherhood and divinity. Where is all the materiel?"

"I got hijacked," Williams said. "I got hijacked in Nevada. It wasn't my fault; I was trying to bring it all back but I got waylaid."

"I don't like that," Father Justice said and spat again. "I do not like the idea of materiel falling into the hands of hijackers. What I wish to know is what made you come back here to begin with without that ordnance? You know how seriously I regret its loss. So seriously that I have already been sending out representatives to discuss the matter with you."

"No more than I regret it," Williams said, "I feel very badly about it, believe me. But something more serious has happened."

"Has it?" Father Justice said softly. "What could be more serious than the loss of much firepower, which our brothers could have used in the unending war for justice? Tell me what exceeds this in seriousness?" The

.38 did not waver. Williams looked at it, calculated the chance that he could take the gun from Justice, wrestle it free and turn it on the man. In some intricate way, all the shifting odds passed on tape through the teletype of his mind; he might be able to do it. The odds were sixty-to-forty in his favor in any event: he had surprise and age on his side as against Justice's obvious alertness and familiarity with the weapon; put it all together and three times out of five he might be able to make it, might actually take control of the situation, but for what? Williams thought: two times out of five, in two worlds out of the five of possibility he would have his brains blown out, and the odds were not good; it was not worth it. Beyond that, Justice was obviously not threatening to kill him, merely pulling out the gun to establish a certain level of relationship, which is the way that the good reverend would approach most of his business dealings. That looked pretty sensible, considered that way. It isn't worth it, Williams thought, and put it out of mind.

"I'm still waiting for an answer," Father Justice said. He looked less ecclesiastic than Williams had ever seen him; but then again, Williams thought, aspects of the Old Testament prophecy called for a hard and unyielding witness. The reverend was merely being faithful to one aspect of the teachings.

"I have no answer," Williams said, "I really have no answer for that. It wasn't done in my interests. Besides, I purchased the ordnance. Wasn't it a straight purchase deal?"

"With an 80 percent refund when they were returned," Justice said. "We expected them to be returned. You agreed that you would return them. It was a rental with a 100 percent full value deposit."

"That's neither here nor there," Williams said. It really wasn't, and abruptly he was tired of confrontation, tired of Father Justice and his .38, tired of the materiel room itself, whose odors brought him back unpleasantly to a time only a few months ago when he had looked at matters in a sick and wrongheaded way that he was still trying to put behind him, labor out from under the color of a disease. "Put that gun away," he said. "This is ridiculous."

"No, you are ridiculous. You have severely jeopardized the cause."

"What cause?" Williams said. "You sell munitions for profit, that's your cause?" Father Justice's face became dense, thickened, seemed in the light to become gray, and Williams said, "There's a small chance that we might be able to get them back, but I didn't come back here for that."

"What did you come back here for?"

"I think that a man might have been here to buy some stuff from you," Williams said.

Justice looked at him bleakly, still holding the gun. Then, with a massive, unwinding sigh, put it back in his robes. "I see that a vindictive approach will not work with you, my son," he said gently. "You are sunk too deep in the great corruption of your ways. Instead, we will have to pray. We will have to pray for you."

"I hope you'll do that," Williams said. "I'm looking for a man who I think would pray for me, and you may be just the one to do it."

"Indeed," Father Justice said. He seemed to have converted himself and his conversation to an amiability so gross that Williams decided that it could be as offensive as the good reverend's aggressiveness. Unfortunately, Justice could not seem to find a proper middle ground; this, perhaps, being the true and final definition of religious fanaticism. "Indeed, I will have to pray for you." He shook his head, looked at the shelves and shelves piled with M-15s, grenades, and Browning Automatics and said, "Let's get out of here. I find it very difficult to discuss salvation in an environment like this."

"No," Williams said, "let's stay here. I have one question. I want to know if a man, a white man might have been—"

"You have already asked that," Father Justice said. "That question has already been asked of me and you may recollect that I did not elect to answer it. I am extremely distressed with you, my son. I am afraid that you are preoccupied with violence. You are, in fact, obsessed with it. Thoughts of violence seem to be central to your brain and spirit, and that, of course, is very bad. We must cultivate love, peace, that peace which passeth all understanding—"

"Now listen," Williams said. With the gun safely tucked within the reverend's robes, with the axis of the conversation seemingly tilted toward him again, the urge was clear: pull now his own service revolver on the good reverend and reestablish that natural balance that should exist between the authorities and the governed. But then again he was no authority, not really, and it could hardly be said that Father Justice would label himself as being among one of the governed. Quite to the contrary, if Father Justice took orders from a higher authority it would be one to whose level Williams could not ascend. He shook his head, bit his lips, dismissed the idea. Fuck it. "Now listen," he said, "let's try to be reasonable about this. You see," he said then, trying to be cunning, deciding that there might be another approach after all with which to entice the good reverend, "that white man, the one who I'm looking for, he might be the one who would know where all that ordnance is. As a matter of fact, that's why I'm looking for him."

"Dissemblance," said Father Justice, "dissemblance is a sin not only in the eyes of God but in those of man himself, and we must deal, all of we poor stricken creatures must deal with man primarily if only as the access route to God. Sin of all kinds blocks our passage to the higher realm, but of all the sins of which we speak, mendacity may be the worst. I—"

"I'm not lying," Williams said, "I mean it. If there was a white man looking for stuff from you, if he was in here to try to check out some armaments, he's very likely the one you want, the one you got your stuff heisted from. I'm looking for him." he paused, tried a careful breath, found it all right, took a deeper one. "If I can find him, there's at least a good chance that you'll get all the stuff back."

The reverend came closer to him. "The sins for mendacity's use are great," he said, "and they will be paid in full in the higher realm; they will—"

"I'm not lying," Williams said, "believe me, I'm not lying at all. If we can find him, we may find the stuff."

"Ah," Father Justice said. "Ah," and paused, his robes seemed to rise slightly as if he were taking deep, gasping breaths, but then again he might have only been preparing himself for a devotion of some sort. "I wish that I could truly believe this, but I detect within you some inner tension, some doubt and indecision—"

"No," Williams said, "it's true," and extended an arm to take Father Justice out of the ordnance room, slowly the reverend extended an arm to meet his, the two of them linking, and then he led him, surprisingly weightless, out of those damp, dense spaces and into the sacristy where Williams felt that he heard murmurous voices, although they might only have come from the sound of the crucifix as it gently brushed against the curtain on the little Harlem winds as they hit the panels of the storefront outside. "All true," he said outside. "Why I think you'd be surprised at how much this man may have to do with the stolen ordnances, how much responsibility he may bear for what has happened to you. I can almost assure you that all the answers will emanate from there once you help me find him."

"Ah. I see. Well," Father Justice said, and in a sudden, spasmodic motion of devotion that Williams might have found quite touching in other circumstances—*the motion of devotion creates commotion*, he thought—"such a man was in here just a very few days ago to request some materials."

"Ah," Williams said, "ah. I thought so."

"Of course I had no idea whatsoever that he is, as you say, responsible for the theft of the ordnance. Otherwise I would not have dealt with him. The eye of duplicity is deep and penetrating, and the antichrist himself will dwell in the form of the familiar."

"That is true," Williams said, "that is very true." The crucifix was rolling and banging around in idle breezes now; it was really amazing how much circulation of air there appeared to be in the church. Of course, there was no saying either what sources Father Justice had tapped into for his power. "I agree with that philosophy."

"I was tempted," Father Justice said. "I was deeply tempted." He crossed himself, a gesture that Williams had always associated with Catholicism, but this was a peculiar offshoot of a sect; one simply did not know of their devices. "I trust that I will be forgiven for this lapse."

"I'm sure you will be," Williams said encouragingly, "forgiveness may be granted for true penitence."

"Do you think so?"

"I truly think so." It was easy when you got into it; it was just a different way of looking at things. "The only sin that is unredeemable, beyond redemption that is, comes from the sinner who will not admit the error of his ways. But for those who grant it, redemption will come."

"That is very comforting. That is truly comforting; I appreciate those words of counsel, my son."

"It is nothing. Really it is nothing."

"Perhaps not. But there is true and real relief nevertheless to hear you say those words."

"I am glad of that," Williams said, resisting an urge to reach out and touch the suffering Father Justice. Perhaps he really was a minister of the Lord, one who merely dabbled in ordnance on the side to support his mission. Then again he might be an arms seller who used the church as a front. That was the more logical explanation, certainly the one he had accepted at the outset. Still, there was no saying. Life and religion were far more complex than you might think at first glance. It was entirely possible that the reverend was indeed supporting his ecclesiastical activities through satisfying a basic demand and then, conscientious man that he was, paying penance for it. One never knew. In Harlem there were at least three levels to everything. "Yes, there was such a man in here. He purchased a machine gun, some grenades, an M-15 rifle, and other miscellany. I had my doubts about serving him but he was sincere and advised us that he would not use these materials in any way to raise up a hand against our people but would instead be supporting our own great and holy mission to restore the world to black peoples as was ordained. So, in my great weakness, I gave unto him according to his demand. I am truly shamed." His shoulders sagged. The crucifix banged, jingling on the rostrum. "I will pay for the vanity of pride, for the sin of greed. I am paying for this already."

"What did he look like?"

"What did he look like?" Father Justice said, and paused. "It is hard,

hard to give a physical description of one who functions as one of the tempters or comforters. He was a tall man, about six feet four inches, in his mid-thirties, who seemed to have had some kind of military background. That, at least, was in his bearing, but this may be a false assumption on my part. God must guard against the sin of pride."

"That is the man," Williams said. "Do you have any idea where he went?"

"Ah," Father Justice said. Benevolence radiated from his features; it seemed that he had come close to having a religious insight, would, in fact, have mounted an altar if there had been an altar instead of merely a flat sunken place in front of the crucifix. "I think that I might have an idea where he went. We have many devoted followers in the brotherhood here, many of whom are willing to cooperate in any fashion that will enable us to complete our mission, to serve our God. Accordingly," he said, "accordingly we felt it best when this white, this antichrist, left our quarters to have him followed, very subtly of course, to that place from which we came."

"Were you able to locate it?" Williams said hoarsely. He was poised on a tip of anticipation; in another moment he might have been on his knees in front of the reverend. "Were you able to locate the place where he is living?"

"I do not know if he is living there, my son," Father Justice said peaceably, "but we were able to, or I should say, certain devoted followers, whose place shall be numbered with the very best, were able to follow him to that place in which I believe his evil schemes are hatched, in which he broods like the great snake itself over his apocalypse."

"Where would that be?"

"Why I have it right here. I have it right here," Father Justice said and went to the altar, stood behind the podium, dug a hand into an empty space underneath the podium and came out with a large manila envelope, his hand splayed outward within it. Williams could see the little extensions his fingers made against the paper, and then Father Justice came out with a slip of paper, which he looked at intently, the lights twinkling in his eyes, bringing a sheen to his forehead, before he passed it to Williams. "Here," he said, "it is believed that he was in residence at this address. Of course in this flawed and difficult world it is a mistake to confuse design with reality; he may not be living there at all. Nevertheless, one of our devoted congregants was able to trace him to this address." He seemed to bow subtly, inclining his head altarwards, his hands gripping the podium then in an embrace. "I hope that it will be of service."

"I'm sure that it will be."

"If it is of service and if you are able to establish contact with this individual, I trust that you will keep our priorities very much in mind."

"Oh, I will," Williams said. "I can assure you of that."

"We would be very interested in dealing with this individual should you find him. It was a serious mistake, a very serious mistake indeed for me to deal with him. Nevertheless, he presents a superficially winning appearance, and the church has long wished to establish that it is devoted to forms of righteousness no matter what color they may wear externally," Father Justice said. "For this reason I allowed myself to fall into the hands of the tempter, but this will not happen again. Truly it can be said that I have learned from this and that never again will I be so persuaded."

"Sure," Williams said, "certainly," and backed toward the door, his business completed. It was time to leave, but it was hard to bring himself to leave the form of Father Justice, now fully embracing the altar, hugging it in fact, moving belly to belly against the crucifix, his back to the podium, which he had abandoned in the last flight toward ecstasy. He seemed to be humming a liturgical chant. "Thank you very much," Williams said again uncertainly and went toward the door, began to struggle for the knob nestled in the midst of the panels.

"One thing," Father Justice said, turning in prayer, his eyes heated and intense, glaring at Williams, "just one thing. The measure of vengeance is sure and terrible, and it would be highly unpleasant for you if you were lying to us. If indeed this white devil of yours had nothing at all to do with the materials you failed to return, it would be you who misled us, and our devoted followers would surely be as unhappy as I. Some of them are overeager; this is a regrettable habit on their part, but then again, until dedication can be tempered by mercy, one has to get along with them. You know the problems of the pastorate in these troubled times."

"Oh yes indeed," Williams said, "oh yes indeed, I do know what problems religion is facing, it's truly a time of transition," and finding the doorknob he wrenched open the door, it came stickily, ungratefully into his hands. He had to struggle with it to hold it into place, and then he was in the street, the decayed, binding smells of Harlem once again around him, and in his hand the precious slip of paper with the location to which Wulff had been tracked.

He looked at it quickly and it was as if even without seeing he had known what it would be; a furnished room in the west nineties. Yes, indeed, it would end where it all began. Everything in life made sense after all; it all came together in a perfect closed circle of unity if you only knew how and where to look. Father Justice was right. He was right:

there was a divine order to things; even the doubter would find it if only
he knew where to look.

Walking down the street, the paper already ripped into shreds and
discarded, feathers to the breeze, he found himself wondering: perhaps
the true religious services of the brotherhood church were in the
transfer of money and guns; perhaps the sacraments were arrived at
through the blood that its ordnance customers ripped from the bodies
of others. Perhaps when you came right down to it the good reverend
himself found his glimpse of the divine in the dull, dead stock of the rifle,
in the hard shell of the grenade, in the shelves in his ordnance room
where all knowledge, transferred to hard, impacted pieces of destruction,
lay piled upon itself ready to be turned at any moment toward the true
mission of the church, which was nothing less—when you looked at it
in the overall sense—nothing less at all than to clean up the world.

If you looked at it that way—and Williams saw nothing sacrilegious
about it—it was an entirely new insight into religion. Perhaps that was
what it had to become: an instrument of vengeance.

He headed downtown on his way to see the wolf.

XI

Wulff had chucked the book of the man who looked like a stockbroker
a long time before, but a couple of names still stuck in memory. One of
them was De Masso. He remembered De Masso well; the name had
rung a connection from his narco squad days. De Masso was worth
seeing; he had put off the idea of visiting him only painfully because the
important thing, the book disclosed, was to get to San Francisco and
head off a shipment due there. But he had abandoned the idea of
seeing De Masso with regret; now he would be able to make up for it.
Make up for the long stopover.

So he went off to greet him.

De Masso had lived and worked in New York until only a few months
before, when he had quite suddenly moved to a high-rise apartment in
Fort Lee. A crossout of his old address and the entering of the new one,
including the date that it was good, in the stockbroker's book had
indicated this; from the date it was also pretty clear exactly why De
Masso had decided to move at that time; there was a happy concordance
between the enactment of the new New York State drug law providing
life imprisonment for convicted drug dealers and De Masso's decision
that bucolic, pastoral living in a high-rise overlooking the Hudson beat
all hell out of struggling along on Manhattan's West Side. If nothing else

could be said for the governor's drug law, you could definitely say this: it was shuffling people around. It was moving them from here to there; a surprising number of people in the drug business had come to the decision that city life was intolerable and what they really needed was to live piled over one on top of the other in some rabbit warren of a high-rise slum in Fort Lee, New Jersey. Maybe the governor had worked in accordance with the Fort Lee real estate brokers and builders. You never could be sure of this; he had connections everywhere.

In any event, De Masso was in Fort Lee, and Wulff decided that it was time to pay him a visit. Nothing to it; he was getting around quite a bit this time, now it was time to see how De Masso was enjoying country living, how all of that west-shore-of-the-Hudson air was agreeing with him. Wulff, carrying a valise, boarded a bus at the Port Authority and rode with the commuters all the way, standing in the aisle, holding perilously to a strap, as the bus, sputtering exhaust fumes, staggered through the tunnel under the Hudson, heading west. This was the life, the commuters agreed with one another. Getting the hell out of the city at five; you couldn't beat it.

At Fort Lee, Wulff got out with the rest of them, walked to a diner a block from the bus stop. He had already worked his disguise over back in the furnished room, using the men's room at the Port Authority only to give it some final touches, to see how it was holding up in public. It seemed to be holding up fine. The moustache and the little dabs of charcoal he had placed under his eyes managed to convey an impression of age and weariness; he might have been a forty-five-year-old clerk/accountant coming home from a difficult day in the municipal building, or better yet he might have been a forty-five-year-old police sergeant, fleeing the city after a day of interrogation, glad to get back to the swamps of New Jersey after a risky and perilous attempt to deal with New York for another nine hours, his face and body clotted with the wastes of the city now, but essentially optimistic: after all he was going home. Oh, it worked, all right; it wasn't the most effective disguise, but then no one on the homeward bound bus at the Port Authority gave a shit about anyone else, and he had to assume that surveillance was not of the highest quality anyway. There was still a high bounty on him, and there were a lot of people who might be keeping an eye out for his appearance. But what he had done in nine cities so far would have to discourage all but the absolute hard core or the financially desperate, neither of whom were the most difficult kind of assassins to defeat. And so many of those people who had carried his name and photograph around in their pocket—well, so very many of them were dead. He had effectively raised the price on himself by cutting by four-fifths the number of potential assassins—which was a crudely direct but highly effective way of going at the problem, of course.

De Masso. He thought about De Masso. The inclusion of the name in the stockbroker's book had not surprised him at all; everybody in narco knew that De Masso was one of the major dealers working within the tight confines of the East Side. He handled Lenox Avenue, around 120th street, east over to Fifth, that was pretty well how they had him mapped on the departmental charts and from the stories of informants. The thing was that there was absolutely nothing to get De Masso on and for that matter no interest in getting him; you could hardly bust him for possession because he was too clever to ever have anything on his person or in his home. And as far as catching him in the act itself, well, how the hell were you supposed to catch a distributor? Could you tap his phones, get a court order, get cameras and tape recorders to bug the critical conversations in which the careful, almost unspeaking arrangements were made? The hell you could. And De Masso, sure as hell, was never going to be found out on the corner of 124th Street and Lenox, hawking heroin at the top of his lungs from a fruit stand. That would be entirely too much to ask.

And besides, narco simply did not work that way. Narco was not after the dealers or distributors at all; at the root narco wasn't after anything. All that narco was there to do was to act as a buffer between the police department public relations division and the newspapers and federal government's war on narcotics, so that PD could say that they were indeed making an effort: for one thing look at the full-time squad they had working on nothing else. Narco worked on hustling cheap informants and doctored reports; occasionally when the heat came up very high they might bust a miserable, sniveling informant or two on a prearranged charge, which would be dropped for lack of evidence in a couple of weeks. But by that time there would have been another murder in the East Village, and the newspapers, hopefully, would be off covering it, meaning that maybe only three or four times a year, five if there were a lot of dull news days, you would feel any heat at all. The rest of the time narco was pleasant, easy work; now and then you could bust a college kid stupid enough to be smoking a joint in public or peddling the stuff to his friends, and that would build up the charts too, but most of the time it was a breeze. Narco, in the late sixties, was absolutely the best place to be; it was a clover detail, almost as good as vice, but vice was too good to be true altogether and had just about been phased out. The amateurs were taking the professional trade away anyway. There just wasn't much percentage in hustling street hookers who were the dumbest and poorest of the lot, and the other ones, the ones operating out of high-rises and studio apartments had plenty of buffer zones between themselves and arrest; and many of their friends worked down at the precinct. So vice was scratched altogether; narco wasn't too bad, but narco had been such fun for all that it too was being scrapped, amalgamated into the federal bureau of narcotics was the way the newspapers had put it. They were phasing it out, which was a spectacular shame for a lot of informants anyway.

But that was all behind him; it left the issue of De Masso. No narco squad could touch him; that made him only riper pickings now in Fort Lee. Wulff, finishing off his coffee at the diner, was thinking of the ways best calculated to make the approach and what he would do when he got to him. Pity about the old bastard he had killed in the furnished room. His thoughts skittered back that way although he did not want them to. Hell, that was finished, the old bastard was dead, the room was cleaned out, Wulff was now in another place two blocks down and three blocks over. It would be weeks until someone decided to check out his tightly-locked room, investigate perhaps the smell drifting through the walls and find out what was lying in there. In the meantime he had all the room to operate that he needed, and that was what the mission was all about. Operating room. Opening up some space for himself in which he could function again, paring open the night with the clear, deadly edge of his assault. The old man in the room that he had occupied would stink and inflate, his body assuming grotesque and comic proportions finally in the onslaught of death, the pure, high scent of him merging with the walls to produce something so penetrating that at last curiosity would draw someone in there. But death on the West Side was such a familiar, completely unremarkable event, death on the West Side was so much a part of the urban redevelopment program itself, that Wulff doubted if there would be any follow up at all. If there would, the hell with it. How were they going to tie him to it, and what good would that knowledge do them weeks after the fact?

At the rear of the diner, there was an intense little huddle around one table, eight or nine people wedged into that tight space, all of them men, all of them conversing intensely. He could pick up scraps of conversation if he wanted; all that it meant would be a slight alteration, a shift of consciousness and he would be attuned to what they were saying. Already little scraps of words were coming out of the huddle, words like *kilo, hash, nickel*, and that could mean that they were talking about only one thing, they were talking about shit, they were talking about its distribution, probably niggling out the last details of a deal. But what, he thought, granted that this was what was going on at the table, what was he supposed to do about it? Enactment of the new drug law along with his own crusade had already driven the vermin across the river and into the towers of the Hudson; it was drug paradise here and nothing to be done to stop that, but what was he, Wulff, personally to do? Was he supposed to lunge over to that damned table, scatter them like fruit, bring vengeance upon them right in this diner? Did you have to clean up the world indiscriminately, taking on evil as you saw it in whatever form, simply because it could not be tolerated, or did you have, as he still believed, to pick your spots?

He did not know. It was certainly better to pick your spots; he had been doing that all the way. Here in New York, although with a harder edge, he still wanted to think that he was selecting the battleground and the terms of attack rather than having it thrust upon him. He had been functioning in a meaner, lower, more emotional gear here than anywhere else, but planning was still paramount. You just did not seize a gun and go out on the streets hunting, shoot any piece of vermin who looked like a junkie or a dealer. Or did you? Did you have to hit them just that way: randomly, violently, without any planning whatsoever in order to play their own vicious game?

Well, it was something to think about. He would worry about it after De Masso. Maybe. On the other hand, maybe he would not. With De Masso it was likely that he would already have all that he could handle. All that he knew was that he was not going to do anything in this diner; he was going to take it one step at a time. One step at a time.

He passed the table quickly, ignoring the glances. There was a flicker, then a flurry of interest as he walked to the door, first one and then down the line, all of them were looking at him. He could see the exchange of intelligence as knowledge passed between them, and he kept on moving, thrust the door open, walked into the winds of Fort Lee, the high winds spinning off the river, and cut in back of the diner into the parking lot, then into a blank field, the fastest way to the high-rise in which De Masso lived. He walked through rubble, feeling little blocks of concrete and stone coming up against his feet. Fort Lee was impermanent, hastily assembled as if by a gigantic child playing with materials on the bank of the Hudson; the high-rises came up fifteen stories or more, cheap plastic and steel glinting, the foundations poking down into rock. In the streets between and behind the high-rises, there were still patches that had not been paved, little ruined houses in which the poor lived, neighborhood groceries, cement-strewn fields of debris on which the children played. The building had been helter-skelter, piecemeal, and no one was responsible for the spaces between the buildings but the town itself, which was too busy raking in payoffs from contractors to be worried about anything as elementary as services. So what you had was a great deal of money and architectural ambition funneled into a town that thirty years ago had been little more in population than any of the cow towns working their way up the east and west side of the Hudson above Peekskill, with the difference that Fort Lee had accessibility. Half of the New York mafiosi lived in these towers.

Oh, it was a mystery all right, Wulff thought, that was for sure, a mystery how all of this had been thrown together, a mystery as to how it was able to continue. Considering the graft and greed that lay behind the assignment of these contracts, it was a miracle that any of these high-rises remained standing; the half-life of the plaster could be measured in months. But someday there was going to be a hell of a judgment. Up and down the line it was going to happen; one by one these blocks were going to fall right into the river, thousands of people were going to be incinerated and drowned, and where would the contractors be then? Well, Wulff did not want to think about that. Surely the contractors at this moment were laughing and working over their balance statements and tax-evasion schemes, and were not concerned about what would happen when their constructions began to topple.

He heard steps behind him in the rubble. Instantly he slowed, worked to the ground. There was nothing here against which to brace himself, nothing to act as cover. The only cover would be in going to ground, and Wulff did it without hesitation. The footsteps might be in his imagination, he might be overreacting, but it would be better by far to overreact and pay the penalty in scraped knees and embarrassment rather than to go up against what he thought he might be facing. The field was almost entirely dark; there was slight illumination coming from a single streetlight about three hundred yards straight ahead of him, the rays of the light half cut off from this angle by the jut of a single building. Wulff could just about see his hand in front of his face, and he cautiously worked a gun into it, kept it leveled, lay on the ground. No sight to shoot by but voice would be good enough, voice would give him an edge. Then he could hear the sounds of the men talking as they scuttled to a stop about twenty yards from him. It was that group from the diner, at least some of them, he thought, say four, maybe five come out to pursue him while the rest stayed back. It was as he had suspected, what he should have known when he had allowed himself to look them over too closely in the diner; they knew who he was. They had identified his face even in the half-disguise of false sideburns he had affected, and now they were seeking an enormous bounty. He should have known it. He should not have looked them over as he had.

It looked like De Masso was going to get awfully lucky tonight.

They were talking urgently among themselves, in low whispers, with little fluttering signs in the darkness that might have been the hand signals with which a group of professionals can communicate almost as well as with speech, can fill in the pauses between. Wulff knew without being able to hear what they were saying to one another: they did not know if he was still in the lot but they were pretty sure he was. It stood to reason, and in the next moment there were a series of nods as if some hastily negotiated decision had come out of this. And a flashlight leaped like a spear from the darkness.

Its strobe pierced the night, coming across the place where Wulff lay in a low arc, just sputtering past, and swung in full radius, paused, began to come back slowly. At this rate they were going to be able to locate him; they knew exactly how to use that flash for maximum sweep, knew how to make quarters of the area to be searched, an old combat technique, and then probe those quarters. As the flashlight curved back through the lot Wulff knew what was going to happen, if not on this sweep then surely on the next; they were going to pin him in that strobe, blind him, hang him like a frog squirming on laboratory pincers and quite remorselessly shoot him. There would be only two sensations, so quickly would they work: first the pain behind the eyeballs as the light lanced him, then the quick, thudding impact of the bullet as it dove into his heart or head, exploded the life out of him. Once he allowed himself to be open to the light, there would be no way he could stave off that second impact. They would not wait, they would shoot him on the spot.

So he had this small moment, this instance of reprieve as the light wove toward him again, and he thought that it was the smallest chance he had yet been given: a small pistol and a hand grenade he had been saving for De Masso, against four of them with reinforcement troops behind. But there was no way out of it. To lie crouched in the lot waiting for the light to come in was merely to huddle like that laboratory frog in the tank and hope that those pincers swooping forward had some entirely different objective, some different frog in mind. But men were not frogs; they did not have to be fools either. The difference between men and frogs was that men were aware of their mortality and could take steps, at least halting and limited steps, to counteract it.

So he fired off the pistol toward the invisible arm at the end of the light, the bullet spattering bone in the darkness, heard the yelp as the man was hit and then the light leapt like a fireball from that hand, went rolling to ground on the lot, spinning, turning. Someone else leapt forward to seize that flashlight but caught the second bullet high in the throat. A hard whimpering sound came from something that had been hit, and then the light went off totally as if a body had fallen on it, was shutting off all light forever, and Wulff did not pause, but in the last flash of light that he had been given before the light was obliterated he got off two more shots, the first one missing—he knew it from the moment it left the gun, you had a feeling about things like that, you could tell the good and bad shots as they emerged from the barrel of the gun even before they had hit; maybe shooting was like sex in that way, knowing a good come from a bad—but the second shot was right on target: he heard a wet sound as if something were being pulped, a vegetable falling open with a splat like thunder from the rottenness pouring out. Then he was on his knees, he was on his feet, first weaving, then running in the darkness, first pausing, then moving, first calculating, then going flat out, and he ran low to the ground holding the gun before him, following the light of the street lamp, breaking the angle, the building falling away, and as he cleared the obstruction he took the grenade from where it had been, pulled the pin and threw it.

It twinkled in the air. He could see it rising in flight in the rays of the street lamp. Then it dove, like a bird, like a stone, toward the figures that he could see in the quick light massed on the ground squawking like chickens, strange sounds of dismay and concern ripping from them as they saw the grenade coming and surmised what it was. And then the grenade was down, rolling, ticking. Wulff in full flight wondered if it was a dud; no, it could not possibly be, Father Justice took great pride in his merchandise. It was inconceivable that in the war for divinity and freedom any of the grenades would be duds, that in the army of Christ there would be any section eights. And down the grenade went, then up, he heard the *oop!* of the explosion, and the night was filled with light, the secondary concussion, rolling in thickly on the heels of the first, and in the air then was only hissing fragmentation. The screams were cut off by that secondary explosion just as the light had been.

Wulff ran. He ran through the streets of Fort Lee. His interview with De Masso, it seemed, would have to be abandoned for another evening; he had had an interruption along the way but it was a worthwhile interruption; trade off four for one. Then, as his pace slowed to normal, as his breathing eased, as the sweat dried on him, he felt the quick rising of the gun within his pocket like a little animal scrambling away in there, and he thought why the hell, what the hell, why the hell not? What did this have to do with the business at hand? He might as well do it anyway.

Temporary interruptions, no matter how pleasant, just should not divert the course of a campaign. That was combat logic for you.

So leaving the lot to the sirens and the vultures of the press and photography corps, Wulff went off to see De Masso.

XII

The slaughter in Fort Lee and a story buried on page sixty about a man who sounded like Gianelli being pulled dead out of a furnished room on the West Side hit the papers on the same day. They hit Miller, who made it his business to read the papers, very hard. For a long time, particularly since the interview with Gianelli, he had felt himself trembling on the verge of a decision. Now the two events, in concordance, a great pivot seeming to link and hold the two, pushed him over the edge, and he knew that the decision had always been waiting for him. There was no one else to make it. Of course there were plenty of people to make it, but in the war of attrition, Miller had moved further up along the line than he wanted to think.

"I'm going to call it off," he said to the woman lying in bed next to him. Her name was Stella, and she had been going to bed with Miller, first formally, then informally, for something over five years. In the beginning it had been all passion, a shared apartment, candlelight, and heavy seduction; but now it had eased into a long-standing relationship without frills; Stella still had the apartment, but Miller had long since moved back to his quarters and looked upon the rages, convulsions, passions he had felt with her years ago as the characteristics of a different man, one he had long outgrown. Now she came in once or twice a week, more if he felt like it, to fuck him and otherwise stayed out of his life, pursuing a vague career in modeling or some such. On the other hand, he trusted her absolutely, only as a man can trust a woman who would otherwise have been his wife, and he told her everything. She listened, evaluated, and said nothing back to him, which was even better. After five years Miller still could not decide if she was a very bright girl working on being dumb for self-preservation or whether she was indeed as dumb as she seemed but, with the cunning of the attractive, stupid woman, had cultivated the appearance of intelligence behind silence.

In any event she said nothing whatsoever, merely rolled in the bed, placing a hand on Miller's thigh, running her fingers all the way up the surfaces, touching his scrotum lightly in a way she knew he liked. He felt himself twitch, respond faintly, then the impulse to couple was submerged in the urgency of what he was thinking. Also in the fact that he had had her not fifteen minutes before. He did his best, most lucid thinking after a fuck; purged of all desire it was possible to see the world in the cold glass of suspension that it really was. It was only desire, as a matter of fact, that fucked you up, got you involved in calculations that were not suited to reality. If for no other reason than this, Miller was dedicated to Stella: she helped him to cancel desire, keep him thinking rationally most of the time.

"Cut it out," he said, putting his fingers around her wrist and drawing her hand down. It drifted to his knee, lay there warmly. "I'm trying to figure out something."

"Sure," she said and rested her cheek against his. He felt the soft imprint of her lips, then the darker mold of her tongue touching him, moving quickly across the panels of his cheek and for just a moment the temptation was there to immerse himself within her, to seek within her again what he seemed unable to find anywhere else, a total blankness, a total reversal of discontent. But no, it would not work, he was forty-three years old, too old for double-headers regardless of her cooperativeness and his optimism. Besides, he was trying to frame his thoughts. To see this right. "All right," she said, when she felt him moving away from her, they were that attuned to one another after all these years anyway. "All right, I won't do anything." She turned, threw an elbow across his stomach, looked at the ceiling, and sighed.

"I've got to call it off," Miller said. "There's no point in pursuing this any more. He's costing us too much, too much in men and energy, don't you understand that?"

"I don't understand anything. I just listen."

"Right," Miller said, "you just listen. Now he's killing people in Fort Lee, this old man, this friend of Calabrese's who came to me to ask permission for vendetta and I figured what the hell we had nothing to lose, he's dead too. He's bombing out joints in Harlem, he's conducting a one-man campaign here, and do you know something? I don't want to go up against him any more. So I'm going to call the troops off. I'm going to make it clear that we no longer want him; some bounty hunter, someone outside the organization wants to give him a shot, we can't stop him, that's for sure, but we won't cooperate either. We're not paying rewards. We're cooling it in the New York territory."

"Cooling it in the New York territory," she said quietly and nibbled at Miller's earlobe. "Yes, I understand that."

"I mean it's ridiculous," Miller said. "Someone might say that he's beaten us, that I've given up, but it isn't that way at all. Not really. This is completely a business decision, that's all it is. He's wrecking us, we're putting far more into him, taking far greater losses than he's worth. So we've got to cut away. I don't even think that he's attacking us any more; he's just on a guerilla campaign."

"Guerilla campaigns are a lot of fun."

"Not in fucking Southeast Asia they aren't," Miller said. "I just can't justify going on this way any more, that's all. Hell, if we could get him, we would. It's not a matter of guts; I'd face him anywhere if it was just a man-to-man proposition, and I'd get him too. But we're losing more on this now than we can possibly gain. It's ridiculous. I'm calling it off."

"All right," Stella said, "you're calling it off." She was still on his earlobe. "But don't you think you should think about this?"

Sometimes she opposed him; once or twice in the course of a conversation she might pick up on a point and cross-examine in a way that hardly pushed the point. It was one of the reasons why he had not reached a final decision on whether she was smart acting dumb or dumb faking smartness, because she knew that the bright people asked questions. "I have thought about it," he said, "I've thought a lot."

"Because it's a big decision."

"Oh I know that," Miller said, "I know it's a big decision."

"If he's as dangerous as you say he is, should you just let him go on this way?"

"I've thought about that," Miller said. He put a hand on her thigh, ran it up, entwined a finger in her pubic hair, turning it, without desire. Sometimes the greatest pleasure in touching a woman was when there was no desire in it; he would think about this. "But you see I don't think he's dangerous to us any more. He started out, it was a campaign, no question about it."

"I see."

"But the campaign is over. He's not fighting a planned action any more; he's just striking out anywhere, any way he can. There's no rhyme or reason to it. He's just hitting the stops. So it's not a question of protecting our interests the way it might have been at the beginning."

"Oh," she said, "I didn't know it was that way."

"It's that way," Miller said. He turned toward her. She was looking up at the ceiling, curiously inert, curiously absorbed, and he felt once again a touch of desire, a gentle finger of ice pressing him at the base of the spine, radiating out little tentacles of cold to the upper and lower parts of his body. "Believe me it's that way." He began to stroke her in earnest now. He felt better. Sometimes it was that way with decisions; you didn't even know what you were going to say until you started talking, and then the talk framed out the decision that had been there all along. Maybe presidents or heads of state operated the same way, viscerally, didn't know what they were up to until they heard themselves saying it. Then they would have advisers draft position papers justifying all of it after the fact. It was a fairly terrifying way to look at the way the world worked, to think that everything went on this way, but then again you had to accept it.

"All right," she said, "all right," and then she was all over him, her body a fine network, a mesh draped over him, little holes in the mesh through which he was able to brush and just barely touch all of the forgotten, buried sweets that he must have been able to seize fully only in dreams, all of her rising thickly against him, groaning, panting, and he felt her tongue penetrate like wire into his mouth, and he moved down and around her and then very slowly, precisely began to make the motions of generation.

"Good," she said cooperatively, "ah, ah, that's very good," and he wondered if she felt desire or whether all of this was simulated, had been faked from the beginning, nothing within her whatsoever, Stella merely a receptacle. But in the rising or deepening gloom of his energy, he did not think of this any more, and as he worked his way toward orgasm the image that predominated was that of the murdered old man as revealed in the one small clip that the tabloid had printed; the body lying swathed in its blood, the face rolled back, constricted, dead eyes locked to the ceiling. And as Miller came he thought that the old man Gianelli and he might be seeing exactly the same things, Gianelli at death, himself at the come. And then it all came crashing down upon him as he carried himself toward the end of all recollection.

XIII

Williams was the one who made the actual discovery of the corpse. Not that it made much difference; the porter had been damned curious about that apartment, having a feeling that something was wrong inside it. When Williams showed his police credentials, he said that it was just as good that Williams had shown up because he, the porter, had been planning to call the cops about it anyway, quite soon. Something was wrong in that place, he was sure of it; and he didn't like the looks of the guy who had rented it either; he seemed to be a strange type. So it was academic as to who would actually find the corpse in there, although Williams supposed that it was just as well that he had; it would indicate to the deputy commissioner that the Wulff Squad was making progress, at least of some sort, and the deputy probably needed all the help that he could get at headquarters.

The lieutenant had been pleased as hell, of course. Williams had phoned the call into the precinct with full identification, and the lieutenant had been on the scene almost before the homicide squad, beaming and nodding, talking to all of them, giving whispered confidences to the one police reporter that had come up with the squad, and he had taken Williams aside in the hallway while the squad was working to tell him that he thought he was doing a wonderful job. "I haven't found him yet," Williams said, "so what's a wonderful job? As far as I can see, this is just another murder that we weren't able to prevent."

"But it means that we're closing in!" the lieutenant said. "It means that we're throwing the net around him and this is clear evidence, clear evidence of effective progress that we were first on the scene. We're hot on his trail, don't you understand that?"

"I don't think it means anything at all. I got an idea, I got a good lead, was able to track his whereabouts to this place, that's all. I have no idea where the hell he is now."

"But of course you do!" the lieutenant said with wide, astonished eyes. "If you got this close, then you've got an excellent lead on him and it should only be a matter of a short period of time until you apprehend him, right? Of course we'll have reinforcements for you now; you won't have to take him alone. I can tell them," and he motioned back toward the open door, the sounds of the squad working, the presence of the reporter, "I can tell them a capture is imminent, right?"

"That would be very stupid," Williams said, "and what would be even stupider is to release news that there's a special detail to track him. Do you really want to make him aware of us?"

"Oh," the lieutenant said, "ah. I see what you mean," and went away looking rather vague and troubled. The squad had lumbered through its basic details, the meat wagon had come, and the corpse had been taken out of there. Williams gathered that the victim might be some kind of minor mafioso figure, a fringe guy on the edges of the organization. There was something familiar about the face, and Williams suspected that he had operated out of the Midwest. They would check Chicago on this; the teletype was already going through. Williams did not see where the identity of the victim made a hell of a lot of difference, but if it gave them satisfaction to make him, then they could go ahead. He had a far more serious and basic problem: he had the feeling that he had lost Wulff.

He had had his one good shot; he should have had him, he had obviously been just a few hours too late. If he had gone to see Justice faster, if he had not bullshitted with Justice so long but had forced the information out of the reverend at gunpoint (but how would that accord with the principles of brotherhood?) if he had nine-elevened his information into headquarters instead of making the arrogant gesture of trying to get to Wulff himself, he might have gotten him. Perhaps the old man there on the floor would not have been dead. Perhaps some people who Wulff had in mind for his next outing would be alive as well.

He was in a difficult position. It was hard for him, on the one hand, to think of Wulff as a felon, an assailant, an arrest case, but on the other hand he guessed that he agreed with what the deputy commissioner had said. Wulff was too dangerous; he was dangerous not only on principle but example, and if the department would tolerate a campaign of this sort in its midst, it was opening up the possibility for a lot of other people, less principled than Wulff, trying similar campaigns. And that could not be done.

No. He had to be stopped. And Williams guessed the reason that he had not nine-elevened the call in was really quite simple: he had thought that a private confrontation with Wulff might have worked. He owed him that much; maybe he was crazy, he thought that he owed to Wulff the chance to be talked around to reason. But if Wulff did not listen . . .

Well, what then? What was the difference? Why pursue it? Now there was the report out of Fort Lee and that report was very bad, worse than New York even. Here he was up to his guerilla campaign again, and the cost was high, four more bodies and fragmentation that had substantially rocked an adjoining high-rise. It was fortunate that there had been no one surrounding that vacant lot when the incident had occurred, otherwise innocents might have been added to Wulff's death roll of honor.

It was escalating out of sight. Now Williams had the feeling that the real crunch was on.

He told his wife about it. Not the full details, just sketches here and there to give her some conception of what he was going through; a way of seeking out advice. He was back in the house in St. Albans; so was she, so was their month-old son; superficially he was living exactly as he had when all this had started in the neatly mortgaged home protected from the world by the lawn and his civil service job; but inside everything had changed, only part of it having to do with Wulff, and he was sick of living inside himself now; he could not steer a solitary decision as he had before. Solitary decision had driven him away so that he was not even there when the baby was born. Now he had come back but there was a kind of pain that he could never transmit to her and a determination never to do it again. Whatever he did from now on could not come merely from inside himself but would have to be shared with her.

Not that there was much she could do about it, of course. She thought the Wulff Squad was even worse than Williams thought it was. Also, she had met Wulff, she had liked him, there was some kind of feeling there and oddly she had more to say in his defense now than Williams had. The scar he had taken from the knifing near the methadone center still ached, it burned late at night, a flame of implication circling through his gut; sometimes he could not differentiate the pain within from the pain without; maybe they were the same thing. Maybe not. He did not know what he would do if he had Los Angeles to live over again. Wulff and he had attacked each other in the trailer park; if it had not been for the onslaught of the enemy, one of them might have been killed. Knowing this, would he have gone out to Los Angeles still?

"Leave it," she would say to him late at night, sometimes holding the baby, sometimes not, sometimes lying next to him in the bed, sometimes speaking from the high, straight chair she would use in their bedroom to breast-feed the baby, a scene that Williams would have found maternal and touching if there had not been so much desire in it, and if she had not been so conscious but so ungiving of that desire. "If it hurts you that much, if you can't straighten it out in your own head, David, then get off the squad. It isn't worth going through this," she would say in the bed, on the chair, with the child, without the child, clutching her breast to the baby, and sometimes just lying on her back looking at the ceiling. She would not let him touch her breasts or have anything to do with them while she was nursing the baby. That was definite. She had made it clear to him from the first that she would take him back but she would do it only on certain terms, and that was one of them. It had seemed easy then; it did not seem easy now. Still, comparing his life to the lieutenant's or the two patrolmen, did he have the right to complain? "Get away from it," she said, "I can't listen to it any more."

"I can't leave the squad," he said. "My squad is the way back to the PD, don't you understand, if I don't stay on the squad then they'll break me for good. I'm back on probation. I've got to stay, but I don't know what to do."

"Don't do anything," she said. "Don't do anything, let the others worry about it, let it be their decision."

"I can't," he said. "It all comes down to me. I'm the only one who can take him."

"I don't believe that."

"You'd better believe that. He'd kill any of the others on sight. I'm the only one who would have a chance to talk to him."

"But there's nothing to talk about, is there?"

"I don't know," he said, "I don't know," and got off the bed and began to pace through the night as she watched him with that imperturbable, closed-in, mysterious expression that women with infants have; an impression of special knowledge denied everyone outside that circle. "I don't know what to do."

"I think you know what you want to do," she said. "You just don't want to face it. You don't want to face your real feelings, what you know you should feel about this."

And this was almost true, it came so close to being true that he could not take it. So he said, "All right. Forget it, I won't talk about it anymore; I'll work it out on my own."

"Can you?"

"I think I can," he said, "I've got to." He thought of the attack in Fort Lee, the dead man he had seen in the furnished room in the west nineties. "It's starting to come clear," he said. "It won't go on this way any more."

"He's your friend. You don't want to kill him. You're not even sure if you want to stop him."

"I don't know about that either. I don't know whether I do or not. But the squad is doomed. The squad isn't going to work; it's either me or none of them."

"And you can't stand that," she said, "you can't stand having to make that decision."

"All right. All right, I can't, but I've got to make it anyway. There's no way around it. I've got to face up to it and no one else will," and he said no more. Sometimes, after these conversations, he slept; sometimes he closed his eyes and merely looked at the wall of darkness superimposed upon them; sometimes he left the room to sit by himself by the television set staring out through the slats of the blinds at the empty lawns of St. Albans; sometimes he did none of these whatsoever but merely came to terms with all of them in some private way that had nothing to do with the blankness or the darkness, had nothing to do even with his wife.

XIV

De Masso had fallen easily. That was the funny thing; the papers were full of the bombed-out area in Fort Lee, they had picked up on that old man he had killed in the furnished room (Gianelli? was that his name, Gianelli? It was funny: once you got a name to put on a corpse, an entire sense of identity began to filter in along with the complexity that came with murder. Before he had known the old man's name, it was not a murder but merely an administrative act, what you could call an exchange; now he had another to add to the list), but they had missed on De Masso completely. Either De Masso was so obscure that his death was not even worth a mention, because he had thoroughly covered his tracks in dealing or, and this was the more difficult part of it, the De Masso murder was big news, really substantial and they were keeping it out of the press for other reasons. That was something to think about, not that he didn't have enough on his mind already.

But De Masso had been a simple process. He had simply gotten through the unlocked door of the lobby, looked the man up on the building residents' board downstairs, taken the elevator to the seventh floor, knocked on the man's door, had it opened on him, confronted a short, grim man in his late fifties wearing an undershirt, made a voice identification (De Masso? yeah, De Masso), taken out the .45, and shot him in the head three times with the silencer, using his left hand braced into the outer wall for leverage, aiming deep and true. And the man, De Masso, had fallen backwards into his foyer, his palms splayed outward, shrugging and jerking away as if he were apologizing, somehow, for the indignity of his collapse, and lay there on the carpet, his blood soaking into it, little pulpy sounds coming from his throat as his life ran away. It had been a noisy death as so few of them were, De Masso lying there, squeaking his life away. Then a woman in her twenties had come from somewhere behind, had peered out from the living room and seeing De Masso lying there on the rug had begun to scream. The screams had started even before comprehension had settled; reflex action, spastic tremors like frogs in a laboratory, and Wulff had struggled with the temptation to shoot her as well, nothing personal, just cut off the screams . . . but at the last moment he had not, holding back, shuddering with the knowledge of how close he had come to murdering her.

He had closed the door neatly, turned away, and taken the fire exit down, blind staircase, all six flights of it, to a small alley hidden in the bowels of the development, opening up to a small patch of grayish light outside, the street. That exit had carried him far away from De Masso's side of the building, and it had been simplicity itself to clear his way through the streets and back to the bus terminal. In all respects the tenants of these high-rises were transplanted Manhattanites. Nobody came out into these streets at night except on very urgent business. The place was as deserted as the lot had been.

So he had gone back to New York. Again that shuddering feeling had hit him in transit; how close, how very close he had come to shooting the woman. That had not been the point of his odyssey; he was not going to hit bystanders, witnesses, victims, relatives of his enemy, but only the enemy himself. It was going to be a clean series of kills; like the enemy itself, at least in the old days, he had wanted to abide by the principle that the families stayed out of it; what was being settled was an extension of business practices. But he had come to the verge of hitting the woman, not in panic, not even in feeling, but simply because it would have been easier to have done it than not. And there would have been a pleasure in it too. He would have multiplied his fury against De Masso.

So what did that make him? Did it mean that something subtle or not so subtle had been altered within him: that he was turning now into an indiscriminate killer; that the indiscriminate kill itself was the new shape that the campaign was taking? He did not know; what he realized was that in some dark and complex way he was turning the corner, and he simply was not looking at this situation the way he had when he had begun. People changed. *He* changed. The price he had paid in nine cities was too great.

And they had killed Tamara. They had violated their own principles; she had been abducted and murdered only because they knew they could reach Wulff through her. Seeing her dead on the beach, soaked with blood like water, the blood pouring freely from all the vents of her body, Wulff had had a clear insight down the tube and into the bright center of all implication: if you were in the business of death, you could not go into it halfway. Death, like sex, was a totality; you had to follow it through to its logical end, just as you could not, as a mature man, interrupt intercourse, pull out, be courtly, spill all over her piled clothes instead. *That* had been the turn that the campaign was taking. He was bringing death home now; he was killing them viciously and indiscriminately, just as the junk they peddled anointed some with death, others with cramps, many with jail, and a few with great wealth. Wulff's own great wheel was spinning and spinning in the night, and where it came up death was delivered.

Still, the papers had not reported De Masso.

Now, in another furnished room in the west nineties, only a few blocks from where he had murdered the old man, Wulff braced himself against his ordnance and talked to the man that he had brought up from the street—a junkie, nodding and nodding his time away on the sidewalk outside, too offensive to pass by, too pitiful to harass and yet he could not let it go by, had jammed a finger in his back and said *start walking* and now that he had him in his room he literally did not know what he had wanted. "Where did you get the stuff from?"

"What stuff?" the junkie said. He could not have been more than thirty, but he had the posture of an old man, the same quavering delicacy of movement, the same tentative gesture of hand and mouth. "What you talking about?"

"Where'd you get it?" Wulff said again. "Who's your supplier? Who gives it to you?"

"I don't know what you're talking about, man," the junkie said. He had been nodding off even as Wulff had poked him up the stairwell into his bare, bleak room, the open cases of armaments glinting away. But now some comprehension seemed to have seeped into him, some realization that he was not in a run-of-the-mill situation, that he was not dreaming this but coming to terms in some way so complex that he could not get at it. "I don't know."

"Yes you do," Wulff said. He showed the junkie the gun. "You see this? I'll blow your head off if you don't tell me your source of supply."

"Now that's shit man," the junkie said, "that's shit if you think that I know anything about that." He looked at the gun in a querulous, highly interested way, as if he had read about things like this somewhere but had never quite had to deal with them until this moment. "That is fucking ridiculous," he said. "A gun."

"I'm running out of patience."

"I'm sure you're running out of patience," the junkie said. His eyes were large, white, luminous, distended almost like tentacles from the hidden spaces of his skull, "but that don't have nothing to do with it." Those eyes became cunning. "You from the governor's task force?" he said.

"What's that?"

"The governor's task force. Understand he's rounding people up the streets to kick the shit out of them." The junkie blinked. "There's no more supply left in New York," he said. "The governor ought to understand that. His program's working away just fine; you can't get a fucking thing this side of the river."

"All right," Wulff said, showing him the gun, clicking the trigger gently, an old trick that he understood had worked pretty well in the interrogation rooms right up until things had tightened up. "You see this?"

The junkie's face was very weary. "Yes," he said, "I see that."

"I'm going to use it. You know I'm going to use it, don't you? Don't you?"

"Yes. I believe you're going to use it."

"Make it easy for me," Wulff said almost pleadingly. "It doesn't have to be this way at all, you know. You can resolve it very simply. Where are you getting the stuff from? Tell me your source of supply." I've been through this before, he thought. I started this way at the very beginning, back in an Eldorado in Harlem. Started by tracing it up piece by piece. A hell of a thing to be back at the beginning now. But wasn't life, all of it, in itself a beginning? What the hell were you supposed to do when you knew you would have to repeat the same acts over and over again? Deny them?

The junkie seemed to sigh in collaboration; a look of knowledge passed between them then, outside the context of the confrontation as if the two of them might have been old actors staggering through yet another repertory season together: different masks, different sets, different towns to play in but underneath the same script, the same tired, ravaged old faces behind those masks, the same sense underlying the staging. No, you could never really get out of it.

"Tell me," Wulff said again and realized that there was a pleading tone in his voice; nothing to be done about it. He could not cancel out the tone because he *was* pleading. Any fool, even the junkie, could see that the balance had shifted the other way.

"I can't tell you that, man. You know that as well as I do; I can't tell you shit and besides that," the junkie said, "besides that, I'm not really on the stuff anyway. You've got me pegged the wrong way. I'm just being social." His eyes blinked, the whites becoming even more luminous. Wulff leaned forward to find such a clarity there that they might have been tiny screens in which he could see running the clips of his own response as he stared at them. Wide eyes, wide mouth, wide heart, the junkie was telling him the truth, and Wulff could see that. He could no more tell him where he was getting supplies than he could have cut out his heart and presented its palpitating mass to Wulff. In the New York that had been created by the new laws that confidence would be death. Dealing was life imprisonment without parole now; a man facing that would have very little compunction about killing anyone who had put him in that position.

So things had changed. It was not like the old days on the narco squad when you could squeeze out the squalid information you needed from the informants, all of it a game, an end-run against the middle with only a few people hurt and most of them held at bay. The days of the trade-off or the deal were gone now; it was all or nothing. Looking at the junkie, Wulff thought, yes, you could see some merit in the old ways after all. Damn it to hell but you had to face that insight: the narco squad, the old lax drug laws were more workable; at least you could get along in a world that would not have worked at all had it not been for the easy collaborations you had forced. But now it had changed. It had changed for all of them, enforcers, junkies, dealers, vigilantes alike, all of them were pinned on the edge of that drug law, fluttering away like insects. Nothing could be done. Nothing.

He could kill the junkie or he could let him go. But the trail of information would end here.

"All right," Wulff said then, "get out of here."

The junkie did not move. He looked at the floor, spread his palms, looked up at the ceiling. "Out of here?" he said.

"Out. Get the fuck out."

"All right," the man said. He came to his feet in a beaten posture, shuffled, clasped his hands together. "You just going to let me walk out of here?"

"Not if you don't go right now."

"All right. All right, I'll go right now. I can't tell you shit, you understand? Maybe you're law, state police or something like that, right? Well let me tell you that you can't get nothing this way. It won't work. It just won't work."

"Go," Wulff said again, "just get out of here, get out," and the rage overtook him, he was swinging the revolver, butt end before he became quite conscious of it, hit the junkie a blow high on the shoulder, stunning him. The man cracked against a wall, little showers of sweat droplets exploding from him. "I mean it," Wulff said, "I mean get out."

"Yeah," he said weakly. "Yeah, I'm going, I'm going," and turned weakly, went to the door, opened it. The foul, dense odors came pouring from the hall, a mixture of plaster, poison, cooking, grief. "Yeah, I'll go," the junkie said and went out of there, closing the door quickly, quietly behind him, the door on automatic lock clicking once. Wulff could not hear him as he went down the hall.

Gone: he was gone. And so much for that.

Wulff did not like the room. All furnished rooms looked the same in these old single-room-occupancy tenements; all of them served the same basic purposes, but some were more ominous than others, some fell wholly below the line of acceptability. If this room had been his life, he would have had to leave it because the overall effect, the density, the unpainted ceiling through which he could see the bare struts of the building themselves coming through, the flaking walls, the stinking furniture smelling of urine lined up against the walls military fashion: bed, desk, chair—this effect would not have been tolerable for a sane man who found himself committed to these quarters. No, you could understand the drug freaks, the junkies, the acid freaks, the potheads, the hash droppers, the cocaine sniffers, the whole cornucopia of twentieth-century American visionaries, if you could see that they were trying, many or most of them, to escape rooms exactly like this. You had to have sympathy for them. You had to understand as he had finally, confronting the junkie in this room, that all of them were victims.

But not so for the dealers and the distributors.

No, it was not true for them: they lived in pleasant houses shielded by trees, or in high apartments in the better areas of the city. They drove their cars in and out of the areas that festered with drugs, on superhighways that walled them off from sight. They had batteries of lawyers, accountants, corrupt cops to shield them from any consequences of what they had done. No, there could be no mercy for the dealers.

But sooner or later, he thought, you had to make a distinction, you had to separate the two. At the beginning of his war, he had seen all of it as a swamp: everything was mixed into one slimy mass. Dealers, distributors, junkies, pushers, peddlers, occasional users, even the journalists who sympathized, glamorized the drug culture had been in that swamp as he had envisioned it, all of them equally needing to be torched out. Bring flame to the swamp, burn it out, he had thought then. But, no, he had been wrong. There were whole levels of authority and responsibility here, varying levels of implication. The junkies were *not* the same as the dealers; the dealers were *not* in the same category as the potheads. Even within this subculture, and perhaps here more than on the outside, there were whole shadings, gradations of moral confrontation. He had to face it now. All right, he would face it. He was not unequal to it. He had never thought that he had known everything. He had moved into this from a simple position of ignorance, seeing things in clear-cut terms exactly because the fucking liberals who underlay modern police procedure along with the criminals who manipulated and paid off the cops—exactly because *they* would see no discrimination. But there was. There had to be.

The junkie could not, under the new drug law, tell him who his supplier was. For the junkie to have told him this would have subjected the purveyor to life-imprisonment without parole. Who was going to buck those kind of odds? Who would tolerate them?

The dealer had undoubtedly made it quite clear that it was worth the life of anyone who sprung the news of his whereabouts. And that meant the end of the informant system.

It also, Wulff thought, it also very likely meant the end of his crusade. It would be impossible to go back to the beginning and pick up the threads again. And after the big ones he had killed, ending with De Masso, there was nowhere else to go.

There was also little point in indiscriminately attacking the junkies, once you realized they were victims. No, nothing was so simple any more. None of it at all.

Wulff put his head in his hands.

It had seemed so easy at the beginning. At the beginning had been clarity, purpose. You started at the bottom and rode clear through to the top, that was all, and then you moved along the line of the top, killing and killing. Eventually there was no one else to kill and then you were finished. The task had been awesome to confront but it had been nothing more than a lot of work; there had been no ambiguities in it. But now, and for the first time, he saw that there were a considerable number of ambiguities.

Wulff sat in his furnished room, head deep in his hands, his eyes closed shut against knowledge. Leaping like fire against the canvas of his mind came not thought of junkies, distributors, dealers, big men or purveyors, not even the image of cold, white death itself—but rather the image of Tamara, not as he had last seen her bloodstained body, but the Tamara he had held in his arms in Los Angeles and San Francisco, all of her flesh a blanket to cover him, smooth, warm, full against the night, her lips all over touching him, touching him, carrying him past certainty into the cold, final tunnel where the great gong roared.

XV

Williams kept on plugging away at it. The decision was made now; he would have to take Wulff. He would do his best. It had nothing to do with the squad any more, it did not even have much to do with Williams himself. Nothing personal in it. It was just something to be done.

Everything leaves a spoor: the deer in the forest, the needle in the arm, the ruined eyes of amphetamine users, the trails by which junk made its way into the country. Wulff would leave a spoor also; it was only a matter of picking it up from where he had been and tracing through. Knowing that Wulff had been in the one furnished room gave him a way of mapping out his progress from there; there would always be signs, indications, if you were patient enough to look for them, and Williams felt a horrendous patience settling upon him now. He would go as far as he could, as long as he could, until he found the man. He functioned out of time, outside normal motivation, outside any considerations of what would happen after he did face Wulff. He simply did what he had to do. That was all.

So he worked his way across town in the most patient, plodding, monomaniacal investigative work that he had ever done; the kind of work that the detective squad might have been able to do forty or fifty years ago when there was a detective squad and the time and lack of distraction to make this kind of work possible. He wandered up and down the streets; he checked neighborhood stores, he moved slowly and patiently through the well of the city, looking for any scrap that he might turn up. A fleeting glimpse of a man who looked like Wulff seen through a shop window might be the insight that would break the case. Something heard or sensed on a street corner might lead him straight through to what he was seeking. You never could tell, in short, when the case might break; you would slog along for hours or days, weeks or months possibly, getting nowhere, doing nothing, and then the one tiny detail would fall into your fingers like the thread that when severed would open up a cheap suit of clothes. Williams was willing to wait it out. So was the lieutenant. The Wulff Squad had gotten a lot of backlash from headquarters because the dead man was so clearly, as the pieces of background on him started to filter in, Wulff's work. But it was also indication that the squad was on the right track, that they now had him pinned somewhere in the city.

At least Williams thought that he was pinned in the city. So much of this was a matter of instinct and reckoning; so little of it worked out in terms of normal, logical processes. He simply had a strong feeling that Wulff was within a radius of a few blocks on the West Side and that he would not, could not leave. If everything had started here for Wulff, so then would it end, and there was one great piece of unfinished business that Williams could see that would be on Wulff's mind. He could not quite articulate it, found it hard to spot, but it had something to do with the dead girl, Marie Calvante, whose discovery had sent Wulff off on his campaign. He had found her here and here for Wulff her spirit remained; until that spirit was buried he could not leave. Williams could sense that. He could even, he supposed, respect it. Not that it meant anything in terms of his search.

It was hard work. Furthermore, he now had Father Justice to contend with, too. Father Justice was not very pleased at the way things were going. After the Gianelli murder Williams had gone up for the last time to the storefront church to find out if Father Justice had any information that could track Wulff, but the reverend had been almost speechless, whether with rage or grief Williams could not tell. He had refused Williams admission to the church, staring through the slats, saying that there was some kind of service in progress and no outsiders were permitted. When Williams had asked if he had read the papers and whether he had any ideas, the reverend's face had clotted with rage. "Get out of here," he said. "Just get out of here and pray that you find him before my men do, because if my men find him it is not going to be very pleasant. For either of you." So that had been pretty clear, laying it on the line, so to speak: Justice felt responsible because he had not been able to turn up Wulff before the murder and his own ordnance had been used to commit it, which brought him up on a conspiracy charge, possibly, if it was ever traced. This left open the question of why Father Justice, if he had known where Wulff was originally, did not simply attack and bring him out. But the ways of the Lord, as the reverend himself often pointed out, the ways of the Lord were extremely strange and complex, and there was no saying as to how or why He worked. Mysterious and strange, most of this went into metaphysical areas that were not Williams's area of expertise. Anyway, there would be no help at all there, that was for sure. It all came down to him.

Williams felt that he could get him. That confidence had been lurking within all through this; there was no doubt in his mind that sooner or later he would locate Wulff. And would have their confrontation. The question was what he was going to do when he came up against him? He did not know, and that reluctance might even underlay the pace of his detective work. He was proceeding methodically rather than in great, intuitive leaps, possibly because intuition would have worked a hell of a lot better than method. He did not know what he was going to do.

But he had an idea. The idea was forming within him. And when the word came out of the precinct, it was as if that moment of preparation would extend forever, so sure was he of what he was going to do next.

The call came from the precinct only indirectly. Actually it came from the lieutenant of the Wulff Squad on one of Williams's few evenings home. He had given up, knocked off early, gone home at five that night for a change, simply because he was exhausted and the smells of the West Side were deep within his nostrils. Now, sitting in the living room with a drink, listening to the sounds of his wife making dinner in the other room—she was cooking more and more elaborate meals, he sometimes thought, as a means of punishing him—he heard the phone, let his wife answer it, waited while she came into the living room and said that someone wanted to talk to him. Williams went into the kitchen to answer it, conscious of the fact that she was going to the bedroom to pick it up on the extension. All right. She could do that. That kind of thing hardly mattered any more.

"I think the case has broken," the lieutenant said when Williams got on. His voice was high, nervous, Williams had never heard him quite that way before. "I think the case is breaking right now."

"All right. Tell me."

"We got a call in from the sixty-second precinct. I mean, it came into headquarters of course, but they put me onto it because it's our responsibility. We—"

"Come on," Williams said. He squeezed his fingers into a hard ball, looked at his hand suddenly discolored from the pressure. "Tell me."

"They're putting in headquarters detail of course," the lieutenant said uncertainly. "I mean it's a downtown matter, I think the TPF is moving in. But it's our business too, isn't it? I thought so right away. I think we have to get in on it."

"Tell me," Williams said, "for Christ's sake, you stupid son of a bitch, you tell me right now." There was a shrilling gasp on the other side of the phone. He thought it might be the lieutenant, but no, that was less likely than his wife, listening in. Don't blow it, he thought, don't blow it now.

"All right," the lieutenant said. He seemed to take no offense from Williams's curse. As a matter of fact, it seemed to have relieved his mind in some way, as if he had always known he was a stupid son of a bitch and was merely waiting for someone to deliver the word to him so that he would be relieved of the responsibility of sole knowledge. "Our man is in the sixty-second right now. Or someone who sounds very much like our man."

"All right," Williams said, "all right."

"They can't go right in and take him, though. We can't, either. There seems to be a sort of problem."

"What?" Williams said, "what's the problem?"

"It's not clear. But he's got himself barricaded in there and he's holding some personnel for ransom. That seems to be it."

"Son of a bitch," Williams said, "son of a bitch."

"You cursing me again?"

"Yes," Williams said, "no. Yes, no, what does it matter? All right. I'm going in there."

"Be careful," the lieutenant said. "I'll see you up there, I guess. We've all got to go in there. You know where the sixty-second is?"

"Yes," Williams said, "I know where the sixty-second is. And this one I've got to handle myself."

"I don't understand—"

"Forget understanding," Williams said, "forget all of it," and, throbbing with a sense of urgency that came over him like ague, flung down the phone, went from the kitchen, took his service revolver and identification and headed for the door. No time to change into blues, not that that mattered. At the door his wife, now holding the baby, met him, looked at him in a silence that extended toward pain. Williams tried to break the moment, fling himself through the door, but he could not. He could not do it. There was something to be said, he supposed, but he did not quite know what it was.

"Be careful," she said after a while, "for God's sake, be careful."

"Being careful has nothing to do with it."

The child stirred in her arms, opened an eye, looked at Williams. She looked down at it. "Do you have to do it?" she said, "must you?"

"Yes," he said, "I've got to do it. This time I've got to do it."

"Is it the end?"

"I think so," he said, "I think so. I think that this is the end, at least for me," and he leaned down and kissed her once, one light contact on the forehead, feeling the cold, impermeable surfaces of her flesh open up like lips to something like contact. Then, without thinking any more because thought would have been pain, he slammed the door, bolted toward the Ford, got into it and backed it screaming out of the driveway, not even clearing the street, trusting to luck, came into a wide arc on the other side, slammed it into drive and headed toward the sixty-second.

The sixty-second. Central Harlem. Where Wulff had set it up for siege.

And somehow Williams knew exactly what it was all about.

XVI

The idea had occurred to Wulff in sleep or semiconsciousness, hard to differentiate between the two, he had been drifting and dreaming in his room, looking at the ordnance, thinking or not thinking, his mind perfectly blank, whirring at idle as he tried to pick up his next move. And then it had been there, clear, hammered into his mind as if it had been there all the time and he had merely turned his attention to the inscribed words. Clear, clear: it was so devastatingly, hopelessly clear that the only question was why he had not thought of it a long time ago. But it did not matter. The important thing was that he had thought of it now. It was merely a matter of acting on it.

Because it had not begun with Marie Calvante, with the dead girl on the floor. He thought that it had; that was why he had returned to the West Side, to close full circle, to end as he had begun, to unite the end with the beginning. Maybe he had thought that if he went back, if he could clean it up and make it right here at the source, the girl would still be alive, nothing would have happened, he would have cleaned out not only the recent but the total past and all would have been as before: Marie close to him, their engagement an impatient waiting, their marriage a finality. Maybe that was what he had wanted. But he had not understood.

No, he had not understood. This odyssey did not begin with the girl, but somewhat earlier. It had begun with the informant that he had brought under the gun into Harlem's sixty-second precinct, the informant who was carrying and whose insolence and mockery in the neighborhood bar he could not stand—*shit man, you fucking narco, no narco's going to bust anyone but a tip*, the informant's sneer had said—and which had made him bring the man into the sixty-second if only to prove to him that there were limits to defiance. And at the sixty-second there had been the lieutenant, the fucking desk lieutenant, the tall son of a bitch who had put Wulff in one room and the informant in another, made Wulff sweat it out for two hours before the lieutenant had come into Wulff and said that it was false arrest; the informant was not carrying. He had nothing. He had been turned back into the street. How did Wulff think that he was going to do the department any good if he got them into suits for false arrest because of his goddamned stupidity? And although all of this had been said to him straight, there had been a little mad twinkle in the lieutenant's eyes, a little of the same, *man, I'm just shitting you*, that he had seen with the informant. So he had lost his temper, he had been under very great pressure by that time, and had belted the lieutenant in the jaw, just a light one, but hard enough anyway to send the uncoordinated lieutenant lurching back into the wall.

And that was how it had all started. The lieutenant had called narco, narco had busted him back to patrol, patrol had put him into the police car next to Williams, and the next night he had discovered the body of the o.d.'d girl five flights up on West Ninety-third Street. It had started with the lieutenant. The lieutenant had crossed him. Not narco. Not even the monsters, whoever they were, who had killed his girl. No. *The lieutenant.* Because some how, some way, he had called them in on him.

A man who was collaborating with an informant sure as hell would know people a little higher up along the trail. He would pass on information to them. Routinely.

All of this slid into Wulff's mind almost unobtrusively, dropping in like a series of chain gears, like a hoist dropping engines into new cars on the assembly line, one a minute, driving in the works, and the simple clarity of it had brought him out of his chair, his sleep, his reverie, whatever it had been. In that moment Wulff had seen all of it clearly mapped for him: why he had been at loose ends, why he had not known what to do next, why this second New York campaign so far had been such a hit-or-miss affair, such an essential loss of purposes. It was simple. He had never approached the basic problem.

The basic problem was the lieutenant.

No doubt, no indecision now. He knew exactly what he had to do now.

He got out of the chair, armed up with two grenades and an extra pistol. After long consideration he dropped the idea of the machine gun, not because he could not use it, but because its concealment, entering a station house, would be almost impossible. He found it a very easy load to carry, considering all the death packed away. In relation to the damage he could cause, he was carrying one of the lightest packages one could possibly conceive. Combat technique of course—the most artillery in the lightest possible package. Someday they would arrive at the perfect weapon, which would be a mechanism capable of destroying a city, and which one could carry in the palm of one's hand. That would be worth more to the generals than any amount of plutonium bombs; they could wreck the world all right.

He went up to the sixty-second precinct. Coming back to Harlem was an exercise in familiarity. It was for him like a sleeper's blankets being piled over him as he sank back from nightmare into the surge of an equivocal dream. He would have had to come an awfully long way for Harlem to have struck him as an exercise in familiarity, for Harlem to have been comfortable to him, but coming out of the subway that was exactly how he did feel; it was a foreign land but occupied territory. He thought he understood it far better than the barbarities of the East Side, better than all the strange cities he had seen. The despair kindled in Harlem was a New York despair that worked within the landscape rather than being imposed upon it like the angst of suburbia; he could breathe it in, breath it out, shrug his way with it like most of the residents. No, Harlem had been bum-rapped all over the country. The media had dug their tentacles into it as they did into everything. But after all was said and done, Wulff guessed he understood it.

Two brisk blocks to the sixty-second precinct. Rambling through the sidestreets he had the good old Harlem feel, one of blending, meshing with the landscape rather than fighting against it. Even though he was white, a white man in the vicinity of the precinct was not an unusual sight, and he felt no tension as he walked past the crumbling brownstones. The police to Harlem was the occupying army, treated with the sullenness and respect due such an army. Occasionally, like every five years, there would be a flare-up, but it was quickly put down, as almost all of the local revolts were, and things returned to normal. At the sixty-second he saw the private cars of the cops angled up and down the pavement, parked in the street, on the sidewalk in the way that cops had; the only civil service position in town where free parking was considered a fringe benefit, a right not guaranteed by contract but by unwritten understanding. The residents loved that, the cars all over the street, but then they understood that an occupying army had its own rights and privileges, and who were they to protest?

Wulff walked up the steps of the precinct almost humming. Everything was certain now; everything was in place, all doubt and indecision gone. It seemed impossible that he had not known this a long time ago: that the way to attack was frontally and at the base of the problem. Inside, the odors of the precinct house, the stains on the walls, the ruined furniture were as familiar to him as the pictures he made behind closed eyes to ease him off to sleep. He inhaled, grateful to feel at home. Once a cop, always a cop; that was the truth. You could repudiate a hell of a lot of it, know its rottenness and stink, but the rottenness and stink were part of you. It was better to accept this.

The desk sergeant looked at him incuriously; a white man coming in this way could only be reporting a robbery or mugging, but Wulff was moving too slowly for that, seemed to be not agitated. On the other hand, the desk sergeant had watched a hundred a day come in here for eight years; that meant twenty thousand faces coming into the precinct house. He could hardly take any of them as remarkable or as a basis for response, because if he did he would blow himself apart. He merely sat there writing in a book, making painful entries of some sort, probably logging in his pension credits, Wulff thought. The reception room was otherwise deserted; overhead, in the cages, he could hear the faint murmurs of staff, the sound of typewriters. Downstairs in the pit there might be screaming, but there was plenty of insulation in this, as in all the old precinct houses; he would not be hearing this. And things had changed a good deal through the last decade; he doubted if there was such stuff going on now. Nowadays they did it more efficiently and usually out in the street. It was easier to log in a dead perpetrator. And it saved arraignment difficulties and the problem of going to court.

"Yeah," the desk sergeant said finally. He was a small, weary man with a face like a doorknob. "What do you want?"

"What do I want?" Wulff said, "I want—" and then he paused dead because he realized that he did not know the lieutenant's name. Had never gotten it. That was pretty stupid of him, he thought. To go through all of this and not even know the name of the man he wanted. Little foresight. He should have checked it out somehow.

"I'm waiting," the desk sergeant said, "I'm really waiting now," and behind his eyes a little light was kindling, a faint light that only a practiced eye could see, but Wulff saw it and he realized that the desk sergeant was not as dumb as he looked, desk sergeants never were, nor was he as dead, this being an exception in the trade. Some connection had been made, something was worming its way slowly through the mind of the sergeant, something on the verge of recognition working its way through those eyes, and Wulff thought: he's going to make me, he's got me, they've got my picture in their wallets. He stood there momentarily indecisive, not knowing whether the next move was to move right on or out, whether he dared push the sergeant or instead had to retreat. And then the lieutenant of six months ago walked into the room straightening his uniform, pulling his slacks into alignment, strolled over to the desk, and winked at the sergeant without even looking at Wulff. "How you doing?" he said. "I think I'm checking out."

Too much. It was too much, but the wrenching bizarreness of the coincidence was exactly what Wulff needed to enable him to go on. A fat woman was coming up the steps carrying a small weeping child, running a hand through her hair, and this distracted the sergeant, he swung his angle of vision to take her in, then came back to Wulff. Wulff said, "All right. That's it. Let's hold it."

The sergeant looked at him flatly; the lieutenant sighed and said, "Jesus Christ, have we got another goddamned nut case here?" and then he turned and saw Wulff, and everything came together for the lieutenant in that moment. Wulff knew the feeling, he had had it himself a few times, events tumbling, colliding, and then slamming into one another with the majestic precision and solemnity of ships crashing.

The lieutenant went for his pistol, gibbering; the sergeant, puzzled, looking at all of this through narrowed eyes, the child in the woman's hands sniffling and too late, too late for all of them. Wulff held the pistol very level at the lieutenant's midsection.

"Don't do it," he said quietly. "Don't think of a thing. You make a fucking move and you're going to be without a gut."

The lieutenant's hands fell away, his hands shook, the sergeant's face folded over in amazement and the fat woman, still carrying the child, turned and ran at full sprint down the steps and out into the street. Wulff could hear the door bang behind, and then there they were in perfect confrontation—sergeant, lieutenant, Wulff. And Wulff said it as he had worked it out before and knew in the saying that it was going to be all right. It would work. He had the feeling within him that a good pool player would have when he was about to start what he was sure was going to be a hot run.

"All right," he said to the sergeant then. "I'm just going to take this man into one of the interrogation rooms. You'd better get the word out that I've got a hostage here and that if anyone makes a move, any kind of a move to break this up, they're going to lose that hostage. You understand that?"

The sergeant nodded once, very slowly. "I know who you are," he said.

"I'm glad of that. Are you going to listen to me and cooperate, or is there going to be trouble?"

The sergeant looked at him and there was calculation tempered by a certain amount of insight. "No," he said, "there won't be trouble. I'm not going to buck you. You don't knock over precinct houses, you know. We can't stand that. You ought to remember that much."

"I remember plenty," Wulff said. He took the gun then, prodded the lieutenant in the back. The man had not said anything since the gun had been pulled on him; he was sweating lightly, terrified. Probably had never been under the gun before. Not that it made much difference one way or the other; mean bastards came in all forms, some had seen too much of the gun. "Let's go," Wulff said. "I remember where that room is. Let's go and have a talk."

"About what?" the lieutenant said, his voice cracking. He cleared his throat, tried again. "What's there to talk about?"

"There's a lot to talk about," Wulff said, prodding him. To the sergeant: "You'd better tell them to keep their distance if you want to see this man again."

"Do it," the lieutenant said, "don't fuck around with him." He was already walking. "For Christ's sake, he means business. What is there to talk about?"

"A lot of things," Wulff said, guiding him. "For one thing I want to know how you put me here and for another what you expect to do to get me the hell out." To the sergeant: "Tell them they shouldn't fuck around. Tell them I've got a couple of hand grenades too."

On the phone the sergeant looked up, spread his free hand and said, "I never would have doubted it."

XVII

Outside they had the TPF, the emergency squad, floating cars from other precincts, the emergency rescue squad, a cordon of cops ringing the building holding back the crowd, which was five-deep and growing. They didn't know what was up, but in Harlem it was bound to be something bad for them, and it sounded ominous. Williams ignored all of it, pushed his way to the front. "Let me in," he said to the patrolman at the sawhorse. "Let me in there."

"You've got to be crazy," the patrolman said. "No one's going in there. That place is under siege."

"No," Williams said, "I've got to go," and pulled his identification from his pocket, shoved it under the patrolman's face. As the man instinctively reached forward to take it, momentarily distracted,

Williams hurdled the sawhorse and in three leaps was moving up the steps of the precinct into the interior. Another set of police was at the door standing, hands on hips, one of them clawing at his gun as Williams came up. "Get away," Williams said again, "I'm going in there."

"No one's going in there," the cop said. He put a hand on his sergeant's stripes as if wanting to show levels of authority yet feeling vaguely embarrassed about it at the same time. "We can't risk it."

"We've got to risk it," Williams said. "You've got to let me in there. I'm the man he wants!" and while the sergeant was thinking about this, Williams was already through him. The others on both sides made reluctant efforts to stop him, like men snapping flies out of the air, then let him go. If he wanted to kill himself, Williams imagined their thinking was, if he wanted to go into the sixty-second and be a sacrifice, it was his business. Cops were very loyal that way; they were loyal to themselves. They had a fervent belief in the right of brother cops sacrificing themselves if that would take the heat off them and get the cops some sympathy in the media. He was in the precinct house itself now, the murmurs of the crowd dimmed to mutters behind the doors. The desk sergeant, rearing from his post, telephone to his ear, looked at Williams with amazement and then slammed the phone down. "Don't you know what's going on here?" he said. "What the fuck are you doing?"

"I know what's going on," Williams said. "Where the hell are they? Just tell me where they are."

The desk sergeant could not take it. It was as if the multiplication of events had worked its way into him up to a certain point, the circuits taking it with only slight overheating or strain, but now like a computer there was an overload and he was about to shut down. "Don't you understand," he said, "I've got TPF, I've got special units, I've got—" and then swallowing in a constricted way several times he could say no more. His eyes bulged. "I can't take it any more," he said, "I just can't fucking take it any more. You go along to a certain point, and this is a tough precinct, but it's too much. It's too much," he said almost indolently, leaning back from his high chair, the tilt precarious, and then he came slamming forward, his elbows banging hard on the desk. "Get out of here," he said, "just get out of here before I begin to take you seriously, before I believe that there's someone here."

Williams said, "I'm here to take him. I'm on the special squad dealing with him. Tell me where he is and your troubles are over," and he thought, screw this, what was he even bothering to pump information out of the desk sergeant for? It was merely a delaying tactic, a delaying tactic against his own reluctance. The basement; they would have to be in one of the old rubber hose rooms lined up down there. "Let's go," he said, more to himself than the desk sergeant and bolted toward the staircase.

The phone rang at the sergeant's elbow and the sergeant cut it off, Williams could hear him babbling into the receiver. Good enough, let him babble away, it had nothing to do with his own problem. He had run the barricade, but that did not mean that anyone else was going to do so. He charged down a staircase reeking of urine and old fires, little scraps of paper twinkling under his feet, and he found himself in a low, flat basement, the ceilings near his head, down at the end little lights winking from the various rooms. From one of them, way down, he could hear a voice. Wulff's voice.

Williams took out his gun. It felt cold in his hand, more like a sheathed knife than a gun, deadly, present in his grasp. He began to move toward the voice. The fluorescence of the lamps sparkled. He might have been in a street, not the basement, the street lamps winking down at him. It was like the night that he had been near the methadone center, the night before the knife had gone into his ribs. He felt his ribs quiver; a spot of bright reminiscent pain darting from that special place where he had been hit. He put a hand over it, cupped it, eased the pain away and kept on moving. Toward the sound of the voice. Low, maniacal, it had fallen into a chant that now filled the hallway. He went down in an instinctive combat low-crawl and he kept on moving.

XVIII

Wulff had the lieutenant braced against a wall in the prisoner's position, hands high above his head, palms flat to the wall, kneecaps touching, stomach against the plaster. He held the gun in the lieutenant's back and every now and then gave him a small prod, just to keep him alert. He had adjusted the one spotlight in the room so that it came down in a white, heated spot focusing on the back of the lieutenant's skull. The lieutenant's cap was off, ripped off by Wulff, flung to the floor, and sweat was coming from him so profusely that even the back of his head was wet. He breathed in uneven, shuddering gasps, shunting the breath through as if it were passing many obstacles. Wulff knew that if he turned the man around he would see that he was crying. He did not turn him around: he did not need to see him do it. All of the confirmation was in the lieutenant's voice.

"Tell me," he said, "why did you do it? Why did you let him go? You could have booked him, you know there was enough evidence to hold."

His voice was calm, level. He had started by screaming but soon had realized that there was no need for this; what you had to do was to cultivate an absolute sense of control. He had it now. He was completely self-possessed. "You should have booked him," he said, "why didn't you book him? All the evidence was there." He kept on going. He could go on that way now as long as he needed.

"I told you," the lieutenant said, "I don't know what you're talking about." His body quivered. "Please stop this," he said, "it's not doing any good."

Wulff hit him at half-speed in the ribs with the butt of the gun. "No good," he said. "It won't wash. It's not what I need to hear; it's not what I like. Why did you let him go? What had you worked out with him?"

"I don't know," the lieutenant said, "I don't remember. I don't know what you're talking about."

"Yes you do. You know exactly what I'm talking about."

"No I don't. Listen, let me turn around, let me face you, let me talk—"

Wulff hit him again in the ribs the same way. The lieutenant screamed lightly, then went back to the concentrated effort of breathing once more. "I told you," Wulff said, "I don't like it. It doesn't wash. Remember. Tell me."

"I can't tell you anything."

"Yes you can. Try to remember."

"I know who you are," the lieutenant said. "I swear to God that it doesn't affect anything. Listen, nobody here has any quarrel with you. We all think you're doing a real job. All of us here at the precinct—"

Wulff thought of hitting him again, but one more blow might topple the lieutenant and that was not necessary. He did not want to kill him. Not at all, at least until he got the answer. "Cut it out," he said again. "You remember. You remember everything. Why did you let him go? Why did you turn me into the command post? What did I do that you didn't like; who was paying you off?"

"Oh shit," the lieutenant said, "oh shit now, just listen, nobody was paying off. Nobody remembers anything, it's all gone, it's all forgotten," and he turned then, a stricken aspect to his face all that Wulff saw, and then the man was on his knees, facing him. "Please," he said, "please."

Wulff said, "That's no attitude for a cop. Particularly one dedicated to protecting the rights of informants like you were. I'm not impressed. Get off your fucking knees."

"It's all forgotten. It all happened a long time ago; it doesn't really make a bit of difference. You'll never get away with this," the lieutenant said, a shade of cunning moving, then retreating on his face. "They'll storm the precinct. You won't get away with it, you hear me?"

"Yeah," Wulff said, "I hear you," thinking how many times he had heard this before, all of the organization guys, the mob guys, the shrewdsters and the speedsters standing before him telling him that he did not have a chance, that there was no way he could get away with this, that they were going to be rescued, that they would be bailed out, that terrific vengeance would be exacted from Wulff for fucking around with guys as significant and important as them. Oh yes he had heard it, standing in a hundred rooms, listening to a hundred speeches like this, and here he was listening to it once again. Under the gun, cops and mobsters talked exactly the same way; there was a message in that, leave it to whoever was good at digging out messages. As far as he was concerned, he had enough trouble figuring out exactly what he wanted. What was he after? Exactly what did he hope to gain from the lieutenant? There the man was, the man who had started him on the great voyage, the man who in a sense was responsible for a hundred deaths himself: a gnarled, sniveling mass at his feet, as effectively broken as Wulff could ever have hoped him to be, the precinct ringed with troops he was sure, and yet he had not dug out what he wanted. There was something obscure, something he was after, but he could not quite lay his finger on it—and then it was there as if the finger had been *resting* on this one jot of information all the time and had now leapt away, springing free the one damning insight that he had been looking for all this time. Now he knew why he was here; now he knew why he wanted the lieutenant. "Who killed her?" he said. "Who killed her?"

The lieutenant looked up at him. His face was streaked with sweat. "Killed who?"

"Killed the girl. Who o.d.'d her out and left her for me to find in that rooming house? Tell me," he said. He pointed the gun at the lieutenant's head. "Tell me now."

"I don't know what you're talking about," the man said frantically. "I don't know—"

"All of them said they didn't know who did it, that the organization had nothing to do with it. I chased them all over the country and I heard it in nine cities, no one knew what had happened to her but they weren't responsible. I called them liars and one by one I killed them all. All of them. And you know something? The message finally got through this thick skull. I think they were telling the truth after all. I don't think any of them knows who did it; I don't think they were responsible for it."

"Leave me alone," the lieutenant said. It was the most ridiculous, unresponsive thing he could have said; some knowledge of this caused his mouth to arc into a tormented grin. "For God's sake, I don't know what you're talking about."

"I do. I think you do too. Somebody here killed her to teach me a lesson; to make me lay off. To hit me so hard that they wouldn't have to worry about me ever again. And it could only have been a cop."

"Stop it," the lieutenant said. He was rigid in posture, thin blotches on his cheek. "Stop it, you're crazy."

"Only a cop could have picked her up, only a cop could have gotten her trust long enough to have brought her there and done what they had to do. No one else. Anyone else had tried it, they would have had to kill her on the way. She was a fighter. The girl was a fighter."

The lieutenant said, "I don't know what you're talking about. I don't know anything about the girl."

"Yes you do," Wulff said, and indeed he felt that finally everything was falling into place: he was seeing with a dreadful clarity that could only have been accumulated from stepping over a hundred corpses. Win one, lose one, lose yourself but win knowledge. Was it worth it? "You," he said, "it would have been you all the time. Or one of your contacts, some other rotten fucking cop who would have gone along with it. But most likely it was you. You got hurt bad. I put you in a hell of a spot, dragging in one of your own protection cases. So you had to dig for a way to get back at me, and it wasn't very hard, was it? If you know a little investigative technique, if you can reach the local precinct, which any cop could, pull rank, dig out some information, it wouldn't have been very hard at all." He pointed the gun at the lieutenant. "I make it you killed her," he said. "It was you all along. All this time I've been killing hard guys, busting up the trade and you've been sweating it out."

"Listen," the lieutenant said. The blotches had become great spots, circles on the cheeks covering them with red, the trapped blood spiraling upward toward the temples. "You're wrong. If you think what I guess you are, you've got it wrong. I wouldn't; I couldn't. You don't involve someone else in this; it would have been just you and me. Your girl wasn't any part of it. She was out there in Queens—"

"You knew," Wulff said, "you knew she was my girl and out in Queens. That's all I need to know, that and everything else coming together. It's stupid," he said. "I've been going one way all the time when I should have been going the other. It could have been so simple. I could have done this from the beginning." He pointed the gun. "This is it," he said.

"No!" the lieutenant shrieked, the wailing scream of a dying man and Wulff concentrated on the trigger, freeing the trigger and someone behind him screamed: "Stop it, Wulff, don't do it!" His hand shook, the gun shook, the shot went wild, and the lieutenant dove to the floor, Wulff already turning. And there was Williams behind him, the .38 special in his hand, pointing. And as Williams watched, astonished, Wulff shot the gun out of his hand, the gun cracking, spinning against the wall. Wulff looked at Williams under the hot, harsh light of the naked bulb, the lieutenant whimpering on the floor. For the longest time Wulff did not know what to do or what to think, but finally the attitude hit him, the only proper attitude that there could have been, and the maniacal laughter hit him like a pile driver, working through all the spaces of his body, and he fell to his knees looking at Williams, laughing and laughing until the sweat had in that instant come through his clothes and hung them, glistening, to his skin.

Because the way that everything, in these last moments, had all come together was too much for him. There was a neatness and artistry to it that Calabrese more than anyone would have appreciated.

He wished Calabrese, his old and most respected enemy, could have seen it. He might have understood. Wulff was not sure that he did.

XIX

Williams said, "This won't do. Pull yourself together." The advice seemed unnecessary. Wulff was already assembling the various parts of himself, control flowing into him like ice, beginning in the dark chambers of the heart, then carried by the blood through his system. He would be all right. It was the other one, the man in uniform on the floor who Williams was worried about; the man appeared to be in complex shock, gibbering, rolling, grappling with his ankles, humping the floor as if it were a woman, then subsiding to lie there. He belched, a thin stream of fluid coming from his mouth. Williams looked at the man with revulsion and then at Wulff. "Well," he said, "well, it's been a while."

"Yeah," Wulff said, "it's been a while all right." After the maniacal fit of laughter, his control seemed to have returned absolutely; he seemed almost nonchalant, completely unaffected. "I should kill him," he said. "All I want to do is kill him."

"Killing's against the law. There are very stringent rules against that, Wulff."

"For human beings," Wulff said, staring meditatively, "but this is in a different category." He looked up at Williams. "He killed her, you know. I'm sure of it."

"It's too late for that now. She's dead and he's not going to be killing anyone any more."

"I don't know," Wulff said. The lieutenant revolved, lay sighing on his back, blank eyes staring at the ceiling. "There's no saying; he might be doing a lot of things. You can't close the books on a human being until he's dead."

Williams said, "It won't work, Wulff." It occurred to him for the first time that he was unarmed. Wulff held the pistol, moving it between Williams and the man on the floor. Fascinating, Williams thought, fascinating that it should come down to this; that Wulff should wind up being dangerous to him. But he guessed he was. He concentrated on keeping his voice flat and level. "Let's go, Wulff," he said. "Let's get out of here. Let's go upstairs."

Wulff was still looking at the lieutenant. "I can't do that," he said, "I just can't do it, you see. They'll arrest me."

"Not necessarily."

"You know they'll arrest me, David," Wulff said. His voice was low, patient. Williams had never heard him so calm. "And then what will it come down to? Everything's going down the drain, it will be for nothing. That's not right. You've got to admit that that isn't right, David."

"It can't go on," Williams said. The basement was very quiet. He had thought that behind him they might be throwing in reinforcements, a few daring TPF coming under his lead. But police, generally speaking, were more clever than that. Why bother? the thinking was upstairs. If Williams was able to bring him out, save them the trouble, so much the better; he would have taken the load off them. If he failed, if Wulff added one more corpse to his cycle, then that would make him a cop-killer and compound the case. Either way they figured they could not lose. They had him under siege. One thing was quite clear: Wulff was not going to get out of here alive. Under no conditions would they let him, they had him ringed in. So they had all the time in the world. They could wait.

"I've got to kill him," Wulff said again, looking at the lieutenant. The lieutenant, it seemed, had fainted; his respiration was even, his eyes closed. One way or the other now he was out of it. "If I don't kill him it's ridiculous. Everything goes down the drain; it's for nothing, all of it." He turned toward the body on the floor, leveling the pistol. "He killed my girl," he said. "He started off everything."

"They'll deal with that."

"No they won't. They won't deal with anything." But Wulff did not shoot the man. That was the interesting thing; he did not shoot him. Some fine strand of reluctance seemed to have looped his neck, he shrugged, twitched, looked uncomfortable. Williams said, "Give me the gun, man. Let's get out of here."

"I can't do that. Now you know I can't do that; if I give you the gun you'll just take me upstairs and walk me into that net. And then what?"

"That's right, Wulff," Williams said, "I'll take you upstairs and turn you over."

"I'll never make it through there alive."

"Wrong, Wulff," Williams said quietly, "dead wrong, wrong, you'll make it through there alive. They want you in custody, they want to take you in, and I don't think that it's going to be that bad. You see, you're something of a hero. They don't shoot heroes."

"They crucify them."

"No," Williams said again. Strange, his relationship with Wulff from the beginning had been so equivocal, so uncertain; who was the leader, who the follower? Who had created, who had enacted? These questions had torn around and through him to no conclusion, no conclusion whatsoever. But now Williams thought that he saw the answer coming finally as if glimpsed after a long, gasping crawl through high ground to the top of a mountain, the view showing only waste. He was stronger because he was inside. From the inside, no matter how corrupt it was, came strength. He stretched out his hand. "Give it to me," he said. "You want it to be over, Wulff. You want it to be over just as bad as they do, as I do. Otherwise you wouldn't be here."

Wulff looked at the crumpled thing on the floor, the flanks of it heaving. "And that?" he said, "what about that?"

"They'll take care of him."

"Like they've taken care of everything else?"

"They'll settle with him. He won't get away with it. If he did it I'll guarantee that he pays. Even," Williams said, "even if I have to do it myself."

Wulff stood there. The moment extended, reshaped itself, curved back in like a long, floating scarf drifting in wind. Outside it was still very quiet. They were waiting. They would let Williams settle it out. They had conferred and as always they had let the black man do their job. Muck around with the shitwork. Clean up the world.

"You know you want it to be over, Wulff," Williams said softly again. "They're all dead. Calabrese, Marasco, the Nazi in Peru, all of them. You did what you had to do. You've done your job. Now you can rest."

"It's always going to be the same."

"But it's a little different. Every time around it's a little different. Hell, man, you can't clean up the world, not in one shot. You tried. You tried."

"That's for sure," Wulff said, "I tried." He extended the pistol, butt end first, and Williams reached forward, touched it delicately, feeling a hint of resistance from Wulff's fingers, then slowly pulled. The pistol came into his hand. He touched it, gathered it, put it in his pocket. Wulff looked at him then and seemed to smile.

"You forgot the grenade," he said and took something gray and round from his jacket pocket, gave it to Williams. Williams felt it like an apple in his hand, held the place where the pin was locked in securely, put it carefully into his pants pocket. The lieutenant kicked once on the floor.

"All right," Williams said, "let's go."

"And leave him here?"

"I don't know where else to leave him. I don't know any other place, do you, Wulff?"

"No," Wulff said. "I don't." He moved past Williams, went to the open door of the interrogation room and moved out into the hall. Williams came behind him and then they were in the hall. Wulff turned and Williams could see a sudden light kindled in his eyes, a trace of humor perhaps, something that he had not seen there before. Wulff extended a hand, touched Williams on the wrist and then seemed to wink at him.

"You're right on one thing," he said. "You hit the nail on the head one way, friend. You can't imagine how I want it to be over."

They headed upstairs.

EPILOGUE

Williams had a dream. In that dream someone had attacked him during the night and, just like Marie Calvante, had overloaded his system with junk. Now his body had expanded to fit the proportions of the planet; another astronomical body, he drifted within the solar system, gross, distended, seeing the other planets filtered through their surrounding haze, drifting in their orbits around him. He was a million miles in circumference, revolving around a sun that looked like a light bulb, the light burning hard into his eyes, and even though he was impossibly huge, every inch of it was built for pain, and he writhed in the darkness.

He had been overloaded with junk and now he was a world, no longer a man but a specimen, a huge artifact drifting in the solar dust, trapped there, his movements controlled by gravity and by the bombardment of the Van Allen belt, no sense to him, no movement. Someday he would be entwined in ropes and brought like an artifact, a beached whale, to be examined by aliens in some museum. Now he thrashed in orbit in impossible pain and the screams began. He was no longer human, but he had retained all the human capacity for pain; he had the feeling but not the possibility of being human, and this was hell, it was as close to hell as he could come. He screamed and the scream broke him to the surface of what he dreamed to be his condition; he was lying on the floor of a room, a needle in his arm, junk flowing like minerals through his system and as he looked upward he saw the faces of those who had overloaded him, and there they all were, there they were: Calabrese, the two guards, Tamara, Wulff.

He woke up bellowing, shouting, rattling in the sheets, and his wife was over him then, her hands on his body pressing him back, cool from her fingertips, threads of cold pulsing into him, and after a while he was able to lay on the sheets without movement, the quivering slowly working within him like the sea. He shook his head, coughed, then sat up slowly in the darkness, her hands still on him. He put on the lamp. "It's all right," she said finally, "it's all right."

"I don't know."

"Bad dream?"

"I've had better ones."

"It's going to be all right. It's all over now and you can rest."

"That's what I told Wulff," he said. "That's what I said to him, that it was all over. That's how I got him out of there. But I don't know. I just don't know. I don't think that anything's over."

"It has nothing to do with you any more."

The dream had begun to recede; already the outlines, like some great animal dissolving in a swamp, were beginning to merge into the background of the night. In ten minutes he would have forgotten all but the feeling of it, but that would stay, that would stay a long time. "In Los Angeles," he said, "we saw that it wouldn't work, the two of us couldn't work together, so I headed back East but I got kidnapped. I got kidnapped by two men who worked for Calabrese, and I was held in Chicago and Miami for a week." It was the first time he had told her any of this. Before then he had said that that month would have to be shut out of their lives if they were to live again.

"All right," she said, "it's over now."

"I spent a week in a room with a couple of men who were paid, going to get paid for killing me. We got along fine after the first couple of days because they didn't like their job too much, but do you know what it's like to be in a room with a couple of men who want to kill you?"

"It's not good," she said, "it's no good."

"They're dead now," Williams said. "Everyone's dead, except for Wulff and me, and he's in jail and I'm lying here in bed and supposed to go back into uniform next week. So that means that no one's left, do you understand?"

"No," she said, "I don't. I don't understand it."

"Dead," Williams said again. "Calabrese, the girl, the two guys who were guarding me, everybody else, hundreds of corpses, Wulff himself in jail under tight security, and me getting out of it, supposed to go back to patrol work as if none of it ever happened. It's all gone," Williams said, "it's like it never was. It's all covered over."

"That's for the best," she said. She put a hand on his elbow, tugged. "Get back to sleep," she said. "It's five in the morning."

But Williams was beginning to see what the dream had been trying to tell him, what signal had been pulsing from the quasar of distant intelligence there; he could not let it get away. "All for nothing," he said, "all of them gone, all of it gone, everything the same. Sure the trade's been hurt; he hurt it a lot. But there's still junk in Harlem. There's still somebody dying right this moment from an o.d. There are still men hustling it, dreaming it, pushing it. They just have different names and faces in the middle, and at the top it's probably been the same all along, people so high that Wulff couldn't even touch them. People who probably run things. It's still flowing. It was just a campaign."

"This doesn't mean that it failed," she said, but she didn't really know what she was talking about. Williams could see that, sense it, she had missed the point completely, but that was all right, he understood, everyone would miss the point, no way that they could see it. Wulff himself, in the bowels of the police station had missed out; saying only that no one had any idea how much he wanted it to be over. If Wulff missed it, could Williams's wife get it? Of course, Wulff was entitled to be tired. At the beginning he might not have thought this way; he might have seen what Williams was now seeing. But he could be forgiven. At the end, in exhaustion, there was remission. You did what you had to do, that was all; there was nothing that you could do to change the circumstances and breeding that had made you what you were. Wasn't there a name for this kind of thing? Behaviorism? Cultural determinism? Something like that.

Williams leaned over, flicked off the lamp, turned on his side, and lay there. "It's all right," he said. "I can sleep now," and he thought that he could, he really could. His wife came over from her side of the bed, lay against him, an arm draped around his stomach, the fingers touching his chest, drawing him against her, and he felt a thin rush of desire instantly superseded by exhaustion; he could not take her, even now when she was doubtless more accessible than she had been in a long time. He was too tired. It was just fear, that was all it was, less desire than fear and the need to draw him in. "I'll be all right," he said. "I'll be all right now," and closed his eyes, watching the images leap up once again on the screen of the mind.

Wulff in Los Angeles using heavy ordnance to fight off the assailants at the trailer park. Justice in New York, clamping his hands together, his black face pulped with rage as he said he could not tolerate the loss of explosives. Wulff's face when Williams had seen him up on the fifth floor at West Ninety-third Street, his face as he turned toward Williams, the eyes and cheeks riven as if scraped by chisel and behind him the dead girl. Flame around it. Calabrese on the plane to Miami when the old man had told Williams almost amiably that he would have to kill him if Wulff did not cooperate. Tamara, the girl on the beach in the midst of the corpses, the second girl over whom he had seen Wulff standing, keening his song of loss the more dreadful because there were no words or music to it. The look on his wife's face the night Wulff had come to their home. The link that had passed between them that he knew he could neither see nor touch. Santa Anita. Santa Anita in the sun in August where he and Wulff had met.

It was all there and it was not there; close your eyes and the images came swirling up, close them and they were gone. Christmas-tree lights on a circuit breaker: up, down, on, off. Open the eyes and it all dissolved; it was New York and the gray dawn outside; close them and all of it returned shimmering in color. Up, down, in, out. They existed and they did not. They were here and they weren't. Now you see it, now you don't. Voyage in. Voyage out.

Wulff was incarcerated. They were still working on the charges. Maybe he would get out. Maybe he would not. Maybe the war would go on in some way and perhaps it was ended. But the past could not be changed. It had happened. All of it had happened.

Williams stirred, felt himself entering the vault of sleep. This time the beasts of dreams were not inside; it was cool and dense within the vault, filled with the rich air smelling of ozone that poured in from the vents. In the vault was surcease and you crawled into it seven or eight hours a day, every day of your life, a little light glimmering at both ends, and then entrance into the vault forever. Death was already familiar; already the lover for it brushed against you one-third of your life, all of your life, and when it came it was no stranger. It came with the bright face of beckoning and you went into it.

Los Angeles. Santa Anita. Calabrese. Tamara. Marie Calvante. Wulff holding the gun looking at the lieutenant on the floor, that sick expectation in his eyes fading off to something else. Something that might have been knowledge. You did not know. You did not know what was going on.

You could not judge another man.

Always, always: you had enough trouble judging yourself. Always there was that one confrontation to make, to come up against oneself in or out of the vault of sleep and to know another truly. Sleep could do it. So could love, bright death, dark death, circumstance, or the lance of the needle itself. It took all ways. It took all kinds. But at the end perhaps it made sense, and then perhaps it did not.

Breath pouring from him, breath coming in, Williams lay in the vault of sleep. For a long time in the room there were no sounds at all but the sounds of the city gasping to life around them. And time then for another day, for another crack at it, for another possibility, and maybe at the end, at the end of all of it, another life.

26 August 1973: New Jersey

THE END

Afterword:
In The Stretch Turn

By Barry N. Malzberg

"The Heart of the Country...where the holy people go"
—Paul McCartney

"He's dead, Jim"   —Dr. McCoy in *Star Trek*

Phoenix was a would-be Vegas; unlike Harlem it had chosen to shroud reality. Whereas Harlem wallowed, Phoenix, although it was a city that had elements of beauty permitted that beauty to come across in blurred, damaged simulacrum. It really was the kind of place those who could not make it to Scarsdale or the Oakland Hills or Grosse Point would stop. Fifty years ago Phoenix had been nothing; now in pastels it had sprawled across the desert. It had its millionaires, its reactionary Senators, one of them anyway, its bigoted cesspools that moved from the offices of the downtown to determine what part of the desert would be occupied by certain people of forced but better circumstances. It had its hustlers too who were working the pastoral:

> "… estate, two or three acres of underground swamp available now for a limited time for twenty-five dollars down and a hundred a month forever. They were working the El Pastorale out of the boiler seeking sellers just as the Pocono hustlers worked the other heart of the heart of the country."
> —*Phoenix Inferno*

And here it was coming into a smeared and deadly focus, in writing the series it seemed that I was writing history itself, was part of that history, had found in blurred microcosm the state of the Union itself. Wulff was trying to do to the drug trade what Kissinger, Nixon, the seemingly detached draft boards were doing to the country. They were taking it toward a state of utter disconnect in which the wishes, even the basic truths accorded the polity were ignored, debased, made into little other than a dimension of policy, a subdivision of the military-industrial complex. For this was the vision of the country adumbrated here, two novels earlier than the penultimate #13, *The Killing Run*, with its notable (to me anyway) paragraph quoted earlier. It was the gradual and then fierce homogenization driving to reduce the ravaged and glorious country into a single, clotted landscape. Wulff saw this as the haze of druggies' dreams; in the alleys and towers they lay in thick and ugly circumspection, seeing their world now as one size fits all and that clotted clarity, that unreasonable summing up was driving the series toward a fate absolutely foreshadowed from the first bleep of the Cadillac de Ville's fuck you horn in the opening *Night Raider*. From *Night Raider* to *Harlem Showdown* was a clotted passage but it was one-size-fits-all just like the country itself; those novels were built as a self-referential circle eternally driving Wulff back into himself. Bolan was an attempt at a Pilgrims' Progress, a simulation of motion; Wulff and his author (and his publisher too) knew that it was the same old stuff, however you dressed it: lingerie concealed under combat fatigues or the other fashion show of heavy ordnance. At this point it was getting old for all concerned, even Wulff, even the unhappy Nixon voters he had encountered in Miami's hotel corridor. But the force of insistence held on to say nothing of the clarity of the contract. Finish it off.

That was one part of the journey, another and perhaps more essential locus was the degree and pervasiveness of the hatred which had leached through every aspect of the polity. It is difficult to make understood even in the Trump or immediate post-Trump (or perhaps it was to be internal) how deeply loathed the President, Lyndon Johnson, had become in his last two years in office and how his successor had not only taken Johnson's place as the hated but had, in the crumbling masonry of Watergate, exceeded it. That Vietnam and its killing fields were a totally fraudulent enterprise was apparent now not only to the troops, to potential draftees, to the majority of their families had sent ugly and poisonous vapors beyond the walls and stalls of the War to leach into every aspect of the common experience. Matters were becoming so dangerous in the killing fields and the home front, so dangerous that the feeble "draft lottery" was only through its randomness bringing ever harsher life on the nonsensical caprice of fate as guiding destiny that Nixon and Kissinger moved to abolish the draft by fiat. They got it too and it broke the back of the protest movement almost within a fortnight. Personal implication, fear of death's immediacy had brought the protests to the Pentagon and the White House but the draft's abolition in its cynicism soothed the situation just enough to keep the war running even past the election and Kissinger's famous Christmas bombings which rendered "peace with honor" as lying cant. It was into this fatally polluted reservoir that the Lone Wulff and his violent competitors on the newsstands had been tossed and they began to stink in a way which began to affect sales. "You can't run a war like this for many years with even sixty percent support," Hunter Thompson recorded himself telling the Defense Department. "Something like this which goes on and on, you need ninety percent. This is doomed." Counsel from the meanest Boy on the Bus who had also given some to Nixon through the open window of his passing limousine. "Throw the big one, Dick! Go ahead and do it!"

The novels were madly refractory, if nothing else; the novels were a crazy-funhouse-with-mirrors version of the State of the Union. Like Wulff, I drove on toward the gonfalon. There was nothing else to do.

January 2022: New Jersey

Barry N. Malzberg Bibliography

FICTION (as either Barry or Barry N. Malzberg)

Oracle of the Thousand Hands (1968)
Screen (1968)
Confessions of Westchester County (1970)
The Spread (1971)
In My Parents' Bedroom (1971)
The Falling Astronauts (1971)
The Masochist (1972, reprinted as Everything Happened to Susan, 1975; as Cinema, 2020)
Horizontal Woman (1972; reprinted as The Social Worker, 1973)
Beyond Apollo (1972)
Overlay (1972)
Revelations (1972)
Herovit's World (1973)
In the Enclosure (1973)
The Men Inside (1973)
Phase IV (1973; novelization based on a story & screenplay by Mayo Simon)
The Day of the Burning (1974)
The Tactics of Conquest (1974)
Underlay (1974)
The Destruction of the Temple (1974)
Guernica Night (1974)
On a Planet Alien (1974)
Out from Ganymede (1974; stories)
The Sodom and Gomorrah Business (1974)
The Best of Barry N. Malzberg (1975; stories)
The Many Worlds of Barry Malzberg (1975; stories)
Galaxies (1975)
The Gamesman (1975)
Down Here in the Dream Quarter (1976; stories)
Scop (1976)
The Last Transaction (1977)
Chorale (1978)
Malzberg at Large (1979; stories)
The Man Who Loved the Midnight Lady (1980; stories)
The Cross of Fire (1982)
The Remaking of Sigmund Freud (1985)
In the Stone House (2000; stories)
Shiva and Other Stories (2001; stories)
The Passage of the Light: The Recursive Science Fiction of Barry N. Malzberg (2004; ed. by Tony Lewis & Mike Resnick; stories)
The Very Best of Barry N. Malzberg (2013; stories)

With Bill Pronzini

The Running of the Beasts (1976)
Acts of Mercy (1977)
Night Screams (1979)
Prose Bowl (1980)
Problems Solved (2003; stories)
On Account of Darkness and Other SF Stories (2004; stories)

As Mike Barry

Lone Wolf series:
Night Raider (1973)
Bay Prowler (1973)
Boston Avenger (1973)
Desert Stalker (1974)
Havana Hit (1974)
Chicago Slaughter (1974)
Peruvian Nightmare (1974)
Los Angeles Holocaust (1974)
Miami Marauder (1974)
Harlem Showdown (1975)
Detroit Massacre (1975)

Phoenix Inferno (1975)
The Killing Run (1975)
Philadelphia Blow-Up (1975)

As Francine di Natale

The Circle (1969)

As Claudine Dumas

The Confessions of a Parisian
    Chambermaid (1969)

As Mel Johnson/M. L. Johnson

Love Doll (1967; with The Sex Pros
    by Orrie Hitt)
I, Lesbian (1968; as M. L. Johnson)
Just Ask (1968; with Playgirl by Lou
    Craig)
Instant Sex (1968)
Chained (1968; with Master of
    Women by March Hastings & Love
    Captive by Dallas Mayo)
Kiss and Run (1968; with Sex on the
    Sand by Sheldon Lord & Odd Girl
    by March Hastings)
Nympho Nurse (1969; with Young
    and Eager by Jim Conroy &
    Quickie by Gene Evans)
The Sadist (1969)
The Box (1969)
Do It To Me (1969; with Hot Blonde
    by Jim Conroy)
Born to Give (1969; with Swap Club
    by Greg Hamilton & Wild in Bed
    by Dirk Malloy)
Campus Doll (1969; with High
    School Stud by Robert Hadley)
A Way With All Maidens (1969)

As Howard Lee

Kung Fu #1: The Way of the Tiger,
    the Sign of the Dragon (1973)

As Lee W. Mason

Lady of a Thousand Sorrows (1977)

As K. M. O'Donnell

Empty People (1969)
The Final War and Other Fantasies
    (1969; stories)
Dwellers of the Deep (1970)
Gather at the Hall of the Planets
    (1971)
In the Pocket and Other S-F Stories
    (1971; stories)
Universe Day (1971; stories)

As Eliot B. Reston

The Womanizer (1972)

As Gerrold Watkins

Southern Comfort (1969)
A Bed of Money (1970)
A Satyr's Romance (1970)
Giving It Away (1970)
Art of the Fugue (1970)

NON-FICTION/ESSAYS

The Engines of the Night: Science
    Fiction in the Eighties (1982;
    essays)
Breakfast in the Ruins (2007;
    essays: expansion of Engines of the
    Night)
The Business of Science Fiction: Two
    Insiders Discuss Writing and
    Publishing (2010; with Mike
    Resnick)
The Bend at the End of the Road
    (2018; essays)

EDITED ANTHOLOGIES

Final Stage (1974; with Edward L.
    Ferman)

Arena (1976; with Edward L.
  Ferman)
Graven Images (1977; with Edward
  L. Ferman)
Dark Sins, Dark Dreams (1978; with
  Bill Pronzini)
The End of Summer: SF in the
  Fifties (1979; with Bill Pronzini)
Shared Tomorrows: Science Fiction
  in Collaboration (1979; with Bill
  Pronzini)
Neglected Visions (1979; with
  Martin H. Greenberg & Joseph D.
  Olander)

Bug-Eyed Monsters (1980; with Bill
  Pronzini)
The Science Fiction of Mark Clifton
  (1980; with Martin H. Greenberg)
The Arbor House Treasury of Horror
  & the Supernatural (1981; with
  Bill Pronzini & Martin H.
  Greenberg)
The Science Fiction of Kris Neville
  (1984; with Martin H. Greenberg)
Mystery in the Mainstream (1986;
  with Bill Pronzini & Martin H.
  Greenberg)